**Nobody can wr̲ ̲ ̲
like C̲**

Of *Led̲*

"Sensationally sensual…this tale of a forbidden,
guilt-ridden love is a delight. Brimming with diverse,
compelling characters, scorching-hot love scenes,
romance and even a ghost, this story is unforgettable."
—*Romancejunkies.com*

"This deliciously naughty fantasy takes its time
heating up, but it's worth the wait!…"
—*RT Book Reviews*

Of *Taken Beyond Temptation*

"Great characters with explosive chemistry, a fun
intrigue-flavored plot and a high degree of sensuality
add up to an excellent read!…"
—*RT Book Reviews*

"Filled with intrigue, mystery, humor, sizzling
hot love scenes, a well-matched couple, a surprise
ending and a ghost, this story is unforgettable
and definitely a winner."
—*Romancejunkies.com*

Of *Twice the Temptation*

"Well written!… Fans will be delighted to see their
favorites return for brief appearances…"
—*RT Book Reviews*

"Cara Summers has penned two tales in *Twice the
Temptation* which will not be forgotten, but will live
on in the reader's fantasies."
—*Cataromance.com*

Dear Reader,

I love writing FORBIDDEN FANTASIES for Blaze, and so getting the chance to write three in a row is a real treat!

Seven years ago, spurred on by their father's wedding, a bottle of champagne and a serious case of lust for their new stepmother's gorgeous sons, Adair, Piper and Nell MacPherson each wrote down their most secret sexual fantasies about their "ideal" man and buried them in a stone arch on their family's estate. Then they forgot all about them. Almost.

Now, one by one, the Sutherland triplets, Cam, Duncan and Reid, are being drawn back to Castle MacPherson, not only by the erotic fantasies penned all those years ago, but also to right a wrong and restore a stolen bride's long-missing dowry to its rightful owners.

I hope that you enjoy Cam and Adair's story, *No Risk Refused*, and that you will look for *No Holds Barred* in September and then *No Desire Denied*. All three books feature an amazing dog named Alba, who currently resides at the Northeast Animal Shelter in Salem, Massachusetts, but is waiting for her forever home. I hope you fall in love with her just as I did.

For news on my future releases, visit www.carasummers.com. And for more information on the Northeast Animal Shelter and the Blaze Authors' Pet Project, visit www.blazeauthors.com/blog.

May all your forbidden fantasies come true!

Cara Summers

NO RISK REFUSED

BY
CARA SUMMERS

MILLS & BOON

First published in Great Britain 2012
by Mills & Boon, an imprint of Harlequin (UK) Limited,
Eton House, 18-24 Paradise Road, Richmond, Surrey TW9 1SR

© Carolyn Hanlon 2012

ISBN: 978 0 263 89383 0
ebook ISBN: 978 1 408 96926 7

14-0812

Harlequin (UK) policy is to use papers that are natural, renewable and recyclable products and made from wood grown in sustainable forests. The logging and manufacturing processes conform to the legal environmental regulations of the country of origin.

Printed and bound in Spain
by Blackprint CPI, Barcelona

Was **Cara Summers** born with the dream of becoming a published romance novelist? No. But now that she is, she still feels her dream has come true. And she owes it all to her mother, who handed her a Mills & Boon novel and said, "Try it. You'll love it." Mom was right! Cara has written over forty stories for Blaze, and she has won numerous awards including a Lifetime Achievement Award for Series Storyteller of the Year from *RT Book Reviews*. When she isn't working on new books, she teaches in the writing program at Syracuse University.

To my sons, Kevin, Brian and Brendan.
As you've grown into fine young men, I've seen
you do everything you can to protect and cherish
the ones you love. In short, you inspire my heroes.
Thanks! I love all three of you.

And special thanks to the best editor in the world—
Brenda Chin. You have once more pulled one of
my stories out of the darkness and into the light.

Prologue

Glen Loch, NY
Summer 1812

THUNDER CRASHED AND lightning ripped through the sky
while rain lashed at the stone arch over Eleanor Campbell
MacPherson's head.

Perfect, she thought.

It was one of her dreams that had awakened her. She'd
heard Angus's voice again. The sound of the wind had
drawn her out onto her balcony and when she'd seen the
clouds roll in over the lake, blacking out the stars, she'd
known it was time to begin her mission. To right a wrong
that she'd done so many years before.

Slipping out of the castle, she'd raced the rain to the
stone arch and reached it just as the skies opened. The
dreams that had been recurring since her husband's death
had centered here in the place that had played such a powerful role in her life and in Angus's.

Her sons and daughters-in-law, who loved her dearly,
would not be happy that she regularly sneaked out of the
castle in the dead of night. Even less happy that she was

here in the stone arch on a night like this. And she doubted
they would approve of her plan.

So she would make sure that they didn't know.

All her life, she'd been good at keeping secrets. But
since the death of her husband a year ago, one of those
secrets had begun to weigh on her. And the dreams had
begun. Angus was sending them to her. He'd known her
so well, and he'd known that the Stuart sapphires she'd
carried with her to the New World had troubled her conscience.

Thunder roared and lightning flashed so bright and
fierce that for an instant, Eleanor saw everything clearly—
the garden, the elegant facade of Castle MacPherson, the
cliffs beyond and the roiling waters of the black lake
below.

Home, she thought. Whatever mistakes she may have
made, coming here with Angus Daniel MacPherson fifty
years ago was not one of them. She'd turned her back on
her home in the highlands of Scotland, the pride and expectations of her family, and a man who'd claimed to love
her very much. And she'd never looked back.

Not that Angus had given her any choice.

The memory made her smile and set her mind drifting back to that night in Scotland so long ago, when he'd
asked her to run away with him to the New World. She'd
been shocked at the idea, thrilled and frightened at the
same time. They'd been standing beneath a stone arch in
the gardens of her family's home. Its location in an isolated part of the garden made it a perfect place for them
to meet in secret.

And secrecy was essential. She shouldn't have even
talked to him. Even though their families' lands shared
a common border, the MacPhersons and the Campbells
had been blood enemies for years.

And she'd been promised to another man.

But once Angus had kissed her beneath the stone arch he'd completely captured her heart. Her mother and older sisters had warned her about the legend surrounding the stones. They carried a power from ancient times, and the man you kissed beneath that arch would be your true love forever.

And she hadn't just kissed Angus once. Each time she'd met with him she'd kissed him again and again. And each time she'd promised herself it would be the last time.

The night of Angus's proposal, her family had thrown a ball to formalize her upcoming wedding to her betrothed. She was wearing her future husband's gift to her, the legendary sapphire earrings and necklace that had been bequeathed to his family for service to the Scottish court during the reign of Mary Stuart. The queen had worn them at her coronation, so they were priceless. He'd insisted she wear them tonight as proof of his love for her and as a symbol of the union of their two families.

When she'd slipped away from the ball to meet Angus, she'd planned to say goodbye.

She'd been repeating the little speech to herself all day. She was betrothed to another man, she couldn't go back on her word, and their situation was impossible. There was no way that their families would allow them to marry. In fact, her father would probably inflict bodily harm on Angus.

Eleanor slipped her hand into her pocket and closed her fingers around the leather pouches where she kept the sapphires. The only time she'd worn them was for her wedding portrait that hung in the main parlor of the castle. The jewels always reminded her of the man she'd betrayed and left behind. Everyone had always believed that they were her dowry, and she'd kept silent all of these years.

If only she'd left the necklace and earrings behind with

the man who'd given them to her. At least their families would have had the sapphires. But there'd been no time. Angus, impatient, impetuous, irresistible, hadn't allowed her any. And when she'd initially refused to go with him that night, he hadn't taken no for an answer. He'd simply carried her away.

Thank God.

Her heart tightened as she thought of how he'd completely swept her up in his belief in their future.

Lightning flashed again, illuminating the visual reality of that belief. Angus had promised to build a castle and gardens for her in a setting that would remind her of all that she was leaving behind in Scotland. He'd kept his word. The lovely lakes and mountains in the Adirondack region had kept her from getting too homesick during those early years. He'd kept his promise to build a replica of the stone arch in her family's garden. He'd even brought some stones from the original, and when it was complete she'd stood with him here just as she'd stood with him beneath the one in Scotland.

That was when the legend of Castle MacPherson's stone arch had begun. Over the years she'd lost count of the number of times Angus had told and retold the story of how she'd captivated him, heart and mind, that first time they'd kissed beneath the stone arch in her family's garden. And the story had spread, being told and retold throughout the community. Her children had believed in it and they'd each married their mates right here.

The little pain around her heart increased. In the year since he'd passed she'd missed him so much. But she always sensed his presence when she stood here in the place where they'd laughed and loved and dreamed together so many times.

And the stones had played a part in the dream she was

sure that Angus was sending her. In them, she always saw the same thing. A young woman with reddish curls dropping to her knees at the side of the arch and lifting a leather pouch out of a pile of loose stones. Inside, the young woman always found one of the earrings. Not the pair or the necklace.

Eleanor tightened her fingers around the pouch she held in her pocket. As she did, she heard Angus's voice in her ear, just as clearly as she heard it in her dreams.

"Her name is Adair. She believes in the power of the stones enough to bury her own dreams and fantasies beneath them. You must hide one of the earrings in the stone arch for her to find. When she finds it, the Stuart Sapphires will begin to find their way home. You can finally rest easy. Trust me, Ellie—just as you did on the night we ran away."

The rain had stopped, and a few stars had reappeared in the sky. With Angus's words still in her mind, Eleanor stepped out of the arch and began to work some of the stones loose. And when the earring was safely buried and she returned to the castle, she slept peacefully.

1

AN AFFAIR TO remember.

That had been the guarantee that Adair MacPherson had given to Rexie Maitland and her parents when they'd signed the contract to hold their daughter's wedding and reception at Castle MacPherson.

And she intended to deliver. She had to. There were already two big *X* marks in the failure column of her life. She didn't need a third one.

Adair pressed a firm hand to the nerves jittering in her stomach. The first step on her way to her goal, the wedding rehearsal scheduled for today, had gotten off to a rocky start. The high-strung bride had gone into a panic attack when the groom-to-be hadn't arrived on time. But Adair's aunt and business partner, Viola MacPherson, had warded off a full meltdown with a cup of herb tea. And the tardy Lawrence Banes, a suave, sort of George Clooney look-alike with a good fifteen years on the bride, had finally arrived, full of apologies.

Pulling off the Maitland/Banes wedding on Saturday

was crucial to the launch of her new business plan, one that would establish the reputation of Castle MacPherson as a premier wedding destination in the heart of New York's Adirondacks. Adair swept her gaze around the garden.

The setting was perfect. The gray stone castle she and her sisters had grown up in stood on a rocky promontory at the far eastern end of Glen Loch Lake. Three stories high and rectangular in shape, it sat tucked between two mountains, boasted spectacular views, and its gardens, thanks to her Aunt Vi, had graced the pages of several gardening magazines.

The Maitland/Banes wedding would take place beneath the stone arch her several-times-great-grandfather Angus One had built for the stolen bride he'd brought here from Scotland. Now the tardy Mr. Banes was standing beneath it flanked by the minister and his best man. The maid of honor and the flower girl had lined up just behind the arbor that marked the entrance to the gardens. The mother of the bride, Bunny Maitland, had taken her seat in the first row of chairs, and just in front of the stone arch, Aunt Vi sat, her bow poised over her cello, ready to play on signal.

Everything was perfect, except that the bride-to-be was holding Adair's hand in a death grip.

"I don't know if I can do this," Rexie whispered.

Ignoring her plummeting stomach, Adair took a deep breath and spoke in her calmest voice. "This is only a rehearsal. You have to save those nerves for Saturday."

"I know." Rexie, a pretty twenty-two-year-old blonde and heir to the Maitland fortune, smiled tremulously. "I can't seem to help it. I need to know that I'm doing the right thing. I have to know that the legend will work."

"It will." The power of the legend and the stones was

the one thing in her life that she still had absolute faith in. She might be a bit shaky on her ability to keep this wedding on track, but she had no doubt that the stone arch her ancestor Angus One had built for Eleanor Campbell MacPherson had the power to bring true loves together.

This was the young woman's second go at matrimony. A little over a year ago, her first husband had left her to return to his family's horse farm in Montana. Then Rexie had met Lawrence and six months ago, after reading an article on the history of the MacPhersons and the legend in the *New York Times,* she'd contacted Viola to ask about scheduling her ceremony and reception at the castle because she wanted a guarantee of success this time around.

The *Times* article had created quite a buzz because it had dug up all the rumors that had circulated over the years about the missing sapphires that Eleanor MacPherson had worn in her wedding portrait. The writer had even reprinted an image of Mary Stuart wearing a similar necklace and earrings at her coronation and posed the theory that Eleanor's dowry of jewels had been given to her by the Queen of Scots.

Adair could have kissed the *Times* writer for stirring everything up and giving her the idea for a new business plan.

She took Rexie's other hand in hers. "You are not going to fail this time."

That was the mantra Adair recited to herself each morning. Not that she'd ever failed at marriage—she hadn't had the chance. Six months ago she'd come home to Aunt Vi and the castle to lick her wounds, and they were still fresh. The five-year plan she'd so carefully crafted when she'd finished her MBA had gone south. One day she'd been on the fast track, and the next, the company she'd worked for had downsized and derailed her. Her pink slip had been quickly followed by an email from her boyfriend, Baxter DuBois, terminating their personal relationship, as well.

That's when she'd moved back to the castle. Now with her aunt's help and the power of Angus One's stone arch, she was determined to turn her family home into *the* wedding destination spot in upstate New York.

And the success of Rexie's wedding was key. Mr. and Mrs. Winston Maitland III resided on Long Island but also owned homes in Boca Raton, Florida, and Vail, Colorado. They had the kind of social contacts that could make the reputation of Castle MacPherson.

Or break it.

"I've seen proof of the stones' power in my own father's life," Adair said. "He's kissed two women beneath the stone arch, and if he were here, he'd tell you it was the stones that gave him two chances of finding his true loves. He considers himself a very fortunate man."

Adair held back a little on the details. Her father had taken the loss of her mother so hard that even after he fell in love with Professor Beth Sutherland, it had been a dozen years before he married her. But seven years ago she and her sisters, along with Beth's three triplet sons, had stood beneath the arch while her father, A.D., and Beth had exchanged vows.

"And your father's happy?" Rexie asked.

"Yes. There's real power in the stones. When we were growing up, my sisters and I believed in it so much that we used to write down our dreams and goals and bury them in a metal box beneath some of the loose stones. It was my mother's old jewelry box so it had three different compartments and we all used different colors of paper."

She'd nearly forgotten about that box, Adair realized. On the night of her father's wedding, she'd even written down a particularly erotic fantasy involving Cam Sutherland and buried that, too. She hadn't thought of it in years. And she hadn't seen Cam or his brothers since the wedding. They'd been finishing college that year and each had been focused on career plans that kept them very busy. Last she'd heard, Cam was working overseas for the CIA. For an instant his image flashed brightly into her mind and she could see him just as he'd looked that day—the dark, unruly hair, the blue eyes that had always held a dare.

And Cam Sutherland was the last thing she needed to be thinking about right now. If she didn't get this wedding rehearsal on track, an "affair to remember" was going to take on a whole new, horrible meaning.

She focused on the hint of panic in Rexie's eyes. And a solution suddenly occurred to her. "Look, why don't we tap into the power of the legend right now?"

"How?"

"This is just a rehearsal and you won't actually say your vows, but why don't you kiss Lawrence? If you do that today while you're beneath the stone arch, then you should be all set. In the legend, it's the kiss that does the trick."

"Really?" Rexie shifted her gaze to where her groom-to-be waited. He was on his cell phone.

"It's guaranteed," Adair assured her. "Why don't we start? Everyone is in place."

"Except for my father," Rexie said, her lip trembling. "He's taking another call on his cell."

"Mr. Maitland?" Adair spoke in a low tone, but she kept Rexie's hand firmly gripped in hers.

The bride-to-be's father held up one finger, but he never stopped talking into his phone. Winston Maitland, a tall stocky man with thinning gray hair, had pretty much had his cell glued to his ear since he'd arrived. So had the groom-to-be for that matter. The jerks. Adair wanted to shake both of them.

That was when she heard it. Just the whisper of thunder. Damn. Keeping Rexie's hand in a death grip, she angled her head just enough to catch sight of a cluster of dark clouds at the far end of the lake.

A quick glance around told her that so far she was the only one who'd noticed. The sky overhead was bright blue, the garden bathed in sunlight. She sent up a quick prayer that the storm would stay put.

Alba, the white whippet mix her aunt Vi had recently brought home from a shelter, rose from where she'd plopped herself a few feet away on a patch of sun-drenched grass. She shot a look out over the lake, and whined. Adair followed the direction of the dog's gaze and so did Rexie. The clouds were rolling closer.

"Look. It's going to rain," Rexie said. "That's not a good sign. Maybe we should postpone this."

Adair tightened her grip on Rexie's hand. "No. It's still quite a ways off. We just have to get started."

Alba whined again, then made a beeline in the direction of the castle, the bell around her neck emphasizing her departure.

Not a good sign.

Though Alba was deaf, her other senses were spot-on, and Adair was willing to bet she could sense the approaching storm. So could the mother of the bride, Bunny Maitland, who sent her a worried look.

Adair tried for a serene smile. The clouds were still a good distance away, she assured herself. Time enough to panic once the lightning started. She waved to get her aunt's attention.

Viola MacPherson had moved to the castle after Adair's mom, Marianne, had died. She'd been four, her sisters three and one. Their father had buried himself in his painting, so it was their aunt who'd raised them. She'd given up her job at the nearby college and devoted her life to creating a home for them while providing a haven where their father could continue with his landscape painting.

Now in her late fifties, Viola looked and projected the energy of a much younger woman. Adair had inherited her aunt's tiny stature as well as the curse of naturally curly red hair. Viola's cascade of ringlets was gray now, and she managed them by pulling them back from her face. She favored long skirts or wide-leg pants and tunics that went with her gypsy look.

At a signal from Adair, Vi began to play Beethoven's "Ode to Joy."

Thunder sounded faintly in the distance.

Refusing to look out over the lake again, Adair directed the flower girl to start down the short path that led from the rose garden to the stone arch. When the little girl was halfway there, Adair gestured to the maid of honor.

"Daddy's still on his phone," Rexie whispered.

"Mr. Maitland." Adair spoke in a low tone.

Frowning at Adair, the man stuffed his cell in a pocket and moved to his daughter's side. "That was an important call."

Adair smiled at him. "And this is a very important moment for your daughter. Go."

Thunder rumbled—closer this time.

Rexie and her father were halfway to the minister when the dark clouds settled like a lid over the garden with such speed and finality she wondered they hadn't heard a loud clang.

Lightning flashed behind her just as Rexie and her dad made it to the shelter of the stone arch. Adair hurried up the path, grabbing Bunny's arm on the way. Together they power-walked to join the rest of the wedding party.

Cello in hand, Aunt Vi was the last to make it before

the next crack of thunder sounded. Then for a moment, no one spoke as they huddled shoulder to shoulder and watched nature put on a powerful show. Lightning criss-crossed the sky at times so bright Adair found herself blinking. The intermittent explosions of thunder made her wonder if this was what it might be like to be trapped in a bunker during an attack.

And her mind flashed back to the night of her father's wedding. There'd been a storm like this that night, also. The Sutherland boys, Reid, Cam and Duncan, had flown in just for the wedding and then gone back to their colleges right after the ceremony. She and her sisters hadn't seen them since that long-ago summer when the boys' mother, Beth, had been a visiting professor at nearby Huntleigh College and she'd gotten her father's permission to use the library at the castle for the research she was doing for a historical novel she was writing on the MacPherson clan.

That was the summer when Adair's fascination with Cam had begun. Because she'd hated him. He'd been a relentless tease, always pulling her curls and calling her "Princess" because she lived in a "castle." And he'd constantly nagged her to try things she'd never tried before— like climbing over the stone arch.

There were days during that summer when she'd wanted to strangle him.

But strangling hadn't been on her mind the night of her father's wedding to Beth Sutherland. Because in the twelve years that had passed, the Sutherlands had changed. Drastically. From annoying, know-it-all ten-year-olds to attractive young men.

What hadn't changed had been her fascination with Cam. It had flared immediately from the instant he'd arrived at the castle that day.

They weren't kids on a playdate any more. And while

their parents had been pledging their vows beneath the stone arch, her eyes had locked on his, and she'd wanted him in a way that she'd never wanted anyone—or anything. It had thrilled her, terrified her. And it had fueled the fantasy that she'd committed to paper and put into the special metal box that she and her sisters had hidden away in the stone arch.

Lightning flashed again and the thunder roared, instantaneous and deafening, refocusing her thoughts on the present.

Vi whispered in her ear. "This isn't good."

Adair had to agree with her aunt. In all her years growing up at the castle, she'd never seen a storm like this one. And it had to happen the day of Rexie Maitland's wedding rehearsal.

They were so tightly packed in the space that Adair had to crane her neck to meet Rexie's eyes. Panic was what she saw and she felt an answering surge in herself. Pushing it down, she kept her voice calm and spaced her words to fit in between the claps of thunder. "We should go forward with the rehearsal."

Not sure how much Rexie heard in the cacophony of sound bombarding them, Adair pursed her lips and pantomimed a kiss. Then she held her breath, willing Rexie to kiss Lawrence and seal the deal. Not for the first time, she wished she had at least a smidgen of the power Macbeth's witches had.

Thunder cracked so loud Adair was certain the rocks beneath her feet moved. Aunt Vi grabbed her hand and held on hard. Adair kept her gaze on Rexie, her willpower on at full throttle.

Finally, Rexie turned to Lawrence and put her hands on his shoulders to get his attention. A second later, he began to lower his head.

Lightning flashed, so close this time that Adair could smell it, and the ground beneath them shook—enough to tear Rexie out of Lawrence's arms just before their lips met and thrust her backward into the minister. Adair heard stones tumble from the front of the arch before thunder deafened her.

When the earth stilled again, Adair found herself held tightly in her aunt Vi's arms, a cello pressed hard against her thigh. Rexie was in her mother's arms. Not good. Lawrence and Winston had their heads close. The maid of honor had picked up the flower girl and the best man had slumped onto a ledge, his face sheet-white.

When the storm had moved off so that conversation was a possibility, everyone began to talk at once, their voices pitched almost as low as the now-fading thunder. But the main consensus was that the stone arch they were standing under had just been struck by lightning.

Vi was looking at the stones that formed the arch over their heads. "We're lucky they held, but we should have someone check them."

Adair figured checking the stone arch was the least of her problems. The biggest one was headed toward her, elbowing her way through the group. When Rexie reached her, she said, "I'm calling off the wedding." Then she burst into tears.

2

AN HOUR LATER, Adair stepped out of her room and went in search of her aunt. After finally seeing the Maitlands off, she'd spent some time in the shower replaying everything that had happened in her mind, going over the should-have-saids and could-have-dones. Her ex-boyfriend Bax had always criticized her for trying to second-guess herself.

Maybe he'd been right. In the downsizing at her former company, he'd kept his job. She hadn't.

Pushing that thought out of her mind, she went back to her replay. The shouting match that had occurred after the lightning strike and Rexie's hysterical announcement had rivaled the storm for intensity. Mr. Maitland had claimed the lightning strike was a sign they should change the venue for the ceremony back to Long Island, which had triggered a fresh eruption of tears from the bride and a yelling match between her parents. Using the noise as a cover, she'd told the groom that he'd better soothe his bride-to-be.

The fact that she'd had to jump-start him had bothered her. If he hadn't been late for the rehearsal, the storm and the lightning strike wouldn't have been an issue. But he'd said something to Rexie that had calmed her while she concentrated on the parents.

Before they'd driven away, Rexie had agreed to postpone her decision to cancel the wedding. The men had departed for Long Island but Adair had booked Rexie and Bunny into the Eagle's Nest, a bed-and-breakfast in the nearby village of Glen Loch, so they could return to the castle in the morning when their nerves had settled to give her their decision. The one thing that Rexie had remained firm on was that if the wedding was going forward, it would be held at Castle MacPherson.

Which was exactly what she wanted, too. Wasn't it?

And why was that even a question she was thinking about? Of course she wanted the wedding to go forward. What kind of a businesswoman was she? Good ones didn't sabotage their own business plans.

She just had to keep her focus. But it was hard to ignore that lightning strike, or the fact that it had occurred at the exact moment when Lawrence was about to kiss Rexie and seal the deal.

The moment she stepped out onto the veranda that ran along the back of the house and spotted Vi sitting at a table with an opened bottle of wine and two glasses, some of her tension eased. It didn't surprise her that her aunt had chosen this place to wait for her. The back of the castle, with its flagstone terraces dropping in levels to the lake, had always been one of Adair's favorite spots. She noted that the water was calm and stunningly blue, its surface a perfect reflection of the now-cloudless sky overhead. The only reminder of the violent storm was a fading rainbow.

Alba lay sprawled nearby on the flagstones, totally exhausted by the day. Adair could certainly sympathize with the feeling, but her own day had a ways to go. There was a decision to be made.

She joined her aunt and accepted the glass of wine.

Vi clinked her glass to Adair's. "To a job well done."

"I haven't done anything yet."

Vi sampled the wine. "You've weathered a lightning strike, you've calmed down a very upset bride and her parents. And you'll see to it that more rational minds will prevail in the morning."

"And what if I'm wrong?"

"Wrong in what way?"

Setting her wine down, Adair reached out and took one of her aunt's hands. "You know how much I want this wedding to take place on Saturday."

Vi brought her other hand to cover her niece's in a gesture that was achingly familiar to Adair.

"Ever since you were a child, whenever you've set yourself a goal you've achieved it. Not only that, you egged your younger sisters into setting their own goals. Look where they are right now. Piper is working for a famous defense attorney in D.C., and Nell is touring the country on a grant that allows her to teach creative writing classes in disadvantaged schools and at the same time, promote her first children's story."

Adair shook her head. "I'm not doing that well in the goal achievement game anymore."

"Why on earth would you think that?"

"Because the first curveball that life threw at me..." She paused and waved her free hand. "I ran away and came back here. I'm not proud of that."

Vi studied her for a moment. "You're not your father, Adair. If that's what you're worried about."

Perhaps it was, Adair thought. Her aunt had always been able to hit the nail on the head. Perhaps that fear was at the heart of the gnawing anxiety she'd felt ever since she'd left Chicago.

"When your mother, Marianne, died, he did run," Vi said. "He hid for years, burying himself in his art and his teaching at the college."

"I've never understood him. He met Beth Sutherland when I was nine, the summer that she did her research in the library and we had all those long afternoon playdates with the Sutherland boys. Nell saw Dad kiss her once beneath the stones. We thought they might get married and that we'd all become a family. But then she went back to Chicago and he went back to his painting and we didn't see any of them again until the wedding seven years ago. And Beth and Dad are so happy now, traveling the world, each pursuing their dreams. Why did they wait?"

"Because they needed to. They had young children to think about, careers to pursue. She came here to do her research shortly after her husband had been found guilty of fraud and sent to prison. His family was wealthy and they tried to sue for custody. She felt that building her career was essential to holding on to her sons. And your father always had his art to return to. They waited for a better time. That's where you're different, Adair. You don't wait for anything."

Adair blinked. "I don't?"

Vi laughed. "Good Lord, I can barely keep up with you. You didn't even have your bags all unpacked when that feature writer from the *Times* visited us for an interview. I could almost see the lightbulb go on over your head. The very next day you were plotting out a business plan for the castle. And when the article stirred up interest in the legend and Eleanor's missing sapphires, you had brochures printed to hand out to the tourists who started arriving on the weekends."

Adair shrugged. "I just capitalized on the buzz the rumors of a missing and possibly priceless collection of gems created. They'll die down again."

"The point I'm making is that you didn't hesitate to capitalize on that buzz to promote the legend surrounding the stones. I've never known you to hide, Adair. And while you were showering and changing, I'm betting you marshaled together a strategy for handling Bunny and Rexie tomorrow morning."

Adair took a sip of her wine. "I think I've got that covered. Sure, lightning struck during the rehearsal, but did it do any permanent damage? No. The stone arch is still there. Indestructible. So it still has the power to unite Rexie with the love of her life on Saturday. And that marriage will be just as indestructible."

"Very nice argument."

"Yeah. If Lawrence Banes *is* the love of her life," Adair said. "He was late to the rehearsal, and it was his schedule that had required it to take place two days before the wedding. Plus, he was texting on his cell instead of trying to support Rexie when she became hysterical after the lightning strike."

Vi merely met her eyes, saying nothing. It was a ploy that her aunt had used very successfully when she and her sisters had been trying to explain some of the mischief they'd gotten into.

"Okay, maybe he's just a jerk," she conceded. "A jerk she's in love with."

"Or maybe he's just as nervous as the bride. When you first explained your business plan to me you defined our role pretty clearly."

Adair raised a hand, palm out. "Right. We're not matchmakers or relationship counselors. Our job is to provide the perfect wedding and let the stone arch do its work."

She rose then and walked to the low stone wall that

bordered the veranda. Beyond the gardens she could see the curve of the stone arch. Vi joined her and put an arm around her shoulder. "But? I hear a *but* in there."

"I can't help thinking that's what the lightning strike was about. I suggested to Rexie that she kiss Lawrence today during the rehearsal to seal the deal. That way she could walk down the aisle on Saturday knowing that she was marrying her true love. But the lightning prevented the kiss. Maybe the power of the stones is working against this wedding."

Even as she said the words, an image from an old movie filled her mind—a bride running down the aisle. Quickly, she shoved it aside. That kind of thing didn't happen in real life. Did it? "We really need to pull off this wedding, Aunt Vi."

Vi gave her a hug. "Then you're going to find a way to do it. Why don't you go down to the arch now and think about it while I get started on dinner. Use the power."

Shoving her hands in her pockets, Adair moved around the veranda's low wall and started down one of the paths. Gardening wasn't her thing. She couldn't even begin to name the plants that bloomed everywhere in profusion.

Except for the roses. And she'd recognized the lilacs and violets earlier in the spring. Gardening was one of her aunt Vi's talents. Angus One had built the original garden for Eleanor but it had been well tended by their descendants. In fact, all the MacPhersons who'd been born and raised here at the castle had benefitted from a very rich gene pool. Some of them had turned to education. It was one of her great-great-uncles who'd been a cofounder of the nearby Huntleigh College. There were three paintings in the castle that bore Eleanor's signature. And Angus One was credited with the design of the castle. And he had to have had some serious engineering skills to have pulled off the construction of the stone arch.

Stepping out of the gardens, she crossed the grass verge until she reached the row of chairs they'd placed in front of the stones for the rehearsal. The arch itself was ten feet tall at its center, ten feet long and eight feet wide. The summer the Sutherland triplets had played here, they'd measured it off to the inch.

The boys had been ten that year, she'd been nine and her sisters eight and six. They'd been fascinated by the Sutherlands. Cam in particular had intrigued her. They'd taken turns deciding the games they would play on those long afternoons. And the ones Cam chose had been her favorites. There was always a risk involved, something that made her heart race faster.

His favorite game had been "pirate and treasure." More than once he'd chosen her as his partner, and together they'd climbed up the cliff face to the west of the castle. Adair's heart raced just thinking about it. Aunt Vi and her father had always forbidden them to go to the cliffs. But they could hardly admit that to the Sutherlands.

When she realized she was smiling, Adair made herself stop. She hadn't come here to the stone arch to think about Cam Sutherland. She'd managed not to think about him for years. She hadn't even seen him since that night after their parents' wedding, when she and her sisters had come out here with a bottle of champagne to write out their secret fantasies about their ideal fantasy lovers.

She'd written her fantasy about Cam. She hadn't been able to get him out of her head from the instant her eyes had met his during the ceremony. In that moment of eye contact only, no one else had existed. The intensity of the awareness she'd felt, the depth of it, had been something she'd never experienced before. When he'd asked her to dance later, she'd seen the challenge in his eyes. He'd known the effect he was having on her. But she'd refused the dance, preferring the safety she'd felt in his brother Reid's arms.

It was only later, with a little help from the champagne, that she'd given full flight to her desire and her fantasy. Just thinking about it made her knees feel so weak that she sank onto the narrow ledge that ran along the side of the arch. Cam spelled trouble for her. And she didn't kid herself. She'd increased the problem exponentially when she'd written her fantasy down on paper and buried it in the arch.

The whole thing had been her idea, and she'd talked her sisters into doing the same thing. Adair the great planner. In the back of her mind she'd had some idea that if she wrote a fantasy about Reid or Duncan, she could negate what she was feeling for Cam.

Hadn't worked out. The instant her pen had struck paper, it had all been about Cam and no one but Cam.

Calm down. Adair forced herself to breathe in, breathe out.

You've avoided him for years. His job at the CIA has kept him overseas. There's nothing to worry about.

Except the power of the stones.

And there might be a way to lessen that....

Dropping to her knees, Adair traced her fingers along the base of the arch, trying to find the loose stones that she and her sisters had discovered when they were children. Behind them there was a niche just big enough to hold the metal box they'd used for years. Any fantasy that she'd put into the box could be taken out. Then she just might have less to worry about.

None of the stones were loose.

That couldn't be. Lowering herself to her stomach,

Adair squinted at the stones as she ran her hands along them again. There wasn't even a crack she could get a finger into.

Had the lightning shifted things?

The sound of Alba's bell had her scrambling to her feet. Once the dog reached the arch, she wandered around to the side and started pawing at some stones. Adair spotted her aunt as she stepped out of the gardens.

"Find any damage?" Vi called.

"Seems pretty solid." Adair brushed her hands off on her slacks. And she was going to put that box and the fantasies it contained out of her mind. Why on earth was she obsessing about Cam Sutherland all of a sudden? Avoidance had worked so far, and there wasn't any reason to think that it wouldn't continue to work.

Unless you don't want it to....

Pushing the thought firmly away, Adair stepped out of the stone arch. "I have an idea about how to avoid the runaway bride disaster."

Vi smiled at her. "I'm all ears."

"You distract Bunny tomorrow and give me some time alone with Rexie. Maybe she'll tell me what's bothering her. I'd like to know what really happened with her first husband that's making her so nervous about taking a second chance."

Vi smiled. "I can handle Bunny. She's very interested in getting the recipe for the scones I served with her herb tea."

"You never give that recipe out."

"I won't this time either, but I have several older versions of it that I can bear to part with."

Alba's bell jingled again, and she suddenly appeared around the side of the arch with something in her mouth.

The dog dropped what looked like a leather pouch on the ground at their feet.

She and Vi dropped to their knees together. Then Adair picked up the pouch. It was folded like an envelope with another pouch inside of it and another pouch in side of that. "Chinese boxes," Adair murmured.

But when she opened the last one, all she could do was stare. Inside lay a sapphire earring set in gold. The gem was the size of her thumbnail and it dangled from a link of gold chain.

Vi caught her breath. "Oh, my."

Oh, my, indeed. Adair recognized it right away. Eleanor Campbell MacPherson was wearing it in the portrait that hung in the main parlor. And Mary Stuart might very well have worn it on the day she was crowned.

But Eleanor's dowry had been missing for years. The theory was that one of the Anguses had sold it long ago.

With the earring still lying in the palm of her hand, she stood and walked around to the side of the stone arch where Alba had been digging. Sure enough, there was a pile of stones that looked as if they'd shaken loose during the storm.

"Who on earth put this here and why?" Adair breathed.

Alba began to bark. When Adair glanced at her, she saw that the dog wasn't looking at the loose stones but at the wooded hill that sloped sharply upward beyond the stone arch. Alba continued to bark as she raced to the hedge that separated the gardens from the trees. Adair ran her gaze up the hill, trying to see what was upsetting the dog, but she saw nothing.

"There's something up there she doesn't like," Vi said as she moved past Adair to take the dog's collar and pat her head.

Even as the dog quieted, Adair scanned the hill again and still saw nothing.

"We'd better get that earring inside and then we'll have to call your father and let him know," Vi said.

Adair stared down at the earring and as she did, it seemed to glow. She could have sworn that she felt a warmth in her hands. After all these years, a part of Eleanor's dowry had shown up. Why now, she couldn't help but wonder. And why had it been hidden away in the stone arch?

3

Received a call from Mom and A.D. Need our help. Conference call with all three of us at five-thirty?

CAM SUTHERLAND READ the short text from his brother Reid twice. Some things never changed. In spite of the fact that he and his brothers were triplets, there'd always been a pecking order. From the time they were little, if his mom needed something she'd always called on Reid, the oldest. Even now, she used him as her main contact person, and it was his job to relay the information and/or request.

Because his younger brother Duncan had always been studious and a bit shy, he'd always seemed to receive extra attention, too. Not that his mom had a lot to spread around. Her work teaching and her research had always absorbed her. "Absentminded professor" might have been a term coined to describe her. But after their father had been sent to prison, Beth Sutherland's academic success and her publications had been key to keeping custody of her sons. So from the age of ten, they'd all pitched in.

And they'd fallen into roles. Reid had become the leader and organizer, Duncan had offered ideas and analysis, and it had usually fallen on Cam to carry out the missions. Not that he'd complained. He'd always preferred action over giving advice or orders.

His mother didn't turn to them very often anymore, but he had no doubt that he would probably get the assignment. His older brother's new duties in the Secret Service serving on the Vice President's security detail were keeping Reid very busy, and the last time he'd talked to Duncan, who worked as a profiler in the Behavioral Sciences division of the FBI, he'd been consulting on a case in Montana.

Then with a frown Cam read the text again. His mom and A. D. MacPherson were in Scotland, and if they'd taken the time to call, his best guess was that something was going on at the castle. From what he'd last heard, Viola MacPherson lived alone there now. The image of a tiny, energetic woman popped into his mind. He hadn't forgotten her scones or her brownies. Except for Christmas and birthday cards, he hadn't seen Aunt Vi or visited the castle since his mother had married the successful landscape painter seven years ago. That had been his senior year in college and he'd joined the CIA right away. For five years he'd worked a variety of covert operations overseas. He'd enjoyed the travel and the challenge of the assignments, but when an opportunity had presented itself to transfer to the Domestic Operations section in D.C., he'd been ready for a change. He still worked in the field but his assignments tended to be of shorter duration, and as a side benefit he got to work for an old and dear friend.

The last he'd heard, the MacPherson sisters had been as busy as he, his brothers and their parents, and were pursuing career goals. Not that he knew what they were doing exactly. He'd avoided thinking about them for years.

Especially Adair.

He strode to the window of his office, but it wasn't

the scenery that he saw. It was Adair MacPherson's face. The image of her standing beneath that stone arch during his mother's wedding to A. D. MacPherson had been popping into his mind lately. It had been a late-fall wedding. He and his brothers had been tied up in classes so they'd booked flights that arrived on the morning of the ceremony and left that evening.

The picture he'd carried in his mind before that had been of a little girl with red curls and freckles, a face that had frowned easily when he'd teased her, and a temper that he'd enjoyed igniting. Calling her "Princess" usually succeeded in eliciting both responses. But she had a smile that he'd wanted to trigger almost as much as the frown.

What he'd enjoyed most about her during those long summer afternoons when they'd played together was the fact that she was willing to try anything. Eager, in fact. She'd been fun—for a girl.

But what he'd felt at his mother's wedding had been something else. And that was the image that still lingered in his mind. Her red-gold curls were tied back with a green ribbon. He'd wanted to run his hands through those curls. At nine, her body had been sturdy and athletic. At twenty, it had been slim as a wand, and he'd wanted to explore every single inch of it. Desire was far too tame a word for what he'd felt. But it was her eyes that had nearly finished him off that day. He had no clear idea of how long he had looked into them. But he'd never forget the color—a pale and misty green that he could have sworn he was drowning in.

Cam drew in a deep breath and let it out. He'd wanted her that day in a way he'd never wanted anyone or anything before. In a way he'd never wanted anyone since. And he'd been rash enough to ask her to dance. If she'd agreed, if he'd held her in his arms, he still wasn't sure what would have happened. Perhaps she'd had some idea of the possible consequences because she'd turned him down flat.

He wasn't sure why she was popping into his mind more frequently lately. Perhaps because he was back in the States. Perhaps because she'd never really left his mind. Perhaps because it was only possible to avoid something for so long and then…

"Got a minute, Sutherland?"

Cam turned as his boss walked into the room. Seven years ago Daryl Garnett had recruited him to work for the CIA. Cam had trained under the man at the farm and Daryl had been one of his mentors ever since, and he'd invited Cam to join the Domestic Operations section he headed up in D.C.

"I think I just got something on my old nemesis." Daryl moved around Cam's desk and taped two photos on the whiteboard that covered nearly one wall. "Meet Gianni Scalzo."

Cam turned to study the photos. He'd seen one of them before because Daryl carried a smaller version in his wallet, the way a man might carry a photo of his family. But Gianni Scalzo wasn't family. He was a con man extraordinaire who'd put a bullet in Daryl's knee and limited his career as a covert field operative.

Since then, Daryl had been steadily working his way up in the training and management side of the Agency, but he'd made a hobby out of tracking Scalzo down.

In the photo that Cam had seen before, Scalzo had long, curly, shoulder-length hair—Mel Gibson in the first *Lethal Weapon*. In shorts and sunglasses, he looked very much at home on the prow of a sailboat. The man standing next to him in the picture was shorter, less athletic in build, the kind of man that you wouldn't notice if you passed him on the street. Interpol believed he was Scalzo's partner. Daryl agreed. Both men were masters at disguise, but the partner had always stayed in the shadows.

The man in the second photo was older. His short dark hair boasted just a sprinkle of gray and he had a well-trimmed mustache and goatee. Not Mel Gibson but he still had a sort of middle-aged movie star quality. Next to him stood a pretty young blonde.

"What do you think?" Daryl asked.

"It's a difficult call. The more important question is what do you think? You're the one who met him in person."

"Allowing for the passage of time, I'm betting they're one and the same," Daryl said. "I felt it as soon as I saw the picture. I had one of our techs run a facial analysis of the two photos."

Cam moved closer to study the two images more closely. "What were the results?"

"Inconclusive." A tall lanky man in his mid-fifties, Daryl stood shoulder to shoulder with Cam at the whiteboard. "Right now, I'm having someone age the photo of Scalzo on the sailboat."

"How long have you been looking for Scalzo now?" Cam asked.

Daryl tapped the leg that had retired him from the field. "Fifteen years, three months and nine days."

"The age difference is about right. Who tipped you off to take a look at the guy?" Cam asked.

"Ben Slack contacted me an hour ago and I asked him to email me the photo," Daryl said. "He was in your class at the farm."

Cam remembered Ben, and anyone who had been trained by Daryl would know of his interest in tracking Scalzo down.

"Ben says the Securities and Exchange Commission is 'looking at' this guy," Daryl said. "One problem I've always had in tracing Scalzo was that the man avoids getting his picture taken. But this guy is getting married, so he couldn't very well refuse to have an engagement picture published."

"What else have you got?" Cam asked.

"If the Securities and Exchange Commission is sniffing around him, he could be using the same M.O. as Scalzo did in Italy, and the same one that he used in Portland a few years ago. I was nearly in time to get him. He changes looks, identities and locations, but the scam he and his partner run remains the same. They target financial planners—some who handle select clients as well as others who manage pension funds. Scalzo is always the front man. He infiltrates the social strata first—buys an estate, joins the right clubs. That's exactly what this guy has been doing in the Long Island area for the last year and a half. He promises huge returns to his investors and he delivers them. After the recent scandals, that's enough to bring him to the attention of the Securities and Exchange Commission."

"It sounds like the same kind of scam my father tried to run, but your nemesis is much better at it."

Daryl's hand settled on Cam's shoulder. He didn't have to say a word. As the man who'd recruited Cam, Daryl had accessed all the details on his father's background. A rich and pampered young man, Cam's dad, David Fedderman, had relied on his parents to buy him out of scrapes all of his life. Once he'd joined Fedderman Trust, he'd spent all of his time wining and dining clients and traveling to locate new investment opportunities. When it had finally been revealed that he'd been dipping into clients' accounts to the tune of hundreds of thousands, his parents hadn't been able to buy Davie out of serving jail time. They had, however, tried to get custody of Cam and his brothers in a brutal lawsuit. But Beth's lawyer had finally prevailed and she'd immediately changed their last name to hers—Sutherland. They hadn't heard from any of the Feddermans since.

What wasn't in all the files was the fact that his father hadn't been any more skilled at being a father or a husband than he'd been at being a crook. Cam had been ten when it had all gone down, and what he recalled most was that after the arrest, he'd never heard his mother cry herself to sleep anymore.

Daryl looked at him then. "Any chance you could help me out with this?"

Cam smiled at him. "I thought you'd never ask. Do we have any way to connect this guy to the Portland crime?"

"That's what I'll start on next. Scalzo's good." His smile widened. "But the Portland police have a set of prints for the alias he operated under there. I've got a call into the P.D. there right now."

Cam tapped the second man in the sailboat photo. "What about his partner?"

"There's no sign of him. He stays out of sight, out of mind."

"What's your plan?"

"I've got some vacation time coming, so I'm going to take a few days to see what I can dig up on Long Island," Daryl said. "Maybe I can get a whiff of the partner or a glimpse of Scalzo. I think I can recognize him in person."

"Let me know what you need on this end." Then he remembered Reid's text. "But I may have to make a quick trip up to the Adirondacks to check out a family thing."

Daryl grinned at him. "Luck is on my side." He pointed to the engagement photo of the man he was sure was

Scalzo. "My friend here is getting married in this little place in the Adirondacks this coming Saturday. Castle MacPherson. Ever heard of it?"

Cam stared at him. "Yeah. As a matter of fact, I have. That's my stepfather's place."

"So you're familiar with it?"

"Somewhat." Not enough to know that people were scheduling weddings there. He turned to his desk, did a quick search for Castle MacPherson on his computer and found himself looking at Adair's smiling face. The impact of just seeing her stopped him short for a minute. The fancy wedding hairdo was gone. But the eyes were the same pale, mysterious green. He had to remind himself to take a breath.

"A wedding destination spot, huh?"

Realizing that Daryl was leaning over his shoulder reading the computer screen, Cam reined in his thoughts and scanned the web page. By the time he finished, he'd noted Vi's photo also, along with a shot of the castle, the gardens and the stone arch. And he'd clicked on a link that led to a small feature article in the *New York Times* that provided a brief history of the castle as well as the story of the legend and Eleanor Campbell MacPherson's missing sapphires.

"And here I thought that wedding destinations involved sandy beaches and drinks with little umbrellas in them," Daryl remarked. "But I guess a stone arch with the promise of a happy-ever-after would have a definite draw. Do you know if the two women are alone up there?"

"They won't be for long." Turning, he glanced back up at the photos on his whiteboard. "I'm going to be an unofficial guest at the upcoming wedding."

"Thanks." Daryl patted him on the shoulder. "I'll need

a day to get my ducks all in a row and make sure he's my guy. Then I'll get in touch."

BY THE TIME five-thirty rolled around, Cam had his own ducks lined up and he was ready to hit the road for the castle. He answered Reid's call on the first ring and once he and his brothers had exchanged greetings, he said, "Problem solved. I'm about to give Vi a call to let her know that I'll be leaving later tonight." Suiting the action to words, he stepped into the elevator and pushed the button to the garage.

"How did you know Mom and A.D. wanted one of us to go up there?" Reid asked.

"I called her," Cam said. "You sent me the text an hour ago. Just because you're the oldest and Mom always calls you doesn't mean Duncan or I can't take the initiative."

"You tell him, bro," Duncan said, laughing.

"I thought we should discuss it first. What if we all took the initiative and we'd all dropped everything to run up there?" Reid asked with just a trace of annoyance in his tone.

"I checked," Cam explained. "Duncan's in Montana and you're on the way to Dulles right now because the Vice President is flying to Paris."

"How did you—?" Reid began.

"He's CIA," Duncan said. "And, as the middle brother, he always has to show off."

"And I'm usually the one who gets the field assignments," Cam pointed out. "I figured I'd get started."

"Yeah, yeah, yeah." But Cam could hear the smile in Reid's tone.

"Plus, you knew I'd jump at the chance once Mom told me that Vi and Adair had discovered an earring from Eleanor's missing dowry."

"One of the sapphires?" Duncan asked. "Wait. Time out. We're talking about one of the sapphire earrings that was probably worn by Mary Stuart on her coronation day?"

"That would be correct," Cam said.

"If I'd known that, I could have gotten away. The local police made an arrest yesterday, and I'm just hanging around to get some fishing in. Remember all the games we played that summer pretending to find those jewels?"

Cam remembered them well, and the discovery of one of them would allow him the perfect cover to visit the castle. There was no need to let his brothers know that the castle might have other problems, not until Daryl had identified Saturday's groom-to-be as Gianni Scalzo.

"When can you get there, Cam?" Reid asked.

Always the organizing big brother, Cam thought. But all he said was, "My ETA will be early morning. I'll check out the security system and find a better place to secure the earring than Angus One's secret cupboard inside the house. That's were they've put it, and I'm betting that most of the population of Glen Loch knows all about that cupboard, including how to pull the lever to get into it. Have a safe flight, Reid. Catch a fish for me, Duncan."

He ended the call and walked toward his car. He had no doubt he could handle providing security for the earring Adair and Vi had found. The real problem he was facing was how he was going to handle Adair.

4

ADAIR'S EYES SNAPPED open. It took a moment for the rest of her mind to register reality. She was in bed and it was still dark. Moonlight poured through the windows. A quick glance at her digital alarm told her that she must have just dozed off. Three-thirty in the morning and something had awakened her.

Not Cam Sutherland. He'd called Vi and said he'd be arriving in the morning. But she could definitely blame him for the hot, sweaty dream that had awakened her shortly after midnight. That was when she'd opened her balcony doors to cool off.

The sound came again and she recognized it immediately. Alba was barking. Adair let out the breath she hadn't realized she'd been holding. Her aunt's room was in the west wing on the other side of the main staircase, and Vi had mentioned the dog was waking up and barking during the night for no apparent reason. So far she'd managed to sleep through Alba's nightly ritual.

Not tonight. That's what very little sleep, a lightning strike and the discovery of a priceless sapphire earring would do for you. But they were going to keep the discovery under wraps. That's what her father had advised when

Aunt Vi had called him. And he'd said he was going to call
Reid to let him know so that arrangements could be made
to check out the security at the castle. In the meantime,
she and Vi had hidden the earring away in a place that
was as good as Fort Knox—Angus One's secret cupboard.

Alba continued to bark.

Adair stared up at the ceiling. She'd already lost enough
sleep. She didn't need a dog robbing her of the rest of it.
She was about to burrow her head beneath the pillow when
she heard something else.

Not a bark. More of a…what? A creak?

Jumping out of bed, she padded softly to the door,
opened it and listened hard.

Nothing.

Even the dog had gone silent. Aunt Vi had probably
quieted her.

She stood there and counted to one hundred while she
told herself it was nothing. The castle had never had a
break-in. And Vi had assured her the latest updates on
the security system had been installed.

But then she recalled how the dog had barked shortly
after they'd found the earring. Alba had sensed someone
or something in the hills above the stone arch. And she
had been holding the earring in her hand. If there'd been
someone up there lurking or spying, they'd been in a perfect position to have seen it.

Turning, she paced back into her room and checked
the time. Three-forty. Then she strode back to the door
and debated going downstairs. To what? To search for an
intruder? Barefoot and weaponless?

No way. But there was no way she'd be able to fall back
asleep either. She looked around for a weapon. Where was
a large brass candlestick when you needed one? Settling

on a sizable stoneware pitcher, she grabbed the handle and crept softly into the hallway.

At the top of the stairs she paused, listening again. Nothing.

There was half a flight of stairs to a landing where tall stained glass windows filtered the moonlight. Once she reached it, she would be visible to anyone below in the foyer. She had to chance it. Taking a deep breath, she moved quickly down the stairs, rounded the curve of the banister, then slipped into the shadows and flattened her back against the wall.

She made herself take slow, silent breaths—in and out—while she counted to one hundred again. And listened. Nothing moved in the large, open foyer below. Nothing made a sound.

As seconds ticked by, she began to question whether or not she'd imagined the noise she'd heard earlier. It was an old house, she reminded herself.

She was ready to go back to her bedroom again when she heard something. A definite creak this time, as if someone had stepped on a board.

Seconds later, she heard it again.

Her heart thudded against her rib cage and she tightened her grip on the handle of the pitcher.

Security system or not, she was not alone in the house. She scanned the foyer again but the shadows didn't budge. Step by step she started down the stairs. Slow and easy, she told herself. At the bottom she paused and listened again. To her right was a door that opened into the dining room, and an archway that led to the west wing that housed the library and the kitchen. To her left was a door that led to the main parlor.

Wood scraped against wood, and this time the creak was loud and familiar. Adrenaline spiked and her heart thudded even harder as she pinpointed the sound. The main parlor. And she knew exactly what was making it.

Someone was breaking into Angus One's secret cupboard where she and Aunt Vi had put the earring. Temper surged through her, pushing fear aside. She was not going to let anyone steal that earring.

She moved quietly toward the door to the parlor and saw that it was ajar. The crack wasn't wide enough to see inside the room. For a couple of seconds she debated what to do. If she called out, asked who it was, she'd alert them.

Not her best move.

The creaking sound came again, then the scrape of wood against wood. Then nothing.

Except for the footsteps. The carpeting muffled them, but they were getting closer. No time to debate her best move. She climbed onto the seat of a chair flanking the door and raised the pitcher over her head.

The opening in the door slowly widened. She stopped breathing. When the figure stepped into the foyer, she brought the pitcher down hard on his head.

He fell like a tree and the pitcher clattered and rolled across the wooden floor until it thudded into a wall.

He wasn't moving a muscle. And he was big. The foyer was a good twelve feet wide and the man's body filled a great deal of it.

Was he dead? Had she killed him? Her knees went so weak she nearly tumbled as she climbed down from the chair.

He moaned.

Relief had her sitting down hard in the chair. Not dead. She drew in a deep breath and the burn in her lungs told her she needed the oxygen.

The figure on the floor moaned again, then his hand snaked out, grabbed her ankle and jerked. She fell hard, the impact singing through her as he rolled on top of her and crushed her beneath him.

He was even bigger than she'd first thought. Still she fought. She went for his face but he blocked the move and pinned her hands over her head. His chest was like a slab of rock. So were his thighs. When she tried to kick he scissored his legs, trapping hers. Finally she screamed, but the only sound she mustered was a squeak.

"Princess?" Releasing her hands he levered himself up, taking some of his weight off her.

Shock was her first response. It was dark in the foyer but she knew that voice. And there was only one person who called her that. "Cam?"

For a moment neither of them moved. Adair felt as if her mind had become a clean slate, and something was happening to her body. All the fight had gone out of it and it was softening, sort of molding itself to his. Flames ignited at every contact point.

His body seemed to be growing even harder. She was intensely aware of every plane and angle, and the thrill of lying there beneath him was so much better than she'd ever imagined in her fantasies. His mouth was close, too. She could feel the warmth of his breath on her lips.

Panic spurted. She had to do something. Push him away. But her muscles seemed paralyzed. And her brain wasn't doing much better.

She was going to have to rely on her mouth. "Get off of me."

When he rolled away and rose to his feet, Adair realized that she'd never said anything more contrary to her desire. She'd wanted him to continue to lie on top of her; she'd wanted his mouth on hers. She'd wanted him to touch her the way he had in the dream she'd had a few hours ago. She'd wanted...

Stop, she said to herself.

Get back down here, she wanted to say to him.

"I'm going to have a hell of a headache in the morning, Princess. Are you all right?"

The easiness of his tone and his use of the nickname he'd given her helped her to gather her thoughts. So did the fact that he'd backed a few steps away and didn't offer her his hand as she stood up. If he had…

Don't go there.

"I'm just fine." That was a total lie. She still couldn't feel her legs, but she managed to fist her hands on her hips. "I'll be a lot better once you answer some questions. First, what are you doing breaking into the castle in the middle of the night *and* into Angus's secret cupboard? Second, how did you even know about that cupboard? It's a MacPherson secret. Last, but not least, where is the earring?"

The barrage of questions made Cam smile. Even in the dimness he could see the flash of fire in her eyes. The heat they'd generated together a few seconds ago threatened to erupt again. He'd been right about the hairtrigger effect she'd have on his senses. It had taken all of his control to get up when she'd told him to. Every cell in his body had been focused on kissing her. And he'd have wanted to do a lot more than that. He still did. He was a man who trusted his impulses, went with them. In two quick strides, he could…

As if she sensed his intentions, she took a quick step back. "Are you going to answer my questions or not?"

She was close to the stairs and if his memory was correct, she was fast. If she ran she might get away. He might be able to let her.

It took a wise man to know when his first impulse wasn't his best one.

"Well?" She tapped her foot.

He held up a hand. "It's taking me a few seconds to process all of the questions. If you ever decide to give up the wedding destination gig, the CIA will hire you. They can always use a good interrogator."

"I could use some answers."

"I'm here because your dad and my mom called Reid. They thought that one of us should check out the earring and the security system. I made much better time than I expected to, and I didn't want to wake you."

"So you broke in?"

"I decided to check out the security system and the earring without bothering you and your aunt Vi. The system is pretty good. It would take a pro or someone with a buddy on the inside to get through it. And since your dad mentioned that you'd put the earring in Angus's secret cupboard, I just wanted to check and see if it was still there. It was."

"How did you know about the secret cupboard?"

"My brother and I convinced your sister Nell to show it to us years ago. And I was a bit worried about how 'secret' it was."

For a moment she said nothing. He felt the pull between them even more strongly than he'd felt it seven years ago, and he knew she felt it, too.

She turned and started up the stairs. "I'll show you to your room."

"Wait." He turned to pick up his duffel, and his hand collided with something else. A stoneware pitcher. It had to have been what she'd clubbed him with. "Way to go, Princess. I've never been taken out by a pitcher before."

"My pleasure," she said as she led the way up the staircase.

"I'll bet." But he didn't say it out loud, nor did he let the chuckle escape as he followed her.

"YOU'RE WILLING TO share your recipe for these delicious scones?" Bunny Maitland sprang from her chair, excitement clear in her voice.

"I'll do more than that," Vi said. "I'll demonstrate. Follow me."

Adair watched her Aunt Vi usher Bunny Maitland out of her office right on schedule and willed away the headache that was throbbing at the back of her skull.

Then she shifted her attention to Rexie. The bride-to-be hadn't talked much during their meeting.

There hadn't been much chance for anyone to talk while Bunny was sharing the good news like a weather reporter on a sunny day. The wedding would go on as scheduled. A good night's sleep with all that magic mountain air and quiet—blah, blah, blah—had settled Rexie's nerves.

Adair sorely wished the "magic" air had settled her own. Fat chance of that after her run-in with Cam, which had fueled more fantasies than the ones she'd already written down.

She hadn't been able to catch more than a few winks of sleep. Not with her mind racing at full speed, imagining what might have happened if she hadn't let him up from the foyer floor.

Thank heavens her arms hadn't been working.

Too bad her arms hadn't been working.

Adair pressed a hand to her stomach in an attempt to quell the heat that had centered there, but it was already radiating out to her fingers and toes.

Cam had clearly felt nothing at all. According to Aunt Vi, he'd left her a note that he'd left the castle early to visit the library in Glen Loch. Research on the missing sapphire jewels. He was obviously totally focused on his purpose in coming to the castle.

And she had to focus on hers. Reaching for her mug, she took a long swallow of her cooled coffee and shifted her full attention to Rexie. She wasn't sure how long Vi could distract Bunny, and this might be her only opportunity to discover what was bothering the young girl.

The best description Adair could come up with for the expression on Rexie's face was resignation.

So she asked the question that she might not want the answer to. "Rexie, do you want to marry Lawrence?"

"Of course." The answer came quickly but Rexie didn't meet her eyes.

Not good.

"Why do you want to marry him?"

Rexie's eyes lifted to hers. "Because I want to do something right. I messed up my first marriage because I didn't choose the right person. Lawrence is perfect for me."

The fact that Rexie's answer sounded memorized only increased the intensity of Adair's headache. "How is Lawrence perfect?"

"My father and mother like him—he's been such a good friend to them. And our marriage will help solidify the merger between Maitland Enterprises and Banes Ltd. This is my chance to help with that. My duty. Lawrence has already bought a beautiful estate for us on Long Island. He has memberships in two very prestigious golf and tennis clubs nearby. He's going to hire a pro to help me improve my game. And his estate has a stable. He's going to let me keep a horse. I used to show horses when I was younger."

Adair studied Rexie. As she'd listed all the advantages of marrying Lawrence Banes, it reminded her of all the reasons she'd listed for herself when she'd decided to date

Baxter DuBois exclusively. Of course, he'd pointed them
out to her. They'd already teamed up on several projects
at the office, and becoming a "team" outside the office
would only enhance that. It would put them on the fast
track for promotions. And the plan had worked at first. But
then Bax's career had begun to advance faster than hers.

She hadn't seen it at first because she'd trusted him.
More than that, she'd trusted her own judgment. It wasn't
until she'd had that final meeting with her supervisor that
she'd learned how wrong she'd been. Bax had been taking
all the credit for their success, even for the last client that
she had brought in. She'd trusted him, and he'd dumped
her the same day she'd been fired. He'd explained in his
email that it might tarnish his image at the company if
he continued to be seen with her. She of all people had
to know how important perception was in the cutthroat
world of career advancement.

She certainly did now. In Rexie's perception Lawrence
Banes was the perfect husband. Was he? "Rexie, are you
in love with Lawrence?"

Panic flashed into the young girl's eyes. "If I marry
him beneath the stone arch, I will be. And I'll be happy.
Won't I?"

Adair heard Bunny's voice, her aunt's laughter. She
needed more time with the young bride-to-be, and she
needed some help. "Why don't we go down there right
now? You didn't have time to check it out yesterday—
what with the storm and all. That way you can get a better feeling about it."

"Could we do that?" Rexie smiled for the first time
since her arrival at the castle.

"Follow me." Adair rose and quickly led the way
through the open French doors. The path to their right
led around the front of the house to the gardens. With

any luck at all, Vi would distract Bunny long enough that she could get what she needed from Rexie. Perhaps Rexie would get what she needed, too.

The morning was a beautiful one, the sky blue, the breeze cool, and this early in the morning the sun had risen just high enough in the sky to shoot bright lances of light off the surface of the lake. Pansies bordered the path and behind them peonies bloomed in various shades of pink.

Wesley Pinter, Glen Loch's gardener and landscaper, a man who'd been handling the maintenance of the castle's gardens since she was a child, was unloading the last planter from his truck. She noted he'd settled them temporarily on either side of the stone arch. The chairs that they'd set up for the rehearsal the day before were still there and Adair led Rexie to the first row. She gestured her into one and sat beside her.

Then she cut to the chase. "Were you in love with your first husband?"

Rexie tensed. "Mummy says it was infatuation. My therapist says we were just too young. We rushed into it and we weren't right for each other. Coming from the same kind of background helps to ensure compatibility."

A wave of sympathy washed over Adair. Those were Mommy's words or a therapist's, not Rexie's. She laid a hand on the younger girl's arm. "Tell me what happened?"

"Why? It's over. My divorce became final six months ago, and Barry returned his signature on the papers by overnight delivery. I'm no longer Mrs. Barry Carlson. I took my maiden name back as soon as I could." There was a trace of grief in her eyes, a mix of anger and hurt in her voice. Not good.

"Where is Barry now?" Adair asked.

"In Montana. His family owns a horse farm there, and his mother opened a wildlife refuge. We met while he was

finishing his degree in veterinary medicine at Cornell. I
was a freshman, and I fell in love with him the first time
I saw him. I could actually feel my heart take a tumble.
He said it was the same for him. We got married as soon
as we could. Barry insisted on that. He comes from a religious family and he didn't want me to just move in with
him. We didn't have time to do a big wedding thing. We
didn't even tell our parents right away. I sometimes wish
we'd never had to."

"That's when the trouble started," Adair said.

Rexie sighed. "They were so upset. My father was furious, my mother hurt and disappointed. Barry's family
wasn't happy, either. Especially when he told them that
he was going to get a job in the East."

"What happened next?" Adair prompted.

"We started trying to make everyone happy again. My
father got Barry a job in a very upscale, very busy veterinary practice on Long Island, and my mother threw a
huge wedding reception for us at her country club. But I
could see that Barry wasn't happy. Neither was I. I barely
saw him, and when I did we always argued. And when his
grandfather died he went back to Montana."

"You didn't go with him?"

Rexie's eyes grew shiny with yet-to-be-shed tears. "He
didn't ask me to. He promised he'd come back. But each
time he called he made excuses. An ailing horse, then sick
animals at the refuge forced him to extend his stay. Then
he sent me a letter saying that we'd made a mistake and
he wanted me to handle the divorce on this end."

A Dear Jane letter, Adair thought. Why was it that men
were so lacking in class?

"After that he wouldn't even take my calls. I'd leave a
message but he'd never call back." She blinked back the
tears and her voice became very firm. "I made a huge

mistake marrying Barry. This time I want a guarantee. Can you give me that?"

"I can promise you that getting married here will give you your best shot at it."

"Rexie?" Bunny's voice was accompanied by the sound of Alba's bell.

Adair turned to see Aunt Vi bringing up the rear of the small parade. Bunny was a bit breathless when she reached them. "We have to leave for the city now if we're going to make the final fitting on your dress. Then we have to get ready for your bachelorette party tonight."

"Our gardener just unloaded the planters," Adair said. "Can't you stay long enough to give them your final approval?"

Bunny waved a hand in the direction of the flowers. "I'm sure they'll be lovely. But we need to make this fitting. The dress has to be perfect. It's a copy of the one I wore on my wedding day. She's going to wear my veil, also."

Bunny gave Rexie a little push toward the car, then spoke in a very low voice to Adair. "My plan is to keep her busy and focused on the wedding. Your job is to make sure that there are no more glitches on this end. She and Lawrence chose this place against my wishes. They've refused to change venues at this late date, and I've agreed because I want my daughter to be happy."

Bunny's smile didn't quite reach her eyes as she continued. "I'm sure you want her to be happy, too. That way I'll have only good things to say about Castle MacPherson."

With that, Bunny hurried to catch up with her daughter. Seconds later the flashy red convertible sped out of the driveway.

"Well, well. There's a core of steel beneath that sweet magnolia exterior," Vi murmured as she stepped to Adair's side. "And none of the 'glitches' yesterday were your fault. You certainly can't be blamed for the storm, nor for the fact that the groom-to-be was late and distracted."

"Well, Bunny can't very well get angry with Mr. Banes. Not when she's so desperate to make sure this wedding takes place."

"What did you learn from Rexie?"

"Her upcoming marriage will be a marriage of convenience."

"Whose convenience?" Vi asked.

"Exactly. There's money involved. And I think Rexie's still in love with her first husband." She glanced through the stone arch. "I've always believed there's a lot of power here. I suppose we should just leave it to the legend. But I'd like to know more about what's going on with the Maitlands and Banes that makes this wedding so important."

"You're still afraid we might have a runaway bride on our hands."

"Or lightning may strike again." She was beginning to think that the stone arch might have more power than she'd ever realized.

5

THE CAR CAME out of nowhere, flying over the crest of the hill and then smacking down to barrel toward him. Cam's reflexes, honed by his training as well as the experience of battling two brothers as he grew up, kicked in immediately. The narrow dirt road in front of him led to only one place. The castle. And it was going to be very tricky to negotiate past the red convertible shooting toward him at race car speed.

Tall pines with trunks as thick as a giant's thighs pressed close on either side. Thanks to that summer he'd spent playing on the castle grounds, he had some knowledge of the road.

The blonde driving the convertible didn't. Or she wouldn't be speeding. She was risking her own life as well as her passenger's. Keeping his hands steady on the wheel, he set his foot gently against the brake.

Tires squealing, the convertible ahead skidded, swerving wildly from one side of the road to the other. Dust spewed and he prayed for it to settle. He couldn't edge over yet. He was going to need a wide angle when he made his turn. And he prayed it was coming up soon.

With a bare twenty feet to spare, Cam spotted the slight

break in the trees he was looking for and pulled his steering wheel hard to the right. His car fishtailed, bringing it parallel to the trees before it straightened and shot forward. Narrowing his eyes, he pressed his foot gently on the brake, aiming the front of the car right between the two giant pines. He thought of the biblical image of trying to squeeze a camel through the eye of a needle. Impossible. But the car whispered through and bumped its way into a shallow gully. He was grinning as he managed to stop just short of the next tree.

Jumping out of his car, he ran back to the road to check on the convertible just in time to see it disappear around a curve. Son of a…

But it hadn't been a son of a bitch driving that car, he reminded himself. It had been a woman and she'd been in as much of a hurry as the Disney villain Cruella de Vil when she'd been hunting down those hundred and one Dalmatians. Turning, he glanced up the hill where dust still hung in the air. There was only one place she could have come from, since the road dead-ended at the castle.

Then he glanced back down at his car. He'd managed to avoid crashing it, but he was going to need a tow out of that gully. The castle was still a couple of miles off. A nice hike if you weren't in a hurry. There was a part of him that was anxious to get back there. But there was still a part of him that was practicing avoidance where Adair was concerned—something that he'd been doing for the past seven years.

Old habits died hard. He'd left a note for Vi near the coffeemaker in the kitchen that he was going into Glen Loch to let the sheriff know about the earring. He'd also wanted to stop by the library to refresh his memory about Eleanor's missing dowry.

Both were perfectly valid excuses—but not the only

ones he'd had for wanting some time before he came into contact with Adair again.

Cam moved quickly down the incline and grabbed the bag the librarian had given him to carry the books and copies he'd made at the library. His mother had used the Glen Loch library when she'd researched the missing sapphires for her book. It was always best to look at the primary data. Partly that was his CIA training talking and partly it was the curiosity he'd always had about those missing jewels. When he and his brothers had played with the MacPherson girls during that long-ago summer, his favorite game had been "pirates." And the treasure they'd always sought had been the sapphires.

His mother's research had never turned up even a hint of what had happened to them. But the proof of their existence had always been right there in the main parlor of the castle in Eleanor Campbell MacPherson's portrait. When his mother had been researching, she'd picked up on the story that the sapphires had once been worn by Mary Stuart and that they'd been Eleanor's dowry. But exactly when or how they'd disappeared was still a mystery. And no one knew exactly how the sapphires had come into her family's possession. The mystery had always drawn him. And it was one of the reasons his mother was in Scotland right now researching the Campbells and MacPhersons on that end.

And mysteries surrounding the sapphires had drawn someone else to the Glen Loch library that morning. The librarian, a tall, spider-thin woman with sharp eyes, had greeted Cam warmly as soon as he'd identified himself, telling him that she remembered when his mother had brought him and his brothers to the library that summer when they'd first visited the castle. And she'd been very willing to tell him about the stranger who'd come in the moment she'd unlocked the doors. He'd asked for help in locating anything on the missing MacPherson sapphires. She couldn't give Cam a name, but she'd described the stranger as a man with brown hair, a receding hairline, mid-forties, with a portly build. He'd been wearing khaki slacks, a baseball cap and glasses. And he'd printed copies of some of the materials he'd accessed on their new computers.

There were two things that bothered Cam about the guy. His timing and the fact that he was a stranger. His own reason for visiting the library, besides avoidance, was the fact that he knew one of Eleanor's earrings had surfaced. Was it just a coincidence that a stranger had dropped by the library the same morning to gather information on the missing sapphires?

Cam had never put much faith in coincidence. He wasn't even willing to bet that it was some kind of coincidence that had pulled him back to the castle right now.

Shouldering the bag, he started up the hill. Adair was different for him. He'd sensed it on a bone-deep level seven years ago when she'd stood beneath the stone arch with him while their parents exchanged vows. He trusted his gut instinct, something that had always served him well at his job. And working for the CIA had also honed his skills at analyzing data. What he'd learned from his encounter with her on the floor of the foyer last night was that avoiding her hadn't changed a thing. She was still different for him. And he still wanted her.

This time he couldn't just leave the way he'd done when he was twenty-two. He was stuck here until he'd done what their father had requested and thoroughly checked out the security. For now, he'd made sure that the earring was safe. But there was someone else who was suddenly interested in the sapphires. And there was still the job that Daryl had asked him to do. His boss hadn't contacted him yet, which meant he still hadn't been able to definitely identify Saturday's groom as his longtime nemesis. But Adair or Vi might know something about Lawrence Banes that would help him out.

So avoidance time was over.

He hadn't even kissed her yet. But in spite of the fact that he had a lot on his plate, he wasn't sure that he could resist the urge to taste her for very long. And they weren't twenty and twenty-two anymore.

Last night he'd lain awake in the guest room reliving what it had felt like to have every soft curve and angle of her body pressed against his, and the devouring heat, the churning in his gut, that the contact had triggered. The sensory memories had kept him from sleeping for hours.

Cam reached the top of the hill the red convertible had shot over and caught his favorite view of the lake, the sturdy castle with its terraces and balconies nestled in the tall pines, the lush gardens and the blue lake glimmering like a sapphire below it. From this spot, he could even see part of the stone arch. He knew how to do his job. What he still had to figure out was what he was going to do about Adair. And as he started down the hill to the castle, he wondered if he had a choice.

ADAIR DRAGGED THE last potted plant into position, then stepped back to survey what she'd been able to accomplish since the departure of the Maitlands. Her aunt had returned to the kitchen to work on the groom's cake. The mix of lavender hyacinths and purple irises offered a stark contrast to the gray stones, and the colors would pick up the tones in the maid of honor's and flower girl's dresses.

The physical exertion of moving the pots into place had helped her get a clearer perspective on Rexie's wedding.

Focusing on a task and finding a solution had always been one of her strengths. But that skill hadn't worked for her in Chicago. In hindsight, she could see that she'd been so focused on the projects she'd been doing with Bax that she hadn't picked up on the fact that he was taking all the credit for them.

Maybe she just didn't have good judgment when it came to men. Which made it very good that her attraction for Cam Sutherland was one-sided. And he'd no doubt be leaving today. How long could it take to check out their security and reassure her father?

Pushing the thought out of her mind, she backed up to the first row of chairs and sank down. She had a wedding to pull off and she was going to do her best to ensure it went forward. Everyone wanted it to, including the bride.

In her mind, she pictured the bridal couple standing beneath the arch and imagined what she hadn't seen yesterday. The minister saying, "You may now kiss the bride." Rexie wrapping her arms around Lawrence and kissing him.

Visualizing your goal was essential to achieving it, just as important as writing it down. That was business school 101. It had been hammered home in every self-help book she'd read, every entrepreneurship course she'd taken. Even her ex-boyfriend, Bax, had talked about it. He probably believed that she'd been axed and he hadn't because of his superior visualization skills.

Or had the problem been that she hadn't been able to "see" what he'd been doing? Maybe she hadn't wanted to see reality. Instead she'd wanted to believe in the fantasy she'd created in her mind of their perfect partnership.

Focus. Bax was history, and Cam soon would be. What she needed to concentrate on right now was the upcoming wedding. The fate of her new business plan depended on its success.

Closing her eyes, she summoned the image to her mind. *Rexie kissing Lawrence. Rexie kissing Lawrence.* Digging into Rexie's first marriage to Barry was not her problem. Pulling off the second one to Lawrence was. Slowly her imagination delivered. Pretty Rexie, her blond curls all pulled up with pearls threaded through them. And the groom, holding her close.

Keep your focus. Wait for it.

The image grew clearer and closer. A tall man with lean, chiseled features and sandy-colored hair finally lowered his mouth to Rexie's.

But he definitely didn't look anything like Lawrence Banes.

Cut. Stop action.

Adair snapped her eyes open, but the stranger's mouth had been brushing Rexie's before she'd pushed the image out of her mind.

She pressed her hands to her temples. *Think of something else.* A quick glance at her watch told her that she still had forty-five minutes until her next appointment. A prospective client who'd called first thing that morning. Nathan MacDonald. He'd been driving through the mountains and stopped at the diner in Glen Loch, and the patrons had been talking about the upcoming wedding. He and his fiancée were looking for the ideal place to schedule their own wedding. Adair had set him up for a brief tour.

She dragged one of the chairs out of its straight line and propped her feet on it. Leaning back, she closed her eyes and just for a minute, she made her mind go blank. She concentrated on the sensation of the warm sun on her face, smelled the scent of fresh mulch, pine and flowers.

In the distance she heard the rumble of the lawn mower and much closer the chattering of birds, the hum of bees.

As she let herself drift, another image filled her mind. It was blurry at first, but as it slowly came into focus she saw that *she* was standing beneath the arch, not Rexie. And the man holding her? Hard to see in the shadows cast by the stones. But she grew steadily warmer as the features slowly sharpened in her mind—the dark unruly hair, the lean face with its slash of cheekbones. Familiar.

The hands were not so familiar, but as they gripped her waist and pulled her closer, pleasure rippled along her nerve endings. She tipped her head up as he lowered his. He was close now. In another second, his mouth would… With a sigh, she let herself sink into the kiss.

THE INSTANT THE driveway curved past the stone arch, Cam spotted Adair. He'd taken three steps toward her before he realized he was moving. She had her feet propped up on one chair, her eyes closed, and her head resting on the back of another. A wiser tactic might have been to turn around and continue on to the castle. He wanted to ask Vi to give him her take on the bridegroom in the upcoming wedding.

But a good agent took advantage of every opportunity to gather all kinds of data. It had been too dark in the foyer last night to get a good look at Adair. This was his chance to study her. If he could pinpoint just what it was that drew him, he might be able to figure out a solution.

While he crossed to her he had time to refresh his memory of that neat, trim little body. She was wearing shorts, and he noted that the legs were longer than one might expect in someone of her slight stature. She was still slender, but the hint of curves she'd had at twenty-one had fully matured.

As he drew closer it was her face that drew his gaze and stopped him in his tracks. Maybe it was because he'd never seen her asleep before that he hadn't noticed how fragile she looked or how really delicate her features were. He'd nicknamed her "Princess" to annoy her, but he'd never thought of her as one. Princesses needed white knights to rescue them and fight their battles. When he was ten he'd never thought of her that way. If he'd had to play with a girl, he'd figured she was okay. She could handle herself.

But right now, nestled on that chair with a curl tumbled across her cheek, she looked vulnerable, someone a white knight would want to protect and cherish. And it wasn't a fire he felt spreading through his blood; it was something much warmer. He found it nearly as intriguing as heat. And probably more dangerous.

Still, he ignored the impulse to walk away and said, "You've got to stop slaving away like this."

The voice had her eyes snapping open but her mind still clung to her dream. In it, Cam's mouth had been on hers. Now reality registered slowly. Blearily, she made out long legs clad in worn denim. She shifted her gaze upward, taking in the narrow waist. The chambray shirt was rolled up revealing muscled forearms. A big man, she thought, broad shouldered. One hand gripped the handles of a canvas bag; the other was long fingered and resting on narrow hips.

But even when she managed to raise her eyes all the way to his face, it took a second for her mind to fully focus. Her heart had already begun to race, her body to weaken before recognition slammed into her.

"Cam?" She blinked again, trying to gather her thoughts.

"Forgotten about me already, Princess?"

"Adair," she corrected automatically. Some of her

strength returned. "I must have fallen asleep." And he'd sneaked into her dream just as he'd sneaked up on her when she was asleep.

Asleep?

She shot a panicked look at her watch, then let out the breath she'd been holding. If she'd drifted off, it hadn't been for long. But her brain still seemed to be operating on a three- or four-second delay. She got to her feet and found herself craning her neck to meet Cam's eyes. She hadn't had to do that in the foyer last night. Not when she'd been face-to-face with him on the floor.

The Sutherlands were all tall, but she could have sworn that Cam had grown even taller since she'd seen him last. And he'd changed. At her father's wedding he'd still been partly a boy. Now she was facing a man, and as she looked into those blue eyes her throat went dry and something was happening to her knees.

No one had ever affected her this way. She had to get a handle on it. She couldn't afford to let some man befuddle her brain again. Pushing past the dryness in her throat, she said, "What are you doing here?" Brilliant. "I didn't hear your car."

"Some bat out of hell ran me off the road."

Her eyes widened. "When?"

"Half an hour or so ago. Red convertible. She looks like Marilyn Monroe and drives like she's in the Indy 500?"

Adair nearly smiled. "That was Bunny Maitland, the MOB, otherwise known as the Mother of the Bride." She ran her eyes over Cam again, stifling the urge to linger. "You look fine. How's your car?"

"Needs a tow." He set down the canvas bag. "But I enjoyed the walk. Is Blondie the MOB in this Saturday's wedding?"

She narrowed her eyes. "How do you know about the wedding?"

"Sheriff Skinner mentioned it when I dropped in to tell him that you and Vi had discovered one of Eleanor's earrings. According to him, the whole village is talking about the rich couple from Long Island who are getting married here. They're hoping they'll spread the news about what a lovely spot you have here and increase the tourist trade."

"That's the plan," she said. "What's yours? Has our security system passed muster?"

"Not yet." Cam had to bite back a smile. This was the Adair he remembered, just a little on the pushy side. "Can you show me where you and Vi found the earring?"

"Over here." When she started to tug on one of the heavy pots overflowing with blooms Cam grabbed the other side to help her shift it.

Pointing to the rocks and stones that still lay strewn at the base of the arch, she said, "This is where we assume Alba found the earring. We heard her digging around on this side, but we didn't actually see where she found the leather pouch. Aunt Vi and I searched through these stones to see if we could find the rest of Eleanor's dowry, but they're essentially where we found them."

Cam swept his gaze over the side of the stone arch. It was about ten feet long and the height stretched to about ten feet. The rocks varied in size and offered enough small ledges and handholds that he and his brothers had scaled the thing countless times. In fact they'd even had team relay races with the girls. He'd always chosen Adair because she hadn't been afraid.

Angus One was supposed to have built it himself but Cam figured he'd had some help lifting the bigger slabs, and he must have possessed a natural talent for engineering. The thing had stood there for over two hundred years.

"Did it take a direct hit from the lightning?" he asked.

"If not, it had to be close. We were in the middle of the wedding rehearsal, and when the storm thundered in, the closest place to take shelter was here. Most of the wedding party was already beneath it. When the lightning struck, the impact was enough to tear the bride out of the groom's arms and into the minister's."

Cam pictured the scene in his mind. "If I were the groom I might take it as a warning and back out."

"He's not the problem," Adair said.

Cam studied her. "He's not?"

She shook her head. "The wedding will solidify some business arrangement that he has with the bride's family. So her parents are on board, too. And the bride is depending on the legend to provide her happy-ever-after. It's all good."

Her words were saying one thing, her eyes another. Adair's eyes had always been so easy to read, and she was worried. She might have more to worry about than she knew. The business merger side of the wedding fit in perfectly with Gianni Scalzo's M.O., and that argued Daryl's instinct might be right.

He shifted his gaze to the stones and spotted a small crevice where the rocks and smaller stones might have fallen out. Dropping to his knees, he slipped his hand inside.

"There's nothing there," Adair said. "I told you Vi and I already checked to see if there was another pouch."

"There are more loose stones." He pulled one out, half the size of his palm, and poked his hand in again. He pulled out an even-larger one.

Adair dropped to her knees and tried to get a look around his shoulder.

"I can't quite finesse this next rock, but I can feel space behind it." He grunted, then said, "Yeah, I think we've got something here."

6

"WHAT? Another pouch?" Adair asked.

"Can't tell. First I need to get past this stubborn rock. If I could just get a good grip…"

"Let me." Moving on her knees, she wiggled closer until she was practically plastered to his side. "My hand's smaller."

She slid it into the opening. When his rough palm slid over her skin, heat streaked to her toes. "Get your hand out, so I can try—"

He turned his head and suddenly they were face-to-face. All she saw were his eyes. They were so dark, the color of the sky near twilight.

"Try what?"

The words had her dropping her gaze to his mouth. That was exactly what she wanted to try. The taste she'd sampled in her dream hadn't been enough. When his hand wrapped around hers, she felt the heat sear through her right down to her toes. His lips were close, only an inch away. All she had to do was eliminate that small distance and all her dreams and fantasies would become real. She would finally feel the pressure of his lips; she could finally taste him. Lord, she could smell him. Soap and water and something that was different. Male. Just breathing in had the intense and achy need inside of her sharpening. And it wasn't going to go away. Unless—

"We should—" she began.

"Yeah."

Later, Cam wasn't sure who moved first. All that mattered was that their lips brushed, met. And clung. Heat exploded at the contact and spread like electricity along a hot wire. Then, each scrape of teeth, each tangle of tongues upped the wattage.

He streaked his free hand up her side and around to cover her breast. Then he pulled his other one out of the crevice so that he could hold her fully against him.

Blood roared in his ears. Desire hammered at him with a sharpness he'd never felt before. He wanted her, wanted to peel those clothes away and explore every curve and angle. He wanted to feel her skin grow hot and moist beneath his hands. He wanted her beneath him again. No woman had ever taken him this far with only a kiss. In another moment…

Cam had no idea what finally gave him the strength to pull back. They were both panting. Nothing else marred the silence other than the distant hum of a hedge trimmer, a soft breeze at the tops of the pines.

"That was…" She broke off as if at a loss for words.

"Yeah." That was the single one he could latch onto.

"Crazy."

"Insane," he agreed. And Lord help him, if he could just kiss her again, he'd take the straitjacket.

"You and me. It would be a mistake."

"Probably." He moved his hand to the back of her neck and fastened his mouth on her throat. Her scent was stronger here—fresh flowers and sunshine. He found it incredibly erotic.

"We can't… We have to… Stop."

That one word had him struggling to latch onto a thin thread of control. He raised his head, but he couldn't take his eyes off hers. And he saw himself completely enclosed in the misty green.

"Just one more taste." She fisted a hand in his hair and drew his mouth back to hers. Heaven, she thought. And hell. His mouth was so skilled and much more potent than she'd ever imagined. With his teeth and tongue he nibbled, then devoured, seduced and then possessed.

Oh, she'd expected the heat, welcomed it as it flooded through her again. But the intensity of it—the way it sizzled and burned, singeing, then melting everything in its path. That was so new. So amazing. She wanted more. She wanted to crawl right into him until she dissolved and the terrible need inside her eased.

When he ran his hands down her sides, she felt his touch in every part of her body. Her breasts ached, her thighs trembled. When he drew back she wanted to cry out from the loss.

"Adair, we have to finish this inside."

"Inside?" The word floated into her consciousness through a thick fog. "Finish this?" Finally, his meaning penetrated. Shock tore through her when her first reaction was to say yes. Still, it took all her focus to say, "No."

He dropped his hands and sat back down on his heels. She had to brace herself against the stone arch or slide bonelessly to the ground.

What had she been thinking?

The answer to that was pretty simple. She hadn't been thinking at all. Except about what it might be like to kiss Cam. And now that she knew…

"We have to think about something else." Fast, Adair

thought. "We were searching for the rest of Eleanor's jewels."

"Right." It shocked Cam that the jewels had slipped entirely from his mind. There'd been no room for anything but Adair. Before this, desire had always been enjoyable, simple. It had never slashed through him until the wanting had been...everything.

Think about something else.

Edging farther back, he dragged his gaze away from her and glanced at the crevice.

"You think the rest of the jewels might be in there somewhere, don't you?" she asked.

"I think it's odd that you only found one earring."

"Okay. So we need to check it out. But this time we take turns. I'll go first and try to loosen the stone you were working on. Once I have it out, you can work on the next one."

Cam had to smile as he edged even farther away and gestured her toward the small hole. "This is only a temporary solution to our problem."

She shot him a look over her shoulder. "I know. But I need to think about it."

"Go ahead." He knew the value of analyzing data. He just wasn't sure how much time either of them had for that.

Adair reached in and slid her fingers around the edge of the rock. Then she began to wiggle it back and forth. "It's coming. Slowly." She had to use both hands to pull it through the opening. Then she moved carefully out of his way. "Your turn."

The instant Cam reached in, his fingers brushed against something with more defined edges than a rock. Dipping one of his shoulders, he leaned closer to the opening so that he could get a better grip. Carefully, he slipped his fingers over the top and finessed his thumb beneath it. Then he tugged.

"You've got something," Adair said.

"A box, I think. But it's snugged in pretty tight." His fingers slid off, but not before he felt it give a little. He tried again, and this time it moved a couple of inches.

"It's coming." The next sixty seconds seemed to go by in slow motion, but inch by inch he tugged and pulled the box closer and closer until he could get a good enough grip to drag it all the way out.

Once he set it on the ground between his knees and hers, Adair could do nothing but gape at it. She was looking at the box she and her sisters had buried seven years ago.

Cam fingered the tiny padlock. "Shall I do the honors?"

"No." Snatching it up, she clutched it to her chest, out of harm's way.

"That lock is pretty flimsy, but if you'd rather, I have a set of lock picks in my room."

"No. You can't open it. Eleanor's jewels aren't in here."

Cam studied her for a moment. "And you know this because?"

Her cheeks burned with embarrassment. "Because my sisters and I buried this box on the night our parents were married. What's in here is very private."

"Really?" Cam looked at the metal box.

Adair frowned at the intrigued look on his face.

"How in the world did you get it in there without coming across the pouch with the earring?" he asked.

"We didn't bury it on this side. We loosened some stones on the inside of the arch."

"And you're not going to let me see what's inside?"

Adair narrowed her eyes. "What don't you understand about the word *private?*"

Cam held his hands up, palms outward. Adair was about to say more when they heard a car on the graveled drive.

Adair shot to her feet. "That's my one o'clock appointment." She looked down at her dirty knees and scowled. She didn't even want to think about what her hair might look like. No time for a shower. But she could at least tidy up.

Amused, Cam watched her bolt into the garden and race for the back door of the castle with a death grip on the mysterious metal box. Not that it was any of his business.

But secrets had always intrigued him.

Whatever they were, they'd caused a very pretty blush to spread up her neck and across her face as she'd warned him off. Discovering people's secrets was one thing he was very good at, and working in the CIA had honed that particular skill. One way or another, he was going to find out what was in that box.

But there was other business he needed to take care of. Taking out his cell, he punched a number he always kept on speed dial.

Daryl's voice mail picked up. That meant that he must be totally engrossed in his investigation. Cam passed on what Adair had told him about the Banes/Maitland wedding being connected to come kind of business merger. And he wished he didn't have a gut-deep feeling that the bride might not be getting her happy-ever-after on Saturday.

TEN MINUTES LATER, Cam found Viola MacPherson exactly where he'd expected to find her—in the kitchen. And she was frosting a delicious looking cake. For a moment as he stood in the doorway, he was transported back in time to his tenth summer. Except for her gray hair, Viola looked the same.

The dog was new. The medium-sized mixed breed was out for the count in a rectangle of sunshine not far from Vi's feet. The security system they had was pretty good, and he trusted that Vi and Adair were religious about securing the castle at night. And the dog provided added protection. But like most people, when they were home during the day they left doors such as the one he currently stood in open.

"I don't suppose I could talk you out of a piece of that cake," he said.

She whirled, set down her knife and beamed a smile at him. "Cam."

The dog raised its head, jingling the bell around its neck, and rose to its feet. Vi signaled the dog to sit as she moved to wrap her arms around Cam. The gesture tightened something around his heart.

"You seem taller since the wedding," she said as she stepped back.

"You're not." He glanced over her head at the cake.

"Don't even think about it. That's the groom's cake for the wedding on Saturday. The whole affair is dicey enough without the cake disappearing. Sit. I'll pour you some iced tea, and I have fresh scones."

Grinning at Vi, he sank into the chair she'd pointed at. "The MOB ran me off the road just before I got to the twin pines."

Vi ran a quick look over him. "You look okay. The car?"

"Not a scratch. I talked to your gardener, and he said he'd tow it out and have the young guy working for him drive it up here."

"Wes is a good man." She poured two glasses of iced

tea, piled scones on a plate, then carried everything to the table and sat down.

"When I spoke with Sheriff Skinner, he suggested I tell your gardener about the discovery of the earring. The news is bound to leak out—it may have already." He told Vi about the stranger who'd visited the library. "On the days he's up here working, Wes can be on the lookout for trespassers."

Vi nodded. "Are you expecting trouble?"

"After two hundred years, part of Eleanor's dowry has shown up. A lot of people are going to assume that the rest of it is around somewhere. I told A.D. and my mom I'd make sure you and Adair would be safe here." Cam took a sip of the tea and reached for a scone. When the dog moved to his side and plopped her head on his knees, Cam broke off a piece and passed it on.

"I can put her out on her leash," Vi said.

"She's fine," Cam said. "How long have you had her?"

"Six months. I went to the animal shelter to find a good watchdog, and the moment I saw Alba I had to bring her home. She's deaf. But even though she may not hear in the same way you and I do, she senses things."

"What made you want a watchdog?" Cam asked.

"A feeling more than anything. I started waking up in the middle of the night. I never really heard anything, but now Alba wakes me up with her barking. I still never hear anything else—even after I settle her down. But I feel safer."

"What about Adair? Has she ever heard anything?"

"No."

"No signs of intruders or a break-in?" Cam asked.

"No. And I've looked. Nothing is missing." Vi tapped the side of her head. "You're going to tell me it's all up here."

"Not at all." He also didn't intend to tell her how easy it might be for a professional to get past their security system. But usually a break-in was a onetime thing. This had been going on for some six months—long before the earring had been discovered.

Cam slipped another bite of scone to the dog and turned to his original purpose for seeking out Vi. "Adair's worried about this wedding on Saturday, and you said earlier it was dicey enough."

By the time he was biting into his third scone, not counting the one he'd shared with Alba, he had Vi's version of the story. "So in a nutshell, what you've got is a bride who wants a guarantee for a happy-ever-after because she didn't get that the first time around. You've got an MOB pressuring you and Adair to make sure everything runs smoothly on Saturday. A business deal hangs in the balance, and the bride-to-be might be still in love with her first husband."

Vi nodded.

"How does Adair feel about all of this?" Cam asked.

Vi sighed. "She's torn. She wants our wedding business to succeed more than anything since that horrible fiasco in Chicago."

Cam frowned. "What fiasco?"

"She was working with a young man who charmed her into believing that the two of them could make an unbeatable team both inside and outside of the office." Vi used her fingers to put "unbeatable team" in quotes. "Then he passed her projects on to upper management as his own. Long story short, he's still working there and she isn't. And he dumped her on the day she got her pink slip."

"Bastard." The anger Cam felt didn't surprise him. What did was the bitter coppery taste in his mouth. Jealousy?

"Adair has always succeeded at everything she's set her

mind to. She believes that if she pulls this wedding off on Saturday, the future of Castle MacPherson as a wedding destination spot will be assured. If not…"

It was Cam's turn to frown. "If not, she'll find another way to accomplish her goal."

Vi smiled at him. "Of course she will. You know that and I know that. But she has to rediscover that about herself."

Cam didn't like the fact that he might play a role in ruining the wedding. If Banes turned out to be Scalzo… For now he decided to put it out of his mind and pursue another question that was lingering there. "Adair was showing me where Alba discovered the earring, and we came across a metal box with a little padlock. She wouldn't let me see the contents."

Vi laughed. "Of course she wouldn't. She and her sisters used to write down their secret dreams and aspirations and put them in that box from the time they were little kids. When they were teens they came up with the idea of burying it behind some loose stones in the arch as a way to make them all come true."

Interesting, Cam thought. But it wasn't a childhood dream that had made Adair blush and become so territorial about the box.

And solving the mystery of what was inside the metal box was not why he was here at the castle either. "Do me a favor, Vi?"

"I have no idea what's in that box."

He smiled. "I want to know where your bedroom is with regard to the rest of the house."

At the question in her eyes, he continued, "I'm wondering if there might be a reason why you and Alba are having your sleep disturbed and Adair isn't."

"I'll do better than tell you," Vi said. "Let me show you."

7

"THANK YOU SO much. My fiancée will have to approve, of course, but I'm enchanted with this place."

Smiling, Adair shook the hand Nathan offered. She liked him. He wasn't a handsome man, but he had intelligent eyes and a blustery, enthusiastic energy that she found engaging. She guessed he was in his mid-forties. His waistline had begun to spread a bit and gray had begun to dull both his mustache and beard as well as his nearly shoulder-length red hair. This was his first marriage and he wanted to do it up right.

"I'll look forward to hearing from you," she said.

He patted the professional-looking camera that hung at his side. "You will. These pictures are going to sell the place to my sweetheart."

Adair certainly hoped so. The man had taken enough of them. She watched him walk to his car, and when he reached it and turned back to her she gave him a final wave.

She'd shown him the gardens, the ballroom, and at his request she'd even taken him into the parlor to view Eleanor Campbell MacPherson's portrait. Nathan had mentioned he remembered reading about Eleanor's missing jewels in the *Times* a while back.

Even though they were not offering the use of the main parlor in any of the wedding packages, Adair supposed she might as well put it on the regular tour from now on. If the word got out that one of Eleanor's earrings had shown up, she figured more than one potential client was going to ask to see the portrait.

She thought the appointment had gone well, considering that more than once she'd felt her mind wandering. Back to that metal box and the fantasies she and her sisters had buried in it all those years ago.

And back to Cam Sutherland and that kiss they'd exchanged.

As the last little whirlwind of dust settled from Nathan MacDonald's parting car, Adair turned and walked back to her office. She was going to have to figure out what to do about Cam. And herself.

Closing the door behind her, she strode to her desk, sank into her chair and stared at the small metal box. She was responsible for this. It had been her idea to write out the fantasies and bury them in the stones. And she wasn't going to blame the champagne. Earlier that day when she'd met Cam's eyes beneath the stone arch, her heart had raced, her breath had stopped and her whole world had tilted.

So for the first time in her life, she'd done something rash. And now it was coming back to haunt her.

Big time.

She could be the poster girl for the "Be careful what you wish for" warning. What was worse is that she wanted that wish to come true.

She pressed her fingers against her lips and found them warm. Now that she'd seen him again, lain beneath him and kissed him until her brains had practically leaked out of her ears, she didn't want the fantasy anymore. She wanted the reality.

The problem was she did not have time to indulge in the reality of having an erotic adventure with Cam Sutherland right now. There were so many things she had to check on to ensure the success of Rexie Maitland's wedding. Pulling a pad of paper closer, she began to jot down notes. Aunt Vi was handling the cakes and overseeing the catering service. The firm she'd hired would arrive early Saturday morning to set up the tables in the ballroom. Cocktails and champagne would be served on the terrace overlooking the lake.

When Adair realized that her eyes had shifted to the box, she focused on her list again and wrote at the top: (1) Check in with the florist. (2) Call Rexie.

Tonight maybe. She'd sleep better if she knew that the young bride-to-be's nerves had definitely settled.

(3) Call first husband Dr. Barry Carlson.

Adair dropped her pen and stared at what she'd written. Call Barry Carlson? Why was she even thinking of doing that? Hadn't she decided Rexie's first marriage wasn't any of her business? Then she thought of her conversation with Rexie that morning and the look in the young woman's eyes when she'd said, "He refused to talk to me." Hurt that Rexie hadn't recovered from yet.

Dammit. She fisted her hands on her desk. It wouldn't hurt to look up the phone number. Rexie had mentioned that Barry's parents had horses. Lifting her notebook computer out of the top drawer, she booted it up and searched for the Carlson Horse Ranch in Montana. A few clicks got her to the web page.

And there he was—Dr. Barry Carlson. To her surprise, he looked vaguely familiar. She thought of those moments

where she'd been sitting in front of the arch, using her visualization technique to picture Rexie kissing Lawrence
Banes. But the man her imagination had summoned up
had looked a lot more like Barry than Banes.

No, that couldn't be. She'd never met Barry Carlson.
Her mind was just playing tricks on her. When she caught
herself jotting down the phone number of the horse farm,
she dropped the pencil and stared at her hands. They were
playing tricks on her, too.

And it was all because she was trying so hard not to
think of that box and Cam Sutherland. So much for avoidance.

Thoroughly annoyed, she pulled it toward her. Cam
had been right about the lock not providing a challenge.
Over the years the flimsy thing had rusted enough that
she was able to pull it away with one jerk.

Taking a deep breath, she opened the lid. And there
they were—the three compartments with folded sheets of
different-colored paper in each one. It had been Nell's idea
that they use different-colored paper for privacy. She'd
chosen yellow. That night she'd written on a legal pad and
the sheets lay there right on the top of her section.

Unable to resist, she took her fantasy out and shoved
aside her day planner and To Do list. Then she unfolded
the pages and spread them over the surface of her desk.
There was always the chance that she'd find her adolescent fantasy amusing or even laughable. Perhaps just reading it would put it in perspective and she could get her
focus back.

But her lips didn't so much as curve as she read the
words she'd written so long ago. She barely recognized
her own handwriting. She'd written at such a rate of speed,
wanting to keep up with the images that had flooded her

mind. They were as compelling now as they'd been seven years ago. And they were even more erotic.

Being swept away by a stranger had been a fantasy of women for years. And she'd learned in a female studies class she'd taken freshman year that the fantasy was grounded in what had been the reality of many women's lives for thousands of years.

But the fact that it had been *her* fantasy that long-ago night—the fact that it was that particular fantasy that had gripped her imagination and flowed out of her pen had shocked her then.

It shocked her right now.

The pages she'd written that night were all about being transported by a man and by the danger of the adventure. As she skimmed the words, she could see that she'd incorporated elements of *Romancing the Stone* and *Indiana Jones,* and even the first Jason Bourne movie.

The most exciting thing she could think of that night was being swept up in a life-threatening adventure with a man. The sex had to be hotter when it was layered with fear and the adrenaline of the chase. It had always seemed to be that way in the movies.

And it wasn't just the lure of danger and excitement that had captured her imagination, it had been the man she'd imagined doing everything with her.

Cam Sutherland.

He was the man she'd imagined lying beneath. He was the man who'd kissed her, touched her and thrust into her.

And now that she wasn't operating on imagination, now that she'd had a taste of reality and experienced the promise of what might lie beyond the kisses they'd exchanged…

Her blood heated, raced, and something deep inside of her tightened.

She pressed a hand against her heart to keep it from

pounding right out of her chest. How could she possibly reconcile her response to him with the woman she was and had always told herself she wanted to be?

Women who ran off with sexy strangers, chased bad guys in cars, dodged bullets and plunged into mountain streams were...just...not her.

She was organized, goal oriented. She made lists and liked to follow them. She made five-year plans for heaven's sake. So what if her first one had crashed and burned? That only meant she had to concentrate fully on the next one. There was zero room in her life for unplanned and unwanted adventures. Lightning strikes and missing jewels were not on her agenda. And neither was hot-as-you-can-imagine sex with Cam Sutherland.

And if all that were true, why was she losing her mind every time he touched her?

She dropped her head in her hands. Before she did something really stupid, she had to think about this. She had to get some kind of a handle on it and come up with a plan.

Gathering the papers on the desk, she put them back into her compartment and closed the lid. She had to think this through, and her favorite thinking place had always been at Tinker's Falls. After replacing the lock, she tucked the box into her bottom drawer. Then she hurried out through the French doors and headed into the woods.

CAM SLIPPED TO the side of the French doors just as he saw Adair start toward them. When he'd arrived on the terrace she'd had her head dropped in her hands. The posture was so unlike her that he'd stopped short to study her. Once again her vulnerability tugged at him. Had her meeting not gone well? He'd glanced around the room, then arrowed back to the flimsily locked metal box. Was that what was upsetting her?

For a moment all he'd wanted was to go to her, to draw her to her feet and just hold her. But before he could give in to the impulse she lifted her head and gathered up the papers on her desk, put them back in the box and tucked everything away in a drawer.

When she had risen from the desk he'd stepped to the side of the open doors, and now he watched her cross the terrace and head to the path that led to the woods. The energy in her movement, the intent way she'd left the office, reminded him more of the Adair he thought he knew than the woman he'd glimpsed with her head in her hands.

He waited only until she disappeared before he stepped into her office. The space was roomy and might have once served as a second parlor. There were bookcases flanking a stone fireplace, double doors on another wall that opened into the entrance foyer, and to the left, French doors that led into the main parlor.

He had a theory now about why Vi and Alba were having their sleep disturbed and Adair wasn't, and it also might explain why neither of the women had noticed anything missing from the castle. Vi's room was situated over the castle's library, a two-floored room that hadn't been used in years. It still housed a dust-covered but extensive collection, some of it dating back to Angus One. According to Vi, the last person who'd used it for any length of time was his mother. That room was where she'd spent most of that summer when he and his brothers were ten.

If the castle did have an intruder and he or she had confined themselves to the library, that might explain why Adair's sleep had never been disturbed. But that theory opened up a lot of questions. Such as, why would someone want secret access to the library? Why not do what his mother had done and simply ask permission?

Or maybe he was totally off the track. But he'd wanted to talk to Adair about it. More, he'd wanted simply to see her. For a moment he found himself torn. There was a part of him that wanted to follow her and another part that was curious about the contents of the mysterious box.

And he might not get another opportunity like this one. Glancing over his shoulder, he checked to make sure that she was out of sight. Then he crossed to her desk. It was typical Adair, with its day planner and To Do list. He skimmed the first two items, then studied the third. *Call first husband—Dr. Barry Carlson.*

So she really was torn about the wedding. Perhaps her gut instinct was giving her a message similar to Daryl's. Something wasn't right about Lawrence Banes.

He opened the bottom drawer and lifted out the box. She hadn't bothered to latch the tiny lock, so he removed it and opened the lid.

It was divided into three compartments. One was stuffed with folded pieces of colored paper: the one on the left with yellow, the center one with blue and the final one with pink. Organized. He recalled what Vi had said about the three girls writing down their hopes, their goals and their dreams on colored papers and burying them in the stones.

That scenario didn't fully explain the acuteness of Adair's embarrassment. Cam removed the folded colored papers on the top of each section and spread them out on the desk. The date in the top right-hand corner told him that each had been written on the night that his mother had married A. D. MacPherson seven years ago. Each was a different length, each was in a different handwriting, but they had one thing in common. The title at the beginning of each one read: "My Fling With My Fantasy Man."

Totally captivated, Cam sat down in the chair and picked up the first one.

Half an hour later his view of the MacPherson girls had undergone a transformation. They might have been young when they'd penned the fantasies, but they'd had active and inventive imaginations. Though they'd definitely been written from a woman's viewpoint, he'd been caught up in each of the fantasies. Enough that he could use a cold shower.

He'd immediately recognized Adair's as the first one he'd read. It had been on yellow paper. Not that he hadn't confirmed his judgment by checking the handwriting against her To Do list. That neat block lettering was a dead giveaway. And of course he'd had to read the other two. A good agent had to be thorough and look at all the data.

They'd each been incredibly arousing. Sex on demand, any time you want it, any way you want it, no strings, no holds barred. He could relate to that fantasy, all right. And the other one was interesting, too—a string of scenarios in which the woman was the seductress and always the initiator. Every man's secret dream.

They just weren't Adair's. Hers was the longest and it was all about erotic sex on the run with that added spice of adventure and that hit of adrenaline. Even when they were kids she'd had that desire for adventure. It was why he'd been drawn to her and why he'd wanted to partner with her instead of her sisters. Because she could take a dare and she could issue one.

He glanced down at the block letters on the yellow pages. She'd certainly issued one now. He wanted to make the fantasy real for her, for them both. They were adults now—why not enjoy the fantasy and each other before they had to go their separate ways?

Right. Rising, he paced to the French doors, then walked back to the desk. You didn't work six years for the CIA and not learn that things were seldom that simple.

He glared at the box. Curiosity was a very dangerous thing. It had killed the cat and it had caused Pandora to inflict chaos on the world. Now he had a feeling that it was going to play havoc with the life he'd built for himself. One that he'd been totally satisfied with until he'd seen Adair again.

He folded the papers, put them back in the proper compartments and replaced the box in the drawer. Then he strode out of the office, across the terrace, and followed the path Adair had taken into the woods.

ADAIR STRIPPED OUT of her T-shirt, then slipped her sandals off and wiggled out of her shorts. Beneath, she wore a white string bikini that she'd put on that morning just in case she had a chance to get a swim in before lunch. Then she folded her clothes and placed them on a flat rock at the edge of the water. The pond that lay at the base of Tinker's Falls was one of her favorite places on the castle property. The falls themselves were part of a stream that wound its way down the mountain. Twenty-five feet above, the water narrowed, then dropped in a clear curtain to the pond below. Behind the curtain there was a secret cave.

For as long as she could remember she and her sisters had used the place as their own private swimming pool. Flat ledges of rock flanked the top of the falls on either side and made perfect spots for sunbathing. Or diving. She walked to the edge of the pond.

It was about thirty feet long and twenty-five wide. And it wasn't really a pond. In sixth grade science she'd learned that it was a deep plunge pool left behind when the glaciers had melted. There was plenty of room for the lap swimming she'd done at college.

Anticipating the shock, she dived into the water, then

surfaced with a thrilling shiver and set out for the other end. A vigorous workout usually helped her think clearly, and Lord knew she could use a little clarity.

What in the world was she going to do about Cam Sutherland? Reaching the other end of the pond, she tucked, curled and then pushed off with her feet. So much was riding on establishing the reputation of Castle MacPherson this summer. She might have come up with the business plan on the fly, so to speak. In fact, she might never have thought of the potential business opportunity at the castle if she hadn't been fired. But lightning strikes and possible runaway brides aside, she was beginning to enjoy the wedding business. It was exciting and satisfying to help young couples plan the most important day of their lives. She even liked the constant challenges. Not that she wanted any more lightning strikes.

She just didn't have time for a complication like Cam. She surely didn't have time for some adolescent action/ adventure fantasy. Did she?

She let the question hang there for three more laps before she ruthlessly shifted her attention to another equally pressing problem. Barry Carlson, Rexie's first husband. There was a good chance that Rexie was still in love with him. Was Barry still in love with her? She let herself consider that for five more laps. Calling Montana to find out what Barry's feelings were was about as smart as kicking a hornet's nest.

And just about as risky as thinking seriously about giving in to her attraction for Cam Sutherland. How in the world had she become a woman who was so attracted to living on the edge?

But wasn't that one of the reasons she was so drawn to Cam? He was dangerous for her in a way that Baxter DuBois had never been. Bax had represented what she'd convinced herself she wanted in a man. Someone who had the same goals and wanted the same lifestyle. She'd felt comfortable with him. Maybe that's why she'd let him talk her into the team partnership idea. And look how well that had turned out.

She'd never felt comfortable with Cam. He'd always stirred her, aroused her, challenged her. And those feelings had grown even more potent over time. What else could he make her feel? She wanted to know how much more there was.

This time when she tucked, curled and turned, she struck out for the left side of the falls where she'd left her clothes. Reaching it, she pulled herself out of the water and climbed up to the ledge of rock that bordered one side of the falls.

The sun was hot overhead, the wide, flat rock warm beneath her feet. Inviting. A quick glance at her watch told her that she could afford to stay long enough to dry her swimsuit. That would be practical.

And it struck her suddenly that there had to be a practical way to solve the situation with Cam. They both wanted the same thing. A fling. Why couldn't she just look at it like a wedding plan, a short-term event that fulfilled both party's dreams? And then life would go on.

As she stretched out on her back, using one arm to shield her eyes, she started working out the approach she would take with Cam. But it was kicking hornets' nests that she was thinking of when she fell asleep.

CAM STOPPED AT the edge of the trees to watch her climb out of the pond. She looked like some kind of nymph with her hair slicked back, the water sliding off of her body. She wore nothing except two scraps of white that had his mouth going dry as dust. And her legs—he'd gotten some hint of them before, but with nothing marring their length they were making him sweat.

She was strong, he noted as he watched her climb to the top of the ledge. When she rose to her feet and stretched her arms upward, it wasn't a nymph he thought of—but a goddess. Her guts he'd never doubted. But the fearlessness he saw now and the vulnerability he'd glimpsed earlier were new. And they fascinated him.

He'd done his best to avoid thinking about her for years. Now he couldn't stop. And he wanted to know more. Still he didn't move toward her.

Everything should be simple. She wanted him and he wanted her. More than that, he was beginning to learn the way her mind worked. He thought he knew the approach to take. A practical one.

So why wasn't he moving? No woman had ever made him hesitate before.

Dammit. He strode forward into the clearing and circled the pond, approaching the ledge from the back side. When he made it to the top he stopped again, surprised to see that she appeared to be sleeping and hadn't heard his approach.

He glanced around. There was no one upstream. The trees pressed in on all sides of the falls, offering at least the illusion of privacy. His approach as well as any noise he'd made climbing up the rocks had been totally masked by the crash of the falls below.

He shifted his gaze back to Adair and stopped thinking of anyone or anything else. It had only been a matter of a few hours since he'd kissed her. The desire to do so again had only grown as he'd imagined her in each of the girlish fantasies he'd read. That was a hell of a lot of foreplay for a man.

And what she was wearing—or more specifically, not

wearing—nearly had his tongue hanging out. Her skin was the almost-translucent color of fine porcelain and nearly all of it was showing.

He dropped to his knees, not fully recognizing that's what he'd done. Then he simply couldn't stop himself from touching her. Reaching out, he traced one finger over her cheek, then down her neck, and he felt the shock of the contact shoot through him with the intensity of a flame. All thought of his simple straightforward strategy slipped from his mind as he continued to run his hand lightly over her skin.

ADAIR DREAMED SHE was floating in a bubble of warm, sleepy pleasure. Something, the sun perhaps, was caressing her skin, stroking gently over her cheek and down her throat to trace a delicate path along the curve of her breast. She sighed even as she shifted, arching slightly into the caress. She could picture the languid fingers of sunlight stroking over her, arousing and seducing so delicately as they moved, as soft as an artist's brush, over her rib cage to her waist and then down her thighs and back up. Slowly, achingly, the pleasure built layer upon layer upon layer as the pattern was repeated.

Warmth gradually edged into heat—little flicks of fire that raced outward along her nerve endings and seeped deeper and deeper into her center. She was melting now, and she wanted to. It was no longer the sun she imagined stroking her but a lover's hands.

And the caresses were growing more demanding. When the fingers brushed again along the curve of her breasts they seared her skin. Her heart raced and she commanded her eyes to open. Blinded by sunlight, she couldn't bring anything completely into focus. But as she reached to ease the burning sensation, her hand collided with, then gripped, a solid masculine one.

Reacting purely on instinct, she sat straight up, fisted her other hand and aimed an uppercut to his chin. The figure grunted, then landed on his behind just as she recognized her opponent. "Cam?"

"Hey!" He rubbed his jaw with one hand and extended the other, palm outward, to forestall another blow. "You seem to be determined to hurt me. First a stone pitcher and now an uppercut."

"Sorry." Maybe it was the mix of shock and admiration on his face or his rueful tone, but she had to struggle to turn a laugh into a hiccup. "Really, I'm sorry." She covered her mouth with both hands as the laugh broke free. "So sorry."

"I'm glad I'm such a source of amusement."

The dry tone had her stifling another giggle. "You might stop sneaking around."

"Where's the fun in that?" But he smiled.

Then after a beat of silence, he said, "I'd apologize for touching you while you were asleep, but it would be a lie."

The words made her vividly recall exactly what he'd been doing before she'd decked him, and she remembered what she'd decided before she'd drifted off. Straightening her shoulders, she clasped her hands together in her lap. "I don't want an apology. I've been thinking, and I believe I have a solution for what's going on between us."

"I'm all ears." He had a solution, too, and he'd been about to demonstrate it just before she'd decked him. "But make it fast. I can't guarantee how long I can keep my hands off of you."

"It's simple really," she said, her voice a little breathless. "We're both very busy right now. What we need is a plan."

"A plan?"

"Yes. When couples come to the castle to plan their weddings, the first thing we do is sketch out the parameters before we negotiate the details. But in our case I think we both want the same thing—a short-term, mutually satisfying physical relationship with no strings and no complications. After all, in a few days you'll be going back to Washington and I'll be working on the next wedding here at the castle. So while we have this time together I'm suggesting we have what my friends in Chicago always called 'buddy sex.' "

"Buddy sex?" All Cam could do was stare at her. She might just as well have punched him again. What she was suggesting didn't fit with her fantasy at all. Was it the arrangement she'd had with the boyfriend back in Chicago? The thought made him furious and brought that coppery taste back to his mouth.

"Surely you've heard of it." Her tone was pleasant, earnest. "No expectations. No worries about tomorrow. Just hot and very satisfying, on-demand sex between two people who want each other but don't have time for all the problems of a relationship. It's perfect for us."

For the first time he noted that her hands were clasped tight, her knuckles white. Nerves.

The fact that she was feeling them was enough to ease his temper as he met her eyes again. "You've had some experience with buddy sex, I take it?"

She lifted her chin. "And you haven't?"

"You're right. I have." He'd not only had those kinds of relationships in the past. He'd made them his specialty. But buddy sex hadn't been the fantasy she'd written on those yellow pages seven years ago. He was more certain of that than ever. Reaching out, he covered her clasped hands with his. "Tell me what you really want, Adair."

"I want to get everything straight going in so that neither of us has unrealistic expectations. No hurt feelings. Do we have a deal?"

The bastard in Chicago had hurt her. That meant she deserved an honest answer. "The problem is there are no guarantees. Certainly not in my line of work. And I'd bet that in spite of the fact that you like to cross all your t's and dot your i's, weddings are pretty unpredictable, too."

"Yes, but surely we can—"

"Try." He smiled as he pulled her to her feet. "Let's try this." He gripped her hips, lifted her, then strode to the edge of the ledge and jumped.

They hit the water. The cold hard shock of it, the thrill of it, sang through her system as they plunged deep and then deeper. She had no choice but to hold fast and go along for the ride. She didn't want any other choice. By the time their momentum slowed and they kicked upward, her heart was racing, her lungs burning.

When they broke through the surface of the pond they were eye-to-eye. His were so dark and glittered so fiercely that choice was snatched away again. All she could do was sink into them just as she had into the water.

"Breathe," he said. But he barely gave her time before his mouth crushed hers and they went under again.

With one arm, he kept her pressed against him and with the other he touched her—sliding his hand from the nape of her neck down her back to her hip. But his touch was no longer gentle the way it had been when she'd been half dreaming. It was hard and possessive—the way she'd always fantasized it would be. In spite of the icy water surrounding them, heat coursed through her system. She wanted nothing more than to melt into him. Nothing.

They were going to drown. The thought flickered like a guttering candle in some part of his brain, but Cam couldn't find the strength to heed the warning. The completeness of her surrender had him falling hard and fast into a world where there was nothing but the two of them and this terrible need she'd triggered in him.

His foot hit the bottom before he got enough of a grip on reality to kick them both back to the surface. This time when they broke the water, they were gasping and coughing. Latching onto a glimmer of sanity, he kicked to the side of the pond and pinned her against the rocks.

"Look at me," he said.

When she did, he skimmed a hand possessively over her hip and slid two fingers into her. He watched those misty green eyes darken and glaze as she embraced him and gasped his name.

"I've imagined doing this to you," he murmured as he began to move his fingers, coaxing her into a rhythm. "There's more I've imagined." So much more. He was going to show her.

She was moving faster now. He knew he could take her right here against the side of the pond. Fast and hard. The speed might ease some of the terrible pressure building inside of him. But there was so much more he wanted to give her. More he wanted to take.

Then her mouth nibbled at his neck, her teeth scraping his skin in fast, greedy bites, and he felt his control start to slip. He wanted everything. The hitch of her breath, that husky, hungry sound she made each time he stroked his fingers in and then out, in and then out. And the heat—her body seemed to be on fire, and he wanted nothing more than to be consumed by the flames. Then she clenched his fingers, her hungry mouth fastened on his, and they slipped beneath the water again.

The climax streaked into her, blasting a path from where his fingers pressed through every pore in her body.

Reeling from it, she kept her mouth fused to his and demanded more. He gave her more and more as they sank into a dark primitive world and unspeakable pleasure peaked again.

"Breathe," Cam ordered when they reached the surface.

Her lungs burned when she did.

"Got to get you out of here."

Water was streaming down her face, but he filled her vision, the dark hair slicked to his head, the fierce eyes.

"More," she said.

He groaned and shifted his face away when she tried to capture his mouth. "We could die."

"The...cave," she managed between nips at his bottom lip. "Behind...falls."

Cam remembered then. He should have before. And thank God she had. But getting there was going to be a challenge. Holding her close, he struck out for it, using his feet to propel them toward the waterfall. But those long, silky limbs were tangled around him, trapping him. Her mouth was so close, the waterfall so far.

Talk, he told himself. And then he thought of her fantasy and whispered in her ear. "I'm a pirate. For weeks, I've watched you from my ship. Every day you come down to the rocks to bathe and then rest in the sun. I've watched you, fantasized about you, wanted you."

"Yes," she breathed in his ear.

"You've felt my eyes on you."

"Yes." She nipped his earlobe, and Cam nearly lost his focus again. "I've wanted you for so long. Kiss me again."

Not yet. He didn't dare. Carefully, he negotiated the waterfall and they reached the shallower water that bordered the cave. "Today I couldn't resist you any longer, so I swam ashore to make love to you. To make you mine."

Finally, his foot hit a rock ledge and he found enough

balance to shift both of them onto the floor of the cave. She lay beneath him now just as she had in the foyer the night before. He could see her eyes, the dark gleam of them and nothing else as he lowered his mouth to hers.

Now he could explore all those flavors that he'd only sampled before. But as he tasted her, as the flavors poured into him, he felt as if he were drowning again.

And he couldn't seem to get enough. Each time he changed the angle of the kiss, he discovered something new. Beneath the incredible layers of sweetness, there was the darker flavor of desperation. The richness of her tastes, the depth of them, ignited a fire in his blood that started in his gut and radiated to the tips of his fingers. Fingers that trembled as they drew away the wet material that still clung to her breasts.

Her body arched up, offering more, and he had no choice but to take. He told himself to go slowly, to savor when what he craved was to devour and possess. Her skin was slick and so hot that it burned his lips as he moved them down the slim column of her throat. Using teeth and tongue, he lingered at her breasts, teasing, tormenting, taking. He felt her heart beat against his lips and his own nearly stopped.

Each time she shuddered, each time her nails dug into his shoulders, a fresh thrill threatened to shatter his system. Wherever he touched or tasted, her response was so generous, so beyond his experience, he could never have imagined it. Ever.

"Cam."

He could barely hear his name above the rush of the waterfall and the pounding of his blood, but he knew she thought only of him. The power of that nearly pushed him beyond reason. But each time he thought he had to end it, he found more to tantalize him. Lured by the slim line of her torso, entranced by the dip at her stomach, he journeyed lower.

When he found himself blocked by the strings of her bikini, he ripped it away.

"Cam."

Adair had no idea whether she said the word aloud or whether she'd only managed to shout it in her mind again and again. It echoed through her, streaming through her veins, filling her. The story of the pirate and of the woman who'd waited replayed in her mind. Their longings, their needs, couldn't possibly be as great as hers. She'd waited so long for Cam. For this.

Too long.

No one had ever made her feel this way. The need he'd triggered was primal and raw. It terrified her. Electrified her. And just when she thought he couldn't possibly take her further, he did. Each press of his fingers, each scrape of his teeth showed her how much more there was. And when he used them on the skin of her inner thigh, she cried his name again and arched her hips upward. And he pressed his mouth to her core.

The orgasm tore through her, erupting again and again in aftershocks that only left her craving more. There was only Cam, the taste, the smell, the sight of him. When he rose above her again, she fisted her hands in his wet shirt and ripped it apart. Buttons flew.

"Again," she demanded. Then, as desperate as he to taste, to touch, to devour, she rolled with him across the floor of the cave. Legs and arms tangling, they struggled to pull down his wet jeans and strip off his shirt.

"Hurry," she demanded.

"Trying to."

But when she would have dragged him back on top of her, he sat back on his knees and shifted her so that she was straddling them. Then he dug his fingers into her hips to hold them still. They were eye-to-eye, nearly mouth-to-mouth. "Protection," he managed to say.

He dug his fingers into the pocket of his jeans and they fumbled with the condom together.

"Hurry," she said again.

He watched her eyes and nothing else as he lifted her hips and plunged inside of her. She was all he knew, all he wanted. And in that moment, she was everything. They moved together then. And when she climaxed, clamping those long legs around him and crying out his name, power and triumph, heady and sweet, streaked to his core.

Then he built the pleasure again, for both of them. Her nails raked his back as he fought against the mists that threatened to blur his vision. He wanted to see her. Had to see her as they both rode a new and towering wave of sensations. Her face beaded with water, her eyes, witch-green, were fastened on his. They trapped him as surely as the lust. He felt something inside of him that wanted to break out, something strong. He tried to hold it back but her name broke free from his lips as he took her with him over the edge.

9

AFTERWARD THEY CLUNG like wet rag dolls against the wall of the cave. They didn't speak. Adair wondered if her vocal cords might have been cauterized by the heat they'd created. She'd known that Cam would be different for her, but nothing in her experience, nothing in her imagination had come close. No one had ever done the things he'd done to her. And she'd never even dreamed of the things she'd done to him. They'd gone so far beyond her fantasies.

And they were real. She'd never felt like this, so weak, so feminine. So totally satisfied.

She sat snuggled on his lap, her arms and legs wrapped around him, her cheek pressed cozily against his. She would have been content to stay just as they were for a very long time.

But that would be dangerous. She'd outlined their relationship quite clearly, and he'd been ready enough to agree there were no guarantees. The important thing would be to stick to the plan she'd outlined and enjoy what they could have together as long as it lasted.

When Cam turned his head and met her eyes, something fluttered right under her heart.

"You know, I have to be honest with you," he said. "I don't think we did that right."

She stared at him. "We didn't?"

"You said you wanted buddy sex—convenient, no harm, no foul. And you nearly killed me."

The mocking note of accusation in his voice caused a laugh to bubble up and break free. "It was your idea to jump off the ledge. You're the one who nearly killed us both."

"Well, maybe we just need more practice. I'm sure we'll get better at it." He was about to prove his point by actions when he heard his cell phone beep. He managed to keep hold of her as he finessed it out of his jeans.

"How did your cell phone survive?" Adair asked.

"Special CIA issue. Waterproof," he said as he glanced at the text Daryl had sent.

Fingerprints of the man who ran a Scalzo-like scam in Oregan match Lawrence Banes's. I'll be joining you soon.

"Important?" Adair asked.

"A friend of mine is close to tracking down an old enemy." What was good news for Daryl was definitely going to be bad news for Adair's wedding on Saturday. But he couldn't even warn her until Daryl was sure. That worry faded from his mind when he glanced up and noticed movement on the other side of the falling water. Lowering his head, he spoke close to her ear. "Don't move. We may have company."

Easing Adair onto a ledge of rock, he pulled up his jeans and found his shirt. Someone standing on the shore of the pond couldn't see into the cave because of the thick fall of water and the darkness. But he and Adair could get at least a blurred image of anyone who came into the clearing.

Two people had. Cam crawled to the far side of the falls where there was a narrow gap between the crashing water and the side of the cave. Pressing his face against the rock, he peered out.

Because of the spray he still couldn't get a clear image. Two men stood at the far end of the pond. One had his back to the falls and stood with one foot propped on a rock, his forearm resting on his thigh. He wore slacks and a white shirt, and he was tall and broad-shouldered enough to partially block the other man's face. That one held a camera with a telephoto lens. He, too, wore city clothes—slacks and a golf shirt. He was shorter and on the chunky side, with longer hair and a mustache and beard.

And they were not happy.

Though it was impossible to overhear their conversation, they were clearly arguing. The man with the camera used his hands in staccato gestures. The other one shook his head vehemently.

"Let me see." Adair pitched her voice low as she wiggled in front of him.

He eased back so that she could try to see through the narrow gap between water and rock. "Recognize either one of them?"

"Maybe," she murmured. "The mist blurs everything, but the man I had an appointment with just before I came out here, Nathan MacDonald—he had a camera. The hair and the build are right. I gave him a tour. He was particularly interested in Eleanor's portrait. He'd said that he'd seen the photo in the *Times* article and he'd love to see the real thing."

"You showed it to him," Cam said.

"Sure. It's not in the regular tour I give, but many people ask to see it."

"How about the other man?"

Even as Cam asked the question, the two men started up the path into the woods. For as long as she could she studied the back of the taller one who brought up the rear. Something seemed familiar, but she couldn't place it.

"No. I don't know."

Cam turned her around so that they were kneeling on the floor of the cave facing each other. "This Nathan Mac-Donald could have decided to come back and take his own private tour of the rest of the estate. But that doesn't explain the other man."

"He mentioned bringing his fiancée back. But I didn't get the idea it would be today. And he didn't mention that his fiancé was a man."

"But their visit could still be legit. He might want to get the fiancé's reaction before filling you in on all the details."

"Yes. And what we saw was just a little lovers' spat?"

"Maybe." The presence of the two men could be perfectly legitimate. But he had the same feeling he'd had earlier when he'd been driving back from Glen Loch, that sense that he should get back to the castle.

"Okay," Adair said, "we've established a semiplausible reason for Nathan MacDonald and his companion to be here with a camera and being a little secretive about checking out the estate. But you're still worried."

"Because we can't be sure how many people know about the earring yet. Vi mentioned to your dad that Alba barked at someone or something in the hills behind the stone arch right after you and she opened the leather pouch."

He filled her in on the stranger at the library who'd been

so interested in Eleanor's missing dowry. "And I think that someone may have been breaking into the castle at night for the past six months or so—ever since your Aunt Vi started waking up in the middle of the night."

Adair frowned at him. "But how? We activate the security system every night. And nothing is missing. We would have noticed."

"I've been thinking about that. There are times during the day when you deactivate it because you and Vi are home. You're seeing clients. She's in the kitchen and wants to enjoy the breeze from the lake. Depending on their motivation someone could sneak in late in the day. Or if they have the skill they could bypass the system just as I did. And maybe whoever it is just needs access to the castle for a specific reason. Your aunt's rooms are over the library. She and the dog are waking up and you're not."

"You think someone's looking for something in the library?"

"My mom spent a whole summer there doing research. And the *Times* article renewed interest in Eleanor's sapphires. I went to the library in Glen Loch first thing this morning to look them up and to check out what's available to the public. If I were looking for some jewels that could be traced back to Mary Stuart, I'd gather data. And the castle's private library would be at the top of my list to find more. But I'm just theorizing, posing possible explanations."

Like the one he'd just posed for the two arguing men, which seemed less and less plausible by the minute. "At any rate, I'd like you and your aunt Vi to look at the library. Let me know what you see. Let's get dressed."

"Easy for you to say," she muttered. "My clothes are out there where I dropped them, and you destroyed my bikini. Not that I didn't enjoy that part. But there's always a price to pay."

"I could promise to make it up to you later."

She grinned at him. "I'll hold you to that."

Vi WAS WAITING for them in Adair's office when they got back. Alba lay at her feet. "Someone broke in here while you were out," she said.

Cam mentally cursed himself as he glanced around the room. He'd noticed the obvious flaws in the security and hadn't acted quickly enough to prevent this. And he'd been so focused on going after Adair that he couldn't recall whether or not he'd even closed the terrace doors.

Adair crossed to her aunt. "Are you all right?"

"I'm fine." She glanced at the two of them. "What happened to the two of you?"

"We took an unexpected tumble into the pond," Cam said. "Did you see who broke in?"

Vi shook her head. "I was putting the last touches on the groom's cake when Alba started to bark and then she ran out of the kitchen. By the time I caught up with her she was scratching on the door to Adair's office. The doors to the terrace were open, and the second I let her in she bolted out through them and just barked for a while. I heard a car start up, but even the dust had settled by the time I circled around to the front."

The driveway had been empty when they'd stepped out of the woods. There'd been no sign of Nathan MacDonald or the man he'd been arguing with.

Vi gestured to the patch of sunlight Alba had stretched out in. "Now I can't get her to leave this room."

"Take a look around, Adair," Cam said as he secured the terrace doors. He'd already taken a quick scan of the room. The metal box was now on her desk and the contents had been overturned. Colored papers littered the floor. As she crossed to her desk, he said, "Is anything else out of place that you can see?"

She turned then and looked around the room, the first time quickly and the second time more slowly. He did the same but he didn't notice anything else that looked disturbed.

"Everything looks fine." Adair gathered up the papers that were scattered across her desk and on the floor and put them into one of the drawers. It didn't look as if any of them had been unfolded. Then, because her knees felt weak, she sank into the chair behind her desk.

"Someone was in here," she said. "And it's not too big a leap to think they were looking for that earring."

She shifted her gaze to Cam. "Someone could have seen you and me this morning when I pulled out the box. I put on quite a show, clutching it and running into the castle with it when my appointment showed up. Nathan MacDonald could have seen me dash for the house with it, and it was right here on my desk the whole time I talked to him. Even if he didn't know about the earring Alba dug up, he might have been curious about the box. That could be the reason he came back."

"Who's MacDonald?" Vi asked.

Adair filled her in on the man's earlier appointment and about the two men they'd seen arguing at the falls.

"If they were the two who did this, it was a crime of opportunity and not very well planned," Cam said. "Let's see if they searched anywhere else." He led the way through the French doors into the main parlor. The portrait of Eleanor Campbell MacPherson hung in place, but the door to the secret cupboard beneath it stood wide open. "Looks like they did."

"The earring—" Adair couldn't finish the thought.

Cam put a hand on her arm. "Sorry. I forgot to tell you earlier. I took it out of there last night as soon as I got here. Angus's hidey-hole was mentioned in the *Times* article, and with the way that news and rumors can be counted on to go viral in this community I didn't want to take the chance of leaving it there."

Adair whirled on him, not sure whether to hug him or hit him. She compromised by shaking off his hand. "You lied last night."

"I told you the earring was safe." He lifted his pant leg and Adair saw the slight bulge beneath the flesh-colored tape he'd wrapped around his ankle. Tapping his fingers against it, he said, "Special waterproof CIA issue tape. Until we get the security updated around here and lay down some ground rules, the sapphire earring's bonded to me. I promise you I'll keep it safe."

In her imagination Adair pictured armed guards at the wedding. "What exactly do you have in mind?"

"What I'm suggesting for now is that we all be more careful about shutting and locking the outside doors to the terraces during the day, and that we activate the security system whenever someone is alone here, like Vi was earlier. I'll call Sheriff Skinner in Glen Loch and let him know what's happened." Cam punched a number into his cell.

Adair began to pace back and forth in front of the portrait. As he relayed the information to the sheriff, Cam watched her. Whatever blow she'd taken when she'd seen her metal box upended or when she'd initially thought the earring might have been stolen, she'd bounced back and now she was totally focused on the problem at hand.

She had a quick mind. It hadn't taken her long to figure that MacDonald might have had a reason to ransack her office. And when they'd been in the pond and his brain cells had completely shut down, she was the one who'd remembered the cave.

"Sutherland, you still there?" Skinner asked.

"Yes." She was distracting him. Taking his mind off business. He couldn't recall a woman who'd ever had that kind of power over him.

"I can spare a man to come out there for the wedding tomorrow—unless you think you need someone tonight."

"Morning will be fine," Cam said. "Thanks."

Then he turned his attention back to Adair. One of the reasons she could distract him was because there were so many layers to her. And each one was so intriguing. There was the woman who'd had the courage to come downstairs last night and hit him on the head with a pitcher. Then there was the woman who'd punched him on that ledge. And the generous and passionate woman who'd met his every demand in the cave. And she'd done more than that. She'd made her own demands, and if she had more he wanted to meet them. There was more to learn about her. More he intended to discover.

"Something doesn't quite make sense here," Adair said. "I can understand that Nathan MacDonald could have just been in the right places at the right times and decided to take advantage. But his knowing about the secret cupboard argues that he has invested a little more time in his research."

Turning to Cam, she waved a hand around the room. "And how does all of this relate to your theory about a person who's been breaking into the castle for about six months?"

"What theory?" Vi asked.

Cam filled her in on his idea that someone might have been making nocturnal visits regularly to use the library. "After you showed me the room this morning I took a quick walk-through, but the two of you have been here for years. I'd like you to take me on a little tour and tell me what you see."

Cam led the way down the hall and ushered the two women into the long, narrow room. A spiral staircase offered access to the balconies that rimmed the second floor. On three walls, bookshelves stretched from floor to ceiling except for the space taken up by a fireplace. The fourth wall was filled with tall windows and sliding glass doors on both levels, and dust motes danced in the afternoon sunlight. Books were everywhere—stuffing the shelves and spilling into piles on tables, chairs and even the floor. Their scent filled the air.

"We haven't used this room in years," Adair said as she walked down the center.

"A.D. locked it up after the girls' mother died," Vi said. "It was Marianne's favorite place. The last time anyone spent any time here was when Beth did her research."

When she reached the terrace doors, Adair turned back to face him. "What are we supposed to be looking for?"

"Evidence that someone has been in here. If I believed Eleanor's jewels existed and I had the time to devote, this would be a good place to start my treasure hunt. I went to the library in town first thing this morning to see what they had, which was easy, as public libraries have a catalog. Everything is arranged in order. That's not true here. It's one of the reasons Mom had to spend so much time here that summer."

The two women went about their task methodically. Adair checked the doors first and found them locked just as he had. "How did this person get in?" she asked.

"There are ways around alarm systems," Cam said.

Adair and Vi split up to start checking the shelves. By

the time Adair got to the end of the room where they'd entered she had noticed exactly what he had.

"There are different levels of dust on the shelves. The farther I go, the less I find—as if he's working his way down the room book by book. Is that what you think this person has done?"

Good eye, he thought.

"Now that you mention it," Vi said, "I can see the same pattern on the shelves over here. And I think I can see where he sits to do his reading."

Cam and Adair joined her in front of the fireplace where a stack of dustless books sat in a pile next to a leather chair.

"So someone has been just coming in here to go through this library book by book to find Eleanor's dowry? Who in the world has that kind of patience?" Vi asked.

"A true treasure hunter—someone who believes that Eleanor's necklace and earrings are somewhere in the castle or on the estate. Maybe someone who's come across concrete evidence that supports that belief. So far they've been willing to go slowly."

Adair held up a hand. "Okay. So we may, on top of everything else, be dealing with a professional thief who is very focused on finding Eleanor's dowry. Today's break-in seems a bit ham-handed for a patient treasure hunter or superthief."

Cam spread his hands. "This break-in today may be the work of someone else."

"We're back to Nathan MacDonald."

"And the man he was arguing with. Or maybe both of them," Cam said.

Adair closed her eyes. "In other words, we're probably dealing with multiple treasure hunters."

"What do we do?" Vi asked.

"We go on doing business as usual. The two of you have a wedding to prepare for. I'm going to dig through the stuff I brought back from the library in Glen Loch and see if I can find what might have convinced someone that the sapphires are still here somewhere on the estate. But what we're all going to do is be very careful. With one of the earrings already discovered, our thief may lose his patience and get desperate."

"You're trying to scare us," Adair said.

Cam glanced from Vi to Adair. "I want you to take precautions. From now on, no one goes anywhere alone—not into town, not down to the lake, not even for a walk. And we all shut the terrace doors whenever we leave a room. I'll work in the main parlor this afternoon."

"You don't think you're being a little paranoid?" Adair asked.

"Humor me," Cam said. "I'm the one who thought Angus One's secret cupboard wasn't a safe hiding place for the earring. You and Vi focus on the wedding," Cam said. "Let me worry about the rest."

"Okay." But she was already worried about the rest. Because "the rest" for her included him.

One thing at a time, she reminded herself as she left the room. Mentally she made her list as she climbed the stairs. Shower first. That would clear her head and help her to think. Then she'd check in with Rexie. That had been on her To Do list earlier, hadn't it?

She thought of the papers that she'd gathered up and crammed into her desk drawer.

So she'd just make another list. And as far as dealing with what had happened between Cam and her, the only thing she was absolutely sure of was that she wanted it to happen again.

10

IT WAS NEARLY two o'clock when Adair finished the sandwich Vi had brought to her office. The stinging spray of the shower hadn't helped her to clear her head. Or get Cam out of it. Instead, all she'd been able to think of was what had happened at Tinker's Falls. That breathless, heart-stopping jump off the ledge. And what had followed. Especially what had followed.

Just thinking about it had her heart thundering again. Cam had made her fantasy come to life. That little realization hadn't fully struck her until the shower water had turned cold.

Why did that terrify her and thrill her at the same time?

And Cam was not all she should be thinking about right now. But between Bunny and Vi, all the details of the wedding were under control. Caterers, florists, photographers, arrival times. She had a chart on her wall detailing everything. Of course, she and Vi would supervise the setup in the morning. But for now all she had to worry about was the possibility of a runaway bride.

And Cam. Pulling a mini legal pad out of her desk, she tore off three sheets and lined them up in a neat row.

The way she saw it, she faced three major problems:

the Cam Problem, the Missing Sapphires Problem and the Maitland/Banes Wedding Problem. With a pen she labeled each of the papers.

Then she frowned, annoyed that the first problem that had popped into her mind was Cam. In a quick movement she picked that page up and put it in third position. Where it belonged.

Because she wasn't sure she wanted to solve it?

Nonsense. As far back as her memory took her, she had always taken care of herself. She had faced and solved problems all of her life. Practical ones, emotional ones, important ones, trivial ones. They all had to be dealt with by mapping out plans and making decisions. Okay, she'd made a bad one when she'd trusted Bax.

So she'd learn from her mistakes. The trick would be to avoid doing anything rash. She flashed back to that wild plunge she'd taken with Cam off the ledge. Just thinking about it had her heart taking a tumble. But he'd been the rash one. He'd taken the decision right out of her hands—lifting her and stepping out into space.

This time when her heart tumbled, she pressed a fist against it. But what had happened after that, what had happened in the cave—well, she'd been a willing participant in that.

And so what if it had been rash? A girl was entitled to do something outrageous once in her life. Or twice. Or—

Adair lifted the piece of paper with Cam's name on it and turned it facedown on the desk. This was not the problem that she needed to focus her attention on right now.

Neither were Eleanor's sapphires. Cam seemed to have his attention totally focused on solving that one.

She flicked a glance at the French doors that led into the main parlor. Sheer curtains covered the glass squares on the doors, and when she'd passed by them earlier she'd spotted him in silhouette standing at the foot of the portrait, studying it.

When he'd talked about the treasure hunter with the single-minded focus, he might have been describing himself. The sapphires were the real reason he'd come here and if the rest of Eleanor's jewels were still here on the castle grounds, he'd find them. Then he'd go back to his life of adventure with the CIA.

Turning the sapphire paper over, she focused her attention on the problem that deserved her undivided attention. The Maitland/Banes wedding.

Like it or not, the possibility of calling Barry Carlson had been on her To Do list earlier, spurred by the fact that she'd envisioned someone other than Lawrence Banes beneath the stone arch. Someone who looked a lot more like Rexie's first husband than her intended second. Sure, it could have been a figment of her imagination.

But could she depend on that? What if the stones were trying to tell her something?

Right. And why didn't they come and just cart her off to Looney Tunes-ville right now?

She tapped her pen on the paper. What would the harm be if she gave Barry Carlson a call? If Barry turned out to be the cad that Rexie had described, then she'd have some solid information to use in case the bride got cold feet and went into another meltdown.

Opening the desk drawer, she pulled out the jumble of papers she'd crammed into it when she and Cam had first returned to the house. The To Do list had the number of the Carlson Horse Farm on it. Methodically sorting colors into compartments, she slipped everything back into the metal box, placing the larger folded sheets of paper that contained the fantasies on top.

No To Do list.

Pushing back her chair, she dropped to her knees and glanced under her desk.

Nothing.

Crawling around the corner, she peered into the wastebasket. Nary a scrap of paper greeted her inspection.

She was still on her hands and knees, scanning the rest of her office floor for the elusive list, when she heard someone knock on the terrace doors. Starting, she saw an expensive pair of Italian loafers first. Then she took her gaze on a swift journey up perfectly creased trousers and a pristine white shirt. She breathed a sigh of relief when she recognized Lawrence Banes.

Jumping to her feet, she moved forward and hurriedly opened the doors. "Mr. Banes, what a surprise."

And she had a feeling from the expression on his face that it was not going to be a good one.

AN HOUR OF poring over the materials he'd taken from the Glen Loch library convinced Cam that he'd run up against a solid brick wall. Leaning back in the carved oak chair, he planted his feet on the desk in the main parlor. He'd come across an article in the *Glen Loch Gazette* that featured pictures of Angus's secret cupboard, open and shut. But nothing he'd looked at shed any light on the current whereabouts of the rest of the sapphires. They'd been part of Eleanor Campbell MacPherson's dowry, and the only evidence of their existence other than the painting was the earring that Vi and Adair had discovered yesterday.

He'd left a message on his mother's cell but he didn't kid himself that her response would be timely. She and A.D. were taking a working vacation in Scotland, and one of the things that his mother and his stepfather shared was an ability to tune out the rest of the world when they were working. A.D. was painting landscapes for a gallery show and she was doing research for her next historical novel, which would feature the Campbell clan that Angus One had stolen Eleanor away from.

It was a long shot but his mother might have some insights on Eleanor's dowry based on the new research she was doing, and when one of them called back he could fill A.D. in on the security situation.

In the meantime he wasn't any closer to dealing with his other problem—Adair. The curtained French doors that separated the main parlor from her office had allowed him to surreptitiously check on her, more times than he was comfortable with over the past hour. All he knew for certain was that he wanted to make love to her again.

The low rumble of a male voice had him rising and moving quietly to one side of the French doors. She hadn't said she was expecting anyone. With two fingers he pushed against the edge of one of the curtains. The man seated in one of Adair's client chairs had his back to the French doors. He had dark, neatly trimmed hair and the hint of gray told Cam that he was probably somewhere in his forties. Adair's smile was easy and bright but there was a tension in her shoulders. Not fear, he decided. Nerves.

He twisted the knob, eased the door open a crack, then leaned back against the wall to listen.

"I'M SORRY IF I startled you, Ms. MacPherson, but I wanted to see you privately."

Adair's mind raced as she tried to ignore the knot of nerves in her stomach. Even in casual clothes Lawrence Banes looked as if he'd just stepped off the pages of *GQ*. "You've made a long drive for a private conversation."

"Not at all. At Bunny's request I stayed in town overnight at one of the bed-and-breakfasts. She wanted me to be close by because of Rexie. We were all worried about her. But it turned out my help wasn't needed after all. In fact, we decided that a mother-daughter evening was just what Rexie needed to soothe her nerves."

He propped one loafered foot on his knee just as his cell phone vibrated. He slipped it out of his pocket, frowned, then set it on the edge of her desk. Finally he glanced up and smiled at her.

It was the first time that Lawrence Banes had turned the full strength of his charm on her and Adair realized why Rexie might find this man attractive.

"When they left my office two hours ago the wedding was definitely on. Didn't they tell you?"

"Yes. Bunny sent me a text, so I left Glen Loch shortly after they did to keep a business appointment in Albany. About an hour ago Bunny called me back. She told me that Rexie talked to you about her first husband and it evidently stirred up memories."

Adair took a moment to study him. The last person she'd expected to walk into her office unannounced was Lawrence Banes. And in spite of the smile and the casual attitude he was trying to project, there was a tension in him. Albany was a good forty-five-minute drive from the castle, and nothing he'd said so far seemed to warrant him circling back out of his way before returning to Long Island.

"Is that what you wanted to talk to me about?"

"Yes. Bunny and I feel that it's a mistake to remind Rexie of her first marriage, especially when she's feeling so fragile. How much did she tell you about it?" Lawrence asked.

"Not a lot. She told me she and Barry met at Cornell and it was love at first sight. But they came from very different backgrounds." That was about as bare bones as she could make it. Adair hoped that Lawrence would fill in some blanks.

"Different *worlds* is the best way to describe what they came from," he said. "Rexie has led a very pampered life. Her parents have always provided everything for her."

"And you believe you can offer her that same kind of life, the one her parents want for her," Adair said.

"Exactly. Her first husband wanted her to give up everything and go back to live with him in the wilds of Montana. Can you picture that? Anyone can see she doesn't have that kind of strength."

"When did you and Rexie meet?" Adair asked.

"Eight months ago. It was at a charity event the Maitlands were throwing on their estate. Several of my clients were there and they'd offered to introduce me to Bunny and Win. When I first saw Rexie she looked so lonely. Her husband had gone back to Montana for a funeral and stayed. At her mother's suggestion I offered her a sympathetic ear."

"There's quite an age difference between you."

Banes's smile turned wry. "Why is a difference in age always remarked upon? The fact that I'm a bit older than Rexie is probably why I was able to help her get through a bad time."

Banes's phone vibrated. With a slight frown he picked it up. "I have to take this." Rising, he moved quickly to step out onto the terrace.

CAM MOVED AS close as he could get to the doors that opened from the main parlor to the terrace that adjoined the one outside Adair's office. He'd already guessed that the man who'd dropped in on her unannounced was Lawrence Banes and very probably Gianni Scalzo.

He watched Banes walk to the far end of the terrace before he took the call on his cell.

Whatever he said into the phone was muffled by distance. Cam stepped onto the terrace and, using potted trees for cover, edged as close as he could before he dropped down to his knees behind one of them. Luckily Banes was facing in the other direction. If the man turned his way the plant might not offer enough of a shield.

"…told you…I had to talk to her," Banes said.

Cam couldn't make out what the person on the other side of the call was saying. But he could catch the tone. Anger. And he had a lot to say. Cam counted ten good beats before Banes cut the person off.

"I'm going to marry Rexie Maitland." Banes's voice was soft but there was anger there, too.

Banes paced to the far end of the terrace, out of earshot. When he reached the low wall of stones he propped one foot on the top of a flat rock and rested his forearm on his knee.

The stance had recognition streaming through Cam. He was looking at one of the men who'd been at the pond earlier. He would have bet good money on it.

Moving slowly, he began to inch his way back toward the doors to the parlor so that he could be in position when Banes returned to the office.

ADAIR WATCHED THROUGH the open terrace doors as Lawrence Banes lifted his foot to rest it on one of the flat stones bordering the terrace. The instant he placed his forearm on his thigh, his stance and the tension in his body triggered the blurred image that she recalled seeing earlier through that tiny gap in the waterfall. The longer she looked, the more convinced she became that the man she'd seen talking to Nathan MacDonald by the pond had been Lawrence Banes.

How were the two men connected? And why had they been in the woods?

When Lawrence took his foot down, she backed away toward her desk. Shooting a quick glance at the French doors that connected to the main parlor, she was almost sure she saw the shadow of someone through the curtains. So Cam was eavesdropping.

"Sorry about that, Ms. MacPherson." Banes returned to his chair and placed his cell phone on the edge of her desk. He ran a hand through his hair. His smile seemed a bit thinner, his face more tired. "What were we saying?"

"Rexie says that you and her father are involved in some kind of business merger and that the marriage is connected to that," Adair said.

Banes's eyes narrowed. "Win and I are going to sign a partnership agreement right after the ceremony. It's not a secret, but I'm not sure exactly why you've brought it up."

"You seem to be concerned about what Rexie and I talked about this morning. She told me that the deal between you and her father is one of the reasons she's determined to go forward with the wedding."

"Ah," Banes said, relaxing a little. "That sounds like Rexie. She always wants to please her parents. Which is why I wonder how she ever got herself mixed up with the Montana cowboy. But—" Banes raised his hands and spread his fingers "—you know how women are...."

"I do." Adair managed to keep her smile sweet. "But Rexie's first marriage, a mistake or not, was for love. And neither she nor you has mentioned love as one of the reasons for your upcoming marriage."

"Of course I love her," Banes said, his tone a bit hurt. "I was under the impression she loved me. I knew she had concerns about marrying again so soon, and when she read about this place and insisted on having the wedding here I championed her cause. I knew the legend would set her mind at rest."

Adair said nothing.

"I'd expect that you'd be grateful for that, that you'd want this wedding tomorrow just as much as I do. You have a lot riding on it."

"I do." She kept her voice pleasant. "I'm the last person in the world who wants Rexie to call off the wedding. What I don't understand is what you want me to do that I haven't already done."

Lawrence Banes drew in a deep breath and seemed to collect himself. "Sorry. It's just that this wedding means a lot to me. Rexie means a lot to me. Bunny's call upset me because I don't think it's good for Rexie to be thinking about her first marriage. You have no idea how long it took to get her past the divorce papers. She's in a very fragile state. Moving on is the best thing that can happen to her. Once the wedding takes place everything will be fine—for all of us."

In spite of her growing doubts about that, Adair kept her smile bright. "I want you to know that I'm going to do everything possible to make sure that the wedding goes very smoothly on Saturday."

"Good."

As Adair rose, Banes unfolded himself from his chair and glanced at his watch. "I have a pressing appointment. But now that we understand each other, I'm going to leave the matter entirely in your hands."

Adair waited only until Lawrence Banes exited out onto the terrace doors before she circled her desk to follow him. She was only halfway there when Cam stepped into the room.

"I'm almost positive that my nervous about-to-be bride-groom was one of the men we saw at the pond," she said in a low tone.

He smiled at her. "You've got good eyes. And I'm in total agreement."

"But what was he doing there?"

"Very good question. I could go after him and ask him."

Adair saw the reckless gleam flash into his eyes. "Or?"

"We could follow him and see who his pressing appointment is with. Knowledge is power."

"Much better idea. Give me time to tell Aunt Vi."

11

It took Adair three minutes to give Aunt Vi the condensed version of what had happened while Cam alerted Wes Pinter, who was still trimming hedges, that they were leaving. Cam was behind the wheel of his sporty black convertible with the motor running when she slipped into the passenger seat.

"Buckle up," he said. But he didn't wait for her to finish the task before he sent the car flying forward. She clicked the belt in place and clutched the edge of the seat as he floored the gas pedal. By the time they reached the end of the drive and hit the graveled road that twisted away from the castle, the speedometer read fifty and rising.

"Banes has quite a head start," she managed to say as they squealed around the first curve.

"Maybe not so much. Wes Pinter says my car has been the only one parked in the drive since your Mr. MacDonald left."

"So Banes didn't park near the castle, and he lost some time walking to his—" She broke off to suck in a breath as he twisted the car sharply into the next curve.

When the road straightened again he shot her a grin. "Hopefully he has an ego car with less maneuverability."

"Ego car?"

"You know, a sleek, dark colored sedan that shouts, 'I'm successful,' and sucks on a curve like this one."

As he negotiated the next curve, Adair's heart was racing almost as fast as the engine.

"You're good at this," she said.

"CIA training."

As the road leveled for a stretch, she managed to take her eyes away from it and she fastened her attention on Cam. His hands were so sure on the wheel, just as sure and competent as they'd been on her. And he was grinning. She should be scared out of her mind but she wanted to grin, too. "Is this why you went into the CIA? For the excitement? The car chases?" she asked.

"Partly. I love my mom and my brothers, but they're so different. Duncan and my mom are addicted to burying themselves in books and research, although Duncan does get out in the field when his team is working a case. In fact, right now he's in Montana on a big case—tracking a serial killer. Reid loves the straight and narrow. He's totally focused on climbing to the top rung of his job at the Secret Service. I like the variety of the CIA and the fact that I don't always have to follow the rules."

She'd known that Cam was someone who wouldn't be bound by rules the first time she'd ever looked into those twilight-blue eyes. She'd always been attracted to that part of him. Even though she liked rules, relied on them and believed there had to be a reward for following them.

As they crested the hill and shot down the other side, gravel spewed and pinged. Adair held tight and laughed as Cam twisted the car around the next curve. To hell with the rules.

"I eavesdropped on your conversation with Banes. Do

you believe he's marrying Rexie for love or money?" he asked.

She thought for a few seconds. "Yesterday I would have said his motives were strictly business. He was so detached at the rehearsal. He seemed more interested in talking on his cell phone than he was in what was going on. But then he stayed in town last night. And he came to see me today. Maybe he has some feelings for her."

"His cell was keeping him pretty busy while he was talking with you today."

They'd reached the bottom of the hill. Ahead of them the road threaded this way and that before climbing again. Adair spotted a car, a sleek, dark sedan, nearly at the top of the next crest. She pointed a finger. "Looks like an ego car to me."

"Hold on," Cam warned as he floored the gas pedal again.

"The only thing that I'm absolutely sure about is that Lawrence Banes definitely wants to marry Rexie tomorrow. And he doesn't want me to contact the first husband. I had calling Barry Carlson as a possibility on my To Do list, and I couldn't find it when I sorted through the papers I stuffed in that drawer."

"You think Banes might have been in your office before his trip to the pond and saw it?" Cam tapped the brake as he eased into a tricky hairpin curve.

"I'm thinking he took it. And he was worried enough about the possibility of my calling Montana to come back to caution me against it."

"His visit with you didn't go down well with whoever he was talking to on his cell. I couldn't hear everything but Banes did mention that the wedding was on, and the guy on the other end didn't seem pleased. And he and MacDonald were definitely arguing at the falls."

Cam had decreased the speed in order to maneuver through the twists and turns as they climbed the next hill.

"I wish I had a pad and paper so I could draw a timeline," Adair mused aloud.

"Just picture it in your mind as you talk it through," Cam said. "That's what I do."

"Banes says he stayed overnight in Glen Loch to be on call if Bunny needed him. But she didn't. Then this morning he claims he went to Albany for a business meeting and doubled back when she called and told him that Rexie had spoken to me about her first husband. Nathan MacDonald also says he was passing through Glen Loch and heard about Castle MacPherson from the locals."

"We can ask Sheriff Skinner to check it out," Cam said. "Be nice if someone saw them together. Be even nicer if Banes is on his way to meet MacDonald right now." Easing the car around the last of the curves Cam pressed his foot harder on the gas.

"Is it too big a leap to think that one of them might have stirred Alba up when Aunt Vi and I unwrapped the earring yesterday?"

Cam grinned at her. "Theorizing possibilities is a key part of an agent's job. Go with it."

"I'm favoring MacDonald. He had that camera with him and it has a telephoto lens. Maybe he was just hiking along the trail that winds through the hills above the castle gardens and he happened to see Alba dig up the earring. Next morning he calls for an appointment and arrives in time to see me racing up to the house with that metal box clutched in my hands."

"He sees it on your desk, then leaves and waits for you to take off for a walk," Cam said. "It's not long after that I follow you and he can walk right into your office and into the main parlor."

"Maybe he calls Banes to join him. Maybe Banes shows up on his own. But they don't find the earring or the rest of the jewels, so they follow us into the woods," Adair said.

"And they have an argument. They leave, but Banes comes back. And whoever contacted him on his cell was not happy about that."

"Then we've got the interesting fact that Banes didn't park his ego car at the castle. Who was he hiding from?" Adair asked.

"Good question. You've got the mind of a good operative."

"Yeah, well, maybe it will be my fallback career if the Banes/Maitland wedding suddenly crashes and burns."

Cam took one hand off the wheel to give hers a quick squeeze. "One thing my CIA trainer always told me—it's not over until the fat lady sings.'"

They were nearly at the top of the hill when the noise erupted, a squeal of tires, then the crash of metal and glass, once, twice, then a final time. The silence afterward was almost louder than the sounds that preceded it.

They crested the hill, and at first they saw nothing. Cam floored the gas pedal and they were halfway down before he spotted the first signs of the skid. Easing his foot onto the brake, he followed the marks around a sharp curve. To their right a fender lay against the trunk of a thick pine.

"Over there," Adair pointed.

Cam braked and pulled to a stop. To the left the land dipped into a gully. Another fender lay close to the road but the sedan had left a trail of crushed saplings in its wake before plowing nearly head-on into a third pine tree.

"Stay here and call for help," Cam ordered as he climbed out and ran toward the sedan.

Adair had already punched in 911 and was talking to

an operator when she reached the side of the road. Cam was pulling the driver's door open.

"He's alive," he shouted up to her. "Unconscious."

As she relayed the information to the 911 operator, Cam dropped to his knees and leaned into the car. She reached him just as he got to his feet.

"I told you to stay put." He gripped her arm to steer her away from the car. But she caught a good glimpse of Lawrence Banes's face. Its pallor had her stomach lurching.

"You're sure he's alive?"

Cam slid his hand down to hers and linked their fingers. "His pulse is steady. He'll be fine. But tell the operator one of his legs may be broken. I don't want to move him. Ask them how long before they can get someone here."

The simple list of orders helped her to breathe again and to focus. When she'd passed along the information, she said, "The EMTs who are on call at Huntleigh College are on their way. Their ETA is less than ten minutes."

"Hey, Sutherland, is this your work?"

Adair whirled around to see a man move away from a large black SUV and start down the hill toward them. He was tall with tanned skin and liberal hints of silver threaded through his jet-black hair. Dark glasses hid his eyes and added a hint of danger to his sharply sculpted features.

Any apprehension she might have been feeling was completely erased when Cam met him halfway up the hill and hugged him warmly. "I got your text earlier but I have to say, your timing is excellent. There's someone I want you to take a look at."

Cam led the way down the incline. "I want you to meet Adair. This is my boss, Daryl Garnett," Cam said.

Adair studied the two men as they reached her. Though

she guessed Garnett was old enough to be Cam's father, they looked more like brothers.

Daryl caught her hand between both of his. "Cam has spoken enough about you that I would have been able to pick a beauty like you out of a crowd."

Adair found herself returning the smile. It seemed to be her day for running into male charm, and Daryl Garnett had a very potent brand.

Daryl glanced over at the car. "Did Sutherland here run this unfortunate man off the road?"

"No," Adair said. "We were just following him."

Daryl glanced at Cam. "Why?"

"We think he might have been involved in a little break-in at the castle, and we were interested in who he might be meeting," Adair said. "He didn't even know we were following him. And we were still quite a ways behind. So Cam isn't to blame for this. Banes must have lost control on that hairpin curve."

"Banes?" Daryl asked.

Cam gestured toward the open car door. "Meet Lawrence Banes. He's supposed to get married at the castle tomorrow."

"Is he dead or alive?" Daryl moved to the open car door.

"Alive," Cam said. "Ambulance is on the way."

Adair began to get a bad feeling as she watched Daryl check for a pulse and then continue to study the man.

"You recognize him," Cam said.

Daryl gestured them to follow him away from the vehicle before he answered Cam's question. "Yeah. It's Scalzo all right."

"Scalzo?" Adair asked.

Daryl glanced back at the car. "And if you didn't facilitate his accident, I'm wondering if someone else did. Wait here."

Adair might have followed Daryl back to the car if Cam hadn't put a hand on her arm. "Who is Scalzo?" she asked again as they watched Daryl drop to the ground and wiggle his way beneath the back end of the car.

"What's he doing?" Adair asked.

"Checking to see what may have caused the skid," Cam said.

"Got an answer there," Daryl grunted as he eased himself out from beneath the car and got to his feet. A second later he joined them. "Someone cut your Mr. Banes's brake lines."

As Adair shifted her gaze from Daryl to Lawrence Banes, her stomach plummeted. "Someone tried to kill my bridegroom?"

"That would be my guess," Daryl said as he pulled out a handkerchief and wiped grease and dirt off his hands.

"Why?" Adair asked.

"It could be that someone recognized him as Gianni Scalzo or one of the other names he's used, or they figured out the investment scam he's currently running and got to him before I did."

"What scam?" Adair asked, glaring at both of them. "And who is Gianni Scalzo? This time one of you better answer me."

Daryl nodded at Cam. "Go ahead."

As Cam told her about his boss's experience with Gianni Scalzo, Adair's stomach plummeted even further. A lightning strike was bad. This was definitely worse. There was no telling how seriously Lawrence Banes was injured, but as soon as he recovered the CIA wanted to put him behind bars.

How many ways could a wedding go wrong?

"I learned today that right after the wedding ceremony the father of the bride, Winston Maitland, is going to transfer millions into Banes's so far very lucrative real estate investments," Daryl added.

"What's wrong with that?" Adair asked.

"Nothing, if the real estate exists somewhere besides on paper. But Scalzo's specialty is running Ponzi schemes and they're only lucrative for a certain length of time. Then the investors lose a lot of money."

A siren sounded in the distance.

"I'm sorry," Cam said. "I couldn't tell you until I had confirmation. There was a chance he wasn't Scalzo."

She raised a hand. "I get it. You're CIA. You specialize in covert, sneaky ops."

Cam winced. "You can deck me if you want."

"Why? Any way you look at it, the wedding is history. There's an injured bridegroom. The CIA is waiting to arrest him. And someone else wants him dead."

There was a moan from the car.

"The two of you go on." Daryl backed away. "I don't want him to see me quite yet."

Adair reached the car first. Lawrence Banes's eyes were open and filled with pain.

"Ms. MacPherson?" he said in a breathy voice. "What—"

She took one of his hands in hers. "Don't try to talk. You've had an accident."

"The wedding…" He broke off, wincing.

"Don't worry about that now," Adair said. On the road above, an ambulance pulled to a stop. "The EMTs are here."

As the young medics rushed down the incline, Banes's eyes drifted shut but his grip on her hand tightened. "Call Bunny. Tell her…wedding is on. I'm marrying Rexie tomorrow."

Stunned, Adair walked back to Daryl with Cam. "He still wants to go through with the wedding."

"Perfect," Daryl said.

"Perfect?" Adair stared at him. "Someone wants to kill him. You want to put him in jail."

"I have a plan," Daryl said. "How would you like to be part of an undercover op?"

12

"I DON'T LIKE IT." Sheriff Morris Skinner made the announcement after Cam and Daryl had taken turns with Adair in filling him in on what had been going on at the castle, up to and including Lawrence Banes's—or more accurately Gianni Scalzo's—car accident.

What the sheriff specifically didn't like was Daryl's plan—the one he'd outlined while the EMTs were transferring the bridegroom to the ambulance. Adair wasn't sure she liked it either since it involved letting the wedding go on as scheduled.

Learning the truth about Lawrence Banes had hit her like a Mack truck, and for the past hour she'd felt as if she'd been sitting on the sidelines watching the men handle everything.

The waiting room in the clinic at Huntleigh College was barely bigger than a walk-in closet, and once Sheriff Skinner had joined them the space had been filled to capacity. The upside of the cramped quarters was that it offered them privacy, and only a soundproof glass wall separated them from the area where Lawrence Banes was being examined and diagnosed by Dr. Barnhill, a young woman in her early thirties who ran a tight ship.

She'd made one appearance in the waiting room to inform them that her patient was suffering from a broken leg
and she'd know more about his condition after they'd taken
some X-rays. The only thing that she was certain about
was that he was determined to get married the next day.

That had been Daryl's cue to explain his let-the-
wedding-go-on scenario to Sheriff Skinner.

Skinner pinched the bridge of his nose and sighed.
"You're telling me that this Banes/Scalzo guy is an inter-
national crook, but I shouldn't arrest him until after he
gets married up at the castle tomorrow."

"Correct," Daryl said.

Adair had already played the nightmare scene in her
mind. Several times. The setting was the ballroom of the
castle with guests looking on. As Lawrence Banes signed
the papers with Maitland Investments, law enforcement
agencies—some in helicopters, others in black SWAT out-
fits—would all swoop in to make the arrest of the century.

And each time Rexie Maitland would collapse in tears.

The scene made her head spin so much she couldn't
come up with a coherent argument to counter Daryl
Garnett's plan. Her groom-not-to-be had created Ponzi
schemes across the globe and robbed thousands of people
of their savings. The Maitlands and their friends and clients were only the current focus of his business schemes.
But if the deal went through on Saturday Banes would
be caught. And both she and the sheriff were being asked
to be good little soldiers and hold off on letting anyone
know until the knot was tied and the papers were signed.

Skinner, a wiry man in his early sixties, set down his
notebook and scratched his head. "I've been sheriff here
for thirty years, and I've never seen anything like this." He
looked at Garnett first. "You say the Portland P.D. has this

guy's fingerprints when he was operating under a different alias. Can't they arrest him and take him into custody?"

"Sure," Daryl said. "But the fraud he perpetrated there was twelve years ago. Lots of things can happen in a trial, especially when twelve years have passed. But if we catch him in the act, we've got him."

"I'd like to question him," Skinner said.

"So would I," Daryl agreed amiably. "But that could spook him. The man can disappear faster than the kind of ink they sell in kids' magic kits."

Skinner frowned. "I get that. But I'd like to know who cut his brake lines."

"I've been thinking about that," Daryl said. "Scalzo has always worked with a partner—a man many suspect is the real brains behind their cons. It could be they've had a falling-out. And it would be a real coup if we could catch him, too."

Skinner turned to Adair. "I'd also like to know how one or both of them is connected to the other stuff you think is going on up at the castle. A little trespassing aside, I've never known there to be trouble up there." He shifted his gaze to Cam. "You think someone's been breaking into the castle on a regular basis for the past six months. Could that be Scalzo or this MacDonald character?"

"Scalzo has a social schedule to keep on Long Island," Cam said. "All we know for sure about MacDonald is he seemed interested in Eleanor's missing jewels and he had a run-in with Scalzo at Tinker's Falls."

"Maybe he's Scalzo's elusive partner," Adair said.

Cam exchanged a look with Daryl. "It's a possibility."

"Maybe Banes can help us out there," Skinner said.

"It would be better all around if we didn't question him about his connection to MacDonald," Daryl said. "He doesn't know that Cam and Adair saw them talking in the woods. Better to leave those questions until after the wedding and the arrest."

Skinner encompassed all three of them with his gaze. "I'll talk to Edie who runs the diner in town. She's the best investigator I've got. Everyone goes in there and everyone talks. Maybe she can dig up a connection between the two men that isn't merely theory. In the meantime, I'm going to ask Mr. Lawrence Banes is if he knows who might have cut his brake lines."

Cam exchanged a look with Daryl, then nodded. "Be good if he had a nominee. But Adair here should talk to him first. To firm up plans about the wedding."

As if she were responding to a cue, the young doctor appeared in the waiting room doorway. "Mr. Banes is a lucky man. The fracture was clean. He'll be in a cast for a while, but his tibia will heal nicely. He won't be walking down the aisle or dancing, but he should be able to make the big wedding tomorrow. He's groggy from pain meds." Dr. Barnhill held up a finger. "I'll allow one visitor before he gets his MRI."

Adair rose and followed the doctor into the examining room. The distance was short, but she felt as if she were walking the last mile.

Look at the bright side, Adair. Obviously Lawrence and Rexie were not meant to be. Thank heavens the lightning strike had prevented the young woman from ever kissing the scumbag during the rehearsal. And going along with Daryl's plan would put a very bad man in jail.

What she couldn't quite get out of her mind was what the whole thing was going to do to Rexie. The young woman didn't deserve this. Adair had some idea of what it was like to be dumped unceremoniously by a man. But she was finding it hard to get her mind around what it might be like to discover your second husband was a world-class criminal.

And she couldn't seem to come up with a plan that would give Rexie a second chance at happiness. Formulating solutions, solving problems—those were supposed to be her strong points.

Stepping closer to the bed, Adair studied the man lying there. His eyes were closed and he looked older to her than he had before. She reached out and took his hand. "Mr. Banes?"

His eyes fluttered open, but they looked glazed.

"It's Adair MacPherson."

"Mac...Pherson?" He struggled to focus. "Nurse took my cell. Have to call Bunny. Explain."

When his lids fluttered shut, Adair's stomach knotted. Call Bunny? Why did he want to call Bunny? Why didn't he want to call Rexie?

His eyes opened again and he gripped her hand almost as hard as he had in the car. "You call Bunny. The...wedding. Still on."

"I'll call."

Two technicians in lab coats appeared in the doorway.

"Mr. Banes has to have his MRI now," Dr. Barnhill said.

When she tried to disengage her hand, his eyes opened, and this time they were clear. "Let Bunny know."

She waited as the two young men loaded him onto a gurney.

Bunny? And not one mention of Rexie. Well, Rexie was the person she was going to call. And then she was going to make the phone call that she'd had on her To Do list that morning.

Instead of turning right toward the waiting room, Adair

detoured into the ladies' room. She found Rexie's number on her cell and made the call.

The fourth ring transferred to voice mail. "Sorry, I'm unavailable. Please leave a message after the tone."

Adair disconnected, then frowned. She didn't want to leave this message on voice mail. And it wasn't Rexie whose voice she'd just heard. She could have sworn it was Bunny's voice. Did she have the wrong number?

After checking, she dialed again. Once more it was Bunny's voice apologizing on the voice mail message. Why hadn't she noticed that before? Had she ever called Rexie directly before or had it always been Rexie calling her?

With a shrug, she checked Bunny's number and tried it.

Rexie's mother answered immediately. "Ms. MacPherson, don't tell me there's a problem."

Good afternoon to you, too. "I'm calling for Mr. Banes."

"Lawrence? Then he's talked to you about not upsetting our Rexie again."

"Yes, but he asked me to call on a different matter. He's been in a little fender bender with his car. He has a broken leg, but he's going to be fine. And he wanted me to tell you that the wedding will definitely happen on schedule."

"He's broken his leg?" Bunny's voce was laced with panic and concern. "I want to talk to him."

"I think the doctor has confiscated his cell until he's a bit more coherent. I just saw him and he asked me to call you specifically. But I'd really like to get in touch with Rexie. Since I've actually seen Lawrence and talked to him—"

"I'll tell Rexie. I can handle her, Ms. MacPherson. Talking to her about her first husband just reopened old wounds. I don't want my daughter hurt again. So you need to devote your full attention to making sure this wedding takes place on schedule, and I'll take care of my daughter." Bunny disconnected.

Adair stared down at her phone. Why were both Lawrence and Bunny so concerned that she'd talked to Rexie about Barry Carlson?

A knock sounded on the ladies' room door. "You all right, Adair?"

Cam. "Fine. I'll be right out." She waited until his footsteps faded before she got the number of the Carlson Horse Farm from Information and punched in the number.

After four rings, a female voice came on. "Dr. Carlson is busy with the animals. Please leave a message and he'll get back to you."

"This is Adair MacPherson. It's really important that Dr. Carlson call me. It's about his former wife, Rexie Maitland. The matter is urgent." Then she left her cell number.

It certainly couldn't hurt to find out why in the world Bunny and Lawrence Banes were so upset that she'd talked to Rexie about Barry. Turning, she faced herself in the bathroom mirror.

"In the meantime, there has to be something you can do about the wedding fiasco tomorrow. Think."

WHEN ADAIR JOINED the three men in the small waiting room Cam could feel the change in her energy level. He'd been worried about her ever since Daryl had revealed Banes's real identity to her. She had to be feeling that the sky was falling on her head, and the hell of it was, he hadn't been able to cushion the blow. Nor had he been able to come up with a better scenario than Daryl's.

But she had. He could sense it even before she spoke. "Mr. Banes wants nothing to stand in the way of the wedding. But I've decided that I do."

Daryl stared at her. "I thought you agreed that we need to catch this guy."

"I do. But he doesn't even want to talk to his bride-to-be. He just wants to talk to his mother-in-law-to-be. To make sure she gets her daughter to the wedding. And I don't want Rexie to have two failed marriages on her hands."

"Ms. MacPherson, the man you know as Banes—"

Daryl broke off when Cam put a hand on his arm. "She's got a plan, Daryl. Wait for it. Go ahead, Adair."

"There's no reason why the wedding has to be real, right? All we have to do is convince Banes it's real. We're going to run our own scam."

"I think I'm going to like this," Cam said.

She beamed him a smile before turning to the sheriff. "You can handle it with Reverend Foley, can't you? He can get sick, send in a sub at the last minute?"

"Someone who has no legal authority to marry them." Skinner's eyes sparkled. "I think I might be able to arrange that." Then the sheriff shifted his gaze to Daryl. "With that one modification, I'll agree to go along with your plan."

Daryl raised his two hands in a mock surrender. "I've got no problem with running a scam on a scam artist."

Skinner nodded. "After I interview Banes about his accident I'll post a discreet guard on him here at the clinic. My deputy Timmy can pass for a college student. He also has some technological skills. I'll see if he can plant a bug in the room. In the meantime, I think the three of you might want to get back up to the castle. If I wanted to have some uninterrupted time to search the place, I might figure staging a little accident like this would be a good way to focus everyone's attention elsewhere."

"I'll follow you back," Daryl said to Cam as they left the clinic.

Once they were pulling out of the parking lot, Adair pulled her cell out of her pocket. After the fifth ring she said, "Aunt Vi?"

Turning to Cam she said, "Aunt Vi's fine, but Alba has disappeared."

13

Hearing the real worry in her aunt's voice, Adair turned her speakerphone on. "Aunt Vi, we're on our way back right now." She glanced at her watch. Nearly four-thirty. She quickly calculated. "We'll be there in five minutes. Cam is listening, too. Tell us what happened."

"Alba started acting strangely shortly after you and Cam left. I was working in the kitchen and she began growling at the terrace doors. I had them locked just as we all agreed. Wes Pinter was working on the hedges that run along the back of the garden and I assumed he was disturbing her. Though he never has before."

"What else, Aunt Vi?"

"I settled her down, but she wouldn't move away from the terrace. About half an hour ago she started barking again and scratching at the glass. So I let her out and she tore off through the garden. I didn't catch sight of her again until I got to the edge of the clearing by the stone arch. She ran right through and then she disappeared into the woods beyond. I chased after her, but I slipped and fell on some loose stones on the floor of the arch."

"Are you hurt?" Adair asked.

"No. But stumbling slowed me down. By the time I

reached the trees there was no sign of her. She'd started growling again and I heard a yelp. But I can't even hear her bell now."

"Where are you now, Vi?" Cam asked.

"I'm at the stone arch. There's no one here now. I think Alba chased them away and they may have hurt her."

"Where's Wes Pinter?" Cam asked.

"I can't see him anywhere. I tried him on his cell before Adair called. He didn't pick up."

"Stay right where you are and keep your phone line open," Cam said. "We're only minutes away."

Adair gripped the armrest with all of her might as Cam careened the car onto the dirt road that wound its way through the hills to the castle.

"Aunt Vi?" Pushing down hard on fear, she turned to Cam. "She's not answering. I think I've lost her."

"Almost there," Cam said.

In the rearview mirror she could see Daryl Garnett's car through a cloud of dust. Both men could drive like the devil, but she wished they could go even faster.

"We never should have left her there alone," she said, finally giving voice to the guilt that was plaguing her.

"She isn't alone. Pinter is there. Plus, your aunt's a smart woman."

Adair hung on to all those thoughts as Cam shot his car over the crest of the hill that ended in the castle driveway. Wes Pinter's truck was parked close to the castle. Cam pulled in behind it, and the instant the tires screeched to a halt she jumped out of the car and circled the hood. She could just see the stone arch, nearly a football field away. Pines grew thick and tall on the hill that rose sharply behind it. She started toward them. "Aunt Vi?"

Cam grabbed her arm. "Wait." Then he turned to Daryl,

who'd parked behind them and was already approaching. Quickly he filled him in on their conversation with Vi.

By the time he finished, Vi had appeared from the back of the arch and was running toward them. Adair raced to meet her.

"They make a pretty picture," Daryl murmured to Cam as the two women embraced. Then he strode forward, his hand extended to Vi. "I'm Daryl Garnett, ma'am. I work at the CIA with Cam."

"Viola MacPherson," Vi said as she took his hand.

"Where was the dog the last time you saw her?" Daryl asked.

"She was running into the woods behind the stone arch. That was ten minutes ago. I haven't heard anything since." Vi's hand was still clasped in Daryl's when she turned to Cam and Adair. "I'm worried about Wes Pinter, too. Right after I talked to Adair, I tried to reach him on his cell phone again. I thought he could help me look for Alba. But he didn't answer."

"Why don't we split up?" Daryl suggested. "Ms. MacPherson and I will look for Alba and you two can check on your gardener."

"Sure." Then Cam watched his boss and Vi start back toward the stone arch.

"He sure works fast," Cam murmured.

Adair stared at him. Then she shifted her gaze to Daryl and Vi. "You think he likes Aunt Vi? They just met."

Cam met her eyes. "Sometimes it happens just that fast." That was how it had happened to him. One long look beneath that stone arch and he hadn't recovered since. He couldn't quite get his footing even now. He caught one of her hands and raised it to his lips. "Some of us are just slower realizing it."

The quick flash of understanding and panic he saw in

her eyes was such a perfect match to what he was feeling that it steadied him. He grinned at her. "We have some time to make up for. But first, we have to find Wes Pinter."

Keeping her hand in his, he strode through the garden toward the terrace at the back of the castle. The place was silent except for the noise of their footsteps on the path. But there was no sign of Pinter, nor was there any sound except for the lap of water against the shore below them and the hum of bees. The terrace was empty too and the sinking sun slanted long shadows across the pavers. Nothing looked out of place.

"It's too quiet," Adair said, echoing his thoughts.

The sliders to the kitchen stood open, but the door that led to the rest of the castle was closed. Cam moved toward it.

"Aunt Vi said whoever Alba was barking at was outside," Adair said.

"I just want to check the library." The door was only a short distance down the hall. He still believed that somehow the library held the key they needed. Once he opened the door he said, "Stay close, and see if you notice anything that's been disturbed since we were here earlier."

They walked together down the narrow room, stopping to check the chair near the fireplace where Vi had been sure someone had been sitting quite recently.

"It all looks the same," Adair said.

"Yeah." But he drew her with him all the way to the sliding glass doors that opened onto another terrace. They were locked.

Outside a hummingbird hovered at a bright red feeder, but it shot away like a bullet as soon as Cam opened the door. There was no view of the lake on this side of the castle; instead, paving stones bordered with green moss separated the castle from a well-tended lawn before the treed hillside sloped sharply upward.

Tucked into one corner of the space was a gardening shed, its door slightly ajar. Adair's sharp intake of breath told him that she spotted the boots through the open door just as he did. They broke into a run and found Wes Pinter seated on the floor and rubbing the side of his head.

Cam squatted down. "You all right?"

"Headache. Came back here to put away the hedge trimmers and he sneaked up on me. He slammed the door into me and I must have hit my head pretty good when I fell."

The hazel eyes that met Cam's were undilated and clear.

"I got a look at him," Pinter said. "Shorter than me. Had a mustache and a beard. Longish hair."

Cam glanced at Adair.

"Sounds like MacDonald," she said.

"Is Vi all right?" Pinter asked.

"She's fine." Cam's cell phone rang. After a few seconds, he turned to Adair. "Alba's fine, too. They found her halfway up the hill. Daryl says she was knocked out, as well."

FIFTEEN MINUTES LATER, Cam leaned his hip against a counter while the others sat at the table sipping tea. Wes had fully recovered. And Alba, who sat on Daryl's lap being fed scones, looked as if she was also back to normal.

Not only that, she'd gotten a piece of the bastard who'd hit her. Daryl and Vi had found a good-sized piece of khaki cloth clamped in her jaw, and it had a trace of blood on it.

Wes's description matched with MacDonald, but what had the man been after? Whatever it had been, he hadn't bothered to look in the library for it.

"There are a couple of ways to upgrade the security system here," Daryl was saying to Vi and Adair. "I've no doubt that Cam has several suggestions in mind."

"I do, but I don't think this guy wanted to break into the house today," Cam said.

Adair turned first to look at him. "Why not?"

"He took the time to take out Wes." He turned to Vi. "And you were in the kitchen from the time we left until you let Alba loose, right?"

She nodded.

"He could have seen that. You and the dog were safely inside. Wes wasn't. That's why he knocked him out."

"And Alba found him in the stone arch," Adair said, rising from the table. "That's what he was interested in."

"And he didn't want to be interrupted," Cam said. "I'll check it out. The rest of you stay here with Daryl."

"Not so fast. I'm coming with you," Adair said. "You're the one who made the rule that nobody goes anywhere alone."

"You need any backup, you've got my number on your speed dial," Daryl called after them.

Cam was silent as they walked through the garden to the stone arch. Annoyed, Adair guessed. She'd sensed it in the kitchen while they'd been talking. His jaw was set, his body tense. More than annoyance. He was worried, too.

"Whoever whacked Wes and Alba is long gone," she said.

He glanced up at the hills that rose around them on all sides. Clouds were rolling in fast over the lake, darkening the sky. "He's watching right now. I'd put good money on it. And my instinct tells me that he's getting desperate. He or she didn't foresee that the earring would be discovered in the stone arch."

"I've been wondering about that, too. And why just the one earring? Why split up the pair?"

They'd reached the arch, and Cam glanced up at it. "Maybe the rest of the jewels are here, too. That's what I'd be thinking. I should have taken more precautions with you and your aunt."

"You can't seriously be blaming yourself."

He faced her then. "I was supposed to come up here and keep you and Vi safe. Instead I talked you into chasing after Banes, and that allowed MacDonald or whoever he is to attack an old man and a dog. If we hadn't gotten back here when we did…"

Not just annoyance and worry. There was anger in his eyes and even in the hushed tone of his voice.

Anger at himself.

Her first impulse was to argue with him that she and Vi were perfectly capable of taking care of themselves. But she had a hunch that little lecture would fall on deaf ears. So she tried another approach.

"So now you're rehashing all the should-haves and could-haves. Crying over spilt milk. Is that what they teach you in the CIA?"

He frowned at her. "Of course not."

"Then don't. When one plan fails, what you have to do is concentrate on the next one. That's what I've always done."

Cam stared at her then. "That could be it. If he's the guy who's been visiting the library, he must have been certain that something in there would pinpoint the location of the jewels. Now that he knows where one of the earrings turned up, he's switching to Plan B. You're a genius."

"I am?"

"Bet on it." He pulled her close and gave her a quick kiss. At least she sensed that was his intention. But the moment their mouths met, everything changed. It was as if she'd been struck by lightning.

She felt the heat first, primal, powerful, raw. Then the shock of an electric sizzle shot through her system and thrust her heartbeat into overdrive. Greed followed and it was enormous.

There were other sensations, too—the scrape of his teeth, the thrusting movement of his tongue, the press of those hard hands as they gripped her waist and lifted her to pull her closer.

Each separate, staggering thrill built layer by layer on the earlier ones until she felt as if the pleasure might shatter her. Shatter them both.

Cam couldn't breathe. But there wasn't time to worry about it. He needed more of her.

Her taste consumed him. The variety and uniqueness of her flavors flooded his system until she was once again all he knew. The suspicion lurked in the back of his mind that he might search the world, and no other woman would please him this way or suit him so well.

When she wrapped her arms and legs around him, he wanted more. Needed more. He took two staggering steps forward, pressed her against the wall. And reality came back in an icy rush.

He lifted his head, drew in a breath. "Dammit."

He pried her loose from him, and she sank down on the ledge of rock that ran along one side of the arch. He slapped one hand on the wall to steady himself. Because he couldn't feel his knees. Even then it took him a moment to fully focus. "We need to see what that bastard was doing in here. Figure out his Plan B."

Saying the words aloud helped him focus. He'd lost himself in her. The shocker was that once he'd pressed his mouth to hers he'd been powerless to do otherwise.

Even more terrifying was the fact that he wanted to lose himself in her again. He shifted his gaze away. He'd come here to find what the guy was doing in the stone arch. "Vi said she slipped on some loose stones, right?"

"Yes."

Thunder rolled overhead and he noticed that the sky had gone very dark.

When she made a movement to rise, he said, "You're going to stay here. Right where I can see you and you can see me."

"I know every inch of the inside of this arch."

"Then you can tell me if I'm missing anything."

Pulling out a penlight, he snapped it on. "Stay right here." Then he began to make his way along one side of the wall. One thing he was sure of. However dangerous the threat that the intruder posed, Adair MacPherson posed an even bigger one for him.

Adair watched him move away. She didn't intend to stay put. The feeling would return to her legs any second and she would catch up with him. In the dim backwash of light, she could make out Cam's shadow hugging the wall, his head ducking now and then because of the uneven way the stones arched. He was thorough, running his hand down to the floor and testing for any loose stones.

Closing her eyes, she thought of those hands and the way they could make her feel. And she wanted them on her again. She wanted his mouth on hers again. The first drops of rain splattered loudly on the stones overhead, and the sound had her eyes snapping open.

Her heart took a long fall and then bounced when the realization struck her.

She'd just kissed Cam Sutherland beneath the stone arch.

No! That wasn't supposed to happen. A fantasy fling was one thing. Anything else was...

Lightning flickered and thunder rolled again.

Impossible. Absolutely impossible....

She pressed a hand to her heart and felt a surge of relief that it was beating in the right place. Then she took a deep breath and reached for calm. It was just the fantasy that was coming true, she lectured herself. What better proof did she need than the kiss they'd just exchanged? It was...better than anything she could have imagined. The true stuff of fantasies.

And their purpose in being here was not related to her fantasy or the legend. They had a problem.

She jumped to her feet. "Find anything?"

"Nothing loose or out of place on this side." He started back to her, using the light to sweep the opposite wall as he moved.

He hadn't taken more than a few steps when she heard the crunch of stones beneath his shoes and watched him squat down.

She rushed to his side. "You found something."

"What part of 'stay there' didn't you understand?"

"I'm with a CIA agent, right?" She was already on her knees, running her hands along the base of the wall. "There are some bigger ones loose. Maybe he found another part of Eleanor's dowry."

Cam moved his penlight along the lower part of the arch. One larger stone jutted out. "Looks like he replaced some of the stones."

She met his eyes. "No reason to do that if what he found was the rest of Eleanor's dowry. Unless he wanted to hide something."

"Our minds are running along the same path."

Before he could stop her, she ducked low and worked

a small rock out of the wall. Then she began to work on the larger one.

Cam grabbed her wrists. "My turn. We don't know what we're going to find."

But she had a feeling it wouldn't be good as she backed up and let him shoot the light into the space she'd cleared. He freed another stone, then handed her the light. "Hold it steady."

Fear shot ice up her spine at what he pulled out next. It was small, no bigger than the metal box she and her sisters had buried their dreams and fantasies in. But it was encased in plastic and there were wires that connected two small canisters.

She swallowed hard. "Definitely not Eleanor's missing dowry."

He met her eyes. "You've got good nerves. This is a type of bomb I've worked on before. Military issue. That's good news. It means he's not cooking up homemade stuff in his cellar."

"Great."

"More good news—there are no other loose stones. I checked. He only had the time to plant one. And there's nothing ticking, no lights blinking. Otherwise we'd both be running like hell."

"I notice you're not doing a happy dance. What's the bad news?"

"This little puppy works on a remote detonator. All our guy has to do is press a button. But even that's good news."

"In what alternate universe?" she asked.

Cam's laugh was soft, and the smile remained on his face when he met her eyes. "I never know what you're going to say next. But the fact that he's using a bomb with a detonator probably means that all he wanted to do today was plant it so that he can set it off later."

"So what are our options?" She was voting for running.

"Make sure he can't set it off. Ever. I'm going to need your help. You game?"

"Sure." He certainly was. In fact, she was pretty sure he was having fun. The look he shot her was cocky, confident. And totally Cam. Her heart fluttered.

"Hold the light steady."

She was surprised that she could, that her hand didn't tremble. His certainly didn't. She watched fascinated while thunder rumbled and rain pounded steadily on the stones overhead. His movements were as deft and quick as a surgeon's as he isolated wires and then used the blade of a small professional-looking penknife to cut them.

When he started to slip the bomb back into place, she said, "Why are you leaving it here?"

"He's got eyes on this place. I don't want him to suspect that we found it."

"He's bound to suspect something if he decides to use that detonator."

Cam met her eyes then. "Then he'll have to try again. And we'll be ready for him."

She stared back down at the device. She knew that the danger was just beginning to sink in when her hand started to tremble. "What did he hope to accomplish with a bomb?"

"I'm thinking maybe it was his Plan B and that it was born out of desperation. The earring was found in here. He's not the only one who's going to speculate that the rest of the dowry is hidden somewhere in the stones."

"Even if he did manage to blow up the whole place, it could take days to sort through the rubble. He's got to be crazy."

"That's one possibility." He finessed the last stone into place. "Our mission is accomplished."

Adair drew in a deep breath and let it out. "What do we do next?"

Thunder roared and lightning flashed brightly enough that for a moment she could see him quite clearly.

"Let Daryl and Vi know. Notify Sheriff Skinner so that he can get someone up here to stake out this part of the garden starting tonight. Then we wait."

"That's it?"

Cam met her eyes. "I know your affection for detailed plans, but aren't you ever tempted to just go with the flow?"

Only with you, she realized. They were kneeling together on the smooth rocks that formed the floor of the arch. Even in the dim light that radiated from the penlight she'd set aside, he looked triumphant, like some warrior that had just won a battle. And she wanted him more than she'd ever wanted anything. Anyone.

And she'd just kissed him under the stone arch.

Panic streaked its way through desire. The kiss didn't matter, she told herself again. It couldn't matter. If any two people were mismatched, it was Cam and her.

Which was why he made the perfect fantasy. That's what fantasies were about. The impossible. The things you think can only happen in your wildest dreams. But she and Cam *were* happening.

"I do like plans. And missions. Right now I have another one for you." Carefully, she set the flashlight down. "We won't need this." Then she tugged his T-shirt out of his jeans. "You won't need your clothes either."

"Sounds like my favorite kind of mission."

He helped her pull the shirt over his head. Even in the shadows she saw the excitement in his eyes darken to something else, something that had fire racing along her nerve endings. But when he lowered his head, she angled hers, avoiding his lips at the last moment.

"No kissing yet. Once we start that, my brain turns to toast." She gave his ear a quick nip. "I want to touch you first."

"Touch away."

She ran her hands over his shoulders, then slowly down his chest. There was so much to absorb—the smooth taut skin, the hard muscle beneath. Even the tickle of hair under her palms sent a separate thrill rippling through her.

"I can't seem to stop wanting you," she murmured as he moved her hands lower.

"It's a mutual problem."

His breath hitched when she slipped her fingers beneath the waistband of his jeans. Their fingers collided, then tangled as they worked on his belt. When it was finally freed, she pushed his hands away.

"My turn. I'll let you know when it's yours."

The sound of his jeans unsnapping seemed as loud as the rumble of thunder overhead. And the rasp of the zipper as she eased it down was exciting, erotic and irresistibly enticing.

"There was no time for me to do this in the cave."

"We were busy with other things. Let me have my turn and—"

The sentence broke off as she slipped her hands beneath his briefs, found him and freed him.

Their gasps intermingled, then thunder rumbled again.

"Oh, my," she breathed. Her experience wasn't vast, but what she was looking at went beyond anything she'd imagined. She ran her fingers up the length of him and felt the tremor move through him. "When you have toast for brains, you miss things."

"There are other things you're missing. Right now. Say the word."

"Not quite yet." The huskiness of his voice had added one more thrill to the mix as she wrapped her fingers around him. When he groaned, power sang through her bringing fresh pleasure.

"I have a plan," she murmured.

"It better not take long."

With a soft laugh, she met his eyes. Then before she could lose her resolve, she leaned in and gave his ear a quick nip, then licked the pain away with her tongue. "I just want to taste you. Try it. You might like it."

Cam wondered if he had a choice. Ever since she'd closed her hand around him, he'd lost all the strength in his arms. By the time she'd used her teeth on his shoulder and moved lower to take his nipple into her mouth, he was sure he was losing his mind. Each flick of her tongue, each scrape of her teeth, each flutter of her breath on his skin created sensations so sharp, so intense they took his breath away. Her mouth left a trail of heat that seemed to sear away his flesh right to the bone.

And all the time, she moved her hand gently on his shaft, up and then down. Up and then down, guiding him into a rhythm that she controlled.

Then she was finally where he wanted her to be, but he still wasn't prepared for what he felt when she flicked her tongue over the head of his penis. The intensity of the pleasure was so great, so consuming. And the ache that it left in its wake was something he'd never experienced.

The only thing he could seem to move was his eyelids. So he watched her as she used her tongue on him. Moving lower to the base of his shaft and then up again as if she were devouring some delicious treat that she'd been starving for.

New sensations battered his system. Agonizing. Amazing. When she took him fully into her mouth, he thought his heart would simply burst out of his chest. No other woman had ever aroused him like this. Seduced him like this. Destroyed him like this.

The power was hers. His entire world had seemed to narrow to the wet heat of her mouth as it drew him in, then released him. And each time she did, he felt parts of himself melting and merging with her.

He wanted it to stop. He wanted it to go on.

Adair was drowning in him. How could she have known that a man's skin could have so many textures, so many flavors? Or that making a man tremble, making him moan, could be so arousing? So amazing? She'd never imagined that she had this kind of power, the kind that brought only pleasure.

Nor could she have imagined her own greed. She couldn't get enough of the taste of him. The textures fascinated her, steel wrapped in velvet. Sensations poured into her, filling all the empty spaces.

When he reached for her, his hands trembled at first, then gripped her and lifted her so that she straddled his thighs.

"Adair." His voice was barely a rasp, but when she started to move, he held her still. "Protection."

Once the word registered in her brain, she met his eyes. "I'm good. Pill. Still my turn."

Then lifting her hips she lowered herself onto him.

The moment she took him in, enclosed him, he began to move. She felt the storm that she'd been building in him since her first touch break free. His thrusts were desperate, violent. This was what she'd wanted. Dreamed of. Then he drove her beyond what she'd ever imagined into a pleasure so dark, so intense that she was blind from it.

"Cam." He was all she knew as he poured himself into her and she shattered.

ADAIR WASN'T SURE how long they lay tangled together against the stones when the ringing of a cell phone forced them back to reality. Cam managed to get to his just as it rang for the third time.

"It's Daryl." Holding it so they both could listen, he said, "Problem?"

"Not on this end. But the storm ended about ten minutes ago, and Vi's beginning to worry about the two of you."

"We're fine now that we've dismantled a very nice military issue bomb."

"No shit," Daryl said. "Sorry I missed it. But Sheriff Skinner called to check on Vi and he's on his way up here. Seems that using Edie at the diner as his investigator has paid off. Hazel Gallinger who runs the General Store caught our friend Banes talking to a stranger on one of her security cameras. Skinner wants to know if the guy is MacDonald."

"Do me a favor and call him back," Cam said. "Tell him we need that extra man he offered to send up here tonight. And tell Vi we're on our way."

14

It was just before seven when Sheriff Skinner inserted the security disc from Hazel Gallinger's store into the DVD player in the main parlor. One of his deputies along with Skinner's dog were currently on stakeout duty in the stone arch. Another of the sheriff's men was patrolling the grounds. Daryl and Wes had checked the security system and made sure all the windows and doors were locked.

While they'd provided Skinner with more details on the bomb they'd discovered and the attacks their latest intruder had made, Vi had fixed sandwiches and tea and wheeled the refreshments in on a cart.

In Cam's opinion, they made a pretty motley-looking crew. Skinner looked tired as he pressed a button on the DVD player and then pulled up a ladder-back chair. Daryl had chosen a spot closest to the screen on a love seat next to Vi with Alba snuggled between them.

As the TV screen flickered on, Cam's gaze shifted to Adair who sat cross-legged on the floor. While they'd waited for Sheriff Skinner to arrive, he and Adair had used the excuse of getting caught in the rain to fit in a quick shower and change of clothes.

She wore a T-shirt and jeans and her red hair curled

wildly around her head just the way it had when she was a kid. But she wasn't that kid anymore. Nor was she the young woman who had jarred his hormones into overdrive at his mother's wedding seven years ago.

She was so much more.

He thought of the way she'd held so steady when he'd discovered the bomb. She had courage. He knew that she had to have mixed feelings about letting the wedding go on as scheduled, but he'd studied her face when Daryl had spoken about the hundreds of people that Banes had stolen from over the years. And she'd agreed to the plan even though it might put her dream of establishing the reputation of Castle MacPherson as a prime wedding destination in grave jeopardy.

She wasn't anything he'd expected or even thought he wanted. All he'd known was that she would be different for him. What he hadn't counted on was how different. Or that she would take him so far beyond his expectations— or even his fantasies.

He wanted—no, he needed more time with her. They hadn't had much yet. He also wanted to make love with her again. And he had a feeling that he wasn't going to stop wanting that anytime soon.

When her eyes slid to his, he got that same feeling he'd gotten when they'd been making love—that his whole world was suddenly becoming very narrow. Very centered. The feeling had his stomach skittering and something tightened around his heart.

"This is one of the aisles in Hazel Gallinger's store," Skinner said.

Cam focused on the TV screen.

"She was in Edie's Diner when I came in to ask about any strangers in town. She said she saw two early this morning."

Skinner leaned forward to tap a finger on the screen as a man entered. "She noticed the Banes guy right away because of his fancy shoes and shirt. The next guy came in a few minutes later."

Adair felt the hairs on the back of her neck stand up as the second man entered the store. The screen only showed his back, but he had a camera hanging from a strap over his shoulder. And the hair was the right length for Mac-Donald. She waited, wanting to be sure.

He strolled up the aisle and when Banes turned to him, there was surprise on his face followed by a frown.

"Not a stranger to Banes," she murmured.

"That would be my guess," Skinner said. "And Banes doesn't look happy to see him."

The two men stood face-to-face. It was the shorter man who seemed to be doing all the talking. Then Banes glanced at his watch and nodded. The other man turned away from Banes and the moment he did, Wes Pinter said, "Mustache, fancy beard. That's the guy who attacked me."

"That's also the man who introduced himself to me as Nathan MacDonald." Adair turned to meet Cam's eyes. "And that's the man we saw arguing with Lawrence Banes at Tinker's Falls."

Daryl leaned forward and spoke to the sheriff. "A beard and a mustache, especially one that people remember, is a great disguise. If you'd be willing to lend me that disc, I can get a good enough image off it to send to a tech I know. He'll run it through a facial recognition program minus the beard. Then we might know who we're dealing with." He turned to Cam. "It may match up with that old photo I have of Gianni Scalzo's partner."

Skinner ejected the disc and handed it over. "Banes claims that he has no idea who might have tampered with his brake lines. He's going full steam ahead with the wedding. By the time I left his room, he was pestering Dr. Barnhill for a phone so that he could to talk to Bunny."

Bunny again. Adair frowned and found herself looking at Cam. She wanted to talk to him about the fact that Banes hadn't once mentioned talking to Rexie. Something about that was still rubbing her the wrong way. She wanted his take on it, and she just wanted time to be with him. Everything had happened so fast between them. And time was slipping away. After tomorrow, after he and Daryl and the sheriff were able to arrest Banes, they'd probably have to go back to Washington. She and Vi would have their hands full with the fallout from the wedding disaster.

All her life she'd focused on mapping out plans for her future. No one had ever made her want to live so totally in the moment. In the now.

"I wish we had a better handle on what the hell is going on here," Skinner said.

Adair shifted her focus back to the conversation.

"All we've got are theories or suppositions." Cam stretched his legs out. "If MacDonald is the guy who's been poking around in the castle for the past six months, I'd say his goal is the sapphires. Something must have convinced him that they exist and they're here. Maybe it started out as a hobby. But now he's convinced they're in the stone arch, and he's determined to get them before the hills come alive with other fortune hunters."

"If he's Scalzo's longtime partner and he cut Scalzo's brake lines, the partnership is obviously on the rocks. The question is why?" Daryl said. "And why now? They've been together for years. Why have a falling-out the day before a wedding that promises to net them millions?"

"He could be both our nocturnal visitor and Banes's partner," Adair said. "The Maitlands signed the contract for the wedding about six months ago, the same time Vi started to have her sleep disturbed and brought Alba home. If MacDonald is the man behind the scenes, his job could be intelligence gathering, right?"

"That has always been my assessment," Daryl said. "What are you thinking?"

"Maybe MacDonald decided to take the jewels on as a private project and didn't inform Banes," Adair continued. "Then the earring shows up and Banes gets wind of it and MacDonald doesn't want to share. They argue. MacDonald tries to eliminate Banes."

"Damn good theory," Daryl said.

"Ninety-nine percent of marriages that break up do so because of differences over money. I imagine the same thing could happen to a partnership," Vi said.

"And with this kind of money at stake, it might explain why things are getting so volatile so fast," Skinner said. "Whoever he is, the MacDonald guy is dangerous. And he's had professional training."

"Plus, he's versatile," Daryl said. "He cuts Scalzo's brake lines, takes out Wes here and a dog without leaving permanent damage, and plants a bomb."

"A regular one-man army." Skinner rose from his chair. "Before Wes and I leave I want you to fill me in on the schedule for tomorrow."

"I can take you into my office," Adair said. "The entire day is on the wall."

CAM PACED BACK and forth in his room. They'd done all that they could do for the moment. Daryl had a tech working to identify Nathan MacDonald. Banes was being guarded by Skinner's deputy in the hospital, and two of his other men were working surveillance on both the stone arch and the castle grounds.

He glanced at his watch. It was late—well past midnight. Adair had a full day tomorrow. They all did. He should let her get her rest. He should get some of his own.

Moving to the sliding doors that led to the balcony, he stepped outside. The storm had cleared and a full moon bathed the garden below him. He could even see the outline of the stone arch. As he watched, two figures stepped off the garden path and started across the clearing toward the stones. He recognized them immediately. Daryl and Vi. When they reached the shelter of the arch, he saw Daryl take Vi into his arms.

His boss clearly wasn't wasting any time.

And hadn't he already wasted enough? For seven years he'd avoided Adair. And those were years he could never get back.

Turning, he stepped back into his room, locked the slider, then strode to the door of his room and reached for the handle. The thought struck him just as he was about to step into the hallway. He was close to being obsessed with her.

Just as obsessed as Banes was with his wedding and this Nathan MacDonald seemed to be with the sapphires.

How in hell had he let it come to this?

ADAIR LAY ON her back counting sheep. Fifty-seven of them so far. But about every five sheep or so, she lost her focus and started thinking about Cam. And wanting him.

Opening her eyes, she stared up at the ceiling. Twenty-four hours ago he hadn't been a part of her life. She hadn't seen him in seven years. And they'd only made love twice. Surely it took longer than that to develop an addiction.

Yet, as ridiculous as it seemed, she wanted him now—so badly that she couldn't sleep. Sitting up, she twisted around and punched her pillow several times, then lay back down and closed her eyes.

Seven sheep later, her mind drifted right back to Cam as if it were on a magnetic tractor beam.

After the sheriff had left, he'd told her that he was going to work with Daryl for a while and that she should get some sleep. They all had a big day ahead of them.

Rolling over on her back, she stared up at the ceiling. It promised to be a big day all right. A big disastrous day.

She hadn't been able to speak with Rexie yet. Bunny had called to confirm their arrival time for the photograph session, but Rexie was busy with her bachelorette party and couldn't come to the phone.

And Dr. Barry Carlson had yet to call her back. She'd tried him again earlier right before she'd joined everyone in the main parlor for the viewing of Hazel Gallinger's security disc. She'd reached the answering service. Again.

Had Rexie found it that difficult to get in touch with him when he'd originally moved back to Montana?

And then she remembered that she'd wanted to talk to Cam about it. And why shouldn't she? She had a perfectly good excuse to go to his room in the middle of the night— one that didn't mean she was becoming a sex addict.

Throwing the covers back, she leaped out of bed and rushed to the door. Just as she reached it, there was a soft knock, and she threw it open to find Cam.

Grabbing his shirt, she pulled him into the room. "I need to talk to you."

Talk was the furthest thing from Cam's mind once the moonlight poured over her. She was a vision—red curls tumbling over porcelain skin, a shimmer of lace and silk that skimmed her breasts and dropped only to the tops of her thighs. And those eyes, a dark gleam of green. She stopped his breath.

When she nudged him onto the bed, he sat. His legs wouldn't hold him up.

She paced. "Rexie's first husband. I want to get in touch with him."

Cam struggled to focus on what she was saying and found it helped if he fastened his gaze on a point beyond her. "The first husband?"

"Dr. Barry Carlson. He's a vet and they met at Cornell when he was finishing up and she was just starting. It was love at first sight, they got secretly married and then the fact that they came from very different worlds came crashing down on them. The families were not happy. His parents expected him to come back to Montana, and hers pictured her stepping into a well-established social circle on Long Island. They went with her parents' scenario. Not surprising once you've met Bunny."

"The charmer who ran me off the road."

"Exactly. It's such an old story." She waved her hand in an "and so forth" gesture. "But something about the way they broke up keeps nagging at me. It's not like I don't have a big enough worry list. There's a wedding to-morrow that has to go off without a hitch so this Scalzo person can be brought to justice. And there's this Nathan MacDonald still skulking around out there with his martial arts training and his bombs. And there's the rest of Eleanor's dowry. But I can't seem to let Rexie's first marriage go. Does this ever happen to you when you're working on a case?"

"Yeah." She had his attention now. He couldn't help but notice that what was happening between the two of them hadn't made her worry list. And it seemed to be right at the top of his.

She climbed onto the bed near the headboard and

crossed her legs beneath her. "Then maybe you can help me. Tell me I'm wrong."

"First, what bothers you about the breakup?"

"Rexie's still in love with him. I could see it in her eyes. It was the kind of love at first sight that she'll never shake loose. Do you know what I mean?"

Something skittered through Cam's stomach. Ridiculous to think he might know exactly what she was talking about. What he said was, "Classic. Like *Romeo and Juliet* without the feuding families."

"Precisely." She scootched a little closer to him on the mattress. "You may be on to something. If Romeo hadn't killed Juliet's cousin and had to flee the city, how long do you think it would have taken for the Montagues and Capulets to get together and put an end to the marriage?"

"Probably not long. They were blood enemies and they'd each want their child back. They might have been able to handle the friar because his goal all along was to end the feud."

"And the Carlsons and the Maitlands weren't even feuding. In fact they might have had a common goal, a dream for their only child that they wanted to see come to fruition. To fulfill that dream, they needed their child back."

Cam studied her as he thought about the possibility she was suggesting. "You actually think the parents might have had a hand in the breakup?"

"I'm beginning to wonder. Bunny Maitland is a very focused woman. She's got a daughter who in her view has married the wrong man. Then enter from stage right the perfect man for her daughter—Lawrence Banes. Ta da! In Bunny's eyes he's Prince Charming, and in his eyes, Rexie's the ticket to getting a small fortune from Maitland Investments."

"You think Banes was just lucky or did they team up?" Cam asked.

"It may have started out as accidentally serendipitous, but they're certainly working as a team now. When I talked to him right after the accident and then again in the clinic, he wanted me to call Bunny and say that the wedding was definitely on. Bunny, not Rexie. Maybe one of them got the Carlsons on board. I'd put good money on Bunny for that. Think about it. Two mothers with a common goal—they want the happiness of their child. A funeral might have started it all, but it got Dr. Barry to go back there—and then the communication lines break down. Rexie claims he stopped returning her calls. When I try to call either one of them, all I can do is leave a message. And it's Bunny's voice on Rexie's voice mail that tells me to leave it."

"Shades of *Romeo and Juliet* again," Cam mused. "Messages gone astray or intentionally blocked."

"Exactly. I want to fix it," Adair said. "If I could just figure out a way to get Barry and Rexie in the same room together."

He tilted his head to study her. Each time he was with her, he learned something new about her. "This wedding destination thing isn't just business for you. You're a true romantic."

She stared at him, shocked. "No. My sister Nell is the romantic. Piper is the cynic. I'm just plain practical."

But he was beginning to see that beneath the surface, she wasn't. She might work hard at giving off that vibe, but did a practical woman bury her secret goals and sexual fantasies in a stone arch because she believed it to have special powers?

For the first time since he'd come into the room, he took his eyes off her and swept his gaze around the space, noting even in the moonlight the feminine lines of the little love seat tucked away in an alcove and the vase of flowers on a nearby table. And there were candles in various shapes and sizes on a carved cherry dresser and more on the small nightstand.

It wasn't the way he would have imagined her room, but he thought it fit the woman he was coming to know—the woman who'd penned an action-adventure fantasy and buried it in a legendary stone arch.

"I have a plan." Two plans, he thought, as he rose and began to light the tapered candles. One of them would have to wait a bit. The other wouldn't.

"I'd say don't keep me in suspense, but I'm guessing that you're lighting the candles as a part of a plan to seduce me."

"All that covert training wasted." He found her CD player, selected an album and pressed a button. Debussey poured softly into the room. "I hope you won't rat me out to Daryl. He'll have me sent back to the farm for a brush-up course."

"My lips are sealed."

"And they're lovely lips," he said as he joined her on the bed again.

Surprise flickered in her eyes. "You don't have to say that."

No, he didn't have to say it. More importantly, he hadn't ever said it before. "Shhh." He leaned forward, brushed his mouth over hers.

Words. He'd found them for other women. Why was he having problems finding them for her? Drawing back, he met her eyes. "Do you remember the day our parents married?"

"Of course, I do."

"You were standing there on one side of the stone arch

with your hand on Reid's arm. Your dress was pale green and your curls…" He reached out to twine one of them around his finger. "They were all tumbled down like they are tonight, and there was a green ribbon the color of your eyes threaded through them."

Adair stared at him. "You remember my hair and what I was wearing?"

"I remember everything about you. I couldn't take my eyes off of you. And then you looked at me. Do you remember?"

All Adair could do was nod.

"My heart stopped."

Hers was stopping now.

He dropped the curl and ran just the tips of his fingers along her jawline. "I wanted you in a way that I'd never wanted any woman before."

The words weakened her so much that she could do nothing but stare at him.

"And I want you even more now."

They sat on the bed, their faces close, their mouths only inches apart. But when he moved, it wasn't to close the distance. Instead he rose and began to take off his shirt.

Without speaking, she got off the bed, as well, and they worked together to take off his clothes. Not too fast this time. The shirt came first, and when her hand encountered that firm warm flesh, she absorbed the first shock of heat. It took them longer to discard the jeans and shoes. But there was more pleasure as she watched the denim move down narrow hips and strong thighs.

When he was naked, he surprised her by lifting her off of her feet and then lowering them both to the bed. "My turn," he murmured. "I want to look and touch."

And he delivered on the words, tracing her face with

his fingers, rubbing her lower lip with his thumb, then trailing it lower to her throat where her pulse beat so fast.

"Your skin is so delicate looking in the candlelight. Like one of the porcelain dolls my mother used to keep locked away in a cabinet. She wouldn't allow my brothers and me to touch them for fear they'd break."

"I won't break."

"I know." He brushed his thumb over her collarbone, then moved his hand down the silk camisole to where it skimmed the tops of her thighs. "I think it's always been the contrasts in you that fascinate me. I thought of touching you like this the day of the wedding. Here." He trailed his fingers down her thigh, then up again and beneath the lacy hem of the nightie.

"Here." He began to trace a lazy pattern over her panties. Layer after layer of pleasure radiated through her from the clever movement of his fingers.

She arched up, trying to get him to the right spot, then went totally limp when he pushed the lace aside and slipped two fingers into her.

Only then did he lower his mouth to hers. As he slowly took the kiss deeper, matching the movements of his lips and tongue to the rhythm of his fingers, Adair felt everything else slip away.

There was only Cam. There was only this incredible pleasure he alone could give her.

As he guided her slowly higher and higher, he felt the surrender. Savored it, wanted to prolong it. But the first thread of his control slipped.

She was his. Knowing that, treasuring that, he had no thought but to give her more. And to take more.

As greed built, as the need to possess grew, his kiss became more demanding. Linking her arms around his neck, she moved with him, demanding more, taking more and more. His pulse pounded in faster and wilder rhythms as she fisted around his fingers. He knew the moment the pleasure grew unbearably tight inside of her, felt her shudder beneath him when it broke free.

Her arms were still around him holding him tight when he raised his head. "Look at me, Adair."

Her eyes, still filled with the pleasure he'd given her, met his.

"My turn again," he said. Then he let control snap.

The soft, dreamy pleasure he'd trapped her in vanished the instant he drove into her. The shock of his fast powerful thrusts, the glory of it had her crying out, wanting more. And he gave her more. Gave them both more.

Aroused. Thrilled. She met the demand, matching his unreasonable speed beat for beat. Her orgasm was fast too, ripping through her, then lingering in little aftershocks, until it erupted again when he reached his own release.

Afterward, when he could think again, Cam found that she was still beneath him, holding him tight. When he shifted to the side so that he wasn't crushing her, she snuggled into him.

"Don't go."

The words were barely a whisper, but they triggered a warmth that spread through him like a slow-moving river. He'd had no intention of leaving her to go back to his own bed, he realized, as he tugged up the covers.

That was a first for him, too. Though he couldn't explain it, watching her fall asleep on his shoulder in the flickering candlelight felt quite simply right. He lay there absorbing the feeling, relishing it, until her breathing had steadied and he was sure she slept. Slipping quietly from the bed, he retrieved his cell phone, then moved out onto the balcony of her room as he punched in his brother Duncan's number.

Duncan picked up after the first ring. "Trouble or a favor?"

Cam laughed softly. "We always call each other for the same reasons, don't we?"

"What are brothers for? Which is it?"

"A favor," Cam said. "If you're still in Montana?"

"Until tomorrow. I'm still fishing, but if you need—"

"The favor I need you for is in Montana." He gave Duncan the short version of the situation at the castle, the wedding problem, and then explained what he had in mind. "Can you do it?"

"It's an extraction operation, right?" Duncan asked. "You want me to go to the Carlson Horse Ranch and bring this Dr. Barry Carlson to Castle MacPherson. Doesn't the CIA usually send in a team to do this kind of thing?"

"It's not a CIA operation. And it has nothing to do with the sapphire earring or the other problems here at the castle. It's personal."

"How soon do you need him?"

"In the morning would be nice. Afternoon would do it. How soon can you get him here?"

Duncan snorted. "If I were Commander of the Starship Enterprise, I could beam him to you in a matter of moments."

Cam didn't reply because he could almost hear the wheels in his brother's head beginning to whir. Although it was the research angle that had drawn his brother to the FBI profiling unit, Duncan was very effective in the field.

"What are you planning?" Cam finally asked.

"I've got the location of the farm. It's about an hour from Billings, hour and a half from where I am. I'll have a couple of scenarios in mind by the time I get there."

"I just bet you will."

"Luckily I still have our team's private jet at my disposal, but you are going to owe me big-time for this."

"Keep me posted," Cam said.

"Ditto."

After disconnecting, Cam quietly slipped back into bed with Adair.

ADAIR HUMMED A little tune in her head as she stepped out of her room into the hallway. It was the first time in her life that she'd ever started the day with lovemaking, the first time she'd ever showered with a man. The first time she'd ever been in love.

That last little item on her mental list had her stumbling down the last step onto the landing above the foyer.

In love? When she felt that little flutter again right under her heart, she pressed a hand hard against her chest. The gesture did nothing to stop the sprint of panic. She was not in love with Cam Sutherland. He was her fantasy fling.

And she could not think about this right now. It didn't help that her gaze was fixed on the foyer where she and Cam had rolled on the floor that first night.

Which was barely a day and a half ago.

Don't think about it.

With her free hand she dragged a list out of her pocket. At nine o'clock Sheriff Skinner was supposed to arrive for an update. By eleven the caterers would arrive. And by one in the afternoon Bunny and Rexie Maitland and the wedding party would be here for photos.

But the first thing she needed was coffee. Taking a sharp right, she hurried down the hallway to the kitchen, then stopped short in the doorway.

Daryl Garnett and her Aunt Vi were locked in an embrace.

Before she could recover enough to make a quick retreat, Daryl drew away. "Adair is here."

Vi turned and beamed a smile at her.

Daryl signaled Alba, who was stretched out near the terrace doors. "I'll take the dog out for a run."

Even after Daryl had shut the sliders behind him, Adair still couldn't think of what to say. And she almost always could.

"I've shocked you," Vi said, a blush rising in her cheeks.

"No." Adair went to her then and took her hands. "You really like him, don't you?"

"Yes. Don't you?"

"Yes." Adair realized that it was true. She'd liked Daryl from the moment he'd walked down that incline and greeted Cam with a hug. "Cam thinks the world of him."

"When I first saw him, he reminded me a bit of Clint Eastwood—the *Dirty Harry* movies—dangerous, competent. He knew just what to do with Alba, finding the bump on her head, checking her eyes."

She turned then to look through the glass doors as Daryl threw a stick. Alba raced off to fetch it. "She loves him now."

It certainly seemed so, Adair thought as the dog raced back to drop the stick at Daryl's feet. He crouched down, and she licked his face lavishly.

"I love him, too," Vi said.

Adair stared at her aunt, uneasiness and happiness making a queasy mix in her stomach. "You're serious."

"Yes." Vi met her eyes and smiled. "It was love at first sight. I thought that only happened in books or movies or for Angus One and Eleanor. But I think I fell in love with Daryl from the moment he took my hand and told Cam that we'd go find Alba."

She drew Adair with her to the table so they could both

sit down. "It makes my knees weak to think about it. And I know exactly what you're going to say."

"You do?" Adair wasn't sure at all.

"You think it's too soon to know for sure and that falling in love and planning a future with someone takes a great deal of thought and a detailed plan."

A future? The queasiness in her stomach intensified. But it wasn't her aunt and Daryl she was worrying about now. How could you possibly plan a future with someone when you never knew what it would bring? Or how soon it might end.

"Aunt Vi, are you sure?"

"I've never been more sure. Oh, it flustered me at first to believe a man could be attracted to me after all these years. And it was a shock to realize that he could make me feel this way—giddy and…beautiful. He makes me feel beautiful, Adair."

Adair squeezed her aunt's hand. "Then I love him, too."

Vi leaned closer and kept her voice low. "I did the riskiest thing last night."

"You made love with him, I hope."

Vi blushed prettily. "Oh, yes. But first I took him out to the stone arch, and I kissed him. I wanted to make absolutely sure that he's it for me."

The women were holding each other and laughing when Cam entered the kitchen.

"Sorry to break this up, but the sheriff just pulled up. I think our strategy session is about to begin."

HALF AN HOUR later, Adair was perfectly clear on one thing. Her first big wedding at Castle MacPherson, as promised, had turned into an undercover op. Daryl had begun their meeting by having everyone coordinate their cell phones so that they could reach each other instantly on speed dial. They also had a code word to use if they needed help. "Angus" meant that there was a problem. "Eleanor" meant they had a full-out code red.

One day she was going to look back on this and laugh. For now she merely refilled her coffee mug. The tea seemed to be equally good. Vi had poured Daryl three cups. Her aunt looked like she was having the time of her life. Her cheeks were flushed, her eyes bright. Even brighter when she looked at Daryl Garnett.

"Essentially," Daryl said, "we've got a groom running a major scam and he has to marry the girl to get the money. And we want him to sign the agreement with Maitland before we arrest him. Otherwise we've got him only on intent to defraud and we'll have to hope that the chain of evidence in Oregon hasn't deteriorated or disappeared. Not to mention that if Scalzo makes bail on those charges, he'll pouf again."

"There's one other little twist we can add to the mix," Skinner said. "My deputy has learned that at Banes's request Bunny Maitland has hired a security service to provide protection for him. They arrived at the clinic late last night and they'll be transporting him to the wedding."

"So he's more worried about the cut brake lines than he wanted to admit to the local sheriff," Daryl said.

"And he may have a pretty good idea of who cut them," Cam said. Then he turned to Adair. "Why don't you take us through the schedule one last time?"

Adair went to the wall chart. Bunny Maitland had taken her over it so many times she could have recited it in her sleep. "The florist and caterers will arrive at eleven and begin setting up the ballroom for the reception. That's in the east wing." She pointed to the large room at the back of the castle.

"The bride and her parents along with the maid of honor

and the flower girl will arrive at one, and they'll use a suite of rooms above the ballroom to dress." She shifted her finger on the floor plan. "The groom and his best man and his new security entourage will arrive at two and they'll use a room over in the west wing. A team of photographers will cover all of that. Guests should start arriving at three-thirty, and the actual saying of the vows will occur at four-thirty, followed by champagne and food and dancing in the ballroom and the cutting of the cake at five-thirty or so."

She turned back to face the others. "If the groom hasn't been arrested by then."

"But the signing of the partnership agreement and any wire transfers that Banes will make—that could take place at any point in any room," Skinner pointed out.

Daryl rose to stand in front of the floor plan. "Maitland has held off on the signing until Scalzo actually marries his daughter. I'm betting that they'll close the deal directly after the ceremony." He tapped a finger on the floor plan. "They could use the groom's suite for privacy. Plus, it's close to the garden and almost on their way to the ballroom."

"Logical," Cam said. "Unless they make the signing part of the official celebration—a sort of welcome-to-the-family thing."

"We should be able to cover either option and pick up Banes as soon as he drives that proverbial nail into his coffin," Skinner said. "I've still got my deputy on him at the clinic. He'll follow Banes and his bodyguards and see that he gets here. But that still leaves us with the problem of this MacDonald guy. His agenda doesn't seem to be as clear."

"I've got an idea about that." Daryl moved back to his chair to pick up the folder he'd been carrying earlier. "I had time to play around with Adair's computer last night. I sent some images to a good tech man and he was able to send me these."

He opened the folder and passed each of them side-by-side enlarged photos of two men. "I had my guy age an old photo I had of Scalzo's partner. Then I had him take the beard and long hair off our friend MacDonald."

For a moment there was complete silence as they all studied the images.

"If it's not the same man, they're related," Skinner said.

The nods in the room testified to everyone's agreement.

"And he and Scalzo have had a falling-out." Cam leaned back in his chair, crossed his legs at the ankles. "Both of them were in the area when the earring was discovered, so both of them could have it on their radar. Which gives MacDonald two reasons to show up at the wedding. One, to finish off Banes, and two, to get the earring."

"If he does show up," Vi said, "Alba will know."

Daryl pulled another set of prints out of his folder. "I've also run off some copies of MacDonald as he appeared in the security disc with the beard. Even though I doubt he'll try to make an appearance in that persona again."

"No," Cam agreed. "He'll choose something that will blend in. That's his M.O."

As Daryl passed the pictures out, he said, "I figure we don't bother the catering and florist people because we don't want to spook the bridal party. But with the sheriff's two men and the four of us, we've still got quite a few people looking for this guy. We all have to blend in, too. This is a small wedding and we can't let Banes suspect that there's a bunch of security people here."

As the rest of them continued to discuss the blending-in part, Cam drew Adair aside. "You're nervous."

"It goes with the job." The concern in his eyes touched

her. "I'd be nervous even if we weren't planning to destroy a bride's wedding, catch a major criminal and try to predict what a crazy man might do."

"We'll all be on the lookout for MacDonald. Skinner's good and Daryl and I aren't half-bad." He leaned down and kissed her nose. "Just focus on doing your job. It's all going to work like clockwork. The wedding will take place, Banes will be arrested and you'll find a way to handle Rexie's heartbreak."

This time Adair felt more than a flutter beneath her heart. As she stood with him while the morning light poured through the terrace doors, she realized that it wasn't Rexie's heartbreak that was worrying her. It was her own.

15

"THEY MAKE A good team," Daryl said.

"I was thinking the same thing." Cam stood with his boss observing the two women through one of the archways that opened into the castle's official ballroom. Alba lay at Daryl's feet while Vi and Adair worked both separately and together to orchestrate an amazing transformation. Two hours ago the room had been an empty expanse of gleaming parquet floors and cream-colored walls. Now linen-covered tables were scattered along the walls to serve as food and drink stations. Flowers were everywhere.

Daryl sent a sidelong glance at Cam. "We're doing everything we can to keep them safe."

Cam knew that. The problem was that no one had so far gotten access to the castle who looked anything like Nathan MacDonald. And they'd been looked at by a lot of people. None of the florists or caterers or any of their drivers bore any resemblance to the images that Daryl's tech man had captured on the prints.

"I promised Vi we wouldn't let anything happen to Adair. So we won't."

No, they wouldn't. Adair was in business mode with

her curls sternly disciplined into a knot at the back of her head. She wore a professional-looking pale gray linen suit. A notebook was in her hand and she kept methodically checking things off.

"I've never met a woman quite like her," Daryl said.

Since the words echoed his own thoughts, it took Cam a beat to realize that Daryl was talking about Vi.

Turning, Cam studied his friend's face. Daryl was looking at Vi as if he simply couldn't take his eyes off of her.

"She was the last thing I was expecting when I came up here," Daryl said. "But she's it for me. She's everything I want."

Cam shifted his gaze back to Adair. She was it for him, too. Hadn't he know that seven years ago when he stood with her under the stones? He turned back to Daryl. "So what are you going to do about it?"

Daryl met his eyes. "I'm going to adjust my plans to include Viola MacPherson. I'm going to ask her to marry me. But first, we have a fake wedding to pull off and an arrest to make."

As if on cue, Cam's cell phone rang. It was Sheriff Skinner. "The bride's side of the wedding party and a photographer have arrived."

"This is where the fun starts," Daryl said.

TWO HOURS LATER, Adair took the stairs two at a time and ran full tilt into Cam on the landing.

"Whoa," he said. "Stop. Take a breath. Everything's fine in the bride's suite."

She narrowed her eyes. "How do you know?"

"I edged the door open and took a peek. Bunny is running the photo session like a little general."

It would be a waste of time to tell him he wasn't supposed to be peeking. "I need to check in with them anyway. The groom and the best man are here safe and sound in their room. The father of the bride has joined them for coffee."

He smiled at her. "Confess. You sneaked a peek in there, didn't you?"

"I didn't have to. Daryl has the room pretty well staked out. And Aunt Vi just took a tray of sandwiches and some tea and coffee in. The two hired security people are going to get Banes to the stone arch in a wheelchair. The doctor hasn't okayed the crutches yet."

"What did I tell you? Everything is proceeding like clockwork," Cam said. "And I have some good news for you."

"What?"

"After our talk last night, I called my brother Duncan and sent him on what you might call a little fishing expedition."

She narrowed her eyes on him. "And that is good news because?"

"He's in Montana. He paid a visit to the Carlson Horse Farm, and he caught quite a big fish."

She grabbed his arms. "Will you stop talking in CIA code and tell me? What did he find out?"

"Your theory about blocked messages and conspiracy were right. And your hunch that the mothers were engineering that part was spot-on. After Barry went home for the funeral, Bunny and Barry's mother became very friendly. Bunny evidently explained in great detail just how unhappy Barry was in the practice on Long Island and convinced the other woman to help her thwart communication between the two kids. Mrs. Carlson came up with a few creative ideas of her own. Barry wasn't even aware he'd sent Rexie a letter asking for a divorce, nor that he'd signed the divorce agreement. His mother ad-

mitted to Duncan that she got his signature both times in
a flurry of paperwork she handed him."

"Duncan found all this out since we talked last night?"

"He's a damned good agent. An even better brother.
He's bringing the doctor here even as we speak. Barry
wants to talk to Rexie. I thought maybe it might help to tell
her that when Lawrence gets arrested and hauled away."

Adair grabbed him and kissed him long enough and
hard enough to make her head spin. "Thanks." She had to
blink to clear her vision. "I'll thank you better later. But I
have to get to the bridal suite."

"Everything's going like clockwork," he repeated before he released her.

Adair hurried up the rest of the stairs. The problem was
that everything *was* going like clockwork. But that didn't
mean squat. Because so far no one had spotted Nathan
MacDonald. The only drama that had occurred so far was
when Alba started barking her head off at the limo that
delivered the bride and her attendants to the front door.
After that, Aunt Vi had banished Alba to the kitchen.

She knocked once and then stepped into the suite she'd
assigned to Rexie and her bridal party. The photo shoot
was in full swing. Bunny had hired a team of photographers. One was assigned to Lawrence Banes, another was
taking candids of the arriving guests. And yet another
had arrived with Rexie, her attendants and her mother
in the limo.

There were flowers here, too, along with the remains of
the champagne and sandwich tray she'd sent up right after
she'd originally escorted them to the room. She'd had no
time to speak privately with Rexie, but the young woman
wasn't nearly as nervous as she'd been at the rehearsal.

Not that she looked terribly happy. More determined.
But even if she was a tad short of glowing, she made a

beautiful bride. The photographer, a woman with straight, chin-length black hair and seriously framed glasses, had Rexie posing in front of a full-length mirror. The maid of honor and the flower girl stood to one side while Bunny peered over the photographer's shoulder.

"Stand up straight, Rexie honey," Bunny directed. Then, stepping to the side of the photographer, she showed the woman a photo. "Make sure you capture the full length of the train in the mirror. Rexie's dress is a copy of the one I wore for my wedding, and I want the picture to look exactly like this one."

"No problem, Mrs. Maitland." The photographer took several shots.

If Rexie was less than glowing, her mother more than made up for it. Adair thought of Rexie's first wedding—an elopement that Bunny had missed. In spite of herself, she felt a tug of sympathy for the woman. And she couldn't deny the amount of work that Bunny was putting in to make sure that this day was perfect—for both of them.

Then Bunny waved the maid of honor and the flower girl into the photo frame. The camera began clicking again.

"Smile, Rexie," Bunny encouraged. "This is the happiest day of your life."

Adair felt her stomach tighten, then ruthlessly ignored the feeling. However bad today was for the poor bride, there were going to be happier days ahead. And one day—soon, she hoped—Rexie would be very grateful that she hadn't actually married Lawrence Banes.

When the photographer paused for a moment, Rexie sent Adair a smile and a wave. Bunny turned around and hurried toward her.

"What's wrong?" she spoke in a low voice as she

reached Adair. "Is it Lawrence? Has something happened?"

"No. He's here. The photographer is taking pictures as we speak. The guests are being directed to parking areas. Everything's moving along right on schedule."

Bunny glanced back at the photo shoot. The glow on her face had faded. "We don't have any shots with the flowers yet. Can you handle that? I have a list of the poses I want."

"Of course."

Bunny handed her the paper. "I need to see Lawrence. I need to know that nothing else unexpected is going to happen."

Adair felt another pang of empathy for the woman. A groom in a leg cast and wheelchair was probably not the way that Bunny had envisioned her daughter's wedding pictures.

And there were worse disappointments to come. She put a hand on Bunny's arm. "It's going to work out." She had to believe that.

"I just want my daughter to be happy. From the time she was a little girl, I've wanted to give her the perfect wedding day."

Adair's heart sank. But she managed to say, "Lawrence wants that, too. And he's here. You have to give him kudos for that."

"Yes. Okay." Bunny drew in a deep breath and let it out. "I still have to check on him. The bouquets are in the adjoining room."

"I'll take care of it." Adair glanced at her watch. Less than a half hour to wedding march time. "When the photographer's finished, I'll bring them all down."

The second she closed the door to the suite behind Bunny, Adair leaned against it and allowed herself one deep breath. The photographer gestured the maid of honor and the flower girl to the side, then shifted to take shots of the bride from a different angle.

"Jennie and I will help you get the bouquets," the maid of honor said.

As Adair followed them, she passed the full-length mirror and she as she did, something in the reflection tugged at her memory. In the doorway of the adjoining room, she glanced back to identify what might have caught her attention.

Nothing.

The photographer had moved to take a different shot. She was a woman in her forties, with a sturdy build and one of those enviably straight, black bobs that no doubt required regular appointments in an expensive salon. And she was good with Rexie, talking softly to her as she raised the camera to take the next shot, then shifting position and lifting the camera again.

Nerves, she thought. And she didn't have time for them now. It wasn't until she lifted the bridal bouquet out of its box that she felt the tug again. And this time she realized what was causing it.

Images flashed into her mind. The photographer's hands, the familiar way they gripped and moved the camera.

Then came the voices. Daryl saying that wigs were standard tools of disguise. Alba barking when the bridal limo had arrived and Vi banishing her to the kitchen. Cam saying that the way best way to get into the wedding would be to "blend in."

Adair shoved down hard on the hysterical laugh that threatened to bubble out. What better way to blend in than to arrive in the bridal limo with the bride and her mother?

Her mind was spinning so fast that she wasn't even

aware she'd moved back into the main room until she heard Rexie's gasp. "Oooooh, they're beautiful."

Jerking her mind back to the present, Adair crossed to the young girl and handed her the cascade of roses and lilies of the valley. The remaining shots had to be taken. And she had to think.

But her mind had switched from fast-forward mode to slow motion. Any small hope she had of being mistaken or hallucinating faded as she watched the photographer take the next series of shots.

She was looking at Nathan MacDonald all right. The hands, even the way he let the camera hang from the strap on his shoulder—it was all so familiar. Why hadn't she noticed it sooner?

There was no time to plan, but she knew what she had to do—she had to separate MacDonald from the bridal party and she had to keep him away. If his goal was to get revenge on Banes by stopping the wedding, Rexie could be in mortal danger. And if his goal was to get the sapphire, well, she could use that as a distraction.

Walking forward, she took Rexie's hands in hers. "It's time to go. Lawrence is already on his way to the stone arch." She barely kept her hands from trembling as she gathered up the train and gave it to the maid of honor. "You're in charge. Once you get to the foyer, go straight out through the front door and then wait on the garden path just as we did at the rehearsal."

Out of the corner of her eye, she watched MacDonald cover his camera lens and move toward his case.

"Aren't you coming with us?" Rexie asked.

"I'll be right behind you. I have a couple of shots to discuss with the photographer. Your mother gave me this list."

Then without another look at MacDonald, she shooed them out of the suite.

IT WAS ALBA's muffled barking that drew Cam from his post in the foyer to the kitchen. He had to nudge the dog away from the door as he entered.

"What's upsetting her?" he asked Vi as he patted the dog's head.

"She wants to go out that door."

As if to prove the point, Alba moved to it and then turned to stare at them.

"I can't let her out," Vi explained. "Not after the commotion she caused earlier when the bridal party arrived in that limo."

Alba didn't move away from the door. She stood her ground even when Daryl entered through the sliding terrace doors.

"Anything?" Vi asked him.

"Everything's running smoothly outside," Daryl said. "The last of the guests are parking. Both Mr. and Mrs. Maitland joined the groom for the photo shoot, and from what I could hear through the terrace doors they intend to sign the papers there right after the ceremony."

"But so far there's been no sign of Nathan MacDonald," Vi said.

Daryl looked at Cam. "Maybe he's decided to keep a safe distance, wait until Scalzo is in the stone arch, and then detonate the bomb."

"I don't think that's the plan. At least not his whole plan, because it doesn't get him the earring. That's got to be what he's after. Scalzo's partner is a patient man. He works behind the scenes, researching the targets, gathering data. So he's had time since the *Times* article to look into the connection between the missing sapphires and the

Queen of Scots. For fifteen years he's been content to stay out of the limelight. That all fits with the person who's been visiting the library. Then suddenly he comes out of the shadows to pay a personal visit to the castle to talk to Adair. That visit to Adair wasn't about Banes. It was all about the earring. The best chance he has of getting it is through Adair. I'm betting she's his target."

He whirled back to face them. "And he had a camera when she gave him the wedding tour. Maybe that's how he's blending in."

"One of the photographers," Daryl said.

"The last time I saw her she was headed toward the bridal—" The ringing of his cell cut Cam off. He glanced at the caller ID. "It's Adair."

But when he held it to his ear, he heard nothing.

16

ADAIR PAUSED AT the top of the stairs, waiting until the two women and the little girl rounded the landing and started down to the foyer. Only then did she slip her hand into her pocket and close it around her cell.

"Thank you, Ms. MacPherson."

The voice sent a chill down her spine. Because it was Nathan MacDonald's voice. Not the husky voice of the photographer.

"For what?" She kept the smile on her face as she turned to face him. Then for just an instant her mind went blank. It wasn't a camera he held in his hand now, but a small, efficient-looking gun.

"For getting rid of the girls so that we could discuss our business."

"Business?" Slowly Adair drew her gaze away from the weapon and met MacDonald's eyes. The large framed glasses were gone now and she could see that his eyes were calm. And cold. Cold enough to send another chill through her system.

"No need to panic," he assured her. "I just have a proposition for you."

"A proposition? I don't understand." Adair struggled

for composure. He was able to read her too well. And she wasn't going to panic. She couldn't afford to. In her pocket, she pressed the number that she hoped was Cam's and sent the call.

"Oh, I think you do. But we can't talk here." He smiled as he gestured for her to move away from the stairs and away from the bridal suite they'd just left. "We need some place quiet away from the wedding party and guests."

"The library. It's in the west wing. We'll be alone." Adair led the way down the corridor.

"You can stop pretending that you don't recognize me as Nathan MacDonald. I have very good survival instincts. I felt it the moment my disguise failed me. I was sure of it when you rushed the bride and her attendants out of the room. And you saved me the trouble of finding an excuse to keep you behind. After all, the wedding must go on, right?"

Right. Opening the door, she led the way along the balcony that formed the second floor of the library. She heard a muffled sneeze behind her and kept walking to the sliding doors that opened onto the outside balcony. "This was Eleanor's favorite room."

Another muffled sneeze.

She had no idea if her call had gotten through, but she'd remembered the code word—"Eleanor" meant code red. That small detail gave her confidence. Turning, she faced MacDonald and the gun.

"Shit." Swearing helped hold off the fear. Cam held his cell pressed to his ear, then nearly tripped over Alba as he led the way out of the kitchen.

"Is Adair all right?' Vi asked.

That was the uppermost question in his mind. "I can barely hear her." But he'd caught one muffled word. *El-*

eanor. Code Red. So MacDonald had her. But he didn't want to say it. Couldn't afford to think about it. Not when he had to keep fear and panic at bay.

In the foyer he cursed silently when they had to pause for the bride and the two attendants cascading down the stairs.

"Where's Adair?" Vi asked them.

"She's right behind us with the photographer," Rexie said. "We're supposed to wait for them on the garden path."

Just then Alba began to bark.

"Where is—" Cam turned, searching for the dog.

"Alba stopped at the door to the library," Daryl said.

Of course, Cam thought. It was the logical place for them to go. And Adair's mind was very logical. She'd want him away from the wedding. And for MacDonald, the library had to be the room he was most familiar with. He'd suspect that the key to finding the rest of the jewels would be there. For the next few minutes—he doubted they had more—he had to think the way Adair and the man threatening her would think.

He took Vi's hands. "You take the wedding party outside and go on with the ceremony. I'll send Adair to you as soon as I can."

Vi met his eyes for a minute, then nodded. "I'll hold you to that."

Then she smiled at Rexie and led her away with her attendants.

"The library." He spoke in a low voice to Daryl as they walked back to where Alba was barking. "Alba knows where they are."

"The damn photographer," Daryl said. "The dog tried to tell us when the bridal limo arrived."

When they reached the door, Cam turned to his friend.
"Here's what we're going to do."

Less than sixty seconds later, he was climbing up the
wall to the right of the library's balcony.

"You're already familiar with the space, aren't you?"
Adair asked. "You've been spending a lot of time here."

He glanced around. "No. You left it off my tour the
other day." He nearly sneezed, but caught himself in time.
His hand remained steady on the gun.

"Let me open the balcony doors and let in some air,"
she offered. If Cam decided to climb up the outside wall,
he'd need access to the room.

MacDonald muffled another sneeze and gestured her
to go ahead. She shoved them all the way open. The only
sound that drifted in was the breeze ruffling the pines.
The wedding hadn't begun yet. But surely someone had
to have noticed she was missing. Bunny would. So would
Vi. Somehow the message would get to Cam. All she had
to do was keep MacDonald talking. "So what exactly is
your business proposition?"

"You seem to be a practical person, Ms. MacPherson,
so I want to make you a deal. You give me the sapphire
earring you found the other day and I'll let you get on with
your big wedding. So much depends on it. The future of
your fledgling business as well as the little sting operation you're cooperating in."

Adair simply stared at him.

He laughed then, but the sound was threaded with
anger, not amusement. "Oh, I know what you're up to. I
waited around to see if Lawrence Banes survived his little accident yesterday. And I recognized Daryl Garnett,
CIA agent extraordinaire, the moment he got out of his
car. I'm not as stupid as my longtime partner. I told him

six months ago that it was time to take the money we'd made and run. The Securities and Exchange Commission was sniffing around. They've become more vigilant lately. But he couldn't pass up the extra fortune he could make by marrying Winston Maitland's daughter. The agreement they sign today will allow my partner to access millions with a few strokes of his fingers on a computer keyboard. The money will be in his offshore accounts before the cake is cut. And I taught him everything he knows."

MacDonald's voice had risen steadily, driven by his growing anger. Adair heard Alba start barking above it. The sound was muffled. Distant. The dog would know where they were, but she had to keep MacDonald talking and distracted so that Cam could make his move. "Your partner wouldn't listen to you."

"No."

For the first time, Adair saw the full strength of the man's fury in his eyes. It bordered on madness. And it had to be fueled by more than a disagreement over money. Outside, she heard the music begin. The wedding party had assembled. The fake minister had taken his place.

"But you stood by him and tried to convince him for six months. What did he do to make you want to kill him?"

"He told me that he wanted to buy me out. He'd give me half the money we'd already made and then I could take a hike. My services would no longer be needed."

He used the fingers of his free hand to tap his chest. "*My* services that planned every con we've pulled for over fifteen years. *My* services that had allowed him to escape the law on several occasions and kept him out of jail."

"He dumped you."

"No. I'm going to dump him. I thought of killing him, but it will be much more satisfying to think of him rotting in jail. Especially when he learns that I used his precious wedding as a cover to walk away with a priceless sapphire."

He dipped his free hand into his pocket and pulled out a small black box. "But I'm flexible on that. If you don't give me that earring, I'll press this button and there'll be an explosion in the stone arch. While it's filled with people."

The music changed, signaling that the bridal attendants should line up near the end of the garden path. The groom and his best man had taken their places beneath the stone arch. She could picture it so clearly in her mind. Where was Cam?

"The clock is ticking," MacDonald said with a smile that didn't reach his eyes.

She caught a glimpse of Cam to the right of the balcony door. But MacDonald still had the gun. She had to rattle him enough to allow Cam to make his move.

"The earring," MacDonald prompted. "I was up in the hills after the rehearsal and I saw you and your aunt find it. You know where it is. I researched this place in your local library this morning. The most obvious place to hide it was Angus One's secret cupboard. It wasn't there. But you know where it is."

"Yes, I know exactly where it is." Adair folded her arms over her chest. "Someone told me once that it's not over until the fat lady sings. And I'm not going to give you the earring."

"You have to." Some of the fury in his eyes was replaced by surprise. "You have to or I'll blow everyone up. I'm not kidding."

"No, you're not kidding." She pointed to the device he held in his hand. "But you're not going to be able to pull it off. That thing won't work. We defused the bomb."

"No. You're lying." But he glanced down at the box in his hand. And in that second of inattention, Cam gripped the ledge at the top of the balcony doors and swung his feet through and up to knock the gun out of MacDonald's hand. He landed close enough to plant a fist in the man's face.

MacDonald fell like a rock.

"Good work, Princess," Cam said as he quickly turned the man over and secured his wrists.

"You good up there?" Daryl called.

Adair saw him step out from beneath the balcony, his gun raised.

"Yeah." Then Cam grinned at Adair. "Get out of here. You've got a wedding to run."

IT'S NOT OVER until the fat lady sings.

Adair kept repeating the phrase over and over in her head as she raced down the garden path. She wanted to make sure that when that song finally came, there'd be a happy ending for Rexie. And there was one thing she still had to do.

The wedding march hadn't started yet. She had time. Careening around the last curve, she caught sight of the bridal party just as her aunt Vi signaled the maid of honor to start down the aisle.

"Rexie," she said breathlessly as she reached them. "I need…a word?"

Without waiting for an answer, she took the girl's hands and drew her out of earshot of her father.

The wedding march began.

"What is it?" Rexie asked, her eyes wide.

Adair leaned close enough to whisper. "Don't kiss Lawrence."

Rexie stared at her. "What about the legend? I thought the kissing part was the whole idea."

"Rexie, it's time." Winston's voice was soft, but very firm.

Over Rexie's shoulder, Adair saw that the guests had all turned in their direction.

"Make some excuse. He's in a wheelchair," Adair whispered urgently. "Tell him you'll make it up to him later. I don't have time to explain. Just trust me."

Rexie nodded, then turned to her father and let him lead her away.

All Adair could think of to do now was cross her fingers. When Vi joined her, she filled her aunt in on what had happened in the library. "Cam and Daryl have everything under control." Now all they had to do was get through a fake wedding and the arrest of the groom. "One villain down and one to go."

She tried not to think about the devastated bride.

Vi took one of her hands and squeezed it as Lawrence Banes took Rexie's hand from her father's. "I want to know what you told her before you sent her up the aisle."

"I told her not to kiss Lawrence. The marriage might not be real, but I just couldn't let her kiss him beneath the stones."

Vi chuckled. "That's my girl."

"Except I ran the risk of turning her into a runaway bride."

"She's not running."

As soon as Winston Maitland returned to the first row of chairs to take his seat next to Bunny, the fake minister began, "We are gathered here together…"

Adair hardly dared to breathe until he pronounced them man and wife.

When Rexie gave her new husband a hug instead of a kiss, Adair clapped her hands in relief while the guests applauded their congratulations.

The wedding party was halfway down the aisle of chairs when Cam joined her.

"Good news," he said. "Sheriff Skinner just got a call from his man who was screening the guests as they arrived, and it seems we have some party crashers."

"Duncan and Barry?" she asked.

"I told my brother to keep Dr. Carlson in the car until we get the bridegroom and the father of the bride back into their suite. Daryl and Sheriff Skinner are running that show."

Vi looked from one to the other. "Dr. Carlson—you're talking about Rexie's first husband?"

"Yes," Adair said. "Cam arranged for Duncan to extract him from Montana. Can you distract Bunny for a bit while I talk to Rexie?"

Vi's eyes gleamed. "I know just what to do. I'm sure she'll want to help me lead the guests into the ballroom." She hurried away.

Cam linked his fingers with hers as they watched Winston Maitland and two security men wheel Scalzo off to the groom's suite. Vi was true to her word. She had Bunny's ear. A moment later the two women were headed toward the castle and the guests were following them down the path.

A photographer was posing the bride and her two attendants beneath one of the arbors.

"You got a plan once you get Barry and Rexie together?" Cam asked.

"I don't have a clue," she admitted, and tried very hard to ignore the nerves jittering in her stomach. "Any advice?"

"Do what you're good at. Jump in feetfirst and go with the flow."

That had never been what she thought she was good at, but she didn't have a choice. "I'm going to send the maid of honor and the flower girl to the castle. Then I'll take

Rexie to the stone arch to talk with her. When I give you the signal, you call Duncan and have him deliver Barry. Then can you go and help Aunt Vi keep Bunny and the guests occupied?"

"Will do." He couldn't have come up with a better plan himself, Cam thought as she walked away.

Once she had Rexie alone, she took her hands and drew her toward the stone arch. "There's someone here who wants to talk to you," she said. "But first, I have a story to tell you."

Adair waited until she and Rexie were seated on the ledge that ran along the inside of the stone arch before she told it. "There's bad news and good news," she began.

"You're scaring me," Rexie said.

Adair took both of her hands and related the Lawrence Banes/Gianni Scalzo story, including the fact that he would be arrested any moment and taken to jail. Rexie didn't interrupt, but Adair could read every emotion on her face—disbelief, shock, horror.

"I married a crook."

"No," Adair said. "I told you there was good news. You're not married at all. The man who presided over the ceremony wasn't a minister. He had no authority to marry you. You're still a single woman."

A sheen of tears appeared in Rexie's eyes, but there was relief, too. "Really?"

Adair squeezed her hands. "Really. And I think I might ·have even better news. There's someone here who wants to talk to you."

"Who?"

Nerves knotted in Adair's stomach. This part could go either way. But she turned and signaled Cam. Seconds later, a man stepped out of one of the parked cars in the driveway and ran toward the stone arch.

Adair stepped a distance away to give the couple privacy. But the look in Rexie's eyes when she'd seen Barry Carlson had told her everything. Hope and love. Those two things were what the legend of the stone arch were built upon. It had been what had worked for Eleanor and Angus One. And when Barry took Rexie into his arms and kissed her, Adair knew exactly what she was going to do next.

In the rose arbor, Cam lingered long enough to see Barry Carlson kiss Rexie Maitland beneath the stones. They would find their happy ever after now.

The question was: would he?

17

CAM WATCHED ADAIR for a moment longer, debating whether or not to join her. He'd told Duncan to hang around and keep an eye on things. And she'd asked him to keep the parents occupied. But first he had to check on how Daryl's sting operation was going down. Not that he doubted for a minute that it would run smoothly.

Turning, he wound his way down the garden path following the last of the guests. The terrace doors to the groom's suite were open. Pausing, he used one of the trees in the garden for cover and looked into the room. Gianni Scalzo sat at a table in front of a laptop. It was running like clockwork, he thought. A couple of strokes on the keyboard and Winston Maitland was offering his new "son-in-law" a cigar. The moment that Daryl and Sheriff Skinner stepped into the room, Cam moved closer so that he had a clear view of Scalzo's face. And the man was good. Even as Skinner read him his rights, Scalzo registered only innocence and confusion. He turned to Maitland. "They're making a mistake. You have to vouch for me. I just made you and your clients very rich. I just married your daughter. I'm family."

Daryl stepped forward with the handcuffs. "You just

tried to fleece him for every penny he's got. And this time we've caught you in the act."

He clamped one of the cuffs to Scalzo's wrists and the other to the arm of the wheelchair. Then he met the man's eyes. "I told you back in Italy we'd meet again."

"You." Scalzo yanked at the cuffs.

"Yeah." Daryl smiled at him. "Payback's a bitch, isn't it?"

"You'll never prove a thing," Scalzo said, his voice rising.

"We've got enough to put you away for a very long time," Daryl said. "But even if we didn't, your ex-partner's going to turn on you just the way you turned on him."

Cam had the very great pleasure of seeing Gianni Scalzo turn pale.

"I don't know what you're talking about."

"You will," Daryl said.

Cam waited until the sheriff and one of his men wheeled Scalzo out before he strode into the room to join Daryl. "You okay?" he asked.

Daryl grinned at him. "It was almost worth the wait to see the look on his face when he realized he's not going to wiggle out of this one."

Cam turned his attention to Maitland then. The man's face was nearly as white as Scalzo's had been. He'd want to be with his wife and daughter. But Adair needed more time. He moved toward him. "Mr. Maitland, why don't you come with Daryl and me?"

A HALF HOUR later, Cam sat with the Maitlands, Vi and Daryl in a small anteroom that offered privacy as well as a view of the ballroom where guests were sipping champagne and enjoying the view of the lake.

Daryl had filled them both in on Lawrence Banes's

real identity and the fact that he'd been discreetly escorted off the grounds by Sheriff Skinner and his men. Then Cam had told them about Barry Carlson's arrival and the bare-bones sketch he'd received from his brother Duncan. Bunny's complexion had paled considerably while he and Daryl were talking.

As Cam wound it up, Maitland turned to his wife. "You actually conspired with Barry's mother to engineer our daughter's divorce? Why?"

"Because I love her." Bunny pulled a handkerchief out of her purse and dabbed at her eyes. "She was so unhappy. And he was trying to convince her to go back to Montana with him. I couldn't let that happen. And then Lawrence came into our circle. He was just perfect. And that's all I ever wanted for Rexie—a perfect wedding day, a perfect marriage."

Maitland shook his head, but he reached for his wife's hand. "The only thing Lawrence Banes was perfect at was running a con."

Eyes sheened with tears, Bunny lifted her head and met her husband's gaze, "You liked him. You were the one who thought up the business merger."

"Maybe not," Daryl said, addressing Maitland. "I'm betting it was one of your clients who introduced you to Banes, and you only brought it up after you heard the buzz about how profitable his investments were."

Maitland frowned as he thought for a moment. "As I recall, it did happen that way."

Cam looked at Bunny. "Was it your idea to get Barry's mother involved?"

It was Bunny's turn to frown. "Lawrence may have suggested it. He was so empathetic to Rexie's unhappiness and my desire to change that. He mentioned that Barry's mother might feel the same way. So I called her and we decided that they'd be happier if they stayed in their own worlds. She just wanted what was best for her son."

"And Banes—did he also suggest that you could help things along if you kept them from talking or communicating with one another?"

"Yes," Bunny admitted. "And it worked."

"Dammit, Bunny. Banes nearly ruined us," Maitland said. "And think what it's going to do to Rexie's happiness when we have to tell her the truth about him."

"He's damn good at what he used to do," Daryl said. "I've been chasing him for over fifteen years."

Bunny glanced through the glass doors at the guests who were now casting curious glances at them. "He certainly ruined my daughter's wedding day."

"Maybe not," Cam said. He'd caught a glimpse of Adair threading her way through the guests with Rexie and Barry in tow.

Once she'd entered the room, she beamed a smile at everyone. "Mr. and Mrs. Maitland, this is a first at Castle MacPherson. Today you are going to get two weddings for the price of one."

IT WAS A double wedding day he would never forget, Cam decided. Two for the price of one is exactly what Adair had delivered. Cam stood with his brother at the edge of the ballroom terrace as Dr. Barry Carlson danced with his bride under the stars. Bunny Maitland was giving instructions to a photographer while Adair stood at the edge of the dance floor waiting to cue the bride's father. The young couple had been remarried beneath the stone arch just as the sun had set on the lake. By a real minister this time.

"Good work, bro," Cam murmured to his brother.

"I'd say it was good work all around." Daryl joined them and passed out beers.

"Compared to the two of you, my extraction mission wasn't much of a challenge," Duncan said. "All I had to do was explain what had evidently been going on to Barry. His mother caved right away and admitted to conspiring with Bunny Maitland. But she'd been having second thoughts for months because her son wasn't happy, and he was still calling Rexie. The truth was he'd been planning a trip back to Long Island to see if she'd at least talk to him in person. I'm really sorry that I didn't get him here in time to help out with the sting operation."

"You did play a role in that," Cam said. "The fact that I was able to let Adair know that you were bringing Carlson back helped her to pull off the fake wedding. And you definitely played a role in getting Barry and Rexie their happy ending."

On the dance floor, Winston Maitland cut in on the groom to dance with his daughter.

"Speaking of our little sting," Daryl said, "I checked in with Sheriff Skinner and he says that MacDonald is still so angry with his old partner that he's singing his head off. Which means that their victims will be getting at least some of their money back. The only thing he won't admit to is breaking into the library. He admits that he knew about the missing sapphires, but never gave them much thought until he saw Adair and Vi unwrap the earring."

Cam frowned. "That means there's still someone out there who has been sneaking into the castle on a regular basis."

"A new higher-tech security system will put an end to that," Duncan said.

"Not if what they're after is the rest of Eleanor's dowry," Cam countered. "And now that one of the pieces has shown up, I'd be more motivated than ever to find the rest."

Duncan sipped his beer. "Since it looks like the two of you will be paying regular visits to the castle, you'll just have to track them down first."

Cam nearly choked on his beer, and Daryl laughed. "We always have room for an FBI profiler. Why don't you join us?"

Duncan raised his free hand, palm outward. "Not me. I'm staying as far away from that stone arch as I can get."

"Good luck with that," Daryl said. "I'm going to dance with my fiancée."

"Fiancée?" Cam murmured as Daryl walked away.

Duncan clapped him on the shoulder. "I had a chat with Vi. Your boss doesn't believe in wasting time."

No, Daryl didn't waste time. A good CIA agent didn't. And Cam felt he'd wasted seven years already. But it was impossible to get Adair alone. The cake had to be cut, the bridal bouquet had to be tossed, an endless number of pictures had to be shot. And everyone wanted to dance with Adair. He'd had to cut in on the groom to get a word with her.

"You worked a miracle today," he murmured as he pressed her close.

"No, the legend did all the work," she said.

"You were the one who talked them into getting re-married here today."

Adair smiled up at him. "I got the idea when they kissed beneath the stone arch. I mean—why not? Their fate was sealed."

Hadn't he thought the same thing when he'd seen them kiss? And his fate was sealed, too. For seven years he'd avoided accepting that.

"We need to talk," he said.

"Sure. Later." She smiled at him as the father of the bride cut in and whisked her away.

Cam tried to use the time as the wedding wound down to come up with a plan. He needed a good one.

THE LAST OF the guests were locating their cars when Adair slipped away to her office. She needed a moment to think. Barry and Rexie were going to stay in Glen Loch in a bed-and-breakfast. She'd arranged that right after she'd made a call to Reverend Foley. And they were going to talk about their future. Before they'd left the stone arch, they'd been talking about perhaps spending part of the year in Montana and part in New York.

The important thing was that they were talking. Nerves jittered in her stomach. They'd been dancing around there ever since Cam had told her they needed to talk. And he was looking for her even now.

Adair sank into her chair and dropped her head in her hands. She knew what he wanted to talk about. They'd made a deal. They would enjoy each other until his work here was done. And it was. Scalzo and his partner were under arrest and her wedding problem was solved. The fat lady had sung.

And she'd gotten just what she wanted—her Sutherland fantasy fling.

Unless you do something about it.

Lifting her head, she looked at the metal box. Then she tore a yellow sheet of paper off of a legal pad and wrote down what she really wanted before she placed it with her other dreams and fantasies. Maybe it was time she tapped into that power again. Grabbing the box, she hurried out of her office.

AFTER SEARCHING EVERYWHERE, Cam found her in the stone arch on her hands and knees. The moment he called her name, she rose and turned. As he walked toward her, the nerves that had been skittering through his system all afternoon intensified. She was the only woman who'd ever made him feel this way. The only one he'd ever wanted to plan for. To plan with.

He just had to pray that he could sell his plan to her.

The air was perfumed with flowers and moonlight gleamed in a bright path across the lake as he joined her beneath the stone arch. For just a moment, Cam had the feeling that they were not alone. He thought of all the couples through all the years who'd stood right where they were standing and who'd found what the legend promised. Looking into Adair's eyes, he knew he wanted what they'd wanted.

"I want to talk to you about us," he began.

Adair felt something tighten around her heart. Maybe she'd tapped out all the power by getting her fantasy fling.

"Things have happened very fast between us."

She couldn't seem to get a breath. He was going to say that they'd had a great time and now he had to go back with Daryl to D.C. and she would have to get ready for the next wedding. He'd be in touch. And he probably wouldn't be.

She didn't want to hear it. "I know what you're going to say. You have to go back with Daryl. You'll be in touch, but—"

"No. Yes." He took her other hand, gripped both of them hard. "Don't put words in my mouth. I'm having enough trouble finding the ones I want on my own. I've tried all day to come up with a plan. And I'm really lousy at this."

"A plan?" She stared at him.

"There hasn't been enough time. I want more...I need more...."

"Time for what?" Then, because she saw some of the turmoil she was feeling in his eyes, she shut up.

Cam took a deep breath and let it out. "I want more time with you. I need more time to—I want to be able to give you your fantasy."

"My fantasy?" Baffled, she stared at him. "Is that some kind of CIA code I'm supposed to crack?"

"No." He released her hands to grip her shoulders. "I'm speaking in plain English. Here's the plan. I want to give you your secret fantasy. I just need more time."

She stared at him. "My secret—"

Then she suddenly got it. She pushed his hands away and then used her own to give him a shove hard enough to send him stumbling back against the wall. "You read what was in that metal box, didn't you? How could you?"

"I'm a CIA agent. I'm curious. And I wanted to know more about you. Dammit, I've been wanting to know more about you since I was ten. And I think I fell in love with you the day our parents got married."

Because her legs had gone suddenly weak, Adair sat down on the ledge that ran along one side of the arch.

"Well?" Cam asked.

For a moment, she couldn't speak. He looked angry. And stunned. She could sympathize with the latter. "That's what you wanted to talk to me about? That you fell in love with me seven years ago?"

"No. I came out here to tell you about my plan. Just because I'm in D.C. and you're here doesn't mean that we can't spend time together." He waved a hand. "I was thinking long weekends. Once we get the security beefed up here. We still don't know who's been visiting the library." He was starting to babble. He never babbled. "I know you like to look at the big picture. And you can feel free to fill in the details."

When she simply stared at him, he paced to the far end of the arch, then walked back. He never paced, either. He was good at improvising, and he was blowing this. Panic bubbled up. "Look, I don't know why or how this happened, but you're right for me. And I want to be the one who gives you your fantasy. The only one. Because you *are* my fantasy. You're everything. Clear enough?"

She studied him for a moment as everything inside of her melted. He was standing there, scowling at her, and the tension inside of her completely eased. Cam preferred to go with the flow, act on impulse. It was one of the things she liked about him. Loved about him. But he'd tried to make a plan for her. And as odd as it seemed, he was right for her, too. He was just simply right for her. And she wanted him forever. That's what she'd written on the yellow paper she'd just buried in the stones.

Rising, she moved toward him. "About this plan—is it a five-year one or longer?"

He studied her for a moment and she could see the tension flow out of him, too. "Longer."

She put her hands on his face and drew it down to hers. "How much longer?"

He was smiling as he lowered his mouth to hers. "I think it's going to take me quite a while to fulfill your fantasies."

"But you did say I could fill in the details. So when you finish, I'm going to start on your fantasies."

He laughed as he drew her in close and held her tight. "That will take a lot of time," he promised. "I have a lot of them. And I'll be making up new ones as we go along."

"Sounds like a plan," Adair said.

They were laughing as they sank to their knees beneath the stone arch that Angus One had built for his true love.

"Tell me again that you love me," she said when his lips were nearly brushing hers.

"I love you, Adair."

"Here's another detail. I love you, too."

And when Cam covered her mouth with his, a whisper of wind sighed across the stones.

* * * * *

Dear Reader,

I'm thrilled to be back with the latest and final installment in the sexy BRADDOCK BOYS series! It's Colton Braddock's turn, and believe me, he's more than ready. Once the brave, courageous leader of *the* most notorious Confederate raiding group during the Civil War, Colton is now a vampire tormented by his past. He's spent over one hundred and fifty years blaming himself for the massacre that killed his son and destroyed his home. No more. He now knows who the real killer is and he's determined to have his revenge once and for all.

His plans are side-tracked, however, when he meets Shelly Lancaster, a strong-willed deputy sheriff with her own agenda. Shelly is tired of reading about hot, mind-blowing sex. She wants to experience it for herself, and so she's on a manhunt to find the perfect partner. When Colton walks into the Skull Creek Sheriff's Office, she knows in an instant that he's just the cowboy for the job.

I hope you've enjoyed riding along with the Braddock Boys these past few books. While I'm saying goodbye to Skull Creek and my beloved cowboy vampires for now, I'll be back in 2013 with a new series featuring the small town of Lost Gun and a trio of wickedly hot brothers named after the most notorious outlaws to ever blaze through Texas!

I love to hear from readers. You can visit me online at www.kimberlyraye.com or write to me c/o Harlequin Books, 225 Duncan Mill Road, Toronto, ON M3B 3K9, Canada, or connect with me on Facebook.

Much love from deep in the heart!

Kimberly Raye

THE BRADDOCK
BOYS: COLTON

BY
KIMBERLY RAYE

First published in Great Britain 2012
by Mills & Boon, an imprint of Harlequin (UK) Limited,
Eton House, 18-24 Paradise Road, Richmond, Surrey TW9 1SR

© Kimberly Groff 2012

ISBN: 978 0 263 89383 0
ebook ISBN: 978 1 408 96927 4

14-0812

Harlequin (UK) policy is to use papers that are natural, renewable and recyclable products and made from wood grown in sustainable forests. The logging and manufacturing processes conform to the legal environmental regulations of the country of origin.

Printed and bound in Spain
by Blackprint CPI, Barcelona

USA TODAY bestselling author **Kimberly Raye** started her first novel in high school and has been writing ever since. To date, she's published more than fifty-eight novels, two of them prestigious RITA® Award nominees. She's also been nominated by *RT Book Reviews* for several Reviewers' Choice awards, as well as a career achievement award. Kim lives deep in the heart of the Texas Hill Country with her husband and their young children. She's an avid reader who loves Diet Dr Pepper, Facebook, chocolate and alpha males. Kim also loves to hear from readers. You can visit her online at www.kimberlyraye.com or follow her on Twitter.

This book is dedicated to all of the wonderful readers who love the Braddock Boys as much as I do. You make writing the best job in the world!

1

IT WAS OFFICIALLY the worst moment of her romantic life.

Shelly Lancaster read the singles ad printed in yesterday's edition of the *Skull Creek Gazette* and the Red Bull she'd guzzled at lunch churned in her stomach.

> SWF seeks single, adventurous, incredibly sexy male for hot, mind-blowing sex (no serious relationship wanted). One night only. Instant chemistry a must. For a really good time, email: shellylancaster@skullcreeksheriff.com.

WTF?

Her chest tightened and the air rushed from her lungs. No. No, no, no, no, *no!*

Why had she gone to all the trouble of setting up an anonymous email account—hookmeup@hotmail.com— when no one had even bothered to use it?

Panic bolted through her and she fought for a breath. At least now she understood why her Monday had been straight out of an episode of the *Twilight Zone*.

She should have known something was up. She'd felt the familiar twinge in her gut yesterday. That instinct telling her that something was about to happen.

Something bad. Really bad.

She'd assumed it had something to do with the new prisoner that had been delivered on Saturday. The entire office was on pins and needles because of Jimmy Holbrook. At only twenty-three, he'd built quite a reputation for prison escapes. He'd waltzed out of all four of the facilities where he'd been housed and the Texas Rangers were determined he wouldn't walk out of number five. Hence the transfer to a maximum security prison in El Paso. But in the rush to get him under lock and key at an adequate facility, there had been a few mistakes with his transfer paperwork. Which meant that Jimmy was currently locked up in a back cell awaiting an armed escort to take him the last leg of his trip. Until the paperwork got sorted out, he and the Texas Ranger parked outside his cell were stuck right here in Skull Creek. Hence the churning in her stomach.

Or so she'd thought.

She eyeballed the extra-large container of chocolate body paint sitting on the corner of her desk, a big red bow sitting on top. Justin Wellborn, one of the hottest cowboys to ever two-step across the floor down at the local dance hall, had dropped off the stuff just ten minutes ago and asked her to go back to his place tonight. Before that had been Will Freeman who'd brought a basket of scented massage oils. Kip Walker had come bearing edible underwear and some guy she hardly knew, who worked down at the Dairy Freeze, had shown up with fuzzy zebra-print handcuffs.

They'd all wanted one thing.

Because they thought *she* wanted one thing.

Because the ad that was supposed to protect her identity and list only an anonymous email address had printed the real deal, complete with her name.

Her *name*.

This was *not* happening.

"Big plans tonight?" Sheriff Matt Keller's voice slid into her head and scrambled her thoughts.

She slapped the newspaper closed and whirled. "Just the usual," she blurted, scrambling for a semi-plausible explanation. Anything better than the truth. All she had planned was a glass of wine, a hot bubble bath and a few hours curled up on the couch, watching Bud & Sissy fall madly in love in *Urban Cowboy.* "I'll probably clean my gun or watch whatever game's on ESPN."

"Must be some game." His gaze slid past her to the risqué gifts sitting atop her desk.

"This?" She waved a hand and played on the off chance that Matt had yet to see the personals. "This stuff is for a friend of mine." Her brain raced. "It's for

her, um, party. A bachelorette party." Hey, it sounded
better than what was really happening. *I hate to be
the bearer of bad news, but your number-one deputy
is sexually frustrated and trying to break a three-
year fast.*

Ugh. Matt had enough to worry about. On top
of Holbrook, the town's annual chili cook-off and
roping festival started in less than three days. That
meant parking issues, drunken festival-goers and
lots of litter. She didn't want to add *hormonal female* to the list.

He eyed the items one more time and smiled.
"Good for you. It's nice to see you're having a little fun."

His choice of words punched a nerve and she stiffened. Shelly recalled going to bed hungry one too
many nights because her mother had been too busy
having *fun* to bother making dinner or earning a
steady paycheck. Fun had its price and it wasn't one
she was willing to pay. She liked having food in her
refrigerator and money in the bank and, even more,
peace of mind.

"I'm just collecting the stuff," she blurted, sweeping an arm across the desk and stuffing it all into
her top drawer. "I'm not actually going to the party.
I'm on duty." She slammed the drawer shut. "So, um,
what time does your flight leave in the morning?"
she asked, effectively changing the subject.

"Seven a.m." He glanced at his watch as if he'd
just remembered something. "Hells bells, I need to

get out of here. I promised Shay we'd have a candlelit dinner to kick off tomorrow's trip."

Which was why Shelly was in this mess in the first place.

Instead of worrying about Holbrook or the chili cook-off, Matt was leaving everything to Shelly and running off on a romantic getaway with his new wife.

The man had fallen head over boot heels and was now living the proverbial happily-ever-after. That coupled with the fact that Shelly's younger sister had just spent the past six months planning *the* biggest wedding the town had ever seen, had forced Shelly to re-evaluate her own love life.

Or lack of one.

She was twenty-nine years old. She'd never been married. No kids. No pets. She spent most Saturday evenings either on duty or catching up on paperwork, determined to make something of herself. To be the best. To be someone.

Anyone other than the timid little girl who'd hidden under the bed while her mother had spent her nights down at the local honky-tonk. Shelly had been so scared back then. So helpless.

Never again.

She could outrun, out-throw, outshoot and out arm-wrestle any deputy in the department. With the exception of Buck Kearney, of course, but he had a good two hundred pounds on her. She'd even won Best Throwing Arm during the department's annual softball tournament last year thanks to a little bit of skill, a lot of luck and the fact that the current champion had come down with a stomach bug from eating too many ribs. She was strong-willed. Competitive. Tough. Fearless. At least that's what everyone thought and Shelly had always been more than happy to perpetuate the myth.

Until now.

She wasn't ready to put on her Grandma Jean's lace wedding dress and waltz down the aisle just yet, however. One day maybe. *Hopefully.*

But right now, she had too many responsibilities. She was on the fast track to becoming the first female sheriff of Skull Creek. Matt was retiring in six months to run a bed and breakfast with his new wife, and Shelly wasn't letting anything derail her between now and then.

She didn't want to shed her image and fall in love. She wanted to *make* love. While she'd had a few sexual encounters over the years—in the backseat of Mikey Hamilton's Chevy back in high school and under the bleachers with Casey Lewis during rookie training—they'd been few and far between. She'd had a very limited supply when it came to sex, and she'd never had really good sex.

She wanted one night with a man who stirred the pulse-pounding, do-me-right-now-or-I'll-die chemistry she'd only read about in her favorite romance novels. A few blissful hours to satisfy her starved hormones so that she could stop fantasizing and get back to work.

Not that she was broadcasting that info to the world. She had an image to maintain, which was why she'd placed an *anonymous* ad in the local singles section. Or so she'd thought. Her plan had been to find a man privately—preferably one from any of the surrounding small towns that subscribed to the *Gazette*—and live out the very explicit fantasies heating up her lonely nights. She would have been able to get it out of her system without any of the locals being any the wiser.

Another glance at the paper and her stomach twisted.

"Don't forget the security specialist coming tomorrow for the upgrade." Matt's voice pushed past her pounding heart.

"Tell me again why we need a security upgrade?"

"Because if we had an upgrade, we wouldn't have a Texas Ranger babysitting our prisoner." He motioned to the door leading to the holding area. "The clearance paperwork should be sitting in my email first thing in the morning. Just give him a tour and he'll take care of the rest," Matt tossed over his shoulder as he headed for the door.

The minute the knob clicked, she snatched up the newsprint and signaled to the assistant deputy sitting at a nearby desk.

"Keep an eye on things," she told the man.

"Me?" Bobby Sparks glanced behind him. He

was fresh from the academy and the newest addition to the sheriff's department. Like any good rookie, Bobby didn't so much as wipe his butt without asking permission first. "You're giving me my first assignment?"

Shelly put on her most intimidating face. "Keep your eyes open and don't let anyone past the front desk while I'm gone or else Ranger Truitt will tear me a new one. The holding area is on complete lockdown until Holbrook moves on."

"I'm on it." Bobby's grin spread from ear to ear as he bounced to his feet. "I've been doing simulated fire fights on my Xbox at home. I'm ready for anything."

Oh, boy.

"I'll be back in ten minutes." Shelly stuffed down the worry that roiled inside of her when Bobby paused to check his gun belt. "I'll be on my radio if you need me. And remember, no visitors in the holding area. *No one,*" she reminded him. He could handle this. And even if he couldn't, Beauford Truitt was parked outside Holbrook's cell keeping watch on things.

Everything would be okay.

She tamped down her worry and focused on the task at hand—killing the ad before it became the talk of the entire town.

And then she pushed through the door and headed for the *Skull Creek Gazette.*

"IT'S JACKSON'S fault," declared Minerva Peters, the editor-in-chief of the newspaper. "He's our typesetter. Been with the paper going on forty years now. He doesn't see as well as he used to since the cataracts set in. But don't you worry—" Minerva gave her an apologetic smile "—we'll refund your money right away."

"I don't want a refund. I mean…" Shelly's mind raced. "*I* don't want a refund because it's not *my* money. I placed the ad for a friend. You were supposed to use her email, not mine."

Realization seemed to dawn and Minerva smiled. "But of course you did. I knew something was funny about this whole thing. Now if the ad had asked for a female, that I could understand."

"Excuse me?"

Minerva waved a hand. "Don't be shy, honey. I'm the eyes and ears of this town. I know *everything*. Besides, it doesn't take a rocket scientist to figure it out. You never date. You go around dressed like this all the time." She waved a hand at Shelly's uniform. "And you beat up Henry Rogers at the town picnic last year. You obviously butter your bread on the other side just like my niece over in Houston. Why, she came out of the closet just last year and settled down with a cute little hairdresser. Gets free highlights now and everything."

She was not hearing this.

Shelly drew a deep breath and tamped down the anxiety ebbing through her. "First off, this is my uniform. I *have* to wear it. And I didn't beat up Henry. I beat him at arm wrestling, and it was only because he had a pinched nerve." She wasn't sure why she blurted out the truth, but there was just something about the way the woman looked at her—as if she had her completely figured out—that made Shelly want to prove her wrong. "I like men," she heard herself say. "A lot. Just so you know."

"Sure you do." The woman winked as if to say *"It's our little secret."*

All the better, a voice in her head whispered.

That same voice had kept her from telling the entire world that she didn't need the basket of massage oils that had been left on her desk. Not because she wasn't interested in those things, but because she already had her own. She also had chocolate body paint and a pair of fuzzy handcuffs. Pink ones, as a matter of fact. Sure, she'd yet to use them. But still. There was more to Shelly Lancaster than just the rough and tough exterior that everyone saw. She was soft on the inside. Feminine. Just like any other woman.

Just like her mother.

She drop-kicked the thought and eyed Minerva. "I don't want a refund. I want a retraction explaining the mistake."

"No problem. I'll get right on it."

"Great." Relief ballooned in Shelly's chest. "That's the best news I've heard all day."

"Next week," Minerva added, her voice like a pinprick which quickly deflated any relief Shelly had been feeling, "in our very next issue."

"But we need to fix this today." Panic bolted through her. *"Now."*

Minerva shrugged. "We're an itty bitty publication, honey, with a piss poor circulation. Sure, we deliver to the surrounding towns, but their populations are small. We can't afford to put out more than one issue every Sunday."

Which meant the paper would be out there for the world to see for five more days. Her stomach dropped and her eyes burned.

She blinked frantically because no way was she going to start bawling in front of Skull Creek's biggest gossip. Talk about the kiss of death.

"In the meantime," the woman went on, "I wouldn't worry. Hardly anybody is reading print anymore what with that damned internet. Why, Henry Jenkins orders five copies just to line his parakeet cages. And if somebody does actually read it, I'm sure they'll realize we made a mistake." Minerva shook her head. "To think *you* placed an ad like *that?*" The woman shook her head. "Why, it's plum crazy."

"It's not *that* crazy," Shelly blurted before she could stop herself. "I mean, somebody obviously believed it, otherwise I wouldn't have these." She held up the handcuffs as if to say *aha!*

Minerva waved a hand. "There are always a few crazies in the bunch. Testimony to the fact that when men get horny enough, they start to lose brain function. Once those desperate souls open their eyes and realize who they're dealing with, they'll run the other way, honey. Guaranteed."

Gee, thanks.

Shelly ignored the unexpected wiggle of regret and focused on the all-important fact that Minerva was right. No man in his right mind would believe the ad was for real. For the few who did, she would simply set them straight.

News of that would spread well before the newspaper could print a retraction.

A day or two and it would all be over.

She knew that. She just wished it didn't bother her so much.

2

HE WAS WATCHING her again.

Not her, in particular, of course. It was the sheriff's newly arrived prisoner that really got his blood pumping. He'd been hanging around the office for the past three nights now. Watching. Waiting. The female deputy was just an added bonus.

He eyed the beige SUV as it pulled up to the curb out front. The door opened and the driver slid out from behind the wheel. The now familiar brunette walked around the nose of a brown and white Ford Explorer and strode up the steps of the two-story brick building.

The sweet, succulent scent of ripe cherries drifted through the open window of his black Ford F250 pick-up parked across the street. His nostrils flared, his gut clenched and his stomach hollowed out. A wave of awareness rolled through him and he shifted on the leather seat.

It was a crazy-ass reaction considering she barely

looked female with her hair stuffed up under a stiff cowboy hat and her body hidden beneath the drab beige uniform. Reacting to her was friggin' certifiable.

If he'd been your average cowboy.

But Colton Braddock had stopped being a run-of-the-mill wrangler the day he'd drawn his last mortal breath. He was a one-hundred-and-fifty-year-old vampire who fed off both blood and sex, and he was hungry.

Starved.

He watched her pull open the door. Her trousers pushed and pulled, outlining her perfect ass for one delicious moment. His gut tightened. A shiver worked its way up his spine. The uniform, the hard facade, the back-the-hell-up attitude were all just a front for what lay beneath—a soft, curvaceous, passionate woman. Call it instinct. A sixth sense. A vampire's prerogative. Whatever. He *knew* and damned if it didn't work him into a frenzy.

Heat zig-zagged through his body and his heartbeat kicked up a notch. He drew a deep breath. Not that it helped, but old habits died hard, even after an entire century.

Easy.

The command echoed through his head and he drew another breath. And another. While the oxygen didn't sustain him the way it once had, the repetitive motion helped draw his focus away from the demanding need. Watching her was one thing. Touching? Not a chance in hell.

He had plenty of bagged blood stashed back in his suitcase at the motel. More than enough to see him through the next few days while he was stuck in Skull Creek, Texas. While it didn't taste half as good as the fresh stuff, he could make do. He *would* make do. The last thing he needed—the very *last* thing—was to get sidetracked by a woman. Even one that smelled better than a prize-winning cherry pie fresh from the oven.

Not no, but *hell* no.

He'd waited too long for this moment.

For revenge.

The door rocked shut behind her and he forced his attention to the plain brick building.

The jail was a throwback to the olden days with its steel bars on the windows and doors. Appearances aside, he wasn't naive enough to think that the place hadn't been modernized over the years. The sheriff himself was a good friend of Colton's younger brother. The man was also a werewolf. While weres were few and far between and usually at odds with most vampires, Matt Keller was a good man. Trustworthy. He often joined forces with the handful of vampires in town when needed, just as he'd done now.

Once he'd heard the reason for Colton's visit, he'd been more than happy to brief him on the security features that had been installed over the past decade.

An automated lock system. Full camera set-up. Silent alarm. While the local jail wasn't a long-term facility, it was more than adequate to house the average prisoner.

Career criminal Jimmy Holbrook was a completely different story.

The man had been convicted of armed robbery this time and was now sitting inside a cell awaiting transfer to a maximum security prison in El Paso to serve out his sentence.

But it wasn't his crime that had him featured in every newspaper this side of the Rio Grande and a shitload of YouTube videos. It was the fact that he had a "knack" for escaping. At least that's what the media called it.

Colton called it an accomplice.

The sun had set a half hour ago. The overhead spotlights had kicked on, bathing the steps in a soft yellow glow. The place seemed calm. Peaceful. Quiet.

Too quiet for a vampire hell-bent on rescuing her only kin.

While his three brothers felt certain Rose Braddock would come to help her one and only descendant, just as she had time and time again since his first arrest at the age of fifteen, Colton wasn't so sure. She'd turned her back on family once before.

He could still see the billows of black smoke on the horizon and smell the putrid stench of ashes and burned cattle flesh. It had been one hell of a homecoming after four years raiding for the Confederacy. He and his brothers had given Quantrill and his boys a run for their money way back when, but the effort had been wasted. The South had lost and the Braddock boys had headed home to the Circle B to pick up where they'd left off.

He'd ridden up ahead of the others to find what was left of his beloved home, the buildings a smoldering pile of charred wood, the livestock either scattered or dead. And the people…

His throat tightened and bitterness worked its way up. A half-dozen ranch hands had died that night, burned beyond recognition. And the foreman. And his mother. His son. His wife.

Or so he'd thought.

But Rose was alive.

Guilty.

While he had no idea if she'd started the fire herself, he knew she'd played a part. Thanks to his younger brother Cody, they all knew the truth now. Rose hadn't died that night. She'd fled the scene with another man and left them all to perish.

But Colton and his brothers hadn't burned to death. They'd been saved by a vampire, turned just in the nick of time. Garrett Sawyer had happened on the scene by chance and given them another shot at life.

At revenge.

Ironically, he'd bestowed the same gift on Rose. Unknowingly, of course. The ancient vampire never would have turned her if he'd known that she'd practically murdered her family. When he'd run across her a few miles from the scene, he'd thought her and her partner an innocent couple ravaged by savage Indians.

He'd been wrong.

The past stirred along with images from that night. The burning house. A frantic horse. The limp body of a small boy, his face charred so badly he was unrecognizable.

His fingers tightened on the steering wheel. The metal bent, giving way beneath his strength until his prints were permanently indented.

It had been so long since he'd thought of his son. Too long. But with the memory came the pain and so he tucked it back down deep until the pressure inside of him eased. His grip relaxed, but he didn't let go.

Not of the steering wheel, or the anger. He held tight, feeling the heat as intensely as the hunger that now lived and breathed inside of him.

He'd lost everything because of Rose. She was a liar. A traitor. She'd sold him out, which was why his pride hesitated to believe that she would show up now in support of her last living relative. But his head… His head knew the truth.

The pattern was clear. Every reported escape mentioned a visit by a mysterious redhead just prior to the breakout. It *had* to be her.

And if she'd come all those other times, she would come now.

In the meantime…

His gaze shifted to the front window. Through the bars, he watched the deputy pull off her hat and set it on the corner of her desk. Her breasts trembled ever so slightly beneath the stiff blouse, the motion so subtle that he doubted anyone inside even noticed.

He did.

He noticed everything. The slight quiver of her bottom lip. The frantic staccato of her heartbeat. The sweet, succulent aroma of a woman who'd gone far too long without a man.

He fought against a wave of heat, but it was a fight he was destined to lose. He was burning up from the inside out after seventy-two hours cooped up on surveillance. Hungry. Desperate.

For an up close and personal look of the jail, he reminded himself. He'd been biding his time, sleeping during the day and watching all night, waiting for his ticket inside so he could vampire-proof Jimmy's cell in preparation for Rose.

It wouldn't have been a problem if Jimmy had been your average prisoner, but the jail was on lockdown with all deputies on high alert and a ball-busting Texas Ranger parked inside. While Sheriff Matt wanted to help the Braddock boys, he couldn't jeopardize his reputation in the process. Colton needed a believable cover and proper clearance if he wanted access.

Enter Brent Braddock. Colton's brother was an ex-security specialist with friends in high places. He'd managed to get to the right people and pull some strings. Soon Colton would enter the Skull Creek Sheriff's Office as a county-contracted security consultant. His job? To evaluate and perform an upgrade on the current system.

His ticket inside would be ready first thing in the morning and he could quit watching and start doing.

Tomorrow.

He just had to hold out a little longer, bide his time a few more hours. That's what Colton told himself, but damned if he didn't slide from behind the wheel and start across the street anyway.

3

It was too quiet.

Shelly came to that conclusion the minute she sat down at her desk and realized that Bobby was nowhere in sight. Not hunched over his computer or playing video games on his phone or standing in front of the coffeemaker. Her gaze shifted to the men's room.

No doubt the double cheeseburger he'd had at noon had finally caught up to him.

That's what she told herself, but she couldn't shake the strange feeling that something wasn't right. Something besides the local diner's lunch special or the fact that Monty Darlington had left a message on her voicemail asking her if she wanted to get busy back at his place tonight.

Take that, Minerva.

"Bobby?" She tapped on the door. "You okay?"

The only sound that prickled her ears was the steady hum of the air conditioner. She knocked harder. Once. Twice. Her hand tightened on the knob. A loud creak and she found herself inside the one-stall bathroom.

Empty.

Panic sizzled through her for a split-second before she tamped it back down. He was probably out back, talking the hat off the Texas Ranger on duty with Holbrook. Probably shooting the shit and drinking coffee.

She turned toward the containment area, ready to prove her theory when Bobby's voice crackled over the dispatch speakers.

"Mama Bear, this is Baby Bear. You copy?"

A few swift strides, and she punched the button on the microphone. "Would you stop with the nicknames?"

"It's not a nickname. It's code. You never know who might be listening."

"I know exactly who's listening. Martin down at the feed store is the only one with a police band radio and he only tunes in on bridge night to make sure his ex-wife doesn't drink too many mimosas and start streaking again. Where are you?"

"Picking up Honey Gentry. We got a call that she was soliciting outside the Sac-n-Pac," he continued. "They needed a squad car out here asap, so here I am."

"But I told you to stay put."

"And I told him otherwise." The grizzled voice came from behind her and she turned to see her resident Texas Ranger standing in the doorway that led to the cell area.

Rumor had it Beauford Truitt was the oldest Texas Ranger still on active duty and, some said, the toughest. He had snow-white hair, a weathered face and a pickled expression that said he wasn't too happy to be stuck in a one-horse town with Texas's Most Wanted prisoner in tow.

He held a cup of steaming black coffee in one hand and a half-eaten bear claw in the other. "Ain't no sense in him neglecting his duties. Just go on about your business and leave Holbrook to the professionals."

"We *are* professionals."

Yeah right. His expression read loud and clear and Shelly had the fleeting thought that she was in over her head. It was a feeling she'd had many times before when the job had gotten a little too dangerous or her coworkers a little too condescending.

It was a feeling she'd grown all too familiar with growing up with a mother who didn't love her half as much as she loved her social life. All those nights alone had forced Shelly to step up and take care of her little sister when she'd been just a child herself. And while she'd done her best, she'd never managed to shake the uncertainty.

Not that this guy knew that.

She gathered her courage and met his glare head on. "I give the orders here."

"Sure you do, darlin'." He winked. "The prisoner's my responsibility."

"And you're both *my* responsibility, at least while you're in this Sheriff's office." She narrowed her gaze, making it clear she wasn't backing down no matter how many times he called her *darlin'* or *sugar* or *sweetcheeks* or whatever else his *good ole boy* mentality managed to cook up.

Seconds ticked by before he shrugged and she gave herself a mental high five.

"Get some fresh pastries in here before I choke to death," he grumbled, waving the half-eaten goody at her. "This one's as tough as shoe leather." He walked over to the white bakery box sitting next to the coffeemaker and rummaged inside.

Shelly shifted her attention back to the radio. "Finish up and get back here," she told Bobby.

"Yes, ma'am. Baby bear out." The connection ended and Shelly turned toward her desk, her heart still beating double time.

She blew out a deep, easy breath, careful not to let Truitt know that he'd gotten under her skin. She'd come up against his type too many times to count and she knew the worst thing to do was get visibly rattled. It was all about staying calm. In control. Fearless—

The thought faded into the *whooooooosh* of the front door and the heavy thud of boots.

"I'm looking for Shelly Lancaster," came a deep, masculine voice.

Here we go again.

With Truitt eyeballing her from the coffeemaker, the last thing she needed was a potential suitor carrying another bottle of edible body paint. She had to set the record straight right here and now and put an end to all the nonsense.

"It was a misprint" died a quick death on her tongue when she turned to face off with the man standing in the doorway.

Her heart hitched and all she could do was stare for a long, breathless moment.

He had cowboy written all over him with his straw Stetson and button-down denim shirt. The cuffs had been rolled up to reveal muscular forearms, the tails tucked in at his trim waist. Soft, faded jeans clung to his long legs. A rip in the material gave her a glimpse of one strong, hair-dusted thigh and her throat went dry.

She eyed the scuffed toes of his brown boots before dragging her gaze back up, over his long legs, the hard, lean lines of his torso, the tanned column of his throat, to his face.

Brown hair streaked with the faintest hint of gold brushed his broad shoulders and drew attention to his rugged features. A day's growth of stubble darkened his jaw and outlined his sensuous lips. Blue eyes so pale and translucent they were almost gray collided with hers.

No, it wasn't the way he looked so much as the

way he looked *at her* that sucked the air from her lungs.

"Yes, um, that would be me. At your service," she finally managed to say, her voice breathless and excited and downright giddy.

She stiffened at the realization. No way, no how, would tough-as-nails Deputy Shelly Lancaster let a man—even one as good looking as *this* man—turn her into a pile of quivering Jell-O. She frowned and summoned her most no-nonsense voice. "Is there something I can do for you?"

She had to give him credit. He wasn't the least bit put-off by her tone. Rather, a slow, purposeful grin spread across his face and her stomach hollowed out. "I can certainly think of a few things."

The deep, seductive words echoed in her ears, slipping and sliding along her nerve endings and Shelly knew in an instant that this was it. This was what she'd been reading about. Dreaming of. Searching for.

This was chemistry. Pure and simple.

Potent.

Real.

She enjoyed the heat zinging between them all of five seconds before she gave herself a mental shake that kick-started her common sense. He couldn't know that she'd really been the one who placed the ad. No one could. Which meant she'd better start explaining. And fast.

That's what she told herself, but for a long, heart-pounding moment, she couldn't actually get the words out. There was just something about the way he looked at her, as if he saw every little secret, as if he *liked* what he saw, that stalled the explanation on her tongue.

Instead, she breathed in, drinking in the delicious scent of raw leather and virile male. Electricity hummed through her body and sent tiny shock waves straight to her nipples. Her throat went dry.

"I hate to break up this party," Truitt said, shattering the spell and yanking her back to the here and now and the all-important fact that he'd just witnessed her momentary lapse into desperate female. "But some of us have work to do." A smirk tugged at his mouth as he turned on his heel, coffee cup in hand, and disappeared into the backroom.

She glared after the old man before turning the same look on Mr. Tall, Dark and Yummy. "I don't know you," she finally said, despite the strange inkling that she'd seen him somewhere before. She needed to get back on track. Focused. "And I know everybody in this town."

"The name's Colton Braddock."

She arched an eyebrow. "Any relation to Cody Braddock?" Cody was an ex-bull rider who'd moved to town not long ago. He and his blushing bride were now living happily ever after on the outskirts of town.

"He's my brother."

"You're late. The wedding was two weeks ago."

Something dangerously close to regret flickered in his gaze before fading into those pale, unnerving eyes. "I didn't get the invite in time." He stared at her, into her, and she felt the heat rising up from her feet, whispering through her body and igniting everything in its path. "I've got a cattle spread out in New Mexico. It's a little off the beaten path and the mail isn't what it should be." He shrugged. "But it suits me just fine. I like my privacy."

The words echoed through her head and stirred a completely inappropriate vision of him, the moonlight bathing his naked body as he stood in the middle of a ripe green pasture. He wore the same grin that he was wearing right now and her heart skipped a few beats.

"Privacy is good," she heard herself murmur and his grin widened.

"Oh, it's better than good, sugar." The words stirred another decadent vision and her body trembled. *Trembled,* of all things. It was a reaction straight out of a romance novel. The stuff of fantasies.

But it was real, she reminded herself again.

He was real. And he was here right now.

Thanks to a disastrous misprint.

"I didn't advertise for sex," she blurted, the denial tumbling out before her hormones could block the way.

Surprise gleamed a split second before fading into the pale blue depths of his eyes. A grin tugged at the corner of his mouth. "That's good to know."

"The ad was for a girlfriend of mine," she rushed on. "I placed it for her and the paper accidentally listed my e-mail instead of hers. But if you knew me, you'd know there was no way I would ever do something like that. I'm not the type."

"And just what type are you?" he asked, and she had the distinct feeling that he really wanted to know. That he wanted to know *her*. The fact seemed to startle him if the frown that tugged at his mouth was any indication.

For the first time, she noticed that he wasn't carrying edible undies or massage oils or anything else out of a *Naughty Nights* catalog. Rather, he carried a duffel bag and a clipboard. Realization struck, along with a rush of disappointment.

"You're not here about the personal ad, are you?"

He shook his head. "I'm the private security consultant hired by the county to analyze your current system. I'm sure Sheriff Keller must have mentioned me."

"He did. He also said to expect you tomorrow."

"I finished up my previous job a little early so I thought I'd get a head start." He gave her a disarming smile. "We're not talking any major changes. Just a few added precautions to keep you guys on the transfer schedule with the major prisons. You do take transfers, don't you?"

She nodded. "We had one delivered a few days ago. There was some confusion with his paperwork.

He's sitting here while they sort out the transfer details and then we'll be handing him off to El Paso."

"Perfect. I'll take a look inside, make sure he's safe and secure." His gaze slid past her and for a brief moment, without his full attention fixated on her, she felt a niggle of doubt.

There was something slightly *off* with Colton Braddock. Something she couldn't quite put her finger on.

"It's really late," she heard herself say, "and I've got a lot of loose ends to finish up before my shift ends. Why don't you come back tomorrow? I can show you around then."

"And give you time to check out my credentials?" He arched an eyebrow.

"I have to follow procedure." She shrugged. "I'm sure you understand."

He swept a gaze around the room, seemingly memorizing every detail before his attention shifted back to her, his gaze a brighter shade of blue this time, and she forgot what she was about to say.

Instead, she found herself wondering what he would taste like. Sweet and intoxicating and addictive? Dark and dangerous and forbidden? All of the above?

And then some.

The sound of his voice floated through her head, but his lips didn't move. Instead, they tilted in a sensuous grin that did wicked things to her self control. Her hands trembled and her mouth watered.

She wanted to kiss him so badly.

And he wanted to kiss her.

She could see it in the way his eyes darkened and the muscle in his jaw twitched. He wanted to close the distance between them. Just a few feet and bam, they'd be toe-to-toe.

Touching.

Kissing.

"Tomorrow it is," he murmured. And then, just like that, he vanished. No creak of the door. No click of the knob. Nothing. It was as if he'd disintegrated into thin air.

As if.

She'd been on the job for twelve hours straight, pulling a double shift yet again to prove to Matt that she was more than capable and dedicated. She was starting to get punchy. That was the reason she hadn't seen him turn and walk away. Even more, it explained the crazy disappointment whispering through her.

A kiss?

Seriously?

She hardly knew him and he hardly knew her. Even more, she wasn't going to get to know him because he was only here to tweak their security system. It was business and everyone knew that the town's first female deputy didn't mix business with pleasure.

No matter how hot he was or how sexually frustrated she was.

Rather, she was going to go home just as soon as Bobby got back, drown her troubles in a hot bath and get some much-needed sleep before she came face-to-face with Colton Braddock first thing in the morning.

Until then...

She walked over to the box of pastries, unearthed a chocolate-covered donut and took a big bite. The sugar melted in her mouth, sending a rush of satisfaction through her, albeit a temporary one. They weren't *that* stale. At least not to a desperate, deprived woman.

It wasn't sex, but it was definitely the next best thing.

4

COLTON CLIMBED BEHIND the wheel of his truck and tried to figure out what the hell had just happened.

He'd tried to glamour her and it hadn't worked. Not a lick.

Sure, she'd looked as if she'd *wanted* to fall under his spell with her parted lips and her smoldering eyes and her *take me now* vibe. She'd even leaned toward him once or twice, as if she meant to give in to the pull and cross the room. But then…

Nothing.

Not a damned thing.

She hadn't launched herself into his arms and begged him to come closer, to make himself right at home.

Hell, no. She'd stood her ground and told him to come back tomorrow.

Tomorrow.

If he hadn't been so irritated, he might have actually smiled. It had been a long time—over one hundred and fifty years to be exact—since a woman had faced off with him and actually won.

Women typically melted at his feet when he looked into their eyes. Not that he was proud of that fact.

It was simply the nature of the beast that he'd become and, he had to admit, it had its advantages. He didn't have to worry about showing his true nature when he was having sex. All he had to do was stare deeply into his partner's eyes and will away her memory of him.

But there was too much riding on this moment and he needed inside of that jail too badly to be the least bit amused right now. Or turned on. He needed Shelly's cooperation more than he needed her luscious body.

The thought struck and conjured all sorts of images and he damned himself for thinking with his dick. But that, too, was the nature of the beast.

He wanted her the way he wanted all women.

Okay, so he wanted her a little bit more. She was more sexually frustrated than the average female which meant she had all that sweet, succulent energy bottled up inside of her, just waiting to be unleashed. That made her all the more attractive and damned if he didn't want to peel away her stiff exterior and see the delicate curves hiding beneath.

Hiding. That's what she was doing.

He knew because he'd been doing it himself for

more years than he could count. Living in the shadows, protecting his true nature, surviving.

For revenge.

That's the reason he'd kept going all those years ago when he'd lost everything. The reason he kept going now. He'd dreamt of payback, lusted after it, and now was his chance to have it.

He didn't have time for some stubborn female with a badge. No time for touching or kissing.

Especially kissing.

He played the scenario over and over in his head for the next few minutes. The desperate urge to cross the distance to her, lean forward and touch his lips to hers.

To distract her. Persuade her.

It certainly hadn't been because he'd *wanted* to kiss her. Sex was one thing. It was all about survival. Sustenance. But kissing? Talk about personal. Colton had no intention of getting personal with any woman.

No matter how much he suddenly wanted to.

"There's no reason to sit out here all night."

The deep voice shattered his train of thought, thankfully, and he turned to see his brother slide onto the seat next to him.

"She's not even close." Brent Braddock closed the door and eyed his older brother. "So why don't you give it up and come home with me? Abby really wants to spend some time with you."

Colton arched an eyebrow. "Abby, huh?"

Brent shrugged. "Okay, so maybe I wouldn't mind

catching up myself." He met Colton's gaze. "I know Cody and Travis wouldn't mind it either. In fact, Cody really wanted you to stay out at his place."

"The hotel is working just fine." Or it would be if the eightysomething-year-old woman who ran the place with her grandson would stop banging on his door throughout the day, wanting to change his sheets.

"Suit yourself, but it seems a shame not to take advantage of the fact that we're all together."

"We're here for a reason."

"She won't show up for a few more days at least," Brent reminded him. "My contact at the prison did the transfer really fast and on the fly. Holbrook isn't due in El Paso until the day after tomorrow. If Rose has already figured out he's being moved—and that's a big *if*—she'll be waiting there for him. Add twenty-four hours for her to trace the transfer and identify exactly where he's been delayed once she figures out that something is up. Another twenty-four for her to reach Skull Creek since she can only travel at night. That means we've got at least a week to sit around and wait." He caught Colton's stare. "I can't think of a better way to spend it than getting re-acquainted with each other."

"I'd rather not take any chances."

Brent looked as if he wanted to argue, but then he shrugged. "Suit yourself." He opened the passenger door and paused. "I could hang out here for a little while."

"Go home to your wife."

"You shouldn't have to do this by yourself."

"But I'm going to." Colton met his brother's gaze. "This is my fight, not yours. You know that." While they'd all suffered thanks to Rose, Colton had suffered the most. He'd lost everything and he would be the one to make her pay.

Brent looked as if he wanted to object, but then he nodded. "If you change your mind about tonight, we'll be at my place." In the blink of an eye, he was gone and Colton settled back in his seat to keep watch.

At least, he tried to settle in. But his nerves were wound too tight, his hands clenched, his gut tense.

Not because of Rose. Brent was right about one thing—she wasn't even close. Colton could sense other vampires and while he felt the steady hum from his brothers and the others in Skull Creek, that was it. No prickling up his spine. No tingling in his limbs. No spike of anger in his gut.

Yet.

But she would come eventually and he would have his pound of flesh. That would be the end of it.

The end of him.

Because this wasn't just about defeating Rose. It was about punishing her for what she'd done, and then paying the price himself for not preventing it in the first place.

That's why he'd come here.

Skull Creek would be the end. Of Rose and of the damnable guilt that ate away inside of him.

Until then…

The scent of ripe cherries teased his nostrils. His mouth watered and his gut twisted and he stiffened.

He was in for a long night.

SHELLY WAS ON HER third donut when Bobby arrived with a tall, tanned blonde in tow.

"I wasn't soliciting," Honey Gentry said as the deputy steered her into a chair. "I was advertising."

Although well into her late thirties, the woman didn't look a day over twenty-five. With long, dark blond hair and a figure that would make any Dallas Cowboys Cheerleader insanely jealous, Honey was the sort of woman who turned heads when she walked into any room. Especially wearing skimpy Daisy Duke shorts that accented her long, endless legs and a red tank top that outlined her perfect breasts. Add a pair of red cowboy boots and it was no wonder she'd caused a riot at the Sac-n-Pac.

"Thank God. Finally I can talk to someone who doesn't think with his crotch." Heavily lined cornflower blue eyes shifted to Shelly. "This is all a big misunderstanding."

Shelly arched an eyebrow. "I thought you promised Judge Myers that you were going to turn over a new leaf if he let you off with probation last year?"

"I swear I didn't do anything."

"Not yet." Bobby handed over a hot pink flyer. "I

caught her just in time. She was handing out these. Gave one to the mayor's wife. She's the one who called it in."

"Pinkie Hamilton is as nutty as a squirrel turd. She's just mad 'cause her husband is one of my best customers." Honey beamed. "He loves my honey buns."

"You might want to keep that info to yourself until you talk to a lawyer," Shelly warned.

"I was just advertising my product. That isn't against the law."

"It is if the product is a sexual favor."

"It's not a sexual favor." Honey beamed. "I've expanded from breakfast pastries," she indicated the basket that Bobby had plopped on Shelly's desk, "to cupcakes. It's my new business. I'm a cupcake caterer."

"Yeah, right." Bobby snorted and glanced at the pink flier. "You're trying to tell us that *Decadent Thunder Down Under* is the name of a cupcake?"

"One of my top sellers." Honey flicked her long mane of hair. "And it's the mayor's personal favorite which is why his wife hates my guts. She can't cook a lick." She motioned to the basket. "I've got a half dozen to deliver to him. He got stuck in a late meeting so I thought I'd do a little advertising at the Sac-n-Pac until he finished." She motioned to the basket of sweet-smelling goodies. "It's my granny's recipe."

"Cupcakes, huh?" Shelly eyed the list. "Chitty Cherry Bang Bang and Lickety My Banana Split," she read out loud and her gaze shifted to Honey. "Don't you think those names might be miscon-strued?"

"It's called suggestive branding. I learned it on the internet." The woman shrugged. "It ain't my fault if this whole town's got their minds in the gutter. I'm just trying to beef up my business."

"Well you're out of business for now," Bobby in-formed her as he slid behind his desk and reached for an arrest sheet.

"For soliciting?" Shelly asked the deputy.

Bobby shook his head. "When I told Pinkie I couldn't arrest someone just because of a flyer, she got the owner of the Sac-n-Pac to file charges for loitering."

"But that's not fair," Honey protested. "I wasn't loitering. I was an actual customer. I even bought a large sweet tea and a bag of Doritos before I started handing out flyers."

"Tell it to the judge." Bobby reached for his fin-gerprint kit while Shelly barely resisted the urge to put a stop to the nonsense.

"I'm sure Judge Meyers will throw it out in a heartbeat," she told Honey. "But we have to go through the motions when anyone presses charges."

"This sucks." Honey blew out an exasperated breath. "I'm going to miss *Lost*."

"Maybe not." Shelly made a mental note to get Bobby to move the small television from the back room into Honey's cell. Yes, it violated about ten different rules, but this was a small town and these were trumped up charges. Tit for tat.

She gave Honey an encouraging smile and settled down behind her desk to finish up her own paperwork.

Her thoughts kept going to Colton Braddock and the all important fact that out of all the men who'd crossed her path that day, he'd turned out to be The One. Also known as the answer to her sexually frustrated prayers. Which wouldn't have been such a bad thing except he wasn't here because he wanted to have a little fun. He was here to do a job.

And he was coming back tomorrow.

She stiffened and eyed the basket sitting on the corner of her desk. Icing clung to the edge of the lid and the warm scent of sugar and vanilla teased her nostrils. The trio of donuts she'd had hadn't come close to touching the hunger that gnawed inside of her. She needed something more filling.

She needed him.

Shelly shook away the sudden thought and leaned forward. Her hand was an inch shy of the basket when the door buzzed open and a redhead wearing a pair of oversize sunglasses rushed inside.

"Hide me," said Shelly's younger sister.

"Sunglasses? Really? It's seven o'clock in the evening."

"I don't want to be recognized." As if that would ever happen. At twenty-three, Darla Lancaster was tall and leggy with a killer body and enough sex appeal to have all the men in town chasing after her. She'd slowed down long enough to let one in particular catch up, only to leave him at the altar three days ago with no explanation. She'd been avoiding him ever since.

"Billy Spoon saw me coming out of the Iron Horseshoe about ten minutes ago," Darla said, breathless. "I'm sure he's on the phone right now blabbing to Tom." Tom was the man she'd stood up at the altar. He was also a high powered lawyer and the mayor's son. Translation? He had connections. Lots of them. "I'm not ready to see him yet."

"You left him high and dry in front of a church full of people. You left *me* high and dry in front of a church full of people." Wearing the worst dress *ever,* she added silently. "Don't you think you owe him an explanation?" While the wedding planner had told everyone that the bride had had a family emergency, there'd been no further details as to why the lavish event had been cancelled. Nothing but an "I'm sorry" and "Be sure to pick up a slice of cake for the road."

"How can I explain what happened when I don't even know?" Darla rushed to the window, slid the sunglasses down her nose and peeked past the blinds. "He's rich. Handsome. Nice. *Perfect.*" She turned a confused expression on Shelly. "I left the perfect man at the altar. What's wrong with me?" Before Shelly could respond, she added, "He sent me flowers today. Imported Italian tea roses. Only the best for the best." Her eyes filled with tears. "That's what the card said. Talk about a great guy, right? Tom can give me everything I've ever wanted. Even the sex is good." Her gaze collided with Shelly's. "So why don't I love him?"

"Love is overrated." Shelly had learned that first-hand after watching their mother fall in love over and over again. "Settle for good sex and consider yourself lucky."

"I can't marry him if I don't love him. But if I blow him off, he'll get really mad and then he won't *want* to marry me. Then what if I change my mind and decide I *do* want to marry him?" She shook her head. "I just need to stay out of sight while I try to figure things out. That way I keep my options open."

"That's the most ridiculous thing I've ever heard."

Even more ridiculous, it made sense. At least where Darla was concerned.

Shelly and her sister had grown up on the wrong side of the tracks with little money and few choices. With their mother out kicking up her heels every Saturday night and most nights in between, they'd been left to fend for themselves. Alone. Scared. Uncertain.

Shelly had overcome that uncertainty by working her way through the police academy and joining the Sheriff's department. Her baby sister had done it with makeup and hair extensions. While Shelly could outshoot any man in Skull Creek, Darla could have him eating out of her hand with one sultry smile.

"My shift ended a few hours ago. Bobby can stall him if he comes in while I drop you off on my way home." She motioned to the rear of the jail. "My car's out back."

Darla grinned. "You're the best big sister in the world."

"Remember that the next time you're tempted to force me into a hideous bridesmaid's dress."

"That dress was straight off a Paris runway, not that you would know that, since the last time you actually went dress shopping was—I don't know—*never*. Speaking of which—" She eyeballed her sister. "—since you're going to bite the bullet and find yourself a man, you might want to fix yourself up a little." She stared at Shelly's starched brown cover-everything-up uniform. "Your wardrobe needs sexing up in the worst way."

"My wardrobe is just fine the way it is and the newspaper made a mistake. It wasn't my ad."

Darla smiled. "I knew it! I told Mom that it had to be a misprint, but she thinks you've finally lightened up and are now following in her footsteps."

She glared at her sister. "Just meet me out back."

5

SHELLY WASN'T SURE what bothered her more—seeing Colton Braddock still parked outside the jail at midnight when she'd come back after dropping her sister off. Or the zing of excitement she felt at finding him there.

He sat behind the wheel of his black Ford pickup, his window down, his hat tipped low, his attention fixed on the building directly across the street.

She eased her Mustang up behind him and killed the engine. A few seconds later, she leaned into the open passenger window of his truck. "Nice night."

He didn't so much as glance at her. Instead, his eyes stayed fixed on the jail. "Nice enough."

"You usually start most of your assignments with a stakeout?"

"I like to get a feel for a place before I go in."

"And what's your feel for this place?"

He shrugged one broad shoulder and she had the

same sense of déjà vu that had come over her when he'd first stepped inside the jail.

As if she'd seen him somewhere before.

Duh. You've seen his brother. There has to be a family resemblance.

Probably.

"Typical small town set-up." His voice killed any further speculation and drew her full attention. "Front office. Rear containment area. Two or three cells at the most. Good when it comes to a few drunks and the occasional bar fight. Not so good for a prisoner like Holbrook."

"You're here because of him, aren't you?"

"Maybe."

"Either you are or you aren't." She watched him watch the building. "So which is it? Did the county send you in because they don't think we can handle it?" That *I* can handle it? "Or is this all just a coincidence?"

Her instinct was telling her it was number one. Still, she couldn't help but hope she was wrong.

He didn't seem in any hurry to put her out of her misery. Seconds ticked by before he leaned across the cab and grabbed the door handle. The latch clicked and the door opened.

"Get in and I'll tell you." Challenge gleamed hot and bright in his gaze.

Shelly had never been one to shy away when called out. That, and she suddenly couldn't help herself. While her brain told her to run like hell, her hormones were like heat-seeking missiles and Colton Braddock was a blazing inferno. She climbed in.

Leather shifted as she settled on the seat. Hinges creaked and the door closed with a thud. The rich aroma of sexy male surrounded her, pushing and pulling at her already tentative control. The urge to slide across the seat and cozy up nearly overwhelmed her. It had been so long since she'd felt a man next to her.

Even more, she'd never felt one like Colton Braddock.

An air of sensuality clung to him, as if sex was as natural to him as breathing. The musky scent of leather and male filled the cab, teasing her senses and making her heart flutter. The air between them crackled with electricity.

The chemistry was potent, but she wasn't about to give in to it. The last thing she needed was for him to report back to the county that she was anything but professional. This was her job. Her future. And so she gathered her strength and her composure.

"So which is it?" she asked again. "Are you a babysitter for Big Brother? Because if that's the case, you can head right back to Austin and tell them thanks, but no thanks. I'm more than capable of handling anything that happens here."

"Holbrook is a lot more dangerous than you realize."

"I'm fully aware of his background. I've got two deputies on him right now." John had reported in minutes before she'd left with Darla. "And I'll be back first thing in the morning to keep an eye on things myself. Trust me, he's not going anywhere."

"I'm sure that's what they said at the last four facilities he escaped from." His gaze sparked and the twelve inches of leather that separated them seemed to shrink. Colton half turned toward her, resting one arm across the back of the seat, his hand an inch shy of touching her. "So did you check out my story?" His gaze caught and held hers for a long, heart-pounding moment.

"I texted the Sheriff," she said, staring past him at the front of the jail. "But I don't expect a reply back right away because he's officially on vacation. He and his wife are going on a trip."

"Which means I'm not getting in until tomorrow."

She nodded. "If you are who you say you are." She wasn't sure why she said it. His story fit and she had no real reason to doubt it. There was just something odd about him.

Not in a bad way. Just…different.

Exciting.

She squelched the thought and concentrated on breathing.

"What makes you think I'm lying?"

She shrugged and met his gaze head on. "I just get the feeling there's more to you than meets the eye."

SHE HAD NO IDEA.

The thought shot through Colton's head as he

stared at the woman sitting next to him. Long, dark tendrils had come loose from her ponytail and lay limp and forgotten against her creamy neck. Heat rolled off her, teasing his senses, and it was all he could do to keep from brushing his fingertips across her skin. He was so close. Too close. "Maybe there's more to *you* than meets the eye," he said instead.

Her gaze narrowed and he had the sneaking suspicion that she was trying to intimidate him. "What's that supposed to mean?"

"Maybe you aren't half as tough as you want everyone to think." He didn't miss the faint tremble of her bottom lip before her mouth pulled into a tight frown.

"You don't know anything about me."

"Then tell me something."

"I could kick your ass fifty ways til Sunday if I felt like it."

He grinned, the expression coaxing the tiniest of smiles from her. The sudden tension between them eased just a little. "On a good day, maybe."

"On any day."

His grin widened. "So how long have you been a Deputy Sheriff here?"

"Six years. Before that, I did a few years on patrol in a nearby county."

"That's a long time in a tough field. No wonder you're so prickly."

"Very funny." She eyed him. "What about you? How long have you been a security specialist?"

"Not very long." He didn't miss the questions swimming in her gaze. "The ranch isn't earning what it used to and I needed to make ends meet. My brother runs a security firm, so he hooked me up."

"Who looks after things at your place while you're away?"

"I've got a reliable foreman and a few steady hands. It makes turning my back a lot easier." At least that's what Colton had been telling himself since he rolled into Skull Creek to face off with Rose. He didn't have to worry about his animals back in New Mexico. Jasper and the boys would take care of them. Hell, they'd be tickled pink when they found out that Colton had left them each an equal share of his land.

It's not like he would be needing it.

There was no going back after this. No putting the past behind him and settling down. No finding happiness the way his brothers had.

His happiness had died that night right along with his son. He had no illusions about getting over the loss. Killing Rose would give him some sense of satisfaction, but it wouldn't rid him of the damnable guilt. He would never be free. He didn't deserve to be free.

"So you're not married?" her soft voice pushed into his thoughts and eased the sudden tension that had gripped him.

His gaze met hers. *No* was right there on the tip of his tongue, but damned if he could get the word out. "I was once," he heard himself say instead. "A long time ago. But it didn't work out."

"Kids?"

"One. A long time ago. That didn't work out either." When she seemed puzzled, he added, "He passed away."

"I'm really sorry," she murmured and he knew by the brightening in her eyes that she wasn't just being polite. She meant it.

So? Her sympathy didn't change anything. Not the past. Or the future.

Still, he felt the knot in his chest ease just a little.

"What about you?" he asked her. "Do you have a husband tucked away somewhere?" As if he didn't already know. She was too sexually deprived to have a steady guy waiting at home. But he asked anyway because he liked the sound of her voice. "Kids?"

"I'm much too busy to be a wife and mother. Especially a mother." She stiffened as soon as the words rolled out and he knew she'd said more than she'd meant to.

He held her gaze, trying to delve into her thoughts, wanting to for the first time in a long time, despite the nagging voice that told him to *back the hell up.* He didn't need the distraction.

But damned if he didn't want one.

Colton was sick of waiting. Of watching the clock while the minutes dragged on and he grew more and more anxious. He needed some way to fill his time and talking with her suddenly seemed harmless enough.

He eyed her. "You sound like you speak from personal experience."

"My own mother wasn't the most attentive."

"Did she work too much?"

"She played too much. She had no time leftover for anything else, especially me and my sister. It was no big deal." She shrugged. "We managed just fine without her." A smile tugged at her lips. "I learned to make a mean peanut butter and jelly sandwich."

"What about your dad?"

"I never really knew him. He was more of a Saturday night special than marriage material."

"Marriage is overrated."

She eyed him. "Now you sound like the one speaking from personal experience."

"I was the oldest and itching to settle down and carry on the family name, and she was itching to get away from her bastard of a father. It seemed like the right thing to do at the time." But he'd been wrong. Dead wrong. "My son was the only good thing to come out of it." An image of CJ sitting atop his first horse flashed in Colton's mind and he felt a smile tug at his lips.

"What happened to him?"

The question hit like a two-by-four and he remembered that night. The smoke. The blood. The death.

His muscles went tight and his gaze zeroed in on her. "Why did you place an ad for sex?" The quick change of subject caught her off guard and he saw the panic that flashed in her expression.

"I didn't."

"Yes, you did. Otherwise you wouldn't be so dead set on denying it."

Her mouth drew into a tight line. "It's late." She reached for the door handle. "You should call it a night and head back to the hotel."

"Settle down." He touched her then, his hand closing over her shoulder. "There's no reason to get fired up. I don't bite." A grin tugged at his lips. "Not unless you ask real nice."

What the hell was he doing?

He was flirting. Friggin' *flirting*. And damned if he could help himself. He liked seeing the color rush to her cheeks and the sharp intake of her breath. She was nervous and he got the feeling that such a thing didn't happen very often where Shelly Lancaster was concerned.

"If you know what's good for you, you'll move your hand."

"And if I don't?"

"I'll move it for you." That's what her mouth said, but her body wanted something altogether different. Heat rolled off her in waves and she trembled with need. A need she fought with everything she had. Emotion warred in her expression. Desire versus aggravation. Desperation versus full-blown anger.

Forget warm and willing and ready like every other woman he'd come into contact with. She was different, and damned if that didn't draw him more than if she'd stripped off her clothes and planted herself on his lap.

The seconds ticked by and he willed her closer.

She didn't budge and his frustration built.

If she wouldn't give in to the chemistry raging between them, he would just have to do it himself.

Quick and fiery. That's what he told himself as he leaned down and captured her mouth with his own. A fast and ferocious kiss just to satisfy his curiosity and see if she tasted half as good as she looked.

Better.

Her lips were warm and sweet, and in that next instant, there seemed nothing wrong with slowing down just a little and taking his time.

His tongue tangled with hers and he slid his arms around her waist. He pulled her close, his mouth eating at hers, tasting, exploring, *drinking.*

The notion struck as he felt the first wave of energy shimmer through his body. It spilled from her lips, feeding him for a few blissful moments before the shock of what was happening hit him hard and fast.

A climax was one thing, but this was just a kiss. He shouldn't feel such a rush. No heat pouring into him, feeding the coldness inside. No burst of sweet, blissful energy.

"No!"

The protest rang loud and clear in his head. Not his own, though his conscience was rioting pretty loudly at the moment. Rather, the *no* came from her and sent a bolt of common sense streaking through him. He pulled away, cutting off the addictive stream of energy and breaking the connection between them.

Her eyes popped open and she stared up at him. Shock flashed in her gaze, along with a glimmer of disappointment before she seemed to gather her self-control.

Her eyes narrowed. "Good try, but you're still not getting into the jail before the morning." And then she opened the door and climbed out. "Pack it up and get out of here. You're violating curfew."

"You've got to be kidding?"

"Hazards of a small town." She slammed the door shut and stepped back onto the curb. "Now move before I write you a ticket."

She glared and Colton knew beyond a doubt that she had every intention of following through on her threat. He stared at her a moment longer, willing her one last time to weaken, to crawl back into the truck and beg for another kiss, but she didn't budge.

She was a strong one. He had to give her that. And double damned if he didn't like that about her, too.

He frowned and keyed the engine. "I'm not much of a morning person. I'll be in tomorrow evening. Six o'clock." And then he did what he should have done the moment she pulled up behind him—he hauled ass in the opposite direction.

HE'D KISSED HER.

Even worse, she'd kissed him back.

The truth needled Shelly as she watched his tail-lights disappear around the corner.

She'd kissed him back despite every ounce of common sense that had screamed she was being crazy. She knew good and well that he was just try-ing to wiggle his way into the jail a few precious minutes early. The kiss had been a distraction, a way to shatter her defenses and get his way.

Bingo.

She ignored the know-it-all voice and focused on the short drive to her house and the lucky fact that while she'd kissed him back—and wow what a kiss—no one had actually seen her do it. It was his word against hers if he decided to tell the world that there was more to Shelly Lancaster than met the eye.

Much more.

He wouldn't. While he had no trouble calling her out face-to-face, she had the feeling that Colton Braddock was too much of a man to kiss and tell.

Which meant she had only her own conscience to worry about.

She ignored the sinking feeling that she'd made a huge mistake. That one kiss would lead to another. And another. And—no!

She'd been weak, yes, but only because she'd pulled two shifts back-to-back. A hot bath and some much needed sleep and she would surely stop acting like a sex-starved lunatic.

Hopefully.

6

OKAY, SO MAYBE a bath wasn't the best idea after the red hot kiss with Colton Braddock.

Shelly admitted as much an hour later as she peeled off her clothes and sank down into the warm water. Her lips still tingled from his kiss and her nerves buzzed. The heady scent of her favorite bubble bath filled the air and her senses were wide open and raw as she slid the bath sponge over her sensitive skin.

Don't think it.

Her fingers tightened on the sponge an inch shy of her nipple and she caught her breath. She needed to stop obsessing over sex. Block it from her mind. Forget it. *Forget him.*

So what if he was handsome and sexy and they had explosive chemistry? So what if he'd kissed her and she'd kissed him back? He wasn't some anonymous horn dog from a nearby town. He was a colleague, at least for the next few days, which meant she had to keep things purely platonic between them.

Professional, as in no kissing.

Although, maybe if she obsessed just a little in the privacy of her own home now, enough to have one teeny, tiny orgasm, it might ease the knot of frustration so she could actually remember not to kiss him later.

Hey, it was worth a shot.

She touched the sponge to the tip of her nipple and a gasp bubbled past her lips. It wasn't the real thing, but it would do.

She swirled the fragrant soap around the sensitive tip. First one then the other. Delicious tingles danced across her nerve endings. Her lips parted on a gasp as she moved her hands lower, down the silken plane of her belly. Her legs parted and her fingers slid even lower.

Her breathing grew faster, her chest heaving as her fingers parted the silky folds between her thighs. But it wasn't her own hand doing the touching. It was his.

In her mind's eye, she saw Colton Braddock, felt his purposeful touch against her moist heat, his long, deft fingers sliding deep to wring a shudder from her.

Once. Twice. Again.

Sensation exploded, sweeping across her nerves like a brushfire. Only when she'd taken a deep breath, her trembling hands grasping the tub's edge, did she hear the voice.

"I told you I wouldn't bite." The deep, rich voice slid into Shelly's ears, to stir her senses back from their temporary exhaustion.

She drank in a slow, steadying breath and lifted her heavy lids. Through the steam, she saw him standing in the bathroom doorway, his powerful body filling up the small room. He wore the same faded jeans he'd had on earlier, but he'd slipped off his shirt. Muscles gleamed and flexed in the dim light. A pair of matching slave band tattoos encircled his bulging biceps. His eyes pulsed a hot, bright, brilliant purple.

"This isn't real." Her own voice sounded soft and subdued and oh, so far away. She must be imagining things. That's why his eyes were purple now, not pale blue.

She'd finished off two glasses of wine before crawling into the tub. Add to that the sugar extravaganza she'd indulged in at work and it was a wonder she wasn't seeing little green men or even the Easter Bunny.

She pushed to her feet, water drip-dropping all around her as she stepped from the tub. Her heart pounded and the air seemed to thicken with need.

"You aren't really touching me." She moved trembling fingers to her breast. "I'm doing this all by myself." She held his gaze, her fingertips swirling around the tip until it hardened and throbbed and her throat went dry. "And this." She delivered the same careful attention to the other breast.

A battle raged across Colton's features, as if he wanted to reach out but couldn't.

After all, this was *her* fantasy. He could only do as she commanded, and right now she was too busy enjoying the moment to beckon him forward. She liked having him watch. For now.

Her breath caught as she trailed her hands down to the silky strip of hair at the base of her thighs. She followed the sensitive flesh to the slit between her legs. The tip of her finger eased in just a fraction and sensation drenched her. Her eyes closed and her heart rate quickened.

"Holy hell."

His deep voice pushed past the haze of pleasure and echoed in her head. Her eyes fluttered open.

"You're beautiful," he said, even though his lips didn't move, proving once more that she was caught in a very vivid, very erotic fantasy. One that was just getting started.

"Touch me," she finally breathed.

Without breaking eye contact, he closed the few feet between them and dropped to his knees, bringing his head level with her waist. Silky hair brushed her bare stomach.

Impossible.

But in the thick, steamy fog of the bathroom, it was more than plausible. She felt the rough stubble of his jaw against her abdomen, saw the tremble of his shoulders as he leaned forward, felt the flutter of his lips against her skin.

Fire exploded and she tilted her head back. A moan sailed past her parted lips.

"I like touching better than watching." His deep voice echoed in her head at the same time his tongue darted out, licking and dipping at her navel.

Her legs went weak. She grasped his shoulders, her fingers digging into the hard, carved muscle as his lips worked magic on her skin. His tongue caught the diamondlike drops of water that slid down her flesh and her heart beat a frenzied rhythm against her rib cage.

Oxygen bolted from her lungs when his tongue parted the sensitive flesh between her legs. His shoulders pushed her legs apart until she stood completely open and eager and then he devoured her.

He thrust his tongue deep and drank in her essence. She went wild. Heat drenched her. She bucked and her body convulsed and he lapped at her as if he'd never tasted anything so sweet.

He swept her into his arms and a heartbeat later she felt the soft mattress at her back.

"More," she heard herself say when he pulled away this time. She wanted to be embarrassed at the desperation in her voice. Begging, of all things. But this was just a fantasy. An erotic escapade where pleasure took priority over pride. "Don't go."

"I'll be back, sugar. That's a promise."

COLTON FORCED ASIDE the image of Shelly and opened his eyes to the dimly lit motel room. An ancient ceiling fan trembled above him, the blades moving in a lazy circle that barely stirred the stifling summer air. Awareness rippled up and down his arms and he felt the frantic pounding in his chest. Her heartbeat.

No way. No friggin' *way*.

They'd shared one kiss. Sure, it had been a pretty spectacular kiss, but still. That wasn't the way it worked. He had to drink a substantial amount from her to forge a real connection.

A kiss wasn't enough. It never had been in all the years he'd been a vampire and it sure as hell wasn't now.

That's what he told himself, but there was no denying the sweet scent of bubble bath that clung to him or the ripe taste of her luscious sex that lingered on his tongue. He'd been there tonight, all right.

In spirit.

Which meant his damned body was still as hungry as ever. More so now that he'd had a taste of what he so desperately wanted. He needed to feed—*really* feed—in the worst way.

He pushed to his feet and unearthed the small cooler from the bottom of his suitcase. Pulling out a bag of AB-, he headed for the small microwave that sat next to the scarred dresser. A minute later, he dumped the warm liquid into a glass and touched the rim to his lips. The sweet heat rolled down his throat, but it wasn't enough to fill up the emptiness in the pit of his stomach.

It was never enough.

He slammed the thought and took another gulp just as the doorknob trembled. His gaze shifted and he realized a split-second too late that he'd forgotten to secure the door. He crossed the room in a flash and caught the knob just as it turned.

"Turn down service," came the old woman's voice.

"I'm good." Colton pressed the door closed and flipped the lock.

"But I've got free mints for your pillow."

"I'll pass." He reached for a nearby desk chair and wedged the back under the doorknob.

It was exactly what he should have done the moment he arrived in the room. But instead, he'd been too caught up in Shelly and what was happening in her damnable fantasy.

"They're chocolate," Winona added, "not those old hard mints. Special ordered them myself right off the internet. They've got our name on the package and everything."

"Thanks, but no thanks. Have a good night," he added, trying to be polite despite the fact that she was wearing on his last nerve.

She didn't budge and he could feel her curiosity swirling into a frenzy, urging her to whip out the key in her pocket and let herself in anyway. Just to see what her newest guest was up to.

She didn't, but Colton knew it was just a matter of time. Cody had been right. He didn't belong in a motel room. He should have accepted his brother's offer and camped out at his place.

But it was hard seeing them now, remembering the past, the camaraderie they'd shared. The closeness.

Things could never be the same between them. They were different now. *He* was different.

Thanks to Rose.

She'd taken everything from him, and he'd let her. By not seeing her true nature. By not moving faster and getting home sooner. By not seeing the truth.

The treachery.

Never again.

He grabbed a nearby lamp and balanced it on the chair. If Winona tried anything, the lamp would fall and the noise would wake him up. It wasn't the high-powered security system Cody had protecting his spread, but it would have to do.

"Good night," he added.

Another indecisive moment and the old woman blew out an exasperated breath. "Same to you." Footsteps shuffled along the walkway, the sound fading as she made her way back to the office.

Colton damned himself yet again for getting caught off guard. For being antsy and unsettled and frustrated.

Thanks to Shelly.

He downed the last of the blood and shoved the empty plastic into the bottom of his bag. Dropping into a nearby chair, he powered up his computer and spent the next few hours re-reading the articles he'd downloaded about Holbrook's previous escapes.

He didn't learn anything new, but he did manage to kill some time and distract himself until exhaustion closed in and he fell into a deep, consuming sleep.

At least for a little while.

Until the sun came up and the hotel's owner started beating on his door again.

"It's motel policy," the old woman called out. "Everybody gets clean sheets along with a coupon for a complimentary piece of pie from the diner. Best pie you ever had, too."

"I'll pass on the pie," Colton managed to call out, despite the exhaustion tugging him under. "I had a late night. I really need to sleep."

"No problem, sugar. You get some shut-eye."

Thankfully.

"I'll be back in ten."

Forget biting the dust in the coming battle.

At the rate things were going, the old motel owner was sure to aggravate him to death long before he faced off with Rose.

7

"THIS AIN'T EVEN WARM." Beauford Truitt opened the white bakery box that Shelly sat next to the coffee-maker and peered inside. "They're all glazed," he declared, a scowl on his face.

"That's all that was left." Shelly stuffed her purse in her desk and did her damndest not to glance at the clock.

She already knew what time it was. It was two hours past her usual arrival time.

Two hours.

Late.

The truth stirred a memory of a small girl walking into her first grade class long after the bell had rang because her mother had slept in yet again.

It was an incident that had happened time and time again right after her Grandma Jean had passed away. Until Shelly had figured out how to set her own alarm and get herself off in the mornings.

She'd never been late since.

Until now.

Until him.

It had taken her forever to fall asleep after last night's Grade A fantasy, but once she'd managed to close her eyes, that had been it. Not even a full blown alarm or a bedroom full of bright morning sunlight had been enough to wake her.

No, it had taken ten phone calls from Bobby to finally drag her into the office.

"Are you okay?" he asked, coming up next to her.

"I'm fine." She hit the On button and powered up her computer, desperate to ignore the dark, sexy image that rushed at her and brought a burst of heat to her cheeks. Her nipples tingled and her thighs ached and she damned herself for being so weak.

"You don't look fine."

"Well, I am fine."

"You look different—"

"Did you finish the shift report?" she interrupted, desperate to change the subject and stifle the nagging voice that told her he was right.

She *was* different.

Forget calm and controlled and focused.

Her mind raced and her nerves buzzed and awareness rippled up and down her spine.

Sugar and caffeine, she reminded herself. She was hyped thanks to the two donuts and the extra large energy drink she'd had on the way over. The drink had been to wake her up while the glazed duo had been more of a desperate attempt to satisfy the craving that still ate away inside of her. A craving that had nothing to do with food and everything to do with the cowboy who'd kissed her senseless last night.

"I can't put my finger on it, but something's up with you," Bobby declared, his voice yanking her away from the detour her thoughts were about to take, straight into the land of the sexually deprived.

"Don't be silly." She sank down at her desk and opened her e-mail. "I look the way I always do." A quick look through Matt's e-mail verified that Colton had been telling the truth. He was a security specialist from county.

And he was coming back in exactly eight hours and fifty-two minutes and—

Bobby sank down on the corner of her desk, effectively killing her view of the clock. Thankfully.

"What?" she asked when his gaze narrowed.

"Are you wearing lipstick?"

Pale pink shimmer.

She'd bought the tube during a weak moment in Austin last year and stashed it in her dresser along with all of the other cosmetics she would never wear.

But you're wearing it right now, her conscience reminded her. *Right here. Right now. In front of everyone.*

"It's just lip balm," she blurted, pushing to her feet. "My lips were dry." *And tingling from the best kiss of my life. I needed something—anything—to kill the sensation.*

She certainly hadn't swiped it on in a last-ditch effort to look good for *him*.

"Have a donut." She snatched up the box and held it out to him. "I brought two dozen."

"There ain't no bear claws in there," Truitt reminded Bobby. "No long johns. Not even a dang fritter. And all because of Sleeping Beauty there."

"For the last time—I didn't sleep in. I had a broken water pipe."

"In-wall?" Bobby arched an eyebrow as he took a donut. "'Cause my brother-in-law is a really good sheetrock guy. I could give him a call—"

"External," she said. "My sheetrock's fine and I fixed the pipe myself." She whirled and made a beeline for the containment area before Bobby decided to chime in with more questions.

"Hey, where are you going with my donuts?" Truitt called after her.

"They're *my* donuts and I'm going to feed *my* prisoners."

She punched in the combination for the door leading to the back area. The lock clicked and the steel opened, and she left Bobby and Ranger Truitt staring after her.

She walked down the single hallway, the two cells situated on either side, facing each other. To the right, Honey sat flipping channels on the small TV Bobby had set up for her. To the left, Jimmy Holbrook lay stretched out on his bunk, a pair of headphones stuffed into his ears, the cord attached to a small transistor radio Beauford Truitt had allowed him to have. The Ranger's empty chair sat outside the doorway surrounded by a mountain of empty foam cups. The smell of coffee filled the air.

Shelly unearthed two donuts with a napkin and held them out to Honey. "I know the diner sent in breakfast this morning, but I thought you might want a snack."

The woman shook her head, her hair wild and unkempt, as if she'd spent the night tossing and turning. "Thanks, but no thanks. I don't do donuts. Too many calories." She pulled her knees up to her chest and Shelly felt a pang of guilt. Honey looked so tired. So worried. "Tell me again why I'm still sitting in here."

"Judge Myers is fishing in Port Aransas and decided to stay an extra day. He called this morning. He won't be back until tomorrow."

Misery washed over Honey's expression and guilt swirled through Shelly. "I'm so sorry about this. I'd let you out in a heartbeat if I could, but I have to follow procedure." Particularly with Beauford Truitt watching her every move. The man had already raised a fuss about the TV. "Matt's depending on me to run things by the book."

The woman pushed to her feet and paced the length of the cot. "But I've got orders to fill. And I promised Roy McGee I'd do a life-size steer made entirely of cupcakes for the chili cook-off finals on Saturday." She met Shelly's stare. "Daylight's burning and I'm falling more and more behind." Her gaze narrowed as if she'd just noticed something. "Are you wearing lipstick?"

"It's lip balm. My lips are getting chapped. Look, I know this is a pain," she continued, "but you just have to sit tight one more day. In the meantime, I'll drive out and talk to Walt." Walt Hornsby was the owner of the Sac-n-Pac who'd filed the complaint. "Maybe I can convince him to drop the charges."

"And maybe pigs will fly." The blonde shook her head. "He leases the building from Pinkie and her husband, which means he's stuck doing her dirty work and I'm stuck in here." She sank down on the mattress.

"Can I have one of those?"

The deep voice came from behind her and Shelly turned to see Jimmy Holbrook sitting on the edge of his bunk. He pulled the headset from around his neck and pushed to his feet.

He'd peeled off his shirt and wore only a pair of orange pants and a white wife-beater. He had the hard, muscular body of a lot of prisoners who had nothing better to do than spend their days lifting weights out in the yard. A large dragon tattoo covered one arm and crept up his neck, blowing fire around his Adam's apple. His dark hair was cut in a short military style. He looked tough. Dangerous. But there was something oddly disarming when he smiled. His steel blue eyes crinkled at the corners. Dimples cut into his stubbled cheeks and the menacing air that surrounded him seemed to ease.

It was no doubt the very reason he'd waltzed out of four prisons in as many years.

"Help yourself." Shelly held up the bakery box while he extended an arm through the bars and took one of the donuts.

Her gaze met his and a sense of déjà vu washed over her. Her stomach hollowed out and her lips tingled.

"Thanks." He ate half the donut in one bite before turning and walking back over to his bunk.

"Cute, ain't he?" Honey's voice drew Shelly around to find the woman standing at her cell door.

"He's a dangerous criminal."

"With one hell of a body." Honey stared past her and Shelly turned in time to see Jimmy down the rest of his donut and reach for his headset. He stuffed the buds back into his ears, positioned the radio on the bed and dropped to the floor for some push-ups. Muscles flexed and rippled and…okay, so he did have one hell of a body.

"He did push-ups all night." Honey's voice slid into her ears. "And sit-ups. And even some pull-ups on the overhead bar running across the door."

That explained Honey's haggard expression.

Shelly and Honey watched as he pushed up, then down. Up. Then down.

"Maybe I will have one of those donuts," Honey murmured. "Or two. I have a feeling it's going to be a long day."

Shelly glanced at her watch for the countless time, noting that she still had eight hours and forty-one minutes. "Tell me about it.

8

COLTON STOOD IN the shadows several hours after sunset and watched Shelly's car pull out of the parking lot. He'd parked his truck the next street over about an hour ago and had been waiting for her to leave ever since.

Bingo.

He stiffened against a nudge of disappointment and gathered his resolve. Walking into the Sheriff's office last night had taught him one important lesson—Shelly Lancaster was immune to his vamp charisma which meant it would be better, easier, to do what he had to do without her looking over his shoulder.

Kissing her had taught him an even bigger lesson. Shelly Lancaster was more than a distraction. She was downright dangerous. Instead of focusing on the upcoming battle with Rose, he'd spent the day tossing and turning and thinking about Shelly.

About how much he wanted her. And how much he needed her.

Like hell.

The only thing he needed was to avenge his family and silence the demons that haunted him once and for all. It's all he'd thought about since he was turned.

Revenge.

That should be the only thing on his mind, which was why he had every intention of keeping his distance. While he'd connected with her last night, they'd still only shared a kiss. Which meant that the thread that ran between them was fragile at best. It would fade and Colton meant to do everything in his power to speed up the process.

Namely he was staying far, far away from her.

His mind made up, he watched as her tail lights faded and then he started across the street.

The sharp scent of stale caffeine, old meatloaf and Liquid Paper hit him when he pushed open the door and stepped into the office. It was a one room set up with three desks situated here and there behind a large counter that served as the dispatch center. Jason Aldean drifted from a small CD player next to the radio.

Colton's gaze swept the area, drinking in the two most important details—the older gentleman with snow white hair and a pissed off expression who stood near the microwave and the younger man with a blond crew cut who sat hunkered over a pile of paperwork. The blond guy wore a Skull Creek Deputy's uniform, a badge pinned to his chest. He glanced up and his gaze locked with Colton's.

His name was John Cummins. He'd been with the Sheriff's office two years now. Married. Twins on the way. He'd just started his shift and already he was neck deep finishing up Bobby's paperwork because the rookie had been called out to County Road 21 to round up some kids rumored to be throwing cow patties at passing cars.

John paused, pen in hand. "What can I do you for?"

"The name's Colton Braddock." Colton held up the clearance packet Brent had dropped by the motel just after sunset, complete with a badge and ID card. "I'm doing the security upgrade."

Recognition dawned and John nodded. "Shelly said you'd be stopping by. 'Course, we all damn near gave up on you." He glanced at his watch. "It's awful late."

"Better late than never." Colton did another visual comb-over of the room, drinking in the last few details. Four large filing cabinets spread out against the far wall along with a small sidebar bearing a coffeemaker and microwave, as well as five reams of computer paper stacked in the corner.

"What exactly are you planning to do?" John asked, drawing Colton's attention.

"Nothing invasive tonight. Just a walk-through to assess the level of security."

"That ought to take about five seconds." The comment came from the old man. He held a meat loaf sandwich in one hand and a napkin in the other. Swiping at a ketchup smudge near the corner of his mouth, he eyeballed Colton. "Let me tell you, this place is a joke when it comes to security. That's why me and old blue, here—" He tapped the gun at his hip. "—are keeping a close eye on everything."

"This here's Ranger Truitt." John waved a hand toward the old man. "He's helping us out while Holbrook's in-house."

"What he means is I'm doing all the work." The Ranger took another bite.

"I'm sure the folks in town appreciate your support." Colton stared deep into the Ranger's eyes and willed him to listen. *Obey.* "I bet you're tired. Maybe it's time for you to sit down and take a load off." He motioned to a nearby chair. *Now.*

The man looked ready to argue as he swallowed his mouthful, but then his jaw went slack. A glazed look came over his face and his head bobbed in agreement. He stumbled backward a few steps and sank down into the nearby chair, the sandwich in his hands forgotten, his eyes vacant, his mind seemingly a million miles away.

"What the hell?" That's what John was thinking just as Colton turned back to the Deputy.

"You look tired, too, Deputy Cummins," Colton added, killing the man's thoughts before he could speculate any further. "Very tired. I think now might be a good time for you to get a little shut-eye, as well." *Sleep.* He concentrated all of his energy into the silent command and sent it spiraling across the room.

In a matter of seconds, John's expression went from alarmed to passive. He leaned forward and slumped over his desk. His eyes closed and a heartbeat later, a steady snore filled the room.

Colton didn't waste any time. He made a beeline for the door leading to the containment area and punched in the code Brent had given him. The door powered open and in a matter of seconds, he was standing in the hallway that ran between the two cells.

Ranger Truitt's empty chair sat at the very end of the hallway, surrounded by a litter of coffee-stained foam cups. Colton's gaze swiveled past the right-sided cell and zeroed in on the male to his left.

Jimmy Holbrook lay sideways on his bunk, facing the wall. A blanket covered his lower half. His soft, steady snores filled the air.

"Sssshhhh." The female voice sounded behind him and he half turned to see a tall, leggy blonde standing at the bars.

Her name was Honey Gentry and she'd been wrongfully accused of trespassing thanks to a jealous old woman who suspected her of cheating with her husband. But Honey had given up cavorting with half the town's married men to pursue her true passion—baking cupcakes. Only she was stuck here when she should have been working on her biggest order to date and she was damned frustrated about it. And she'd been celibate for over six months on account of she'd joined Sexoholics Anonymous and it was part of her twelve steps.

Her hair was mussed, her mascara smudged due to a stressful, sleepless night courtesy of the hottie across from her. Her hands trembled ever so slightly as she grabbed the bars and anxiety knotted her muscles. He could practically hear the energy bubbling inside her as she pressed a finger to her lips, signaling him to keep quiet.

His gaze locked with hers and, sure enough, he read the anxiety she was feeling. It swirled with a volatile mixture of frustration and hunger that gave her a wired look.

He could definitely relate. His own muscles felt tight and bunched. His fingers still tingled from the feel of Shelly's soft skin. His stomach hollowed out and his gut twisted.

"He just fell asleep. *Finally,*" she whispered. "I'll lose my friggin' mind *and* my figure if you wake him up again." When Colton arched an eyebrow, she added. "He exercises. A lot." She'd never been into bad boys, but seeing all those muscles move and bulge had given her a new appreciation for the dark and dangerous. "If I have to watch him even one more minute…." She swallowed. Hard. "I'll dive back into that box over there." She motioned to the white bakery container sitting on her bunk. "And it won't be pretty."

"I won't wake him," he promised. "If you do something for me."

Desperate blue eyes held his. "Anything."

"Sleep." He held her gaze long enough to send her the few steps back toward the bunk. She sank down and her eyes closed.

And then it was time to move.

Colton pulled a small spray bottle from his pocket. Liquid silver. Cody's friends and fellow vampires at Skull Creek Choppers—the town's legendary custom motorcycle shop—had cooked up the concoction by mixing molten silver with a specially formulated quick-drying paint. The color matched the bars and would blend in evenly once sprayed on.

Colton shook the container for a few seconds the way Brent had told him to, then flicked the nozzle and activated the spraying mechanism. Leaning up, he started in a sweeping motion at the top of Holbrook's cell door and worked his way down.

Forget the age-old myths regarding vampire repellants. Garlic, holy water and crosses didn't stand a chance against a true vampire. Sunlight and wooden stakes posed the only real threats. But silver did pack a powerful punch if used properly. While the metal wouldn't kill on contact, it did burn like a sonofabitch. More than enough to stop Rose and keep her from releasing Jimmy a fifth time.

And then Colton himself would stop her for good.

He finished up with the paint and closed the lid. A drop of paint hit his skin. White hot pain shot through him. He ground his teeth against the sensation until the heat fizzled into a steady throb and he could actually see again. He damned himself for not being more careful and stared down at the raw, smoking flesh. Despite the three bags of blood he'd had back at the motel, the wound wasn't healing.

It wouldn't, not unless he helped it along.

An image of Shelly pushed into his brain, her body slick and wet from the tub, her sweet heat tantalizing against his tongue, her energy so potent and mesmerizing that he couldn't get enough.

But that hadn't been real. Rather, he'd been caught up in her fantasy, seeing and feeling her, but not truly participating. He was still weak. Hungry.

For any woman, he reminded himself.

For one woman.

His gaze shifted to Honey who sat on the bunk, eyes closed, a half smile on her face as if she were dreaming the most pleasant of dreams. His hand screamed and his gut twisted.

"Come."

The command whispered through his head, pushed from his thoughts, and she looked up. Her gaze met his. Her breath quickened in anticipation. She'd been so worked up all day and nothing, not even the sugary donuts had been enough to curb her appetite. But he could. He could give her what she wanted, and take what he desperately needed, satisfying them both.

A few steps and she met him at the cell door. She

really was an attractive female with her long hair and curvaceous figure, and she didn't seem the least bit anxious to hide any of it. She wore shorts and a fitted top that left little to the imagination unlike one infuriating Deputy who made it a point to cover everything up and make him wonder what lay beneath.

After last night, he knew.

He nixed the thought and watched as Honey extended a French-manicured hand through the bars. She held out one delicate wrist.

At the moment of contact, he felt the first bubble of energy. It slipped into his fingertips and crested through his body. But the sensation was weak. Fleeting. She wasn't nearly as warm as he'd expected. As luscious. As stirring.

She wasn't Shelly.

He drop-kicked the ridiculous notion and tamped down on the sudden regret that rushed through him.

"Stay away from Holbrook," he murmured as he stared deep into her eyes. "He's dangerous and you can do a hell of a lot better."

And then he dropped her hand, broke the spell and walked away.

Not because of Shelly, mind you.

No, he had more important matters propelling him away from Honey Gentry than simple infuriating lust over one stubborn Deputy.

He powered open the door and locked it behind him. He'd already pushed his luck with the two men out front. They were under his spell, but it wouldn't last long. Honey was a different story. Females were more susceptible to male vampires and vice versa. She would stay out of it for at least a few hours, the spell fading gradually as the distance between them grew. But the other two?

His gaze shifted from the Deputy who slumped over his desk, to the Texas Ranger sitting stone-faced in a nearby chair. They were still mindless, but there was no guarantee how long that would last. They could wake up any second and start asking questions about the void in their memory. Then Colton would be back to square one, mesmerizing them all over again, wasting more precious time when he needed to get back to his truck and get on with his surveillance.

Just in case Rose showed up early.

He ignored the nagging voice that told him she wasn't anywhere close. That his brothers were right and he was wasting time when he could be resting and gathering his strength instead of waiting. Watching.

Fantasizing.

He left the jail and rounded the building, heading for the back fence that edged the parking lot.

Fantasizing? Hardly.

He was doing no such thing when it came to Shelly Lancaster. And he certainly wasn't running away like a bat out of hell because of her. Because she'd gotten under his skin and the thought of touching another woman had bothered him a helluva lot more than he'd expected. Because he could still smell

Shelly's sweet scent and taste her ripe essence and hear the steady staccato of her heartbeat and—

"What the hell are you doing here?" Her voice echoed and he whirled to find her standing in the parking lot behind him, her keys in one hand, a Red Bull in the other.

She couldn't have looked more different from the bombshell locked up in cell number two. While she'd changed out of her drab uniform, she'd opted for an even more drab pair of gray sweatpants and a matching Texas A & M sweatshirt, the monstrous sleeves pushed up to her elbows. Instead of long and flowing and sexy, her hair was pulled back into a tight ponytail and there wasn't a trace of makeup on her face. No lipstick plumping her lips, inviting his kiss. No shadow accenting her eyes and luring him closer. Nothing.

And damned if she still wasn't the most beautiful woman he'd ever seen.

Instantly, his gut twisted and his chest hitched and he finally admitted to himself that his damned frustration had nothing to do with the need for a real flesh and blood woman and everything to do with *her*.

Because she was the most sexually frustrated woman he'd ever come into contact with. It was her energy that drew him. Distracted him.

And it had to stop now, before it got any worse.

At the rate he was going, Rose would show up and he would be too wired to even notice.

"It's almost ten o'clock." Her gaze narrowed. "Since when is it standard operating procedure to do a security evaluation at this hour?" Without waiting for his reply, she continued, "You should have been here hours ago. I waited an entire day—*all* day," she said accusingly. "I even rearranged my schedule so I'd be free to show you around. I sent Bobby to chase down six of Mr. McGee's cows all by himself because I was sticking around here, waiting for you—"

"We should have sex," he murmured, cutting her off mid-sentence.

Her jaw snapped shut and her head snapped up. Surprise glittered hot and bright in her eyes. Her breath caught and she stared at him for a long, tense moment, trying to comprehend his words. And failing. "What did you just say?" she finally asked.

He stepped closer. "You." Another step. "Me." Step. Step. *"Sex."* And then he kissed her.

9

IT WASN'T THE BEST pick-up line Shelly had ever heard.

There was no smooth analogy. No flirtatious play on words. No seductive wink to punctuate the end of the sentence.

At the same time, it was the only pick-up line—with the exception of "Wanna play hide the summer sausage?" courtesy of Billy Rankin back in the ninth grade—that had ever been directed straight at her. And for some reason that all-important fact packed an awful powerful punch.

Colton Braddock wanted to have sex with her. *He* wanted to have sex with *her*.

The truth echoed in her head for one triumphant moment before realization dawned and she remembered that there was no way she could allow herself to go through with this. They were business colleagues, and Shelly never mixed with business with pleasure. She had an image to protect. She needed the confidence of every citizen in town when election time rolled around which was why she'd called the few men desperate enough to believe the ad and set them straight first thing that morning.

But Colton Braddock wasn't an impressionable voter. He was simply passing through. Temporary. So what if she let her image slip just a little? He was in town for a few days at the most and suddenly there seemed nothing wrong with getting up close and personal.

As long as they set down a few ground rules first.

She stiffened, gathered her strength and pulled away from the best kiss of her life.

She stared up at him and for a few frantic heartbeats, she actually forgot her first rule. He looked so tall, dark and delicious in a black T-shirt and worn, faded Wranglers, the hems frayed around his scuffed boots. He'd left his hat behind and there was nothing except a thick fringe of black lashes shadowing his pale, translucent gaze that swept from her head to her toes and back up again.

In a flash, she had the insane thought that she never, ever wanted to be with any other man. It was him. It would always be him.

Not.

This wasn't about forever. It was about now.

Right now.

"Okay." The word was out before she could stop it.

He seemed surprised for a split-second, before his expression faded into sheer determination. "Let's go—"

"One night," she added, eager to make sure they were on the same page. "And then it's over. You go your way and I'll go mine. And you keep your mouth shut about the whole thing."

His lips drew into a tight line and a muscle ticked in his jaw, as if he meant to argue. That, or kiss her senseless again. His eyes darkened and smoldered. She felt his strong hands at her waist, ready to pull her closer. Electricity zipped up her spine.

The moment held for several fast, furious heartbeats, but then the tension seemed to ease and he nodded.

"Tonight and nothing more."

"*And* you keep your mouth shut. I'm running for Sheriff in six months and I won't do anything that might jeopardize that. I've been working for this my entire life."

A sexy grin tugged at his lips and a gleam danced in his eyes. "Darlin', I never kiss and tell."

His deep voice confirmed what she'd already suspected and a sliver of warmth went through her. Colton Braddock was a lot more likeable than she cared to admit.

"What else?" He arched an eyebrow.

"I need to check in and tie up a few things in the office first." The grin faded and he looked as if he wanted to argue. Fat chance. Shelly had her mind made up. If they were doing this, it was going to be by her rules. "Meet me in an hour. My place."

Surprisingly enough, he didn't protest. Instead, he

dipped his head for one last kiss to seal the agreement, and then he all but disappeared right before her eyes.

A strange sense of *uh-oh* wiggled through her as she stared at the empty spot where he'd stood only moments before, but then anticipation got the best of her. She became acutely aware of her sweat suit and old sneakers and… Yikes.

She turned and hurried around to the front of the building where she'd left her car. She had one hour to pull off the makeover of a lifetime and the clock was already ticking.

SHE'D LIED TO Colton.

Forget loose ends at the office. She'd needed time to trade her sweats and sensible cotton briefs for *this*.

She stared at the drawer full of lingerie, everything from leopard print bras to black sequined thongs. Practically the entire on-line catalog at Naughty Nights. Her very own hidden treasure of indulgence. Perfect for the rendezvous of a lifetime.

She reached for hot pink lace bra and matching thong. A few seconds later, she dabbed on lipstick and a little mascara, and then surveyed the results in the mirror.

For a split-second, time sucked her back and she remembered standing in the doorway, watching her mother get ready for an evening out, praying all the while that she would change her mind and stay home.

Just this once.

She shook away the image and tamped down the urge to peel off the trashy underwear. Unlike her mother, she didn't have any kids to take care of. Even more, she could control herself. One encounter, and then the sexy nothings went back in the drawer where they belonged and Colton Braddock moved on to the next town.

But while she had plenty of lingerie, sexy clothes were a different matter. She turned toward her closet and frowned.

Rifling through a sea of beige cotton, she unearthed her one and only dress—a strappy, summer number that she'd bought during a training seminar in Austin. The dress was white silk with pale yellow flowers and a fringe of yellow lace at the neckline. The tags were still intact, proof that the dress had been more of an impulse buy than anything she would actually wear in her normal life.

But tonight wasn't the norm.

She tugged the tags loose and was just undoing the side zipper when the doorbell rang.

What the...?

Her gaze ping-ponged to the clock. Reality zapped her and she realized that she'd spent an entire half hour angsting over undies.

She stepped into the dress and shimmied and wiggled until she managed to get it up and over her hips. Okay, so trying the dress on when she'd bought it might have been a good idea. But she'd been in a hurry and desperate to do it on the fly while Bobby finished up his lunch at a nearby pub. She'd grabbed it and paid for it and the deed had been done.

Shoving her arms into the straps, she drew a deep breath and pulled the bodice up and over her chest. Frantic fingers plucked at the side zipper, pulling and tugging until she managed to get it up and over her hips. She sucked in a breath to bring it the rest of the way home, but it didn't help. The zipper wouldn't budge past her waist.

The doorbell rang again, sending a message of *hurry the hell up* through her. She fought with the zipper a few more seconds, but it was no use. The dress was a lost cause. She pushed the zipper the opposite way, ready to shed the dress and opt for her sweats, but the metal teeth were stuck. She pushed and tugged, but it refused to budge—

Rrrrrrrriiiiinnnnngggggg!

The doorbell sounded again and she glanced out the upstairs window in time to see Colton Braddock step down off her front porch.

She had the fleeting thought that he might be leaving. Giving up. *No!*

She snapped up her sweatshirt and pulled it down over her head and chest so that it made the sundress look like a skirt. Hurrying down the stairs, she threw open the door. The porch light cast a soft yellow glow that pushed back the shadows and bathed her empty doorstep.

She stepped out onto the porch and scanned the surrounding area, seeing the tiny postage stamp-size yard that she loved so much, the flower bushes lining the perimeter. The familiar black pick-up still sat in the driveway behind her car and relief swamped her.

"I was starting to think you'd changed your mind." His deep voice rumbled in her ear a split second before she felt his presence directly behind her.

"I was getting dressed." She whirled and found herself face to face with Colton Braddock.

He arched one dark brow as his gaze dropped to the sweatshirt. "Weren't you wearing that earlier?"

"Technically, yes. It's a long story. One you'd rather not hear. Trust me."

A grin tugged at his lips and her breath caught. Her gaze collided with his and her heart gave a double thump. He had the most incredible eyes that looked almost silver in the dim light. So hot and liquid and mesmerizing.

She felt herself being pulled into the warm depths. It would be so easy to lose herself. To dive head first and forget about everyone and everything. To strip naked despite the fact that she was standing smack dab on her front porch. Anyone could walk by. Mrs. Fleming from next door could be watering her tulips or Mr. Sandowski could be out walking his dog. Yet staring deep into his eyes, she didn't care. It was about doing this with him, right now, right here, *right now,* regardless of the consequences.

She reached for the hem of her sweatshirt and an image rushed at her, of her mother stumbling in after a late night, tearing at her clothes as she fought to get closer to the man with her. She'd been mindless of her two little girls sitting on the sofa, waiting for her. She'd been a slave to the same desperation that suddenly gripped Shelly.

Her hand stalled and she fought for control. "Not now," she said, her hand trembling. "Not here."

He started to protest, but she pressed a finger to his lips. The feel of his mouth sent a burst of need through her and her body vibrated from the force. She grabbed his hand and led him toward the door. He stalled just shy of the threshold and she glanced back at him.

"Say it," he growled.

"Say what?"

"Ask me to come in."

She nodded, but he didn't budge. She was struck again with the odd thought that something wasn't quite right.

That he wasn't quite right.

But then he leaned forward and kissed her, hard and brutal, and she forgot everything except the heat singing through her body.

"Say it," he murmured again against her lips.

"Come inside," she heard herself say. "Please."

He followed her in. The door slammed shut behind them and she whirled to face him. Her breaths came fast and quick as she grasped the sweatshirt and pulled it up and over her head. Cotton hit the ground at her feet. The cool rush of air from the overhead vent teased her nipples through the lace of her bra and excitement chased up her spine.

"Here," she breathed. "Now." She stepped toward him.

10

HE WANTED TO KISS her again.

The truth struck as Colton stood in the foyer and watched her work at the clasp on the bra. It hit the ground on top of the sweatshirt and his undead heart stopped beating.

Yes, he wanted to kiss her again. But it went beyond the need gripping his entire body. There was something deep inside of him, something urgent and fierce and possessive, that roared to life and propelled him forward. To brand her as his. Now and forever.

No!

He fought the crazy feeling and bypassed her luscious lips. His mouth went to one ripe nipple.

He hauled her close and bent her backward as he feasted on the hard tip, laving and sucking, but it wasn't enough. His teeth grazed her tender flesh and his incisors tingled. Desire pounded through him, fierce and demanding and *different*. The truth resonated through him as he fought to keep from sinking his fangs deep and tasting her sweet essence.

Because *she* was different.

The thought twisted at him as he scooped her up into his arms and turned toward the living room to his right.

Near the large leather sofa, he eased her to her feet, sliding her down the length of his body in a move that made them both gasp. She was so soft and warm and his body trembled.

Their gazes locked as he reached out and touched the zipper of the sundress caught at her waist. His heart pounded and his pulse raced and an ache gripped him from the inside out. He tugged and the zipper gave way. The teeth parted.

She grasped the material and shoved it down as fast as possible. She'd been waiting for this far too long and she didn't want to give herself the chance to change her mind. Even more, she didn't want to give *him* the chance to change *his* mind.

He read the thought before it faded into the heat of her gaze and suddenly he wasn't half as anxious to satisfy his own hunger as he was to slow down and satisfy hers. To prove to her that she didn't need a skimpy dress or barely there underwear to be desirable to a man.

To him.

"Sexy isn't about the package, darlin'," he murmured. "It's a state of mind."

She looked surprised and startled that he was so tuned into her thoughts.

But then the expression faded into a rush of insecurity. "Nice packaging doesn't hurt."

Not that she would know. She'd never wrapped herself up to please a man before. No fancy underwear or frilly dresses. She had an image to protect and she wasn't about to destroy it by giving in to some silly need to play the soft, tempting female.

It was all about being strong. In control.

"There's nothing wrong with letting go once in a while." He dropped his gaze in a slow, deliberate trek down the length of her body before following the same path back up, from her calves to her lush thighs, the strip of lace barely concealing the heart of her. "You *are* a soft, tempting female, Shelly, no matter how much that pisses you off at times."

"It doesn't piss me off." At least it wasn't pissing her off at the moment. No, right now she wanted to sink down to the couch, part her legs and let him inside.

"Do it," he murmured. "Don't deny yourself. Let go. Just this once." He touched her, circling her ripe nipple and she gasped.

Surprise followed by heated satisfaction slid through her and the worried pinch between her eyebrows eased. While he couldn't see every thought because her stubbornness kept shutting the door, he could read her features. The bright flare of her brilliant eyes. The goose bumps that danced up her arms. The pink flush that crept up her neck. The need.

He swallowed, his throat suddenly dry. With a sweep of his tongue, he licked his lips. The urge to feel her pressed against his mouth nearly sent him over the edge. He wanted to part her with his tongue and unleash everything she fought so desperately to keep bottled up. Desire pounded, steady, demanding, and sent the blood jolting through his veins at an alarming rate.

He urged her back onto the couch and surprisingly, she let him. He dropped to his knees between her legs, his shoulders wedging her further apart. His fingertips circled the rose-colored nipple, and he inhaled sharply when the already turgid peak ripened even more.

Leaning over her, he touched his lips to her navel, dipped his tongue inside and swirled. She whimpered, the sound urging him on. He licked a path up her fragrant skin, teasing and nibbling, until he reached one full breast. Closing his lips over her swollen nipple, he pulled and tugged.

He swept his hands downward, over her flat, quivering belly, to her panties. He dipped a hand beneath the lace and traced the slit between her legs. She gasped when he parted her. He pushed one finger deliciously deep. Heat surrounded him, sucking him in and sending a jolt of hunger through him that shook him to his very core.

She trembled and gasped and, just like that, she

came apart. His hand started to tingle as he drank in the sweet, bubbling energy of her climax. The sensation spread through him, pulsing up his arm, into his shoulder, his chest, pushing out the cold and filling him with a hot, vibrating burst of sensation.

He closed his eyes and drank in the feeling, relishing it for a long, delicious moment. Forget plunging his cock deep inside of her. This alone was ecstasy for him. For any vampire.

More than enough.

It was all about a woman's orgasm. About soaking up *her* energy, not spending his own.

"If I didn't know better, I'd say you're enjoying this more than me." The sound of her voice slipped into his thoughts and he opened his eyes to find her staring up at him.

"I'd be a fool not to. You're something else."

He said it with such sincerity that Shelly almost believed him. But this was the heat of the moment and a rock hard erection could impair the sharpest man's thinking. "You don't have to sweet talk me into bed. I'm practically there. Speaking of which, shouldn't we head upstairs?"

His grin was slow and sinful and oh, so delicious. He lowered his head and drew the throbbing tip of one breast into the moist heat of his mouth, and suddenly the only thing on her mind was touching him. She slid her hands over his shoulders, feeling his warm skin and hard muscle through the soft cotton of his T-shirt.

He suckled her, his teeth grazing the soft globe of flesh, nipping and biting the turgid nipple with just enough pressure to make her gasp. Her breast swelled and throbbed.

When he licked a path across her skin to coax the other breast in the same torturous manner, a decadent heat spiraled through her and she moved her pelvis. She wanted him surrounding her, inside of her.

"Easy, sugar," he said as if he read the desperation. "We've got all night."

But Shelly didn't want all night. All night meant a morning after. As in waking up with each other and sharing an awkward goodbye in the bright light of day.

And while she'd never been the one saying goodbye, she'd witnessed it too many times to count.

Never again.

This was about indulging herself right now. About living out a brief, temporary fantasy that wouldn't haunt her in the days to come.

No, she didn't want all night. She wanted one really good climax with him inside of her and her falling apart in his arms. One. And then she could get past the frustration and set her mind on what really mattered—her job.

"I have to be at work early tomorrow." Desperate hands reached for him and he stiffened. "We should hurry up and get to the good stuff. Then you can go home and I'll get some sleep." *And then it'll be over.*

Her hands skimmed his shoulders and drew him closer, but he didn't budge.

"I don't think so." His voice pushed past the pounding of her pulse and she realized that something was wrong.

Her eyelids fluttered open in time to see him push to his feet and stumble backward.

He looked as surprised as she felt.

"What's wrong?"

But he didn't seem to know any more than she did. He glanced around as if desperate for a distraction. His gaze hooked on the bookshelf she'd inherited from her Grandma Jean, along with the dozens of romance novels boxed in the back of her closet.

Rows of how-to books lined the shelves now, everything from gun collecting to softball techniques. All in keeping with the image she'd fought so hard to build.

It was an image that was slipping away as she lay open and exposed to Colton Braddock.

"Please." Her voice was shameless. "Don't stop."

But he had to. She could see it in his expression and while he didn't look all that pleased about it, he shook his head anyway. "It's getting really late. I should go."

"But what about the bedroom?"

His gaze locked with hers for a split-second. "I guess we'll just have to make up for it tomorrow night."

"But that's not part of the deal—" she protested, but he was already heading for the door.

She caught a quick glimpse of his face, the determined set to his jaw, the fire blazing in his liquid eyes, before he disappeared. Hinges creaked. Wood slammed. And just like that, he disappeared and Shelly found herself left with nothing but her fantasies to keep her company.

Again.

11

THE PAST WASN'T just haunting him. It was driving him crazy.

One hundred percent certifiable.

That was the only explanation for what he'd just done. She'd been right there. Open and waiting. *Ready.*

"And then it'll be over."

Her voice echoed in his head and he slammed his foot down on the accelerator, speeding down the road, feeding the distance between them.

He hung a left at the edge of town and headed north, until the pavement turned to gravel and rocks spewed against the underside of the pick-up. The road narrowed, cutting a path between a stretch of rich, green pastureland. To his right, he glimpsed a rustic two-story white rock house in the far distance. He drove another fifty yards, following the instructions Cody had left on his cell, until he got a better view of the structure. A gate marked the entrance, but Colton didn't turn in. Instead, he pulled over onto the side of the road and killed the engine.

It was just half past midnight. Late for regular folks. Early for a vampire.

Lights beamed from the downstairs windows. A rustic Texas star light fixture gleamed near the front door, illuminating a wide front porch and a hand-carved cedar bench.

The house looked so familiar and for a brief moment, time sucked him back and he saw a newly whitewashed two-story house with red shutters and a wide wraparound porch. Curtains billowed at the windows and the scent of his momma's infamous cherry pie drifted from inside.

Home.

The Circle B had been in his family for two generations, passed down from his grandfather to his mother, an only child. She'd loved it and nurtured it more than any man, a helluva lot more than her no-good excuse for a husband did, a man who'd disappeared the first chance he'd had. The loss hadn't phased her. She'd had her home. One she was eager to pass on to the next in line when the time came.

First Colton.

Then his son.

The image of CJ with his bright blue eyes and dark hair faded into that of a woman with red hair and lying eyes. *Rose.*

He felt the familiar tightening in his chest and stiffened, focusing on the heat in his belly. The anger.

Vengeance.

That's why he was here.

Not because he missed his brothers, or because he wanted to make up for lost time. Or even because he desperately craved the peace and happiness they'd all managed to find even if they *were* vampires.

There was no peace for Colton. He'd failed his family. His son.

Because of Rose.

She would pay dearly for her treachery. He would make sure of it, even if it wouldn't come close to easing the guilt. The isolation. The loneliness.

The thought crept up on him so fast that he didn't have time to slam his mind against it.

Lonely?

Fire and damnation, he wasn't lonely. He was simply alone. He liked being alone. That's why he kept his distance from his ranch hands and left their supervision to his foreman. He didn't have to worry over them himself. Over getting too close or too attached. He didn't have to worry about letting anyone down.

Again.

He shook his head against the notion and focused on the bench sitting on Cody's porch. A cuddle bench. That's what his ma had called them way back when. They'd had one just like it sitting on their front porch back at the Circle B.

She'd caught Cody curled up on it more than once with some girl or another and so the name had stuck.

Not that Colton had ever tried it out for himself. He'd been too busy running cattle, desperate to pull his weight and support his new bride the way he'd promised Rose's daddy when the man had come calling with a shotgun and the news that his only daughter was pregnant. She'd named Colton as the father and the man had wanted a proper wedding.

But there'd been no need for that sawed off shotgun. Colton was more than ready to do his duty. Since his father had left at an early age, he'd been carrying the weight of responsibility for his family. Doing his duty was nothing new to him and so he'd done the right thing, determined to be the father he'd never had.

He'd never had the chance.

He slammed his foot down on the gas. Tires spewed gravel as he swerved back onto the road and drove a few miles until he saw the old farmhouse that had once been the only building on Cody's land. He pulled the truck over and killed the engine. While he wouldn't take Cody up on his offer to stay in the main house, he wouldn't mind bunking out here.

Colton was used to roughing it. When he was driving cattle, he slept in a cabin on the back forty of his property. A good sleeping bag and a few well-placed hay bales was all he needed to protect him from the sunlight.

Even better, this place was a good ten miles outside of town, far away from the motel and the nosey old woman making his days a living hell. And far, far away from Shelly and her damnable fantasies.

Boots hit the gravel as he climbed from behind the wheel and started for the old house. The paint had all but peeled off the brown shutters. The once white-washed walls were now gray and weathered. The porch steps were rotted and falling down. It was just a shell of what it had once been, far from the brand spanking new house Cody had built for his bride. Still, it held the same appeal. The same familiar layout that reminded Colton so much of home.

Unfortunately, it wasn't in good enough shape to provide adequate refuge for a vampire. He circled the house and started for the faded red barn that stood out back. While the house had a lot of roof damage thanks to past storms, the barn seemed to be made of tougher stuff. The metal roof was still sound, the structure weathered but sturdy.

Perfect.

The hinges creaked and groaned as he pulled the door open and walked inside. The musty smell of hay and leather and rotting wood filled his nostrils and he felt a pang of regret that his brother had traded this place for the shiny metal barn situated behind his new house.

This place had character, from the kids' names carved into one of the beams, to the old leather saddle still resting atop one of the stalls. A wall of antique tools lined the opposite side of the barn. A hand saw. A circular crank. Several notching tools. A wood stove for heating. He walked deeper inside and saw the work bench. His nostrils flared. His finally tuned senses picked up the faint trace of sawdust that had settled into the beams. Whoever had lived here had probably built the place and even hand-tooled that saddle.

He traced his hand over the leather and remembered the ancient bookcase in Shelly's living room with its scratches and worn edges. She was obviously the kind of woman who appreciated a nice antique, regardless of whether it was a bookshelf, or even a cuddle bench.

Not that he was going to make her one. The last thing he wanted was to cuddle with her, for Chrissake. Their relationship was all about sex. He knew it and so did she.

That was exactly why he'd walked out on her.

He had at least three days to kill and Shelly Lancaster was interested in just one night. All the more reason to slow things down a little. Otherwise he would have to find someone else to sate the hunger that ripped through him.

He wasn't doing that.

Shelly was too perfect. Too ripe. Too ready. Too repressed. She fed the need like no one else and so he meant to take his time. And draw things out for as long as possible.

He wanted Shelly. And he meant to have her.

At least until his past showed up and he said goodbye to everyone and everything.

12

"THANK GOD," Honey declared when Shelly walked into the cell area with another pastry box early the next morning.

Early as in nine-thirty.

Not only had she missed her alarm again, but she'd slept even later thanks to Colton Braddock and his announcement that he wanted to see her again.

Despite her very specific ground rules.

Excitement whispered through her, followed by a quick jolt of anxiety because the last thing, the very *last* thing she wanted was to spend another day like yesterday.

She'd been on pins and needles, waiting, wondering. Distracted. To the point that she'd been acting completely out of sorts.

"Are you wearing lipstick again?" Honey's question drew her from her mental tirade and confirmed the vicious truth.

"It's lip balm," she said, swiping at the Pink Passion with the back of her hand. "The drugstore only had the tinted stuff."

Honey swallowed her mouthful of donut. "Mind if I borrow some?"

"Be my guest." She watched as Honey slathered on Pink Passion, her gaze directed at the man sitting in the opposite cell. He was on his back on the floor, hands behind his head, ear buds stuffed into his ears, music turned up. He counted as he did a continuous rhythm of sit-ups. He'd shed his shirt and his abs flexed each time he folded up. Then down. Then up.

Oh, boy.

Shelly found herself wondering if Colton's abs were as defined. In her fantasies they were, but she'd yet to see for herself.

She wanted to.

She wanted it more than she wanted her next breath, and that scared her more than anything. She refused to get so caught up in a man that she forgot everything that really mattered.

The way her mother had.

No. She wasn't repeating that mistake. Ever.

"Thanks." Honey handed over the tube, but Shelly shook her head.

"Keep it."

"You've got good coloring." Honey slipped the tube into her pocket. "I bet you'd look good in a red lipstick."

"You know everything about make-up, don't you?"

"Been wearing it since I was thirteen. You should try a little eye shadow, too." Honey unearthed a donut from the box and took a big bite, savoring the mouthful for a long moment. "Fix yourself up a little and you might land yourself a boyfriend."

"Maybe I'm not looking for a boyfriend."

"Honey, we're all looking for a boyfriend. At the very least, we'd like somebody to keep things interesting every now and then."

Now would be good, Shelly thought to herself, her nerves still buzzing from last night. Very good.

"Is that how you do it?"

"Do what?"

"Get a guy? You fix yourself up."

"That, and I use a little technique I like to call the three B's." When Shelly arched an eyebrow, Honey added, "Boobs, butt and bending over. It's foolproof. See, you start with a really skimpy dress that's cut down to there." She motioned to her cleavage. "And up to here." She swept a hand to her upper thigh. "That way when you bend over, the dress hikes up just enough to give whoever is looking a sneak peak at your goodies. Then bam, they're following you home for as long as you want."

"And what if it doesn't work?"

Honey smiled. "It *always* works. See, men are visual. Give them plenty to look at and you'll have them eating out of the palm of your hand." She shoved the last of the donut into her mouth. "Just to cinch the deal though," she said in between chews, "I always have a red velvet cake on stand by."

"What if he doesn't like red velvet?"

"The cake isn't for him, sugar. It's for you. After you've wowed him with the dress, or lack of, you cut yourself a big piece of red velvet, or chocolate or carrot or whatever floats your boat, and eat it real nice and slow." She demonstrated with another donut, taking bite after bite, her movements so slow and deliberate and seductive, that Shelly felt her own stomach hollow out. Honey finished by sweeping her tongue along her bottom lip. "No way will he be able to watch that and not jump your bones."

If only.

Shelly made a mental note to pick up a red velvet cake on her way home. While she couldn't imagine that Colton Braddock would put her off another night, she wasn't taking any chances. She was pulling out all the stops and getting him into bed tonight. Then her anxiety would end and she could get back to her life. To being on time—to work and the effin' donut shop.

"No lemon crème?" Honey stared hopefully as she searched through what was left in the bakery box.

"I'm afraid not. They were all out by the time I got there."

"Oh, well." She shrugged and cast a hungry gaze at Holbrook. "It's not like I have to put up with Mr. Fitness over there for too much longer. I'll be out in less than an hour and then it's back to walking the straight and narrow with my cupcakes. Speaking of which, is Judge Meyers in yet?"

"About that." Shelly shook her head. "I know he was supposed to be in by nine, but when I came in Bobby said his secretary had postponed his morning cases."

"She *what?*"

"It seems he had a flat on his way back from Port A and won't be back until lunch."

"I can't sit here until lunch," Honey screeched. "I've got things to do. I've got deliveries coming by my place and cupcakes to bake and a celibacy vow that I'm this close to breaking thanks to him." She pointed at Jimmy. "You have to let me out of here."

"I wish I could. I really do." Particularly since the charges were bogus and Judge Meyers was sure to throw them out. "But Bobby booked you and that means you're in the system. I can't just let you walk without a court order." When Honey's face fell, she added, "But I can head out to your place and sign for the flour and sugar."

"You would do that for me?"

"You bet." Especially since it meant getting away from Bobby, who'd all but freaked when she'd walked in late again. *And* wearing lipstick. Seriously. It was lipstick, for heaven's sake. It's not like she looked that out of sorts. She *was* female.

Then again, that was the point entirely. Bobby didn't see her as the average female. He saw her as an equal and she meant to keep it that way.

In the meantime, she was game for any and everything that kept her busy and out of sight until tonight, regardless of whether it was waiting for a delivery at Honey's, or driving over to the next town to pick up something to wear tonight. And a red velvet cake. Just in case.

"I'm headed out to run a few errands that Matt left unfinished," she told Bobby a few minutes later. "I'll be on my radio if you need me."

To HELL WITH *slow and steady.*

The thought struck when Shelly opened the door later that night and Colton got a really good look at her—from her long, gleaming brown hair flowing sexy and loose past her shoulders, to her pink-tipped toes stuffed into high-heeled sandals.

And everything in between.

The dress she wore was short and tight, cut down to *there* and up to *here.* Hot pink spandex hugged her voluptuous curves and spelled a very detailed picture that left little to the imagination. Not that he needed one where she was concerned. He'd seen every inch of her incredible body, touched it, tasted it.

More.

Lust sizzled and popped inside of him and his gut twisted. His gaze shifted down, drinking in the picture she made, savoring it, before sweeping back up.

At least, he tried for a clean sweep, but his attention seemed hell-bent on pausing at several interesting spots along the way.

The long, bare legs that seemed to go on endlessly. The flare of her hips. The press of her ripe nipples beneath the thin material of her dress. The deep vee between her luscious breasts. The bare curve of one shoulder. The frantic beat of her pulse. The smooth column of her throat. Her full, pink lips.

Need rolled over him and his hands trembled, eager to pull her close and feel her ripe mouth so soft and pliant beneath his own.

A kiss, of all things. He wanted another friggin' *kiss*.

He stiffened and gave himself a fierce mental ass-kicking. Ruthless vampires didn't crave kisses. Not even desperate ones. They wanted sex. Energy. Satisfaction.

Get it together, Braddock. Fast.

He wasn't going to waste time kissing Shelly Lancaster because if he kissed her now, he'd sure as hell want to do it again and again and again. Tonight would be shot to hell and back before it had even gotten started.

No, he wasn't getting that close. At least not yet.

"I've been waiting for you." Her soft voice slid into his ears and swept along his nerve endings. She drew a deep breath. Her full breasts heaved. The dress tugged and pulled in all the right places and his gut twisted.

He narrowed his gaze, determined to resist the sudden urge to push her up against the nearest wall and bury himself hilt deep inside of her, which was exactly what she wanted.

She wanted it now. Over.

One night.

He forced his attention away from her decadent body. His gaze lifted and collided with hers, and damned if the heat in her rich chocolate eyes didn't sucker punch him as much as the sight of her in that slinky, sexy number.

He frowned. "Why are you dressed like that?"

"This old thing?" She shrugged one bare shoulder. "I just grabbed the first thing when I heard the door. Do you like it?"

"It's a little skimpy." He meant the comment as a criticism, to stir her insecurity and put some much needed distance between them.

Instead, her cheeks rosied and a smile touched her lips. As if he'd said just the right thing.

"Really?" She glanced down. "I was worried that it might not be short enough."

"Short enough for what?"

"For the three B's." Before he could ask, she waved a hand. "Don't ask. Just come on in." She pulled open the door and motioned him inside. Hunger flashed in her gaze. "It's time."

He caught the door frame before his legs could waltz right on in. "It's a really nice night." He glanced behind him. "Let's go out."

Disappointment flashed in her gaze, followed by

the briefest rush of fear. Because Shelly Lancaster didn't do relationships anymore than he did.

But this wasn't even close. He wasn't the least bit anxious to get to know her. Not her past or her present or her hopes and dreams. The only thing Colton gave a flip about were the physical nuances that made the chemistry burn so hot between them. The way she trembled and sighed when he touched her just so. The way her cheeks went pink and glowing when she exploded against his mouth. The way her eyes turned a deep, dark, liquid chocolate when she wanted him inside of her.

At least that's what he told himself.

"Listen," she said when he reached for her hand. "I think it's really important that we keep things in perspective. I mean, it's not that I don't like you. I don't really know you, which is exactly the point. I don't need to know you. This isn't about me liking you or you liking me. We're not dating." She voiced the fear in her eyes.

He smiled. "Sugar, this isn't a date." He leaned in and let his lips brush the shell of her ear. Heat zipped up and down his spine and his groin tingled. "It's foreplay."

_13_

"THIS CAN'T BE THE right place," Shelly said fifteen minutes later when Colton pulled the pick-up truck into the parking lot of the local fairgrounds and killed the engine.

Welcome to the twenty-first annual Skull Creek chili cook-off and hot dog eating competition!

Shelly read the words that blazed up on the lit marquis in front of the ten acre dirt parking lot and a wave of apprehension went through her. While it was only Thursday and the real fun didn't start until tomorrow, when Mark Burris and Mitchell Sutherland went head-to-head to see who could stuff the most weenies into their mouth without puking first, the two dozen competition chili teams had already fired up their trucks for the preliminary round of cooking. Tonight would narrow things down to the top five who would go all out on Saturday for first place.

With a whopping five extra teams entered this year, the turn-out was even bigger than expected.

Guilt swamped her and she barely resisted the urge to hop out and start doing a little crowd control. She should be here, keeping an eye on things, doing her job.

Cars and pick-ups overflowed the gravel parking lot, spilling into a nearby field where she caught a glimpse of Bobby directing traffic with his light wand. When he glanced in her direction, she pulled the edges tighter on the duster she'd grabbed before leaving the house. She sunk lower into her seat and damned herself for falling for Colton's ploy.

She'd envisioned a dozen scenarios when she'd climbed into the shiny black truck. Everything from a dimly lit restaurant complete with oysters on the half shell and an acoustic guitar player, to a bottle of champagne and a box of chocolates down by the lake.

Something seductive. Sexy. The perfect aphrodisiac.

But this?

This was a date, plain and simple, and Shelly Lancaster didn't do dates.

In the middle of the fairgrounds, a live band belted out a tune from Blake Shelton while people two-stepped across a make-shift sawdust floor. A ring of cooking trailers surrounded the perimeter. The smell of chili powder and cayenne pepper filled the air and teased her nostrils.

Off to the left, a few carnival rides had been set up for the kids, including a merry-go-round, a Ferris wheel and a gigantic bouncy castle. To the right, a concession stand offered up quart-size cups of beer from a local sponsor. A margarita machine *whirred,* churning out icy drinks.

"There is nothing sexy about chili. Except for Ben Avery." When he arched an eyebrow, she added, "He's the reigning champion. When he isn't winning local competitions with his infamous *Chili From Hell*, he works as a ranch hand."

"And you like ranch hands?"

"Not specifically, but I can appreciate an impressive backside and a pair of rocking abs as much as the next woman."

He stiffened and she had the insane feeling that he was actually jealous. But a man had to care to be jealous and Colton Braddock wasn't the caring type. He'd made that much perfectly clear.

Her mind traveled back to the previous night to the feel of his lips on her neck, her shoulders, her breasts—sex. This was all about sex and Colton Braddock was just what she needed.

But was she what *he* needed? She was starting to wonder. While he'd made the offer himself, it was obvious he was dragging his feet for some reason. Had he changed his mind?

She stiffened and turned accusing eyes on him. "I think we should go back to my place, unless there's some reason you don't want to." She held his stare. "If you've changed your mind, that's fine. Just spit it out."

"Come on." A wicked smile spread across his lips. "It'll be fun."

"I thought we were going for sexy, not fun."

"There's nothing wrong with both." The grin faded from his lips as he eyed her. "What is it you're so afraid of?"

"Nothing," she blurted, because Shelly didn't do fear any more than she did dates. "I just don't think this is the appropriate place to do this." Especially since she was wearing her Triple B dress. Great for private seductions. Not so great for prancing around in front of half the town. She had an image to maintain, after all. A professional, no-nonsense, let's kick butt image that served her well as the Deputy Sheriff of Skull Creek.

She certainly wasn't hesitating because the last time she'd worn a dress had been at her high school graduation when Marcus Sawyer had told her she looked weird.

"You look great." Colton's deep voice pushed into her thoughts and if she hadn't known better, she would have sworn he saw right through her.

Into her.

One callused finger touched a tendril of hair and pushed it back behind her ear. "You don't look weird at all," he murmured and then he climbed from behind the wheel before she could blurt out *What the hell?*

The hair on the back of her neck prickled as he rounded the front of the truck. The door creaked and suddenly he was standing there, his hand outstretched, a challenging light in his eyes as he waited for her to make the next move.

Beautiful.

The word echoed through her head and where she would have refused any other man, there was something oddly compelling about his voice.

For a split second, she forgot everything except the way the deep timbre vibrated along her nerve endings. He really did have a great voice. And he definitely said all the right things. As if he saw deep down inside of her and knew just how to punch her buttons.

As if he cared.

The thought was like a reality check and she stiffened. "Where did the weird comment come from?" she asked, calling him out the way she should have a few moments ago.

He looked surprised, but then the expression dived straight into a blank look. He shrugged. "You seem dead set on covering up and I know how sensitive women can be."

Not because he knew her, but because he knew women. All women. She had no doubt he'd been with more than his share. His expertise last night had proved as much. He'd brought her to the brink with his practiced hands and purposeful movements, and so the explanation made sense.

At the same time, she couldn't shake the feeling that something didn't add up.

Something about him.

"It's a little warm out tonight." His deep voice killed any more internal speculation and she glanced down at the duster belted securely at her waist. "You sure you don't want to leave that in the truck?"

Um, no. "There's a cold front coming through and I want to be ready." She made a big show of shivering.

"It's the middle of July."

"Yeah, well, you know what they say about Texas. If you don't like the weather, wait five minutes."

He eyed her for a long moment. "You don't have to hide who you really are for people to respect you."

"It's called projecting an air of professionalism, and spandex isn't professional. Not that that's why I'm wearing the coat. The Sheriff's department gets a head up on all extreme weather changes." She tucked a strand of hair behind her ear and tried to ignore the sweat already trickling between her shoulder blades. "The temperature is supposed to drop just like that." A sliver of guilt worked its way through her, but she shrugged it off.

The temperature *was* going to drop.

Only eight degrees, but that was beside the point. Bottom line—it was going to be cooler than it was right now. "I hope you brought a jacket."

"The cold doesn't really bother me."

Again she felt a trickle of apprehension, as if they were talking about more than just the weather. "Suit yourself. But don't come crying to me when you're freezing your buns off."

"Sugar, there's enough heat between us to give hell a run for its money. Freezing buns aren't even a remote possibility."

His deep voice stirred and teased. Excitement zipped up her spine, swamping the apprehension until her nerves buzzed.

She drew a shaky breath, suddenly desperate for more air as he took her hand and guided her forward.

"So what's the plan," she asked as they reached the line to get in. "Making out in the bathroom? Groping each other on the Ferris wheel? Going to third base under the bleachers?" The smell of spicy, bubbling chili teased her nostrils and her stomach grumbled, reminding her she'd been so frantic to get an outfit together that she hadn't had time to eat dinner.

"Easy." He grinned. "Why don't we grab some chili and see which one is the best?"

"I thought this was about foreplay?"

"Eating chili *is* foreplay."

"Maybe to an evening spent in the bathroom. I'd rather do more damage in the bedroom."

He grinned. "Foreplay is all about stimulating the senses." He breathed in. His nostrils flared and his gaze sparked. "Just let the place work its magic."

She became acutely aware of the smells teasing her nostrils, the sounds playing at her ears, the bright lights widening her eyes. He was right and suddenly there seemed to be nothing wrong with a little eating and talking and getting to know each other.

In the name of foreplay, of course.

"I *am* a little hungry."

He winked. "Then let's start playing, sugar."

14

"WE'VE GOT YOUR turkey chili, venison chili, vegetarian chili, green chicken chili, white bean chili, chili con carne and chili from hell." Alice Winkle, owner of the local diner and chairman of this year's cook-off, motioned to the array of steaming bowls sitting on the counter in front of her. "Pick your poison," she told Colton.

"The green chicken chili sounds good." And smelled even better. While Colton couldn't grab a spoon and dig in, he could still enjoy the experience. A vampire's sense of smell was extremely heightened. One good whiff of the delicious chili as a vampire would be more satisfying than eating an entire bowl as a human. "What about you?" Colton turned to Shelly.

"Oh, she'll have her usual," Alice cut in, "ain't that right, Shelly?" The woman winked as she reached for a fiery looking bowl from the very end. "Shelly's the only one in town who can eat an entire bowl of *Chili from Hell* without taking a drink or going to the E.R."

When Colton arched an eyebrow, Shelly said, "I won the title last year in the chili-eating competition."

"That's right." Alice beamed. "She beat Harry Farnsworth and ended his ten year winning streak."

"Harry's the chief of the Cherrywood Police Department," Shelly added. "We sort of have this rivalry with them. Matt was supposed to do it last year, but he had a family function so I stepped in and took his place."

"And it's a good thing she did, otherwise we woulda lost like we did all those years before. But Shelly, here, ate the whole danged thing in two minutes and thirty-eight seconds, and now we've got the bragging rights." Alice beamed as she handed over the bowl. "Wait." She added an extra habanera on top. "There you go. Enjoy."

"You guys take your chili seriously," Colton said as they found a spot at a nearby picnic table.

"You should see us during the annual rib cook-off." She folded herself in across the table from him. She reached for the sleeve of crackers sitting at the center of the table next to a roll of paper towels. In a matter of seconds, she'd crumbled half the package into her bowl.

He arched an eyebrow. "Why do you do it?"

"Do what?" She took the first bite and grimaced.

"Fight so hard to keep up appearances."

"I already told you—I'm running for Sheriff when Matt retires. Reliability builds trust."

"It'll also drive you crazy if you do it for too long. You have to cut loose once in a while."

If only.

"That's what my Grandma Jean used to say." A light gleamed in her eyes and a small smile touched her lips. "Of course, she was talking about wearing a red scarf to church as opposed to a beige one, but still."

"A wise woman."

"She was. She knew everything from how to fix her own water heater to how to change the fuel pump on her truck. She said it was because of my Grandpa Ralph. I never knew him, but she said he was a good man. He was sick a long time and so he taught her how to do stuff so that she wouldn't have to depend on anyone. She tried to teach my mom the same, but she wasn't interested in learning how to do things for herself. Or anyone else for that matter. She liked going out a lot more than taking care of two little girls."

"That must have been tough."

"Not at first. We had my Grandma Jean, but then she passed away and my sister and I were left to fend for ourselves."

"How old were you?"

"I was six and my sister was three." Shelly hesitated, as if deciding just how much she wanted to tell him. "I didn't know what to do at first," she finally admitted. "But I learned how to set my own alarm clock and make a mean peanut butter and jelly sandwich." When he arched an eyebrow, she added, "I've never been much for cooking. Anyhow, I managed to take care of myself and my sister, and we made it. Meanwhile, my mom partied all night."

"How are things now?"

"She still lives in the same run-down trailer on the edge of town. Still going out all night and sleeping all day. I drop off groceries once a week and Darla stops by to check on her, but she's no more interested in us now than she was back then." Sadness gleamed in her gaze before she seemed to gather her composure and he had the crazy urge to reach out.

Because he knew how she felt. His own father hadn't given a rat's ass about him or his brothers.

But this wasn't about easing her conscience or soothing her worry. This was about sex. Which meant he wasn't going to touch her.

"That must be tough," he said instead.

"I can handle it." She stared pointedly at him. "What about you? Any dysfunctional parents lurking in your closet?"

He shrugged. "My parents died a long time ago. It's just me."

"And your brothers," she reminded him. "There are three, right?"

He nodded. "Cody's the youngest. Then Brent and Travis."

"Are you guys close?"

"We used to be." He meant to end the conversation there, but damned if the words didn't find a way out before he could stop them. "My dad left when I was really young and so I ended up riding shotgun over my brothers. They didn't like it most of the time, but they sure as hell needed it. They were into everything." He smiled. "And so was I. We did everything together."

"And now?"

His smile faded. "Times have changed." *He'd* changed. He'd failed them when they'd needed him most. He'd failed his own son. He shrugged. "We don't see each other much, what with me being in New Mexico and them being here."

"But you're here now, so you guys can get reacquainted."

If only. He stifled the sudden thought and shook his head. "It's not that simple."

"Sure it is. Just grab a pizza and catch up. That's what Darla and I do when we've both been busy to spend time together. We eat. We talk. She ends up painting my toenails and I end up lecturing her about her latest boyfriend. Just like that we're back to being besties."

She made it sound so simple, but then she didn't know the truth—that he was a vampire hell bent on revenge—and being *besties* didn't figure into the death and destruction that waited for him.

Getting close to his brothers would only make it hard on them when he finished with Rose and ended his own miserable existence. No, it was better to keep his distance.

That's what he told himself, but with Shelly sitting across from him, her eyes gleaming with encouragement, he wasn't so sure he believed it. She made it seem possible.

She made him actually want to try.

He killed the crazy notion and pushed to his feet. "Let's go."

She eyed his full bowl. "Don't you want to eat your chili?"

"Do you really want to eat yours?" he countered.

"I see your point." She followed his lead and snatched up the cracker-laden mess in front of her. "First one to the trash is a rotten egg."

Finally.

Shelly held tight to the realization as she wiped a drop of perspiration from her temple and followed Colton from the main tent. They were leaving.

No more curious glances. No more stifling heat. Soon she could shed the coat and breathe.

Even more, she could have sex. Hot, vibrant, toe-curling *sex*.

Her heart kicked up in anticipation and her steps quickened....

Until they bypassed the Exit leading to the parking lot and stopped in front of a monstrous wagon overflowing with hay bales.

"I thought we were going home." She watched in

disappointment as Colton pulled out a twenty and handed it over to the driver.

"I never said that." The troubled expression that had carved his features back at the table had faded and now he was back to being the wicked, irresistible bad boy. A grin tugged at his sensuous lips as he winked. "I was just saving you from a trip to hell."

"Says you." She eyeballed the two horses hooked up to the front of the wagon. "I grew up in a trailer park. I'm not much into horses."

"There's a first time for everything." He eyed her, challenge gleaming in his gaze. "Unless you're scared, that is."

Them's fightin' words.

At least to a girl who'd grown up trying to prove she was the exact opposite. To everyone around her, but most of all, to herself.

She squared her shoulders, gathered her courage and motioned him into the back of the wagon. "Lead the way."

15

SHELLY WATCHED AS Colton climbed into the back of the wagon. She did her best not to stare at his butt outlined by the skin-tight Wranglers, but it was right there. And she was so hot. And he was so perfect. And…*oh, my.*

He turned and caught her before she could look away. His mouth crooked into a grin as he held out his hand. "My turn to enjoy the view."

"There isn't much view from the front."

"Says you." He motioned to her coat which had slipped open just enough to give him a tantalizing view of her cleavage. He hoisted her up next to him. His hand lingered on hers. "Aren't you burning up yet?"

She swallowed. Hard. "No," she finally managed.

"Don't worry, sugar." He sat down on a nearby hay bale and pulled her next to him. "You will be."

With everyone gathered in the main arena for the upcoming chili tasting competition, the hay ride had been all but forgotten. They were the only two passengers as the driver yanked the reins and gave a quick "Giddyup."

The wagon jumped and the inch of space between them disappeared. Her thigh settled against his as they launched into a steady roll. The sound of music and laughter faded, giving way to the buzz of crickets and the creak of the wagon. Stars studded the velvety sky and the moon sat big and bold above them. Green pasture stretched in front of them and the mirrorlike surface of a nearby lake gleamed in the distance.

Seconds ticked by and she found herself leaning into Colton, lulled by the steady rocking and the peaceful tranquility of the warm Texas night. She felt so far away from everyone and everything.

Fat chance.

The wagon moved at the pace of a turtle and so they were still within earshot when a high-pitched giggle drew her attention. She glanced at two teenage girls who stood on the edge of the fairgrounds. One of them waved, a knowing gleam in her eyes as she shifted her attention to Colton for a brief second and then back to Shelly. She nudged her friend and pointed.

Reality rained down on Shelly and she gave herself a great big mental slap. What the hell was she doing?

She was glued to Colton's side. Practically cuddling, of all things. Before she knew it, they'd be gazing at the stars and sharing their hopes and dreams.

Like how much she wanted to run for Sheriff and how terrified she was of losing. And how she was even more terrified of giving in to the passion blazing inside of her and winding up a slave to it. Just like her mother.

She stiffened, the motion pulling her shoulder away from his and giving her a blessed inch of distance. "I'm still not getting the foreplay aspect of any of this," she said with tight lips.

This wasn't sexy.

No, this was downright romantic, and God help her, but she liked it. She *liked* it.

"You don't have to be so uptight."

She half turned to see him staring at her, into her, as if he could see all of her secrets. "Uptight?" Her gaze narrowed. "It's called being alert, and this is how I am all the time. But then you wouldn't know that because you don't know me very well."

"Ah, but I do." He rested a hand atop her knee and his fingers moved under the hem of her coat until he felt bare skin. "I know you're anxious to get off this wagon because it makes you uncomfortable."

"I don't like to waste time and I just don't see the point to this."

"That's because you're not using your imagination." His expression grew dark and serious and hungry. "If you want to have really great sex, you've got to have a great buildup." A tiny pinpoint of light gleamed in the center of his eyes. "You have to feed the fire until it burns up everything. Your common sense. Your inhibitions. Your fear." Before she could protest, he leaned in and touched his lips to hers in an urgent kiss that sparked the heat already zinging through her body.

Heat that had nothing to do with the warm night air and the coat she was wearing, and everything to do with the passion blazing inside her. Her heart skipped a few beats and anticipation sizzled along her nerve endings.

His hand slid up the inside of her thigh. Slow. Steady. Purposeful.

The air choked in her throat as his finger grazed the slit between her legs. She stiffened and her gaze swiveled from the steadily disappearing fairgrounds to the driver sitting up front.

No one can see. That's what she told herself, her need warring with a lifetime of fear and uncertainty. There wasn't a soul in sight except the driver and he was busy with the horses. No one was looking at them and even if they were, all they would see is Colton's arm partially concealed by her coat. They wouldn't know that she wasn't wearing panties or that he was stroking her or that she *wanted* him to stroke her.

"Don't think about them," Colton murmured in her ear a heartbeat before his fingertip found her slit. He traced the delicate line before dipping inside just a fraction. She gasped and her gaze locked with his.

"Think about what I'm doing to you. What you want me to do to you."

Desire gleamed hot and bright in his eyes, but there was something else, as well. Surprise. Admiration. Respect. As if he'd never seen a woman like her, or wanted one quite so much.

Just like that, her inhibitions seemed to slip away and suddenly the only thing that mattered was the desperation coiling inside of her.

She relaxed and her legs parted in silent invitation.

He dipped a finger into her steamy heat and slid inside slowly.

So tantalizingly *slow.*

Her eyes closed and she would have toppled backward if he hadn't caught her.

A split-second later, she found herself sitting on the hay bale in front of him, his thighs framing hers, her back flush against his chest.

The fairgrounds had all but faded from view, but she no longer cared. She was too aware of him—too desperate for him—to put up a fight when he unbelted the coat and parted the edges. The wool slid free and blessed air rushed over her bare arms and shoulders.

"This is much better." He slid an arm around her waist to hold her firmly in place while he swept a hand up the inside of her thigh. Higher. Higher. Until his thumb brushed the slick folds between her legs. "Don't you think?"

"I…"

He slid the tip of his finger into her and pleasure speared, hot and jagged, through her trembling body. She caught her bottom lip, biting down against the exquisite sensation.

"Yes," she finally managed, the word catching on another gasp as the wagon bounced and his finger slid a fraction deeper.

She tilted her head back and rested it in the curve of his shoulder as she surrendered to the ecstasy beating at her sanity.

He knew just how to touch her, how to push deep until the air lodged in her throat and her senses flooded with sensation. Meanwhile, the wagon rumbled along. The rocking motion fed the intensity of what was happening and increased the pressure.

Winding her tighter.

Pushing her closer.

There.

She braced her hands on his thighs, her fingers digging into the hard muscle as the first vibration hit her.

When he slid a second finger inside of her, she came apart. Shudders vibrated through her body, skimming along her ragged senses in wave after wave of sweet, decadent sensation.

She slumped back against him, weak and damp, her breath raspy, her heartbeat a frenzied rhythm in her chest. His strong arms closed around her, holding her close as if he never meant to let her go.

She knew better.

This was sex and there would be an end to it even though they still hadn't made it to the main event. That was next judging by the rock-hard erection pressing against her.

It would end, all right. He would walk away and she would be glad, and it would be business as usual.

But in the meantime...

She closed her eyes and settled against him.

This was nice.

At least until the ride ended and Bobby found her, frantic with the news that she'd better come quick because all hell was breaking loose back at the jail.

16

"THIS IS BAD," Shelly said as she stood in the outer office near the dispatch counter and stared at the woman on the security monitor.

Honey Gentry sat on her bunk, her hair wild, her eyes puffy and red. Her nose was swollen and running. Tears streamed down her face and mascara streaked her cheeks. It looked as if a tornado had whipped through the room. Feathers littered the floor courtesy of the busted pillow in the far corner. The blanket that had covered the bunk was now in shreds. Honey sat in the middle of it all, frantically tying the ends of the blanket shreds into one long rope.

Uh-oh.

The only upside was that she barely had twelve inches. It wasn't nearly enough to loop over the bars and do anything stupid.

Not yet anyway.

"Woman scared the bejesus out of me," Truitt

said, drawing Shelly's attention to the Ranger standing near the coffeemaker.

As if he'd be any place else.

"One minute I was sitting there doing my crossword," he continued, "and the next, I'm running for my life."

"Did she threaten you?"

"Hell, no. Ain't no little gal gonna threaten me. The dadburned female busted out crying." He gave a visible shudder. "I only put up with one crying woman and only 'cause she lets me have the remote the other three weeks of the month."

Shelly shook her head and turned to John. "How long has she been like this?"

"Since about three. Ever since Millie over in Judge Meyers's office called and said he wasn't going to make it back at all today."

"Another flat?"

"He ran out of gas."

"I swear that man needs a Triple A membership." Shelly punched a button and the camera panned in, giving them an up-close look at Honey and her bloodshot eyes.

Bobby and John gasped. *Men.*

She scanned the camera down, searching for any sort of weapon. While Honey had shred the blanket, she seemed to have done it with her bare hands. After a few seconds scanning the cell's interior, Shelly straightened and caught John giving her an odd look.

She became keenly aware of Colton who stood

nearby, one hip planted on her desk. His muscular arms were folded, his pale eyes hooked on her. Awareness rippled through her and she fought against the sensation.

"What?" she snapped at John, determined to keep her mind focused. This was work and she wasn't going to think about what she was going to do with Colton after work. *Focus*. "You've never seen a woman wearing a trench coat before?"

"Actually, I've never seen *you* wearing a trench coat before." His gaze dropped. "Or a dress. Or high heels for that matter." He swallowed. "I didn't even know you had high heels."

"You'd never catch a Texas Ranger wearing high heels, lemme tell ya," Truitt chimed in, reaching for another foam cup.

Shelly tamped down on a sudden rush of insecurity and glared. "That stuff doesn't come cheap, you know." She motioned to the jar sitting next to the machine. "If you're going to guzzle coffee like that, you need to start chipping in with everyone else." She squared her shoulders, pulled the belt tighter and turned toward the containment area. "I'm going in."

"Not alone, you aren't." Colton was right behind her.

His muscular chest kissed her shoulder blades before she could make it two steps and heat zig-zagged through her. She stiffened and kept walking. "I'm more than capable of handling this."

"I have no doubt. But the department didn't institute a buddy rule regarding dangerous situations for the fun of it." He motioned to one of the numerous posters lining the wall behind Bobby's desk, detailing specifics of dealing with various situations. From first response to containment.

The first rule of any situation? *Always call for backup.* "That's *backup*, meaning another officer." Shelly paused at the security door and eyeballed Bobby. "How about it?"

Bobby took one look at the monitor and shook his head. "If it's a fire fight, I'm right behind you. But my Xbox doesn't simulate hormonal women."

"Coward." Her gaze shifted to John.

He shrugged. "I got two kids to think of."

She turned to Truitt.

"Forget it. It ain't my problem." He glared and dropped a quarter into the jar before taking a sip of his coffee. "I'm on special assignment with Holbrook."

Colton shrugged. "Looks like you're stuck with me."

"Fine then." She blew out an exasperated breath. "But just stay back and let me handle things." She powered open the door.

A moment later, they were inside. Following protocol, she locked the outer door before punching in the code to unlock Honey's cell. The metal groaned and clicked.

"Honey?" She slid open the cell door and took a tentative step inside.

The woman's head snapped up and her eyes lit with a crazed light. "Sssssshhhhhhhh." She motioned to Holbrook's cell. He lay on his side, eyes closed, facing them. "Don't you dare wake him." She shook her head frantically. "I won't be able to take it if you wake him up. He'll start exercising again and I'll go crazy." She shook her head frantically. "I tried, Shelly. I tried not to look, but I can't help myself. He's got so many muscles and this cell is so small and it's been so long since I—" The words cut off as he stirred, rolling over onto his back.

Honey held a finger to her lips, her eyes pleading.

Seconds ticked by and then the soft, steady sound of his snores filled the silence.

"He's still asleep," Shelly mouthed. "I'm coming in." She moved toward Honey, eyeballing every corner of the cell, drinking in her surroundings before her gaze shifted back to the woman. "What are you making?"

"It's a rope."

"Listen…" Shelly sat down on the edge of the bunk. "I know you're upset, but nothing is worth doing something like this."

"You haven't been stuck in this cell for two days."

"No, but I've been in stressful situations before. I know what it's like to feel hopeless. Like you have nowhere to turn. But you do have somewhere to turn. You turn to yourself. You draw on your own strength. And you get through it. You don't give up and hang yourself."

Honey's head snapped up and her gaze locked with Shelly's. "Is that what you think I'm trying to do?"

"Isn't it?"

"Hardly." The woman gave a hysterical giggle before the sound faded and sheer desperation filled her expression. "My lipstick rolled under Ranger Truitt's chair," she said as if she'd just declared the end of the world was coming.

"What?"

"The lipstick you let me borrow." She motioned frantically and Shelly turned to catch a glimpse of gold amid the litter of foam cups. "I accidentally dropped it and it rolled and that can't happen because I need it before he wakes up." She touched her face. "I look a mess. It's no wonder he isn't paying me any attention. But if I get that lipstick, it'll be different." She held up the pitiful excuse for a rope, "See, I figured I'd loop this over the chair and drag it over…" Her words faded as she seemed to think. "You could get it for me," she blurted, grabbing the lapels of Shelly's coat. "Would you do that?"

Shelly realized then that Honey wasn't a woman on the verge of suicide. She was a woman about to spontaneously combust of sexual frustration.

She knew the feeling.

Despite the orgasm during the hay ride, she still felt anxious. Needy. Desperate. She wanted more.

Boy, did she ever.

"Would you get the tube for me?" Honey's desperate voice drew her back to the moment. "I need it now. I really do. *Please.*"

"Forget the lipstick." She took the woman by the hand. "We're getting out of here." While she couldn't solve her own problem and force Colton into bed with her, she could help Honey out with hers.

"Really?" Honey turned hopeful eyes on Shelly.

"Really."

"But what about Judge Meyers? Isn't he the only one who can release me?"

"He's not here and I am. So let's go."

COLTON WATCHED Shelly slide an arm around the frantic woman's shoulders and steer her out of the cell. They'd made it two steps down the hallway before bedsprings creaked and a deep, male voice echoed off the walls.

"Don't tell me you're leaving without saying goodbye first."

Honey stalled and her head whipped back around, her gaze going straight to the man who'd stepped up to the cell door.

"I thought we were friends."

"I—" she protested, but Colton was already in front of her, his back to Holbrook, effectively blocking her view.

His gaze met hers and he sent the silent command. *Just keep walking.*

But it wasn't that easy. Honey was too far gone. She needed another look. She wanted one.

"We are friends. I just—"

"Move," Shelly added, determined to save the woman from herself. She started pushing and pretty soon, Honey was back in motion, headed for the security door.

"Don't I get a free pass, too?" Holbrook's voice drew Colton around just as Shelly powered open the door and pushed Honey through.

"Not this time," Colton said. "Not ever again—" The last word choked in his throat as he got his first good look at Jimmy Holbrook.

But it wasn't the man's resemblance to Rose that tied his gut into knots. No, it was the eyes staring back at him.

Eyes so familiar they could have been his own.

They *were* his own.

Colton's mind rushed back to that night, to the frantic search for CJ. He'd looked everywhere for the body, and he'd found it. A small boy. Burned beyond recognition, but still, he'd known. There had been no other children at the Circle B.

It had to have been CJ.

It *was*.

"Hey, man." Jimmy gave him a disarming smile. "Are you okay?"

He wasn't. He was crazy. Delusional. CJ had died that night. Colton had seen for himself.

He'd smelled the death.

He'd felt the pain.

No!

He moved so fast that he knew he was little more than a blur to Shelly and the other Deputies as he rushed from the containment area and left the Sheriff's office. He needed to get away. To get out there.

To get away from the unimaginable.

Before he actually started to believe that maybe, just maybe, he hadn't lost everything that night. That somehow, someway, his son had survived Rose's treachery, and Jimmy Holbrook was the living proof.

Like hell.

He fought the past as he climbed into his truck and hauled ass out of town. The engine roared and the metal shook as his tires ate up pavement. He needed to move faster, to outrun the vision that dogged him.

Holbrook's eyes.

His eyes.

It couldn't be true. He didn't want it to be true.

That would mean that he'd not only lost his son that night, but that his son had lost his father, as well. CJ would have grown up without *him*. *Without* the one man in his life he needed the most. Even more, he would have thought the worst—that Colton had abandoned him. His son would have learned to hate him the way he'd hated his own father. And he would have had every right.

Colton had been convinced his son was dead. He hadn't looked for him. He hadn't torn up every inch of countryside searching for the boy the way he should have.

No!

Colton had been able to live with his fatal mistake that night—showing up late when he should have been there early—but only because he'd known that someday he would find the killer and make things right. But abandoning his son? He could never make that right.

Ever.

Anguish welled up inside him, along with a rush of rage that gripped him so tightly, he shook with the force of it.

Rose didn't just owe *him* for that night.

She owed their son for all the years she'd robbed him of his father. That explained why she'd been busting Holbrook out of jail every time he wound up behind bars.

But it wasn't enough. It was too small a price to pay for what she'd done.

Anger churned his gut and his fingers tightened on the steering wheel.

She owed much, *much* more and he would make her pay. But there would be no waiting, biding his time. *Hell,* no. He wanted blood and he wanted it now.

Forget Skull Creek. He knew Rose would be coming from El Paso once she discovered Holbrook missing, and so Colton would pick up his stuff back at the barn and get the hell out of town. He would head for El Paso and get to Rose that much sooner.

And then he'd kill her.

He'd extract a pound of flesh for all the pain

she'd caused the people he'd loved. His friends. His mother. His son.

And what if she senses you first and sees you coming?

But Colton was through listening. There were a dozen things that could go wrong. He didn't care. He just needed to get his hands on her, to take out his anger once and for all, to rid himself of the pain and suffering that pushed and pulled inside of him.

A haze of red clouded his vision as he drove toward the barn. Urgency pounded through him, so fierce and consuming that he almost missed the swirl of lights in his rearview mirror.

Almost.

But the blue cut through the haze and reality zapped him. And just like that, he felt the hitch in his chest. The frantic pounding of her heart. The ragged breaths rushing past her lips. The uneasiness urging her faster.

Shelly.

He knew it was her, even though the police car was too far away for him to see who was behind the wheel. He'd drank from her twice now and so the connection was stronger than before. He felt her. Her frustration and anxiety and fear, for him rather than herself.

Because she was falling for him the way he'd fallen for her.

Crazy.

She was friggin' crazy for feeling anything for him. And he was even crazier for wanting her to.

The minute the notion struck, he drop-kicked it right back out the door. No, he sure as hell was not falling for her, and she wasn't falling for him. And he had every intention of keeping it that way.

The only thing he wanted from her was sex. Blood.

Sustenance.

That's all she was to him. All she could ever be because Colton Braddock wasn't some cowboy she could take home to her family or show off at the weekly church picnic.

He was a vampire. A *vampire*.

He clenched his teeth, feeling the sharpness of his fangs cut into his tongue. The salty sweet taste of blood slid down his throat and firebombed in his empty stomach. He damned himself a thousand times for not bending her over that hay bale and working her out of his system when he'd had the chance.

He didn't need Shelly. He needed to drink her blood. To nurture his strength. To *do* something now when he'd done nothing back then.

He slammed on the brakes, swerved the truck onto the shoulder and killed the engine.

It was time to remember who and what he really was, to feed the beast that lived and breathed inside of him.

Starting right now.

_17_

SHE WAS WRITING him one hell of a ticket.

Speeding.

Public endangerment.

Failure to stop at a designated cattle crossing.

The charges ticked off in Shelly's head as she eased up behind his truck and shoved her cruiser into Park.

Violating curfew.

Reckless operation of a moving vehicle.

Walking out on her without so much as a goodbye.

Okay, so that last one wasn't against the law, but it pissed her off nonetheless. She'd barely even caught a glimpse as he'd hightailed it out of the office. No _goodbye_. Or _thanks for a lovely evening_. Not even a _see ya_. She'd barely had time to ask John to take Honey home before she jumped in her car to follow him.

Just who the hell did he think he was?

She held tight to the anger and climbed out, desperate to ignore the worry that roiled inside of her. The niggling sensation that told her something was wrong.

Deep down, she knew there was a problem, she just didn't know what it was. But then he stepped out of his truck and caught the glare of her headlights and she stopped dead in her tracks.

Disbelief pumped through her body at an alarming rate as she drank in the sight of him, her gaze riveted on his face, on his eyes that glowed a vivid, mesmerizing *purple*.

She blinked once, twice, but the color didn't fade into the pale, translucent blue that reminded her of a rain-washed sky on a hot summer's day.

Denial beat through her as the color seemed to shimmer and change. Right before her eyes, they fired a brilliant neon blue, so bright that it actually hurt to look at them.

Not that she could look away. Not with his lips drawn back and his fangs glittering and—

Wait a second.

Wait just a friggin' *second*.

Her heart pounded, echoing in her head, drowning out the steady *beep, beep, beep* of the car door she'd left wide open.

"Mama bear, you copy?" Bobby's voice carried over the radio, slicing through the noise, begging her to turn and climb back in. Respond. *Run.* "You took off outa here like a bat out of hell. What's wrong?"

Fangs. That's what was wrong. He had *fangs*.

Shock hit her like a thunder bolt and she clamped her eyes shut. The air rushed from her lungs and every muscle in her body froze.

No way.

No how.

It had to be lack of sex. That was it. The frustration had finally driven her completely off the deep end. Because there was no way she'd just seen...

That he actually had...

No.

Denial rushed through her, followed by a wave of panic when she opened her eyes again to see him still standing there, looking as ferocious as ever, his gaze still a blinding neon blue, his fangs still glittering in the headlights.

Still a *vampire*.

No. No. No.

There was no such thing. Vampires didn't exist. Only in books and movies and the minds of about a billion *Twilight* fanatics. But they were wrong.

Or were they?

The question beat at her as Bobby's voice blared in the background. "I've got you on GPS. I'm sending a squad car after you. Mama bear, you copy? Shelly?"

"Now you know what I am," Colton murmured, his deep voice slicing through the sound of her frantic heartbeat, drawing her full attention.

"No. You're a security specialist," she insisted. He shook his head and she pressed on. "A rancher."

"Actually, I am a rancher. But I'm also more." His

gaze fired brighter, changing colors again. "Much more."

"This isn't happening. There's no way you're a…" The word stalled on the tip of her tongue and she shook her head. "You're not. This is all some hoax."

"I am," he told her, his gaze pushing into hers. *I'm a vampire.* The deep timbre of his voice whispered through her mind, but his lips didn't move.

"Bullshit," she said, shaking her head frantically.

"You can't deny what you see. What you hear. What you *feel*." Just like that the belt of her robe tugged loose and she glanced up to see him staring at the material, moving it with nothing more than the sheer power of his gaze.

"It's part of who I am. I can control things with my mind. Move objects. Mesmerize people."

She grabbed at the ends, but they slipped from her grasp as if there were hands pushing at hers.

The truth crystallized as she felt the strong, purposeful touches and the brush of his rough skin against her own. And all while he stood several feet away, his muscles tight, his body immobile, his attention fixated on her.

He was a vampire.

A real, honest-to-goodness *vampire*.

A burst of excitement went through her, followed by a ripple of fear that made her hands tremble. Not because she was afraid of him. If he was really a vampire and that was a big *if,* he could have hurt her many times before now. He hadn't.

No, it wasn't Colton who stirred the fear.

It was her reaction to him. The excitement. The urge to rip off the coat and throw herself into his arms, despite the truth staring back at her.

Because of it.

Because she was weak and she didn't care about the consequences. She was lost in the moment, a slave to her own needs.

Just like her mother.

Suddenly she grabbed at the material harder, forcing the edges together, fighting that much harder. No way had Shelly spent a lifetime trying to distance herself from her past only to wind up right back where she'd started. Back under the bed, powerless to stop what was happening around her. Right in front of her.

"You believe me," he murmured.

"I most certainly do not."

"Yes, you do. It's true and you know it. You just don't want to admit it."

"The only thing I know is that you're in a shitload of trouble." She managed to tie the belt back into a knot only to have it slip through her fingers again and come undone.

He lifted his hand and the material rushed from her shoulders. And just like that, she stood before him wearing nothing but her Three B's dress and a tight frown.

"Forget all of the old myths. I don't have any sort of an aversion to garlic or crosses or holy water.

Silver can be painful, but not deadly. I'm pretty much immune to everything except for sunlight and stakes."

"And I can fly like Tinkerbell."

"I feed off both blood and sex," he continued, ignoring her skepticism. "They're both forms of energy that I use to survive, though if I'm having a lot of sex, I can take it easy on the blood and vice versa. And when I drink from someone, it forges a connection." *That's why you can hear me. And I can hear you.*

He couldn't.

That's what she told herself, despite the pieces which had already started to fall into place. The way his eyes changed color. The way he seemed to disappear in the blink of an eye. His overwhelming sex appeal.

She fought against the sudden sizzle of excitement that rushed through her and held tight to the denial.

"I came here because a woman—my ex-wife— set fire to my ranch one hundred and fifty years ago. She killed my family," he stated. "Right now, she's headed for Skull Creek and I intend to kill her when she arrives. That's why I'm here. She took everything from me. Everyone."

"But your brothers aren't dead," Shelly heard herself say as if she were buying this.

She wasn't. He was delusional and the whole coat thing was some kind of magic trick and—

"They were the only survivors," he added, ending her tirade as he went on one of his own, answering the multitude of questions that swam in her brain. "They were turned—I was turned—by a vampire who happened along that night. But Sawyer made a mistake. He turned the murderer, as well. That's why she's still out there—"

"Sawyer," she asked. "As in *Garrett Sawyer?*"

He nodded and the tidbits of information she knew about the man behind one of the South's largest custom motorcycle shops flashed in her brain. Garrett, who worked only at night. Garrett, who had a ranch that could double as a fortress. Garrett, who donated to every charity in town, but kept to himself despite numerous invites to attend this or that event. Garrett, who'd bitten and turned the woman who'd murdered Colton's family. Garrett the friggin' *vampire*.

"He didn't mean to turn her, but I'm glad he did. Otherwise I wouldn't have this chance." His gaze locked with hers and his eyes fired a furious red. "I'm going to make her pay for what she did. I *have* to make her pay." In a heartbeat, he was on her, his muscular body pinning her against the pick-up truck. Regret flashed in his gaze, taking a nose-dive into determination as he stared down at her. "I should have done this a long time ago."

"What are you doing?" she blurted, but she knew.

She saw the hunger in his gaze, felt it in his body, and a wave of apprehension washed through her.

"Feeding," he growled, confirming her worst fear.

And then he kissed her.

18

THIS WAS WHAT she'd been waiting for.

He kissed her, plunging his tongue inside her mouth to explore and savor until she gasped for breath. He tasted so dark and dangerous and forbidden, and she soon found herself caught up in it. Eve in the Garden of Eden.

Her fear melted away and she forgot that she was standing on the side of the road in full view of anyone who happened by, totally mindless of Bobby's frantic voice telling her that John was on his way.

She didn't care about anything as she gave in to temptation. Her own longing boiled over and she kissed him back.

Even knowing that he was a vampire.

Because of it.

Forget good, old-fashioned chemistry. What flowed between them went beyond the ordinary, into the *extra*ordinary.

Lust rolled off of him in huge waves, courtesy of

his vampness, and she couldn't help but succumb to it. Any woman would have. He'd told her so himself. He could seduce with little more than a glance, brainwash with a sexy, seductive smile and hypnotize with a simple thought.

"Not you," he murmured against her lips before pulling away and staring down at her. "I can mesmerize any woman out there." He shook his head as if he still couldn't believe it. "But not you." His words sent a rush of warmth through her. "You're different."

Right. He was a vampire who craved both blood and sex. She could have been any woman.

But at that moment, she felt like *the* woman.

His, and his alone.

The lust that burned inside of her boiled over. She was powerless to resist him and oddly enough, that realization didn't freak her out nearly as much as it should have.

She wanted to feel him, to please him, to make him burn for her the way she burned for him. He made her feel hot and bothered and beautiful.

Her skin still tingled from the reverent way he'd stroked her on the hay ride. No man had ever looked at her like that.

It was her turn.

She reached for the waistband of his jeans.

A groan rumbled from his throat as her fingertips trailed over the denim-covered bulge. She worked the zipper down, tugging and pulling until the teeth finally parted. The jeans sagged on his hips, and his erection sprang hot and greedy into her hands.

She traced the ripe purple head before sliding her hand down his length, stroking, exploring. His dark flesh throbbed against her palm and a wave of electricity sizzled through her. She licked her lips, suddenly eager to taste him.

Insane.

She knew it was, but she couldn't help herself. She didn't want to help herself.

Dropping to her knees, she smoothed her fingers down the dark perfection of his shaft and took him into her mouth. And then she proceeded to show him just how much she wanted this.

How much she wanted him.

HE SENSED THE sudden change in her, the surrender, even before he felt her tongue trace the ripe head of his erection.

He closed his eyes for a long moment and indulged himself. She felt so damned warm. So damned wet. So damned *right*.

Before he could dwell on the last thought, his ears perked. The distant groan of a motor sizzled in the air. His eyes snapped open and his head jerked around. There wasn't a light on the horizon, but he knew someone was coming.

So?

What do you care? You want this. You need this.

He'd waited for this moment, this pleasure, for far

too long. He couldn't stop just because someone was coming or because he knew she would never recover from the embarrassment of having her reputation shot to hell and back. What did he care?

He didn't.

That's what he told himself, but he reached for her shoulders anyway. "We can't do this here."

"We can."

"No." His hand cupped her chin and forced her gaze up to meet his. "We can't." He pulled her to her feet. In a flash, he fastened his jeans, killed the lights and slammed both car doors. Scooping her off her feet, he started to move, racing across the pastureland as fast as his vampire feet could carry him.

In less than a minute, they were over two miles away, inside the old dilapidated barn, the door closed behind them. In a flash, he backed her up against the nearest wall, determined not to take a moment to reflect on what had just happened.

He'd already wasted too much precious time.

He caught the neckline of her skimpy dress and pulled it down to her waist. Her luscious breasts spilled free. Dipping his head, he caught one rosy nipple between his teeth. He flicked the tip with his tongue before opening his mouth wider, drawing her in. He sucked hard until a moan vibrated up her throat. The sound fed the lust roaring in his veins.

Pressing one hard thigh between her legs, he forced her wider until she rode him. Her sweet heat rasped against the denim of his jeans, melting through the fabric, scorching him.

She gasped and a shudder ripped through her. He leaned back to see her trembling lips and her quivering breasts. Her pulse beat frantically at the base of her throat, teasing and taunting, begging for his attention.

His lips parted with a slow hiss and his cock throbbed.

But it wasn't about plunging deep and spilling himself inside of her. It was all about her pleasure, about soaking up the sweet heat of her orgasm.

He shifted, moving and rubbing, working her until she drenched the material between them. The scent of her arousal teased his nostrils and stirred his senses, making him want to be inside of her so bad that it hurt.

Crazy.

He caught her lips in a fierce kiss and plunged his hand between her legs. She was warm and wet and swollen. At the first touch of his fingers, she stiffened. A cry ripped past her luscious lips and just like that, she came apart at his fingertips.

A sizzling heat pulsed through her body and entered him at every point of contact—his hand between her legs, his mouth on hers, his thigh pressed intimately between hers. He drank in the replenishing energy, soaking it up, relishing the dizzying rush of life through his undead body.

But it wasn't enough.

Like hell.

It was all about the orgasm, he reminded himself. The woman's orgasm. That's all he needed to feel totally and completely satisfied. All he'd ever needed.

He sure as shootin' didn't need one of his own.

But he wanted one.

The truth beat at his brain and this time he didn't push it away. He couldn't. Not with her so soft and pliant against him and his own hunger waging a war with his control.

He wanted to plunge deep inside of her over and over until he came so much that his teeth ached. And then he wanted to pull her into his arms and never let her go.

The realization sent a burst of panic through him and he turned, lifting her onto the nearest hay bale. The position put her breasts just inches from his face and he didn't waste any time. He had to sate the beast and kill the crazy urges roiling inside of him.

He stepped between her parted legs, wedging her knees further apart, and caught one ripe nipple in his mouth. His fangs grazed the tender flesh around her areola and his groin tightened. Her nipple throbbed against his tongue as he sank into her just a hair and drew a few precious drops of blood. The salty sweetness sent a dizzying rush to his head. His insides clenched.

He slid his palms around to cup her ass as he tilted her forward, bringing her flush against him. He stroked his head along the length of her slit once, twice, and then he sank his fangs deep, drawing on her, praying that the blood would be enough to kill the need for her.

It wasn't.

The more he took, the more he wanted. He couldn't help himself. He plunged deep inside her delicious heat and just like that, he was home.

His heart beat a thunderous rhythm in his ears for those next few moments as pleasure swamped him. Intense. Consuming. All he could do was stand there and soak it up for a long moment. But then it subsided and need took its place.

The need to get closer. Deeper. *Now.*

He thrust into her, over and over as he drew on her nipple. Her delicious essence filled his mouth and the energy from her sudden climax surrounded his cock, seeping into him at every point where flesh met flesh as he spilled himself deep inside her.

It was the ultimate in fulfillment for a vampire, and it still wasn't enough.

Not the warm, succulent body grasping at him or the sweet essence pulsing in his mouth or the satisfaction that he'd spent himself.

The realization sent him scrambling backward. He snatched up his discarded jeans and yanked them on before walking to the far side of the barn. He needed some distance from her.

From the feelings pushing and pulling at him and the crazy thought that she was the one woman he wanted enough to spend the rest of his life with.

Life?

He didn't have a life to spend. He was a vampire, for Chrissake. No such luxury existed for him. He'd already lived one hundred and fifty years too many.

He'd survived for one reason alone—revenge.

And once he had it, his sole purpose for surviving would end.

He would end it.

He *would.* Even if the notion weren't half as appealing as it used to be.

He forced aside the thought and hit the light hanging above the small work bench he'd set up near his sleeping bag. The smell of sawdust filled his nostrils and chased away the sweet scent of the woman sitting several yards away, watching him.

He needed distance. A distraction.

He picked up the sander and slid it across the block of wood he'd started working on last night. Shavings fell at his feet and the motion eased his tight muscles just a hair.

He heard the rustle of hay as she climbed off the bale, the soft pad of footsteps as she retrieved his discarded shirt. In his peripheral vision, he saw her pull on the soft cotton and walk toward him, her legs sexy and bare, her hair long and flowing and wild.

His gut hollowed out and he worked that much harder, determined to concentrate on the task at hand.

It should have been easy now that he'd replenished his strength. He could feel the buzz through his veins, the rush of adrenalin. *Focus.*

"What are you doing?" Her voice sounded a heartbeat before she stepped up next to him.

"Nothing."

"It doesn't look like nothing," she said, her gaze on the block of wood, as if she were genuinely interested. "What is it?"

"I don't know yet." He shrugged. "I was thinking I might make a bookshelf. Or maybe a table." *Or maybe even a bench.* He killed the notion and focused on the steady movements up and down. "I used to do woodworking a long, long time ago." He wasn't sure why he told her. He didn't like to think about that part of his life—the time before that one terrible night—much less talk about it. But he needed something to drown out the pounding of his own heart. "I made the stock for Cody's first gun. And one for Brent. And Travis."

"How old were you when your dad left?"

"I was twelve."

"That's young."

"Six is young," he said, reminding her of her own childhood. "At twelve I was practically a man. Old enough to look after my brothers, that's for sure."

"They were lucky to have you. You've definitely got skill." Silence settled as she watched him work for the next few minutes. "I'll never forget this one time when I tried making a costume for Darla. She was going to be in the kindergarten Christmas pageant and she needed a white dress so that she could be an angel. It ended up being a disaster, but she didn't care. She loved it anyway. That made me even more determined to do what I needed to do. What my Grandma Jean would have wanted. She was a strong woman."

"You're a strong woman." The words were out before he could stop them, but suddenly he didn't care. While sex with her had been fantastic, this ran a close second. And damned if he could resist her any more now than he had a few moments ago. "The first table I ever made fell over on its side when my momma sat a platter of chicken on it."

A grin tugged at her mouth. "Sounds like some table."

"I gave it to her for her birthday. It had crooked corners and jagged edges. And one leg was shorter than the other."

"I bet she loved it anyway."

"She did." For the first time in a long time, he let the memory come. He saw his mother standing there, a smile on her face as she'd scooped up the chicken. As if it was no big deal that he'd ruined her special dinner. His chest hitched. "I miss her." He'd never said that aloud before and the realization stirred a rush of panic.

Because he shouldn't be saying it now.

He should be focused on that one night. On the pain and death he'd witnessed. And the revenge he would soon taste.

"I'm really sorry for your loss."

"Don't be. It was my own fault."

"I'm sure—"

"Of what?" he said. "You weren't there. You don't know what really happened. You don't know shit."

"I know you were a good son and a good brother."

"Once upon a time maybe." He shrugged. "But I was always so damned set on doing the right thing that I let it get in the way." The memories stirred, welling up inside him. Just like that, the floodgates opened and the words poured out. "We were on our way home from the war for the first time in four years. The first time. And what did I do? I insisted on detouring to Austin to report to General Briggs. He expected a report on our last raid and I was determined to give it to him. That took four and a half hours, plenty of time for my wife and her bastard lover to put a bullet in everyone at the ranch. Time for them to herd all the livestock into the barn and set it on fire." The flames blinded him and the smoke burned his nostrils. "Time for them to kill every living thing that I ever loved and ride away without looking back." Anger and hurt whirled inside of him. "I shouldn't have gone to Austin. If I had been there, it never would have happened. If I had just *been there...*"

The truth hung in the air for a long moment, staring back at him, taunting him. His gut clenched and his chest tightened. And then he felt her arms slide around his waist.

She didn't tell him it wasn't his fault or that he couldn't have known what would happen or that he had to stop blaming himself. She didn't say any of the things he'd heard time and time again from his brothers.

She didn't say anything.

And that said everything.

She understood there were some mistakes that a man just couldn't put behind him and so she simply held him. And surprisingly enough, the knot in his chest eased.

"Did I ever tell you why I went into law enforcement?" her voice was soft, soothing.

"We haven't exactly spent a lot of time talking." He felt her smile against his shoulder blade before the expression faded. He touched the wood again, smoothing the sander over it in a lulling motion that was almost as soothing as her voice.

"I tried to make dinner for the first time and I accidentally set fire to the curtains." Her soft hands settled over his, her warmth seeping into him as she followed his movements with the sander. "The fire department came, along with children's protective services. They wanted to know where my mom was and why I was home alone cooking."

"Why were you?"

"Because my mom hadn't come home for four days." Her hands trembled atop his. "She was passed out in her truck in the parking lot of a local bar, thanks to too much Jack Daniels."

"Did you tell them that?"

"I should have, but I didn't. I lied because the thought of being completely alone was even worse than being stuck with a sorry excuse for a mother. I told them she was helping with the bake sale down at the church. They didn't believe me but Jack Mercer—he was the Sheriff at the time—told them to leave me be. And they listened. Everybody listened when Sheriff Jack said something. They paid attention and that's what I wanted. I wanted people to pay attention to me. To actually *see* me."

The way my mother never did.

The silent thought rolled through his head, even though she didn't say the words. Awareness rippled up his spine and he felt the rush of insecurity that went through her. The pain. Because she knew what loss felt like. She'd experienced it every day of her life that she'd watched her mother walk away from her.

She knew what he felt. The fear. The self-doubt. The isolation.

He turned and stared into her eyes and at that moment, he knew the reason for the damnable hunger that still ate away inside of him. He wanted more than just Shelly's body and her blood.

He wanted her heart.

And she wanted his.

He knew it the moment he saw her gaze, so full of an emotion that she wouldn't admit any more than he would.

Because it wouldn't change anything.

They both knew it. She would go back to her life and run for Sheriff of Skull Creek and he would face off with Rose and do what he had to do to avenge his family and silence his demons once and for all.

No, love didn't mean shit in the end.

But right now… Suddenly it meant everything. And he intended to show her just how much.

19

THERE WAS SOMETHING different about him.

She knew it even before he pressed his lips to hers in a kiss that was so soft and reverent that it brought tears to her eyes.

Love.

That's what brought the sudden about-face. He loved her and she loved him.

She *loved* him.

Instead of fighting against the thought, for the first time, she embraced it. Tonight she wanted freedom. From the past. The future. Her insecurities. Her fears.

The realization hit her as she stared up at him and felt the connection flowing between them. She'd never been so in tune with a man.

She'd never wanted to be.

Until now.

He didn't say a word as he picked her up and carried her over to the far corner of the barn where he'd set up a sleeping bag on a soft mattress of hay. Easing her down, he shed his jeans and simply stood there, staring down at her, drinking in the picture she made.

You're so beautiful.

The words echoed in her head and warmth spread through her, filling up all the gaps and chasing away the emptiness that had plagued her for so long.

Moonlight pushed through the slats in the wood, bathing his features in an ethereal glow that made him almost seem dreamlike.

Almost.

But there was no denying the feel of his hard, hot body as it stretched out beside hers, or the touch of his hand as he traced her turgid nipple, or the flutter of his lips as he leaned over and lapped at the prick points on her breast where he'd drank such a short time ago.

His tongue laved the sensitive spot and sensation bolted hot and raw through her. She gasped.

"A bite can be even better than sex," he murmured. To prove his point, he licked her again and she shuddered. Pleasure drenched her, vibrating along her nerve endings, stirring her senses until she wanted him all over again. Here. Now. Everywhere.

She buried her hands in his hair, holding him close as she arched her breast into the moist heat of his mouth. He pleasured her, sucking and licking as one rough fingertip traced the soft folds between her legs. He pushed inside a delicious fraction and a gasp bubbled up her throat.

Her body clenched and unclenched around the tip of his finger, desperate to draw him deeper, but he seemed determined to keep things slow and easy.

He smiled, his teeth a startling break in the black shadow of his face. Then the expression faded as he gazed down at her. His attention shifted, traveling from her face, down the column of her neck to her breasts, to the spread of her thighs and his finger, which poised at her pulsing cleft.

He pushed all the way in and she moaned, as pure pleasure pierced her brain. The feeling was so consuming and exquisite that it sucked the air from her lungs. She stopped breathing for a long moment while he held still. Her body settled around him and clamped tighter.

"I want you more than I've ever wanted any woman." *You and only you.*

The words sounded so clear and distinct in her head, so sincere, as if he'd murmured them directly into her ear. He hadn't. He didn't have to. He'd invaded her mind as well as her body, and they were linked now.

Connected.

Forever.

A spurt of excitement went through her. She lifted her pelvis, focusing on the pleasure that gripped her as she worked her body around his decadent finger. She swayed from side to side, her movements frantic, desperate, as she pushed herself higher and higher. She wanted—no, needed—to cram as much as she could into this one moment. To brand his memory into her brain to comfort her on all the lonely nights to come.

Because Shelly Lancaster knew that she would never find another man like Colton Braddock. And it had nothing to do with him being a vampire and everything to do with him being *him*.

He was a man haunted by his past, desperate to make up for it.

They were one and the same.

He'd felt the burden of the world on his shoulders and stepped up to the challenge just the way she had.

But while they'd come from the same place, they'd walked different paths. And those paths were now leading them in very different directions.

While she wanted to hope that he would avenge his family and stay in Skull Creek, she knew deep down inside that such a thing would never happen. While Colton felt convinced the world could never forgive him, the truth was, he couldn't forgive himself.

So all they'd have was tonight.

His mouth swooped down and captured hers in a deep kiss that went way beyond the sweet press of his lips. He coaxed her open and slid his tongue inside to draw on hers for several long moments. Until her frantic heartbeat eased and she forgot all about sucking him deeper into her greedy body.

Instead, she wrapped her arms around him, pulling him even closer and relishing his heartbeat so sure and steady against her own.

A heartbeat?

The question swirled with a dozen others, but she wasn't going to play twenty questions. Or a million, for that matter. This moment was about touching and feeling and *loving*.

He canted his head to the side and deepened the kiss. He plundered her mouth with his, exploring and savoring. The air stalled in her lungs and her heart sped faster. A few more seconds and he tore his mouth from hers.

He slid down her body, now slick from the fever that raged inside of her, and left a blazing path with the velvet tip of his tongue. With a gentle pressure, he parted her thighs. Almost reverently, he stroked the soft, slick folds before settling himself between her legs. His hard, hot length rubbed her pulsing clit for a split-second before he thrust deep and impaled her. Sensation overwhelmed her at first.

She anchored her arms around his neck and her muscles clamped down around his erection. She didn't want to let him go, but he had other ideas.

He withdrew and slid back in for a second time. His hard length rasped her tender insides, creating a delicious friction that sent a dizzying rush straight to her brain. He pulled out again, and went back for a third time. A fourth.

His body pumped into hers over and over, pushing her higher with each delicious plunge. She lifted her hips, meeting him thrust for thrust, eager to feel more of him. Harder. Deeper. Faster.

Look at me. I need to see you. I want to see you.

She opened her eyes at his command to see him poised over her, his gaze bright and gleaming with a purple fire that made her entire body tingle. He pushed into her, his penis hot and twitching, and she knew it was his last and final time.

He let loose a loud hiss that faded into a long moan as Shelly arched her pelvis. His penis throbbed, and she felt a spurt of warmth. He bucked once, twice. His jaw clenched. His mouth fell open and his fangs gleamed in the dim light for a split-second before his mouth closed over the side of her neck where her pulse beat a frantic rhythm and he sank his fangs deep.

Like before, there was no pain. Just a smart prickle followed by a flood of *ohmigod* that drenched her senses and consumed her. A gasp vibrated up her throat. Convulsions gripped her body and suddenly she was floating on a cloud of pure satisfaction.

His mouth eased and he buried his head against her neck as she clung to him, savoring the tremors that rocked them both.

A few frantic heartbeats later, he rolled onto his back, pulling her flush against his side, cradling her as if he never meant to let her go.

But he would.

And she would let him go.

At least that's what she tried to tell herself as she snuggled deeper into his embrace and closed her eyes.

20

"Mother Goose? This is Little Boy Blue. You copy?"

Bobby's voice pulled Shelly from the oblivion of sleep. She opened her eyes to find sunlight streaming through the slats of the barn.

It was morning.

She sat up and stared around at the massive room, from the far corner where the work bench sat to the rafters overflowing with hay, to the indentation next to her where Colton had been such a short time ago.

He was gone now.

Duh.

It was daylight and he was a vampire and—

The thought stalled as the images from the past night rushed at her.

The hayride.

Honey's near breakdown.

The high speed chase.

The apprehension.

The truth.

The sex.

She touched a hand to her neck, but the prick points had already disappeared, leaving only a sensitive patch of skin that tingled when she touched it. Her thighs ached and her body felt limp and tired.

And she loved it.

She stretched out and basked in the afterglow of their incredible lovemaking for the next few moments, until Bobby's voice crackled in the air again, telling her that she wasn't alone.

Oh, no.

She bolted to her feet and snatched up the discarded dress. Her coat was back at the road and the only thing she had was a miniscule slip of spandex. She was practically naked and someone from the Sheriff's office was outside.

Panic bolted through her and she snatched up the sleeping bag, draping it securely over her shoulders as she walked to the barn door and peered out to see the cruiser just outside.

Dread rushed through her, followed by a rush of relief when she realized that it was *her* cruiser and the voice was coming from the police band radio drifting through the open windows.

"Mama Goose? You copy?"

She hiked the sleeping bag tighter and walked out into the sunlight. Climbing in, she grabbed the radio. "What happened to Mama Bear?"

"Shelly? Is that you?"

"Last time I looked."

"Thank God. I was starting to get worried. I know a busted pipe can take awhile, but you haven't even called in and you *always* call in and—"

"Busted pipe?"

"That security guy left a message that you two decided to go over some specs last night. He said your pipe busted and you were busy trying to keep the downstairs from flooding which is why you didn't answer our calls. Haven't you found a plumber yet? I told you my brother-in-law can take a look..." Bobby droned on while Shelly fixated on the truth.

Colton Braddock had retrieved her car. And her coat, she realized as she glanced at the pile of wool sitting on the seat next to her. And he'd called in for her. Just like he'd picked her up last night when they'd heard the car approaching and high-tailed it to the privacy of the old barn.

Because he loved her.

She knew it. At the same time, he hadn't actually said the words.

Maybe he'd only picked up the pieces to preserve her reputation so she could go back to her life and he could get on with his.

Probably.

Disappointment ricocheted through her and she shook it away. She should be thankful. Her job meant everything.

Then and now.

One night of hot sex couldn't change that. Even if it had been the best of her life.

"I'm still working on getting a plumber," she told Bobby. "I'll check in later." She hooked the radio receiver in place and keyed the engine. Her gaze stalled on the barn and she had half a mind to head back inside and look for him. He was there somewhere. Hidden away from the sunlight. From her.

But what would she say?

Don't go.

Let's work it out.

I love you.

Crazy.

She shoved the car into reverse and swung the cruiser around. Gravel spewed and brakes squealed.

It's not like she'd thought for even five seconds that they might have a future together. That he could make peace with his past and she could forget hers, and they could both live happily ever after.

Okay, so maybe five seconds.

But that had been in the throes of passion, with lust clouding her judgment. Now, she was sitting smack dab in the middle of the bright light of day, reality blaring in her head.

He was a vampire. She was a human. He thrived on blood and sex. She preferred a good cheeseburger and a milkshake. He crashed during the day and thrived at night. She worked seven to seven and slept like a baby in between.

They were polar opposites. It could never work even if they wanted it to.

Which they didn't.

He didn't.

That was why she had to push last night completely out of her mind, get her act together and get back to work.

Because when Colton Braddock finally faced his past and gave up his life, that's all she would have left.

If only the realization didn't make her want to forget all about work, head home, crawl into bed and cry her eyes out.

SHE FORGOT ABOUT work, headed home, crawled into bed and cried her eyes out.

For a little while.

But then reality intruded. Bobby's brother-in-law showed up on her doorstep to fix her non-existent broken pipe. Darla called about a zillion times to say that Tom had cornered her the night before and they'd slept together. The *Gazette* sent over a copy of the retraction for her approval. Life moved on, and Shelly had to move with it.

Colton Braddock was history.

That's what she told herself as she dragged herself out from under the covers, pulled on her uniform and headed to the office.

"Yes, I'm wearing lipstick," she told John when she walked into work just after lunch. "And blush. And mascara. And a LOT of concealer." She'd been desperate to hide her tired eyes and the sadness that roiled inside of her. "Now put your eyes back in your head and get to work."

Oddly enough, they did just that and Shelly had the fleeting thought that Colton was right. Maybe she didn't have to hide who she really was in order to keep everyone's respect.

She drop-kicked the thought the minute it struck. She wasn't going to think about him. And she certainly wasn't going to worry about him. Or the fact that he was *this* close to facing off with the vampire who'd murdered his family and there wasn't a damned thing she could do to help him.

She had no clue when Rose Braddock would show up, where the confrontation would take place or even when it was going to happen.

A wave of helplessness rolled through her and just like that, she was hiding under the bed, scared and powerless and so very afraid.

Before she could dwell on the realization, Bobby walked in and dumped a major distraction into her lap.

"Honey missed her court date this morning and Judge Myers is about to issue a warrant for her arrest." He headed for the weapons cabinet that sat against the far wall. "I explained the situation, but he's pissed because you went over his head. He says if we don't have her in his office by the end of the day, he's going to call Sheriff Keller and have you suspended."

Uh-oh. "Did you go by her place?"

"First thing. I knocked for about forty-five minutes. I think she's inside, but I have no way of knowing for sure. That's why I came back here." He punched in the security code for the cabinet and the lock clicked. He snatched up several three-inch long cylinders and stuffed them into his shirt pocket and closed the cabinet. The lock clicked. "If she won't come out on her own, I'll just have to gas her out."

"Oh, no you won't." Shelly was right behind him, plucking the cylinders from his pocket. She stuffed them into her pants. Honey might be breaking the law by resisting, but she was no criminal. She was a woman. A stressed out, sexually frustrated woman who was probably terrified at the thought of ending up back in the cell across from Holbrook. She was probably buried under the covers right now, hiding from the world, crying her eyes out. "I'll go get her."

"But—"

"We just got a call from Mr. Rigsby out on Route 9." She handed him the call sheet. "His horse is missing and he needs help finding it."

"You get to have all the fun," he grumbled as he took the sheet and headed back out the door.

Fifteen minutes later, Shelly pulled up outside the small beige house with yellow trim that sat on the east side of town. The yard was about the size of a postage stamp with hedges lining the perimeter. Daisies poured out of the window box near the front door. The light on the porch flickered. Once. Twice.

"Honey, I know you're in there." Shelly knocked on the door. "Open up."

Somewhere inside, Blake Shelton sang about honey bees. A mixer *whirred*. Pots and pans clanged.

"I know you're upset, but hiding isn't going to solve anything. You missed your court date this morning and my ass is on the line."

"I'm sorry." She heard a frustrated voice from inside. "I really am, but I just can't do it."

"You won't have to go near the jail or Holbrook. I promise."

"I still can't go," Honey called out. More pans rattled. "Please don't be mad at me."

Shelly remembered the small cylinders stuffed into her pocket. "I've got tear gas." Not that she was about to use it, but Honey didn't know that. "I'll use it. I swear—"

Hinges rattled and the door swung open. Honey stood framed in the doorway, a flour-stained apron that read *Kiss My Cupcakes* wrapped around her waist. Cake batter smudged one cheek and a clump of white frosting stuck in her hair.

"I'll go straight to the courthouse first thing tomorrow morning," she said, hiking a massive mixing bowl onto one hip. "Cross my heart. I just have to get these cupcakes done first." She stuck her finger in the bowl and licked a dab of chocolate. Determination fired her eyes. "I have to."

Obviously the donuts hadn't been enough to curb

her frustration. She'd gone off the deep end. Straight into a vat of cupcakes.

"You don't have to do this," Shelly told her.

Frustration edged Honey's voice and she nodded. "Yes, I do. I don't have a choice."

"Listen, I know exactly how you feel." The hopelessness. The desperation. Shelly felt both. She didn't stand a chance with Colton. At the same time, she wanted one. "But you don't have to give in to your weaknesses. Don't do it," Shelly said, as much for herself as for Honey. "Don't chuck it all for a little instant gratification. You've worked too hard to get here. He isn't worth it. Holbrook is a criminal. A bad guy. You deserve better."

Honey looked surprised. "I'm not doing this for Jimmy. Landsakes, I haven't even given him a second thought since last night."

"But you were hooked on him."

She shrugged. "I know, but then I came home and I got busy and suddenly he was history." Her attention shifted back to the mixing bowl. "This is for the steer."

Honey's words punched the rewind button on Shelly's memory and reminded her about the steer made of cupcakes being unveiled at the finals for the chili cook-off of Thursday.

"That's tonight, isn't it?"

"Eight o'clock sharp." Panic lit the woman's eyes. "I either deliver on time or I'm out two thousand dollars in commission and the advertising opportunity of a lifetime." A buzzer went off and the lights flickered again. "My mixers," she said. "I've got too many plugged into one outlet. They're overloading my circuits. But a girl's gotta do what a girl's gotta do, right? Hold this." She thrust the mixing bowl at Shelly. "I'll be right back."

A few heartbeats later, the buzzer went silent and the lights stop flickering.

"Don't just stand there," Honey called from inside. "Come on in."

Shelly followed the sugary sweet smell of freshly baked goodies to the kitchen in time to see Honey pull a massive baking sheet laden with fifty cupcakes from one of the three ovens crammed into the small room. Her gaze shifted to the chicken wire monstrosity taking up most of the room. Cupcakes covered half the sculpture making up the animal's head and torso, while the rest sat waiting for Honey to work her magic.

"I call him Bubba," Honey said, reaching for two jumbo cupcakes sitting on a nearby cooling rack. "You're just in time to help me do his testicles."

"I think I'll pass."

"Don't be such a wuss. It's just flour and sugar." Desperation gleamed in her eyes as she held out a spare apron. "Come on. I could really use an extra set of hands. I'll even let you lick the bowls," she added, trying to tip the scales in her favor.

Shelly thought of the alternative—an entire day sitting at her desk, eating stale donuts, worrying over

Colton and the all-important fact that she loved him and he didn't love her back. Life totally sucked.

Or an entire day spent baking—and eating—a gazillion home-made cupcakes.

She wrapped the apron around her waist, rolled up her sleeves and reached for the two massive cupcakes. "Let's give Bubba something to be proud of."

21

SHE WAS EARLY.

Colton opened his eyes to the shadowy interior of the barn and the unsettling truth zipping up and down his spine.

Awareness sizzled along his nerve endings, more intense than the steady buzz he usually felt from his brothers and the Skull Creek Chopper vampires. No, this was different. This was Rose.

Shit.

The sun was about to set and twilight filled the old barn. Colton pushed aside the wall of hay bales surrounding him and climbed to his feet. He ducked his way past the rafters that criss-crossed the ceiling and headed for the edge of the loft. He leaped to the barn floor in one smooth movement that didn't so much as stir the dust beneath his bare feet. He walked over to the far corner and pulled jeans and a T-shirt from his duffel bag. Next, he yanked on his boots, his movements quick, desperate.

Early of all things.

Brent's calculations had been wrong. His brother had estimated they would have at least one more day before Rose showed up in Skull Creek. Plenty of time for Colton to see Shelly again and pour out his heart.

If that had been his plan.

It wasn't.

One more day or fifty, it made little difference. He would never go after her and confess his love. It was over between them and so he had to let her go.

He wanted her to go.

His gaze hooked on the piece of cedar he'd been working on the night before and before he could stop himself, he crossed the room and touched the smooth piece of wood. Shelly's image stirred and he felt the press of her body against his back, her delicate hands resting atop his, her warmth seeping clear into his bones as she'd talked about her past and he'd told her about his.

Warm. For the first time in one hundred and fifty years.

Pure joy leaped through him because he'd finally found the one thing that made him feel whole again. It was followed by a bolt of anger because he didn't deserve it.

He'd messed up. He'd failed his brothers. His son.

Especially his son. And while he took some comfort in the fact that CJ had escaped the torture of a bullet, it did little to ease the knot in his chest. His son had grown up without a father.

His body tightened and his muscles jumped. In a flash, he snatched up the cedar and threw it as far as he could. The wood slammed into the ground and split into two. It was done.

Over.

He grabbed his duffel bag and unearthed the two deadly looking stakes he'd carved himself the night he'd gotten the phone call from Cody telling him the truth about Rose. That she was guilty. That Colton was finally going to get his shot at revenge.

Two matching stakes.

One for the traitor who'd destroyed his family. And one for himself, because when all was said and done, he'd let them down even more than Rose.

He stiffened. Those days were over. He couldn't change the past, but he could keep it from ever happening again.

The sweet smell of cupcakes tickled his nostrils and he stiffened. *Shelly.* Thanks to last night, they were really and truly connected now. She was thinking about him. Worrying over him. Wanting him, despite making up her mind that she wasn't going to do either.

He knew the feeling, but it would end soon.

She would be free and so would he.

That's what he told himself. If only freedom didn't look like an even bigger hell than the one he'd existed in all of these years.

Forcing aside the notion, he shoved the stakes back into his bag and walked out to his truck. Climbing behind the wheel, he keyed the engine, backed out of the driveway and headed into town.

While he would never act on the feelings for Shelly pushing and pulling inside of him, he still felt them. He couldn't let her get caught in the cross-fire because of his own desperate need for revenge.

He wouldn't.

Rose was close. Headed straight to the Sheriff's office. Which meant Colton had to get Holbrook out of there and move him before all hell broke loose and Shelly ended up smack dab in the middle of it all.

As he rolled past, his gaze stalled on the old, aban-doned farmhouse that reminded him so much of the Circle B. It would be the perfect place for him to face off with Rose. To avenge his family and doom her the way she'd doomed them all.

And then?

And then nothing. He would destroy her, and then he would pay for his own sins the way he'd always meant to.

Fighting down a wave of regret, he slammed his foot down on the gas and gunned the engine. The hair on the back of his neck prickled and his nerves buzzed as he sped down the dirt road.

She was getting closer, all right, and the clock was ticking.

AFTER AN ENTIRE DAY spent baking and frosting cup-cakes, Shelly had learned a few things about herself. First, she wasn't half bad when it came to baking—

they'd only had to pull out the fire extinguisher once. Two, she preferred Swiss chocolate mocha cake batter over vanilla bean. And three, she would never be able to forget Colton Braddock.

She didn't want to forget.

She wanted to find him, help him, love him. Regardless of the fact that they were polar opposites. Or that he was a vampire. Or that this wasn't the right time in her life for her to get her very own happily ever after.

Everything was all wrong and yet it had never felt so right.

Up until about an hour ago, that is.

That's when she'd started to feel the panic and anxiety and fear. Not her own, but Colton's. Something was happening and she could only pray that she wasn't too late.

She hurried up the steps of the massive house with its white columns and perfectly shaped hedges. Before she could press the bell, the door flew open and she found herself staring at none other than Cody "Balls to the wall" Braddock.

He had dark hair, striking silver eyes and the muscular physique befitting that of a badass pro bull rider. He'd been the best of the best up until last year when he'd retired to settle down and marry one of Skull Creek's own.

Shelly could have sworn she saw a flicker of surprise when his gaze collided with hers. But then his mouth pulled into a tight line that said he wasn't the least bit pleased.

"You know about us." As if his words had conjured them, Travis and Brent stepped from the shadows and flanked her on either side.

She glanced at both men and nodded. "I also know what's coming and I want to help. But I can't do that without details. I need to know when, where, how—"

"Cody? Why is everyone still standing out here…" The words faded as Miranda Braddock came up behind her husband. She stared past him. "Deputy Lancaster," she said, obviously startled. "I didn't know you were here."

"I'm surprised you didn't sense me."

A smile touched Miranda's lips and her eyes gleamed with an unearthly light that Shelly recognized all too well. "I'm still new at this. Besides, you aren't the only human in the bunch. I thought you were Abby." She motioned to the petite brunette who stepped up next to Brent. "Or Holly." The town's local wedding planner joined Travis and slid her hand into his.

"Not that the situation is permanent," Abby chimed in, eyeing Brent. "We just thought we'd save a little something for the wedding night."

"That's right," Holly chimed in. "'Til death do us part isn't nearly long enough when you love someone."

A pang of envy shot through Shelly, but it faded in the next heartbeat when her gut tightened again and a wave of anxiety hit her. "Please." She eyed Cody. "We don't have much time."

"She wants to know about Rose," he told Miranda when she shot him a questioning glance.

"Well go on, then. She needs to know. She obviously loves him."

"Did you just read my mind?"

Miranda smiled. "I didn't have to, sweetie." She turned and motioned Shelly to follow her inside. "It's written all over your face."

"I WAS WONDERING when someone was going to finally let me out of here," Jimmy Holbrook declared when Colton pulled on leather gloves, gripped the door and slid it to the side.

"The redhead?" Colton pulled off the gloves that were now smoking, tossed them to the side and eyed the young man who reached for his shirt.

Jimmy shrugged. "Red hair, brown hair, purple hair—it makes no never mind. A friendly smile and just like that, somebody's lending a helping hand."

He didn't know about Rose.

Colton saw as much blazing in the man's familiar blue eyes. Forget Rose and her vamp charisma. Jimmy thought it was his own easy charm that had persuaded that guard back in Houston to open the door. His quick grin that had lured the police officer up in Austin into forgetting to lock the handcuffs.

The young man had no clue he had a self-appointed guardian angel, one who was on par with the devil himself.

"What are you doing?" Jimmy demanded when Colton grabbed a wrist and snapped a handcuff around it.

"I'm not letting you out."

"What—"

"You're being transferred." Before the young man knew what was coming, Colton pulled his arm behind his back and went for the other hand.

"What about Ranger Truitt? I thought he was riding shotgun during the transfer."

"He's been replaced." Colton snapped the second cuff into place and shoved Jimmy toward the cell door. "Now move."

If Shelly hadn't already been hopelessly in love with Colton Braddock, she would have surely fallen head over heels after hearing the Braddocks talk about their oldest brother.

Colton had been a loyal, kind, caring man who'd sacrificed everything for his family. That's why Rose's treachery had been so devastating.

The woman had not only turned her back on her husband, she'd killed her own son.

Shelly couldn't begin to grasp how someone could do such a thing to their own flesh and blood, anymore than she could understand how her own mother had turned her back time and time again. But people did bad things all the time. She'd learned that much during her ten years with the department. It was a screwed up world.

Especially for one loyal, trusting cowboy who'd given everything for his family.

As she listened to the story of that night and the years that followed, she gained a new appreciation for the pain and grief that ate away at Colton Braddock. The anger that drove him. The demons that haunted him.

His entire existence was hinged on finding the traitor and punishing her. And now it was about to happen. The Braddock Brothers had found her weakness and lured her to Skull Creek, using her last living descendant as bait.

Jimmy Holbrook.

"I have to get back to the office," Shelly blurted as the truth gripped her as tightly as the fear coiling in her gut.

"We'll go, too—" Cody said, but the radio clipped to Shelly's collar buzzed and Bobby's voice filled her ears.

"Shelly? You need to get back here," the deputy said in a frantic voice. "We've got a serious situation."

"I know. I need you lock down the entire jail and don't let anyone in or out—"

"Holbrook's gone," he blurted. "One minute he was here and the next, he just disappeared. We don't know what the hell happened. Truitt is about to have a friggin' conniption."

Cody exchanged glances with his brothers. "Rose," the three men said in unison, but Shelly knew better.

She knew the truth.

She could feel it pumping through her veins.

The fear.

The anxiety.

The relief.

Because Colton had managed to get Holbrook away from the jail.

"It's Colton. He took him."

"Why?" Cody asked, but Shelly already knew the answer to that. He wanted Shelly safe.

The realization sent a burst of warmth through her, followed by a rush of panic so profound that tears burned the backs of her eyes. Because she knew what was coming. She could feel it.

"Where do you think they went?" Brent asked, but she already knew the answer to that, as well.

She smelled the musky scent of rotting wood and stale air and realization struck.

The farmhouse.

The minute the truth hit her, she knew Colton had read the thought, as well. She felt him stiffen. And then, just like that, the connection severed and there was nothing.

No fear. No expectancy. No Colton.

No!

"I've got to get out of here." She left the brothers staring after her as she turned and bolted for her cruiser.

"We'll go with you," Cody called behind her, but she refused to slow down.

She couldn't.

She'd already wasted enough time. Too much. And now all she could do was pray as she hit gas and headed hell for leather down the dirt road.

Please don't let it be too late.

22

HE'D BEEN WAITING for this moment for one hundred and fifty years.

Colton stood in the shadows off to the side of the house and watched as Rose Braddock stepped up onto the decrepit porch, moving toward the open doorway and the man tied to a chair just a few feet inside.

Clouds had moved in, making the night blacker than ever, but Colton didn't need any help seeing the woman who'd taken everything from him.

She looked exactly as he remembered. Same determined set to her jaw. Same small, petite frame. Her red hair had been pulled back into a tight ponytail. She wore black jeans, a black T-shirt and black high-heeled boots. Her steps were slow, tentative, as if she knew someone was watching her.

Or following her.

She glanced over her shoulder, her gaze scanning the road that she'd just driven down, before she seemed to conquer her fears. She turned back to the house and disappeared inside.

Colton reached the doorway a split-second later.

He watched as she approached the young man who sat there, his arms and legs fastened to the chair, his head drooping down, a steady snore flaring his nostrils, totally oblivious to what was going on, thanks to Colton. She didn't bend down and try to wake him or untie his ropes. She stalled, standing there for a long moment before her familiar voice echoed off the walls.

"You're going to kill me."

She turned and Colton found himself face-to-face with his past. Rage welled up inside him and his body shook with the force of it. "Payback's a bitch," he growled.

He had her by the throat in that next instant. He flew through the air, slamming her back against a far wall. Wood buckled and split and she went sprawling backward into the next room.

Colton was on her in a heartbeat, the stake in his hand, fury gripping him from head to toe. His vision clouded and suddenly everything went a bright red. He lifted his arm, but he didn't send the stake plunging into her heart. Not yet. His hand stalled.

Because as much as he needed to send her straight to hell where she belonged, he needed something else even more at that moment.

"Why did you do it?" He voiced the one question that had eaten away at him for so long.

He didn't think she would answer at first. She simply stared up at him, into him, and he feared that she would hurt him one last and final time by denying him the answer he so desperately sought.

"I never loved you," she finally said. "You knew that." If he hadn't known better, he would have sworn she seemed almost sad about that fact. Regretful.

But he knew better. He knew her.

What she was capable of.

The deceit. The pain. The death.

"I wanted more than a ranch out in the middle of nowhere," she continued. "I wanted to live in town and wear fancy dresses and be somebody other than a bastard's daughter or a rancher's wife." She shook her head.

"Why not just leave?" His fingers tightened on her arm, but she didn't so much as flinch. As if she didn't feel the pain. As if she deserved it. "You didn't have to do what you did. You didn't have to kill them all."

"That wasn't my idea. I thought we were just going to pick up and go. That's what Jacob said.... He said we could take CJ with us and we'd go someplace new. Some place exciting."

"Jacob?" Colton's mind stuck on the name. "Jacob Manning?" The man had been the ranch foreman at the Circle B for ten years. He'd been there that night. He'd died there. "He was the man you left with?"

She nodded. "After you left, we started having an affair. Time's were tight, but he managed to buy me pretty dresses and he made all the right promises. I was so gullible." She shook her head. "I believed him."

"I thought he died that night."

"That's what he wanted everyone to think. That it was an Apache attack. He said we had to do it. That if we didn't, someone would come after us. I didn't want to, but he did it anyway."

"And you were completely innocent, right?"

"No." She shook her head. "I was even more guilty than he was. I let him." She shook her head. "I watched him set the fire and I didn't do a single thing to stop him. I saw what he was capable of that night. That's why I didn't keep CJ with me. I left him at the first town we reached, before I was turned. He deserved something better than me, and a hell of a lot better than Jacob." She closed her eyes. "He's a sadistic bastard." Her gaze locked with Colton's. "I tried leaving him years ago, but he won't let me go. He keeps coming after me and it's all I can do to stay one step ahead of him." Anguish gleamed in her eyes. "He'd be here right now if he knew about Jimmy, but luckily he doesn't. Not yet. I've managed to keep this one secret all these years, but I know he'll catch up to me eventually. And then he'll punish me by taking the one thing I have left."

Colton knew then that Rose was already in a hell far worse than any he could doom her to. She was trapped for eternity with a vampire she hated. A slave to her mistakes. Her past.

She'd kept going all these years, not for her own

selfish reasons, but for their son. For CJ's descendants. For Holbrook.

"But you're here now," she said, a small smile touching her lips. "You can look out for him." And then, before he knew what was happening, she grabbed his hand and lunged toward him.

The stake sunk deep, impaling her, and her entire body started to shake. Smoke steamed from the wound and just like that, her body crumpled, fading into a pile of ashes at Colton's feet.

Rose was truly, finally, dead.

The realization didn't bring nearly the rush of satisfaction that he'd expected. He staggered back a few feet, the past whirling inside him as he turned and reached for his duffel bag. She was dead, but it wasn't over. She hadn't been the only one to blame for that night.

He pulled out the second stake.

"Don't!" The frantic voice rang out a split-second before Shelly grabbed him from behind. The motion caught him off guard and he found himself flat on his back, her knee on his chest, her face looming over his. "You can't do this. I won't let you do it."

"They're dead because of me."

"No one blames you." She eyed him. "Except for you. They've all forgiven you, Colton, but you have to forgive yourself."

She was right. He knew that as his brothers stepped up behind her. He could see the truth shining in their eyes. The acceptance. The love.

They were family. They would always be a family.

"There's been enough death," Brent said. *"Enough."*

"It's time to let it go," Shelly added, reading the turmoil in his eyes, feeling it in his heart. They were one now. The bond unbreakable. Forged in blood and sex and love. Especially love. "I love you, too," she added. "So don't do this. Please." Panic filled her gaze. "If you do, you'll just be hurting me the way that Rose hurt you all those years ago."

"I would never hurt you."

She eyed the stake and challenge gleamed in her gaze. "Then prove it."

He couldn't. This was his last chance to lay the past to rest. To find peace.

But suddenly, he knew there would be no peace in death. Not if he left Shelly. He would feel nothing, but she would be here dealing with the aftermath. Hurt. Devastated.

While he didn't know if he could ever forgive himself the way his brothers had, suddenly he wanted to try.

Wood clattered to the floor. "It won't be easy," he warned. "You. Me. There are going to be lots of complications."

"We'll work through them. Isn't that what people in love do?"

"That's exactly what they do," Cody said.

"Hell, yeah," Brent chimed in.

"You're preaching to the choir, bro," added Travis.

Colton grinned and eyed the woman standing in

front of him. She was so strong. So stubborn. So beautiful. "You're something else, you know that?"

"Something good, I hope."

"Something wonderful." He hauled her close. "I love you. I'll always love you."

"Always is an awful long time."

"I'm a vampire, remember? I've got all the time in the world." And then Colton hauled her close, kissed her for all he was worth, and just like that, he found the peace he'd been praying for all these years.

Epilogue

Two months later...

"THERE'S NO SENSE arguing about this," Shelly told Colton. "I've got my mind made up."

"Don't I get any sort of say so?"

"About this? No." She stared at the man she loved more than anything in the entire world. He perched on one knee on the porch in front of her, a frustrated expression on his face, a very large, very beautiful two carat diamond ring in his hand.

It wasn't exactly a surprise at this point. They'd been living together, loving each other and so she'd seen this coming a long time ago. Colton had taken on Jimmy Holbrook at his cattle ranch in New Mexico as part of a work-release program. If the young man kept up his end of the bargain and worked his ass off, the place would one day be his. In the meantime, he was answering to Colton's tough-as-nails foreman who didn't take crap from anyone. And he was probably hating every minute of it.

But the young man was learning.

Meanwhile, Colton had moved to Skull Creek to settle down with his family. With her.

He'd been ready to take things slow with his brothers, convinced that the years apart had done irreparable damage to their relationship, but determined to try anyway.

But he was fast learning that love had a way of overcoming all obstacles. He was as close as ever to his brothers and had just purchased the two hundred acres that sat next to Brent's property. While the Circle B had been their family's legacy once upon a time, the brothers had overcome their past and were now building a new legacy right here in Skull Creek.

Colton had finally made his peace and now it was time to take the next step. They'd come outside to sit and enjoy the warm summer evening and he'd dropped down on one knee and popped the question.

"Will you marry me?"

She'd wanted to scream *yes* and shout it from the rooftops, but there was still the little matter of Colton being a vampire and Shelly being a human to consider. And while she knew that his brothers had married humans that they would eventually turn when the time was right, Shelly was ready now.

When she pulled on her Grandma Jean's wedding dress and walked down the aisle and said, "I do," she wanted to mean it. No more demons from the past standing between them. No more secrets. No more walls.

No more fear.

"I want this," she told him. "I want you."

"And here I thought you were just using me for my powers." He slipped the ring onto her finger and settled down next to her on the custom-made bench he'd given her just last week. They'd set it up on the front porch and had been using it every night since. "Not that you need another dose of badass. You've got plenty of your own. You'll make one hell of a Sheriff anyway, come the fall."

She shook her head. "I know we've come out of the dark ages with free wifi at the café, but I don't think Skull Creek is ready for a vampire Sheriff just yet."

"I don't know about that. Everybody seems to like Sheriff Keller."

Her gaze collided with his. "Are you trying to tell me that Matt is a vampire?"

"Not exactly. He's half werewolf and half vampire, so he can walk around during the day. But the full moon's a bitch." His gaze touched hers. "If he can do it, you can, too. Don't give up on your dream because of me."

She smiled. "You are my dream."

He settled down next to her for the next few moments as she thought about the past.

Jason Aldean drifted from the radio singing about

green tractors and taking a ride and Colton pushed to his feet. He held out a hand. "Dance with me?"

"Right here?" Her gaze slid to the old lady who stood across the street, watering her grass. She kept glancing at them, obviously waiting to see what would happen next so she could get on the phone and call somebody in her bridge group, who'd call somebody from Bingo, who'd tell somebody from church and so on, until the entire town new that Shelly Lancaster was dancing on her front porch.

Dancing, of all things.

With the man she loved.

She let Colton pull her to her feet and a split second later, she was in his arms and they were swaying to the slow country tune.

And there wasn't a place in the world that she would rather be. She loved Colton and he loved her and nothing else mattered.

* * * * *

A sneaky peek at next month...

Blaze.

SCORCHING HOT, SEXY READS

My wish list for next month's titles...

In stores from 17th August 2012:

☐ Cowboy Up – Vicki Lewis Thompson

& No Going Back – Karen Foley

☐ Tall, Dark & Reckless – Heather MacAllister

& No Holds Barred – Cara Summers

Available at WHSmith, Tesco, Asda, Eason, Amazon and Apple

Just can't wait?

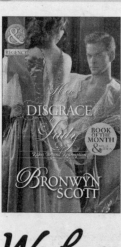

Have Your Say

*You've just finished your book.
So what did you think?*

We'd love to hear your thoughts on our
'Have your say' online panel
www.millsandboon.co.uk/haveyoursay

- 🌹 Easy to use
- 🌹 Short questionnaire
- 🌹 Chance to win Mills & Boon® goodies

*Visit us
Online*   Tell us what you thought of this book now at
www.millsandboon.co.uk/haveyoursay

YOUR_SAY

The World of Mills & Boon®

There's a Mills & Boon® series that's perfect for you. We publish ten series and, with new titles every month, you never have to wait long for your favourite to come along.

Blaze®
Scorching hot, sexy reads
4 new stories every month

By Request
Relive the romance with the best of the best
9 new stories every month

Cherish™
Romance to melt the heart every time
12 new stories every month

Desire™
Passionate and dramatic love stories
8 new stories every month